FATED

Cheyne was thunderstruck. This filthy ragamuffin who had tried to kill him was none other than Laurel Caldwell. God forgive him, he had slapped her.

"I'm sorry I was rough with you, Miss Caldwell, but that disguise was *your* choice, and quite effective. If you take on the role of a male, you must be prepared to accept the consequences."

His words sent her eyebrows skyward. "And once I thought you were a gentleman, Captain Sinclair. Granted, I misled you, but now that you know who I am, I would have expected some slight apology, if not for striking me, then for sinking my ship."

"I didn't sink your ship. Your own poorly maintained cannon sent *The Star* to the bottom."

Her fists were jammed at her waist. "Why do you think I found it necessary to fire my cannons, sir?"

"I have no idea. I thought at the time it was a foolish thing to do."

He watched her control her temper with difficulty. Unfortunately, he found her more fascinating than ever. He remembered her as a beautiful Southern belle in her flowing skirts and bonnet. Now she seemed a mischievous imp, helpless, disheveled, at his mercy, and yet untamed and ready to do battle. What would it be like to embrace her, force her to his will, kiss those lips into utter submission?

PRAISE FROM CRITICS AND BOOKSELLERS ALIKE FOR KRISTA JANSSEN'S FABULOUS SKYE TRILOGY

SKYE LAKOTA

"Krista Janssen blends mystery and passion to craft a fine, entertaining tale."

—Kathe Robin, *Romantic Times*

"*Skye Lakota* weaves magic as it sweeps readers from America to the Isle of Skye. Fast-paced. . . . A great read."
—Jenny Jones, The Book Shelf, Grand Prairie, TX

"*Skye Lakota* is a fun-filled, action-packed tale filled with a romantically delightful couple woven around a great story line."

—*Affaire de Coeur*

"This book has it all. The best of two worlds, the hero is half Sioux and half Scottish—what more can any romance reader ask for! A definite 'keeper'!"

—Annie's Book Stop

"This is the first in the new Skye trilogy, and it's Krista at her best. If you want a gripping tale of the beauty and splendor of London and Scotland in 1815, then buy this book. You'll fall in love with Fletcher Mackinnon, he's what dreams are made of. Krista's writing sparkles in this one."
—Donita Lawrence, Bell, Book, and Candle, Oklahoma City, OK

Books by Krista Janssen

Skye Laurel
Skye Legacy
Skye Lakota
Wind Rose
Creole Cavalier
Indigo Fire

Published by POCKET BOOKS

KRISTA JANSSEN

SKYE LAUREL

POCKET BOOKS
New York London Toronto Sydney Tokyo Singapore

This book is a work of fiction. Names, characters, places and incidents are products of the author's imagination or are used fictitiously. Any resemblance to actual events or locales or persons, living or dead, is entirely coincidental.

An *Original* Publicatioin of POCKET BOOKS

POCKET BOOKS, a division of Simon & Schuster Inc. 1230 Avenue of the Americas, New York, NY 10020

ISBN: 1-4165-0177-0

This Pocket Books paperback printing May 2004

10 9 8 7 6 5 4 3 2 1

POCKET and colophon are registered trademarks of Simon & Schuster Inc.

Cover art by Danilo Ducak

Printed in the U.S.A.

With love to Tom
For countless reasons

Special thanks to Caroline Tolley,
my friend and extraordinary editor

· PROLOGUE ·

New Orleans 1821

Cheyne Sinclair was just fifteen, but he was old enough and smart enough to know he had entered a world where he didn't belong. Standing beside a flowering gardenia bush, Cheyne stayed out of the way and absorbed the sights and sounds and smells of top-drawer society.

Until now he hadn't been nervous about attending a party at the Caldwell mansion in New Orleans's most exclusive neighborhood, because he was tagging along with his friend and mentor, the famous pirate, Jean Lafitte. Growing up on Barataria, with Lafitte's motley gang of privateers, Cheyne had never concerned himself with wealthy folks like the Caldwells. But Lafitte had saved Mr. Caldwell's life a few years ago during the Battle of New Orleans, and that gave Lafitte the right to attend an elegant function such as today's lawn party.

Of course, the Caldwells had gone against their elite society's rules by including Lafitte in their gathering. Jean proably wouldn't have accepted, but he wanted to say good-bye to his old friend Blaine Caldwell, probably for good. Lafitte, who had always treated Cheyne like a son, was being expelled from the United States.

If Lafitte was leaving, Cheyne was leaving.

From his gardenia-scented vantage point, Cheyne was starting to wish he were anywhere but here. He shifted his weight and stared longingly at the cinnamon buns being served on silver trays to the guests drifting among the tables. He was hungry all the time. Jean said he was still a growing boy, but he was already taller than Lafitte and built something like a beanstalk.

He couldn't march into that crowd of ladies with their

swaying rainbow-colored skirts and gentlemen dressed in spotless suits of fawn and gray, and take a bun off a tray. He was dirty from tying up the boat they had used to come upriver from their island stronghold. This morning he'd put on his best shirt and breeches, but that wasn't saying much, since he had only two outfits, one for wearing and one for the wash. His hands were stained, his fingernails encrusted, and his boots caked with river mud. Nay, he'd best stay out of sight till Jean was ready to leave. Surely his friend would bring him something from the table.

Suddenly a large ball rolled from where several youngsters played on the manicured emerald grass. To Cheyne's chagrin, it landed against his boot.

He started to retrieve the ball when a petite child with a mass of blond curls bouncing around her ears, ran up to him.

With her hands planted at her waist, she stared at him. Her crisp white dress was made from endless yards of lace, caught at her plump mid-section by a wide pink silk ribbon and falling to just above her shiny white slippers. She was all froth and honey. The most exquisite creature he'd ever seen.

Her perfect rosebud mouth puckered in distaste as she looked him up and down. "Who, may I ask, are you?"

Suddenly proud of his height, he stretched upward and said in his not yet fully mature voice, "Cheyne Sinclair. I'm a friend of Jean Lafitte's"

"Oh, the pirate?"

"Aye. The famous privateer. I sail with him as his mate."

"Cheyne is a strange name. It rhymes with my father's name, Blaine."

"'Tis not so strange. It's a Scottish name that means *oak tree.*"

"Named after a tree." She cocked her head, her amber eyes sparkling. "Do you know who I am?"

"Nay."

2

"I'm Laurel Anne Caldwell. This is my house. I'm five today and I'm having a party. Pirates aren't usually invited."

"Jean Lafitte is invited. He saved your father's life. And I'm with Captain Lafitte."

Tossing her locks, she said, "I do like Captain Lafitte, but I'm not sure I want a guest who's as dirty as you."

Holding the ball, he frowned at her. He could explain how he got mud on his clothes, but why should he care what this child thought of him? Still, he was embarrassed and annoyed. "I won't be here long. But if I were your father, I'd give you a spanking for being so rude."

Her lips parted in shock. "A *spanking?* My goodness. Some boys will say just anything. Give me my ball."

Angry at the way the girl was making him feel like an unwanted urchin, Cheyne handed her the ball, but accidentally touched her sleeve with the back of his hand. His face flushed when he saw the stain he left on the white ruffle. "I'm—" He was about to say he was sorry when he saw the horror in her eyes as she stared at the spot as if it were a fatal disease.

He clamped his lips.

"Look what you've done!" she cried. "That was very naughty." Without giving him a chance to reply, she spun and dashed back to her friends, the large bow at the back of her dress fluttering with every step.

He stared after her, engulfed with injured pride. On Barataria, he was never spoken to like that. He was respected by all the youngsters and even the grownups for his spunk and his skill with knife and sword and pistol. He'd earned a place on Lafitte's crew, and someday before long, he intended to have a ship of his own.

When the child reached her playmates, she gave them the ball and reached for a bun from the tray offered by one of her servants. Turning to look back at him, she bit into the bun and took her time chewing it and wiping icing from her lips with the tips of her fingers.

He knew she was taunting him, but he supposed she

could act any way she wanted since this was her house and she was very, very rich. He'd be rich someday, he vowed, and if he had a girl child, he grudgingly admitted he hoped she would look like little Miss Caldwell. For the first time in his life, envy struck hard at his insides. To be a part of society like these folks in New Orleans, a person had to be good looking, rich, clean, and above all, legitimate.

Unfortunately, he was none of these.

·1·

Off the Moroccan coast, Spring 1842

In all his days of pirating, Cheyne Sinclair had never felt
death so near. In the hold of a burning slave ship, up to
his hips in icy sea water, his left arm broken and useless,
he was groping blindly through thick black smoke toward his unseen goal.

The dilemma was of his own making. Thirty minutes
ago, his frigate had sent heavy cannon fire crashing on
the slaver plying its way toward America. When the
ship's guns fired back, he had cut its masts with his own
skillful barrage, then boarded it, as was his custom, to
rescue the suffering Africans before the ship could sink.
All had gone smoothly, and he had captured the crew,
freed the slaves, and moved everyone in record time to
his own vessel. But then, a frantic Negro woman had told
him her husband was sealed in a box in the hold of the
burning ship.

Dear God, how Cheyne hated the slave trade. He
remembered well the first time he'd seen African men,
women, and children being sold in the slave market in
New Orleans. He'd heard the pitiful cries of wives torn
from their husbands; he'd seen emaciated children and
men's flesh bloody from chains and the whip. As a lad,
he had envied and admired the wealthy Southerners'
way of life, the elegant and exclusive society he was never
privileged to enter. But when he became a man, and first
boarded a slaver on the high seas and saw what was being
done to the suffering blacks of Africa, he had been
appalled beyond belief. By then, he had made his
fortune as a privateer and had no need to accumulate
greater wealth. Instead, for the past ten years, he had

turned all his attention toward disrupting the abhorrent business of slavery. The New England ship he'd attacked today off the African coast was the third in two months. He planned to turn the crew over to authorities in his home port of Tangier. Fighting the injustice of slavery, regardless of the risk, was his way of repaying the Fates for his great good fortune, the incredible luck he'd enjoyed ever since he had learned the pirate's trade at the side of his hero, Jean Lafitte.

But today, his luck could be running out. Cheyne knew he was in grave danger of dying here in the hold of the sinking slave ship. A few minutes ago, he had rushed below decks to rescue the African. Unfortunately a falling beam had struck him a glancing blow, and he was certain his left arm was broken.

Overhead, timbers groaned as the ship tilted further to starboard. Cheyne was nearly submerged in the frigid water swirling around him. He coughed, trying desperately to get his breath in the smoke-filled enclosure, then continued slogging toward the crate he glimpsed nearby. Pounding came from inside. The poor fellow must be crazy with fear.

Lifting his broadsword, he smashed it against the lid of the box. The wood splintered and two large hands tore at the opening. He saw a dark face with eyes wide with terror.

"Get out!" he yelled. Then he repeated his command in an African dialect.

The man needed no prompting. He pried himself out of his prison and leaped into the water beside Cheyne.

The ship listed perilously. Burning beams fell from above and floating debris slammed toward the starboard side of the vessel.

Cheyne's head was spinning; his breath was knocked out of him as he was thrown beneath the rising water. A strong arm went around him, pulling him up, then heaving him over a broad shoulder as if his six-foot frame had no weight at all. He offered no resistance, knowing that to struggle could be fatal for both of them. With his lungs on fire and his body aching, he felt himself hoisted upward, then lifted into waiting hands. He wasn't sure if the screaming filling his ears was his imagination or the death cries of the doomed frigate.

Briefly, he lost consciousness. When he opened his eyes, he was lying on the deck of the *Monsoon,* his twenty-one-gun warship, and he was staring into the concerned face of his second-in-command, Rafi Hamid.

"Capitaine Sinclair, we thought you would die on the slaver."

Cheyne tried to sit up and discovered his arm was no longer numb but blazing with fiery pain. "Aye, Rafi. I would have, if not for the African." Holding his arm, he lay still, waiting for his head to clear. "Is he all right?"

"He's well, sir. And grateful from the look of him."

"You might say we saved each other. A fair exchange." Grimacing, he pushed to his right elbow. "A falling beam broke my arm. We had better head for home. Take command, Rafi. And be sure those poor devils from the slave ship get some decent food and a bath—with soap. Keep the captain in chains. He deserves nothing better. Later, come to my cabin and see if you can slide this bone back into place."

"Yes, *Capitaine."* Rafi ordered the crew to make sail for Tangier.

Cheyne sat up slowly, then pulled himself to his feet with the aid of the rigging. He'd had a close call, but fortune had smiled again. One of these days, he knew his luck would run out. He was a marked man in America and condemned by the English courts. He was a bastard Scotsman with no country, no family, and a reputation as black as any pirate who ever sailed from the Barbary Coast. For years, he had lived precariously, slipping slowly into pessimism and decadence. If he had died today, he would have died doing what he liked best: throwing caution to the winds and fighting the colossal greed of his fellow man.

But he had beaten the odds once more; he was alive, for better or for worse. He filled his lungs with the fresh, salt-scented breeze and made his way toward his cabin. He'd toast his broken arm with a shot of brandy, alone as usual, out of respect for his Muslim crew's code of abstinence. With today's venture a *fait accompli,* he would soon begin preparations for his voyage to New Orleans. There, in the underground slave markets, he would learn who was buying slaves despite the fact that the United States had declared the importation of slaves illegal over thirty years before. He would infiltrate meetings and learn the traders' routes along the Middle Passage. Then, the Sea Falcon, as he was called by angry Southern planters and irate Northern shippers, would continue his attacks, until people everywhere came to their senses and ended the cruel practice of keeping human souls in bondage.

A week later, Cheyne faced Rafi Hamid in the private quarters of his palace overlooking the sea. His arm still ached, but his mission had been a complete success and the rescued Africans were making their way south toward their home. Preparations were currently under way for his voyage to New Orleans.

"Will the *Monsoon* be ready for a lengthy voyage?" Cheyne asked. "We must be prepared to dodge any spring storms that blow up along our route."

"Yes, *mon ami.* The craft is in excellent condition and scrubbed from stem to stern. All that remains is to load your trunks in your cabin."

"Fatima is preparing my wardrobe now. I'll be hobnobbing with the elite in Louisiana and must look more like a civilized gent than a pirate with a price on my head."

"I would think your old friends there would welcome you."

"A few will, I expect. I'll be meeting with Blaine Caldwell, for certain. Caldwell is the spearhead of our secret partnership. There's always a chance the other plotters will be present this time of year. I've told you about Kyle Wyndford and Fletcher Mackinnon from Dakota. They have large land holdings in the West, but invest in our scheme to free the Africans before the slave ships reach American shores."

"Isn't Mackinnon the Scot you saved from Moroccan rebels a few years ago?"

"Aye. Half Scot and half Lakota Indian. The three of us are sworn to secrecy regarding our abolitionist leanings. If word got out in New Orleans, Caldwell would be doomed for sure. Only one woman shares our confidence, Shannon Kildaire, Blaine Caldwell's adopted daughter. Miss Kildaire owns a lavish hotel in the French Quarter of New Orleans and makes an excellent spy."

Rafi closed his notebook and stood. "Excuse me, *Capitaine,* I must return to the docks to oversee the loading of the foodstuffs."

"Aye. We'll confer once more in the morning before we sail."

After Rafi left the lavish suite, Cheyne stripped off his clothing and lowered himself into the pool beneath the arching glass dome that allowed sunlight to heat the shimmering water.

Relaxing in the warmth, he wondered why luxurious soaking hadn't caught on in sweltering places like Louisiana. Maybe the wealthy did engage in the practice these days. How could he know what took place among that exclusive and closed society in the United States? When he had occasionally managed to get a glimpse into the lives of the privileged class of New Orleans, he had been impressed, awed, in fact. He had spent his youth feeling like a hungry beggar looking into the window of a bakery overflowing with tempting goods, so close and yet totally

9

beyond his reach. He had learned from Jean Lafitte's rejection by the Americans that neither money nor fame nor heroism in a common cause could open the doors to that inner cloister. Not even marriage could assure admittance.

To hell with them. After Jean Lafitte was ousted from Galveston by the Americans, Cheyne had struck out on his own and quadrupled his wealth, then built his own private villa in Tangier, furnished it with treasures from around the world, and hired armed guards to protect it. He would never again envy anyone.

He closed his eyes and rested his head against the cool marble lip of the pool. As often happened, his thoughts drifted to Blaine Caldwell's younger daughter, Laurel. For several minutes, he allowed himself the unparalleled pleasure of picturing the lady, remembering how she looked as a fresh young girl with bouncing golden girls and rosy cheeks, garbed in endless white flounces and ruffles and ribbons, at a soirée he once attended. Laurel had put him in his place when he'd gotten a speck of dirt on a ruffle. She had fixed him with angry topaz-colored eyes and scolded him for being dirty. He had been too tongue-tied to apologize.

Even after all these years, the memory cut to his heart. *Now* he bathed, often and well. Even though he'd learned that cleanliness, fine manners, worldly knowledge, and a vast fortune would never win the admiration of a New Orleans lady like Mistress Laurel Caldwell.

But he'd had the last laugh two years ago when he attended a masked ball in the French Quarter at the invitation of Blaine Caldwell himself. He couldn't risk discovery, so he had stayed for only a short time, spent mostly in conversation with the wealthy rancher, Kyle Wyndford.

And he had danced with Laurel Caldwell.

He had actually put his arms around her petite waist and clasped her delicate hand in his. Her eyes still flashed at him, the way they had done all those years ago when they were children. For one heart-stopping moment, he had thought she recognized him, but then he knew that must be impossible. Many years had passed since the fateful afternoon of Laurel's birthday party, and he had changed from a callow, dirty-faced lad into a weathered man of thirty-four. Besides, the mask he had worn at the ball had hidden most of his face. Laurel had no idea she was dancing with the by-blow of a traveling Scotsman and a camp follower who had abandoned him at birth, a man who had no country and few friends and only hoards of stolen treasure to show for his life of reckless adventure.

Nevertheless, that brief shining moment was like a precious jewel; time had stood still and all things seemed possible. His heart had melted when he took her in his arms, and he sensed her response, saw her fascinated expression, felt her heightened tension mingled with intense curiosity. He'd told her his name was Hammond Brown. Then he'd returned her to the ladies and rushed away to board his ship. Neither God, nor Allah, nor whatever powers ruled the universe, could take away the memory of that incredible experience.

Tomorrow he would leave Tangier and sail toward New Orleans once again. He had much to relate to Blaine Caldwell about this year's successful escapades. Would he see Laurel? Most likely. Would he suffer the usual twin miseries of frustration and desire? Probably. Maybe she had married by now. And why not? She must be in her mid twenties, and a more attractive woman he'd never met. She was fair of face, but much more than that fascinated him. The tilt of her chin, the sparkle in her eyes, the intriguing mixture of intelligence laced with a hint of naiveté. She was as deliciously feminine as any Southern belle, but she had inherited her parent's spirit and determination. Would the man who won her hand appreciate the treasure he owned? By Allah, he hoped so.

·2·

Highgrove Plantation, April 1842

Thank you for proposing, Henry, but I must refuse. I'm flattered, as always, but—"

"You don't have to repeat your usual pretty speech, Laurel. You can turn me down time and again, but I'll just keep asking."

Laurel Caldwell crossed to the tall windows overlooking the tree-studded grounds along the Mississippi. Musing over Henry Beauregard's proposal, she was annoyed that the man wouldn't take no for an answer—a final answer—and find some other lady in New Orleans to pursue. Perhaps he would turn his attention elsewhere when she sailed for Scotland next month. Before she left, she would make it abundantly clear that she would not marry him, or anyone else for that matter, until she had reestablished Caldwell Shipping as something close to the huge success it had been a few years ago. After her return—well, maybe.

Turning, she gave Henry's sullen face a sharp look. "My father prepared me for years to take over Caldwell Shipping. While he and Mother work here at Highgrove, I must manage that enterprise. I have ships to outfit and orders to fill. I simply don't have time for courtship and marriage."

"You have *one* ship remaining after that disastrous fire in Bermuda last year. It's common knowledge in New Orleans's inner circles that the Caldwell bank accounts have fallen sharply, though no one knows why. You've been forced to sell your home in town and rely totally on your plantation's profits, which are reduced enormously because your father has a foolish notion about using free

12

labor instead of slaves. Unless someone takes a strong hand, your family will soon be in dire straits."

"That's not true! I admit we've had some reversals, but my father is doing a fine job running the plantation. I'm leaving soon for the Isle of Skye, where I'll establish a trading port. Besides, Henry, you shouldn't poke your nose into our private affairs."

Henry's dark eyes snapped. "You're a foolish woman, Laurel. If you weren't so damned beautiful, I'd swear there was a man hiding under those blond curls and feminine frills."

"Foolish and beautiful. Your view of me is entirely wrong, Henry. I am not beautiful nor am I foolish. But I *am* a woman, and I like being free and managing the company. I don't need a husband, at least, not anytime soon."

Abruptly Henry crossed to her and gripped her shoulders. "Your looks and spirit are captivating, Laurel. But youth is fleeting, and we both know you're several years beyond your twentieth birthday, toying with spinsterhood, my dear. As for your independent streak, that titillation will soon become more annoying than fascinating."

She stepped from under his hands. "Fine. Then we can settle once and for all that we will be only friends from this day forward. In fact, that's all we've ever been, in my opinion. Do be a gentleman, Henry, and accept my refusal graciously. Only your pride is hurt anyway. There's never been any spark between us, not really."

Frustration and annoyance were apparent in his eyes. She had to admit he was a handsome devil, and terribly rich, with all those acres in prime cotton. Any other woman in New Orleans would kill to be receiving his proposal. At times she had enjoyed their flirtation and the comfort of knowing their families had so much in common, being two of the oldest and most influential names in their elite society. But lately, she had not been able to think of anything but saving Caldwell Shipping. Her father hadn't told her exactly where a substantial amount of their money had gone, but he had always refused to use slave labor, which meant they had a sizable payroll, and even though their horses were some of the best in the area, their profits were slim from selling stock. Their largest trading vessel had burned while in port last year, leaving the aging frigate, the *Star,* their one remaining ship. This past year, she had worked diligently to line up shipping contracts, but only now had she arranged a full cargo to be delivered to Spain while on her way to Scotland. Everyone was pressuring her to plant more cotton at Highgrove, buy slaves, and become rich, but her family would not enslave people in order to make money, even if it meant the end of the luxurious way of life they had always enjoyed and taken for granted.

"We're more than friends, Laurel," Henry pointed out. "I expect you to attend my barbecue at Magnolia next week. We could announce our engagement, and then, if you must make one last voyage, I'll schedule our wedding upon your return."

His persistence was hard to believe. "Yes, I'll be at your party. But I will not consider your proposal until I'm back from the Isle of Skye. I bought the Mackinnon's property on the isle two years ago, and I must spend time determining its value. As a matter of fact, I've invited Fletcher and Elizabeth Mackinnon to visit me on Skye next spring. After that, I expect to return here, but for now, my answer must be no. I wouldn't think of tying you down for such an indefinite period."

His eyes narrowed. "Another year wasted while you traipse around the world like a businessman. It's very unbecoming for a woman of your station, Laurel. I hope I can dissuade you from this nonsense."

She stifled an angry retort and kept her voice calm. "I'll see you next week, Henry. Now, if you'll excuse me,

I must attend to my guests. After all, the Mackinnons have just spent two weeks traveling downriver from Dakota. I don't want to neglect them during their first days at Highgrove."

"I'm leaving. Naturally you may bring the Mackinnons to the barbecue. Though imagining what my guests will think of my entertaining a half-breed like Fletcher Mackinnon is rather unsettling. Do you think he has any gentlemanly manners?"

Her temper was close to the boiling point. "Fletcher and Elizabeth Mackinnon are my mother's cousins. I view them as my uncle and aunt. Fletcher was a lord on Skye before he gave up his title to return to his Lakota people. His mother was an Indian princess. What royal blood do you have in your family tree, Henry?"

"Royalty is a poor substitute for wealth, my dear. Frankly, I prefer a substantial bank account to any royal title."

"You needn't worry about the Mackinnon's financial status. Not since Fletcher has established a thriving cattle ranch in Dakota, and Elizabeth Mackinnon's latest novel is selling briskly in both England and America."

"I said they are invited. In the event my cultured guests are offended by Mackinnon's flowing hair and red skin, I'll explain to them he's *your* relation. I don't believe I've told you, I'm entertaining Franklin Trowbridge, the earl of Croydon, on this occasion. You see, I have royal connections of my own."

Her curiosity was piqued, despite her annoyance. "Really? And how did this come about, may I inquire."

He smirked with pleasure. "So you *are* impressed with titles, after all. As a matter of fact, the earl has come from London in search of a superb horse to enter in Prince Albert's competition next July. The prize is a veritable fortune, and Croydon is determined to win it. He's heard of our southern thoroughbreds and is on the lookout for the best animal in the States."

"I see." Laurel's interest waned. "Then I'll meet *your* royal guest next week, and you will welcome *my* royal cousin. Please excuse me, Henry. I really must ask you to leave now."

He gave her a lengthy perusal. "I realize you're distracted today with your guests from Dakota, but my marriage proposal stands. Nevertheless, I won't wait forever, dear Laurel. I've offered you my hand and my fortune. I could help your family make Caldwell Enterprises extremely profitable within a year. Cotton is where the money is, my dear girl, not delivering trade goods to foreign ports." He bowed and put on his top hat. *"Au revoir.* Remember time is running out."

Laurel stared silently as Henry strode from the living room. What a pompous bore, she fumed. Time running out, indeed. Henry could be incredibly arrogant. She supposed his comment rankled because she realized she was no longer considered prime in the marriage market. She wouldn't care a whit about that, but she did so want to have children of her own. Of course, he was right about the money. Was she being selfish not to take his offer? Her parents would never want to see her in an unhappy marriage. On the other hand, she had grown up knowing Henry and she was certain she could keep the upper hand in their relationship. All of her friends were married. Why couldn't she muster more enthusiasm for the idea?

"Hey, Miss Caldwell, come on out and see Mirage."

Laurel put Henry Beauregard from her mind and smiled at the boy who had rushed into the parlor, banging the door behind him. Badger Wyndford had arrived two days ago from Dakota, along with Fletcher and Elizabeth Mackinnon. He was a rough-cut diamond if she'd ever seen one. The lad was eleven, and was being raised by his Uncle Kyle, whose wife, Skye, was her favorite Mackinnon cousin. Badger's father had been slain by Indians in the early days, and his mother had died two years before. Despite his rascally nickname, Badger was bright and headstrong and already an excellent horseman.

"I'd love to see the filly," Laurel exclaimed. "Why don't we ask your Uncle Fletcher to join us."

"Oh, he's already at the paddock with Aunt Elizabeth. Mirage looks just dandy in her new bridle. I'll have a saddle on her in a week or two."

"Then we must go see her right away." She put her arm around Badger and headed outside. She'd heard nothing but raves about this wonder horse from Dakota. It was time she took a closer look.

In minutes, Laurel was standing under a brilliant azure sky, gripping the paddock railing, and exclaiming over the most beautiful horse she'd ever seen. The animal's coat was pale rose-gray with matching mane and tail. Its build was rather small, feminine and graceful with no hint of weakness. As it pranced about the arena, tossing its head, arching its neck and dilating its nostrils, the yearling was sheer poetry in motion. "So this is Desert Mirage," she sighed, more to herself than to the couple standing beside her. "Tell me again about her breeding, Fletcher."

The tall, bronze-skinned man, his shoulder-length raven hair bound at his neck, spoke with pride. "Her sire is the Arabian stallion I purchased in Tangier two years ago. I believe you saw him when I passed through New Orleans on my way west."

Laurel glanced at Fletcher, remembering how he had barely escaped from Tangier, then had taken his wife to Dakota to establish a ranch near his daughter, Skye, and her new husband. "Yes, I saw the stallion. How fortunate his offspring inherited that remarkable color."

"'Tis caused by the intermingling of white and chestnut hairs. Aye, I'm very pleased," said Fletcher, "though her dam is a beauty, too. Spirit Lady is her name, and she carries the blood of my wonderful Indian pony, Spirit Dog. Mirage won't be tall, since neither breed is known for size, but from the looks of her bones and build, she'll have the stamina she needs for any task required of her. Badger's using an expert blend of patience and discipline in her training." He smiled at Laurel. "We are much obliged to you and your family for having young Badger at Highgrove until next spring." He glanced at the boy, who was busy guiding the longe line for the filly. "The lad just needs a bit of exposure to civilized ways to take off those rough edges."

"Badger's a delight," said Laurel. "We're pleased to have him. Besides, I thought Skye would need to give all her attention to her twin babies this winter."

"Kyle and Skye are surely proud of their bairns," Fletcher said, exchanging a pleased smile with his wife.

Elizabeth Mackinnon nodded, her blue eyes sparkling with happiness. "To think my daughter has outdone everyone in the family. A boy and a girl to fill our lives in Dakota. I told Skye the West needed more people, and she did her part to help out."

Laurel grinned back at Elizabeth. "Two new Wyndfords. I'm overcome with envy just thinking about it." She meant her remark sincerely. Although she was in no hurry to marry, she longed for children. Her young cousin, Skye, had found true love with her Dakota cattle baron. And now Skye had two new babies to make her life complete. Laurel wondered if she herself would ever have everything she wanted in life: freedom, security, love, adventure, children. Someday she might have to make a difficult choice from among the things she desired most. She looked into Fletcher's startling green eyes, a gift from his Scottish father. "I almost forgot, Fletcher. Henry Beauregard was here for a brief visit and has invited all of us to a barbecue next week at Magnolia Plantation. It's quite a lovely place—much grander than Highgrove."

"That was kind of him," replied Fletcher. "Would you like to go, Beth?"

Elizabeth nodded as she adjusted her wide-brimmed straw hat. "I'd love to. Our social life out West is rather limited, I must say."

"Then it's settled," Laurel said. "My parents will also be attending, so we'll have our own entourage. Oh, by the way, Henry said his guest of honor is from London, a certain Lord Trowbridge, earl of Croydon."

Laurel was totally unprepared for the response caused by her announcement.

"Dear God in heaven!" shouted Fletcher.

"No! I don't believe it," said Elizabeth simultaneously.

"What's wrong?" asked Laurel, incredulous at the Mackinnons' reaction.

Fletcher gaped at his wife, his lips parted, his eyes flashing. "What a damnable coincidence," he snapped. "I thought we'd put an ocean between us and that villain."

Elizabeth recovered first and reached for Fletcher's arm. "Don't worry, my darling. We don't have to go to the barbecue, do we, Laurel?"

"No, of course not. But I don't understand. Do you know the earl of Croydon?"

Fletcher met her gaze. "Aye. We know him. The last time I saw Trowbridge, he was plotting to have me hanged for the murder of Queen Caroline of England. 'Tis a long story. For now, let me state with certainty that the man is vicious and without any scruples whatever. Years ago, his false testimony would have sent me to the gallows, if he'd had his way. He wanted the Mackinnon property on the Isle of Skye, and hired my father to murder the queen, then take the blame. When that plot failed, he set me up as scapegoat. If his plan had worked, I would have lost Strathmor Castle, as well as my life."

"Your life? And *my* Strathmor Castle?" asked Laurel breathlessly.

"Aye. The very castle you bought from us and plan to restore. I'm sorry, Laurel, but Elizabeth and I cannot attend the barbecue. If I saw that devil, Trowbridge, I might be tempted to strangle him on the spot. I doubt if your friend Mr. Beauregard would ever live down such a scandal: a murder committed by a half-breed Lakota in front of all his fancy guests."

Laurel nodded her agreement. She would make excuses for the Mackinnons, but she would attend the party with her parents. Her sister, Shannon, would be there, and she was eager to see her. But if Henry Beauregard dogged her every step and insisted she befriend the earl, she would be forced to ignore her careful upbringing and turn a cold shoulder to the two of them.

·3·

Crow's feet!"

"What?"

"Look, Mother, crow's feet. Right here at the edges of my eyes." Laurel squinted into the full-length mirror.

"Laurel Caldwell, your complexion is flawless."

"I can't see the wrinkles yet, but they're there, just waiting, and then they'll be plain as craters."

Rebecca Caldwell laughed and plumped the sleeves of Laurel's sky-blue organdy afternoon dress. "You're as youthful as a girl of eighteen, darling. Whoever gave you such an idea?"

"Henry Beauregard, that's who."

"Henry? But he adores you. I've heard him say you're the prettiest lady in New Orleans."

"He didn't say I had crow's feet, but he said I would soon be a spinster."

"Well . . ."

Laurel whirled to face her mother. "Heavens. Even my own mother is afraid I'll be an old maid."

Rebecca glanced in the mirror and patted her own upswept hair, still richly auburn with only a hint of gray at the temples. "You have passed up some choice young men, dear. Not that I'd want you to settle for anything less than total love like I have with your father. Still, I worry about your following in Shannon's footsteps."

Laurel tossed her head and reached for her bonnet. "I'd be happy as a bluebird to be just like Shannon. She's made herself rich all by herself. She is accepted in the best circles, even if she does own a hotel, and she has plenty of interesting friends. Only—"

"Only what?"

"Only, of course, she doesn't have children."

"Nor will she. Nor will she have a husband to love and comfort her throughout all the days of her life. Keep in mind, we adopted Shannon when she was a waif roaming the alleys of New Orleans. She has different blood from ours and is as independent as a fox. You, on the other hand, have a gentle nature, despite your fine head for business. You'd make a wonderful wife and mother. Laurel, I truly do question your going off alone on this shipping venture. Why not let a professional shipper do the job?"

"Because so much depends on its success. With the profit from this shipment, I can begin to rebuild Caldwell Enterprises. Every detail, here and abroad, must be attended to personally. I've made three voyages with Father, and I know exactly what must be done to insure success. Besides, Captain Harding and the crew have been with us for years. I consider them my friends. I'll be in excellent hands."

Rebecca sighed. "You are your father's daughter, Laurel Anne. But I insist you find a chaperone to accompany you. I'll be nervous as a raccoon treed by hounds until I get a letter from you and know you're safe in Scotland."

Laurel chuckled at her mother's quaint phrase, a residue of Rebecca's backwoods Tennessee upbringing. How lucky her mother had been, coming from such beginnings, to have won the heart of the most eligible bachelor in the exclusive Creole society of New Orleans. Aunt Elizabeth was planning to write about their romance in her next novel. Of course, Blaine Caldwell swore *he* was the lucky one to have found the love of his life, a woman who had given him nothing but joy and devotion these past twenty-eight years.

Laurel picked up her lace gloves. "Henry has asked me to announce our engagement today, but I've declined."

"Again? I'm amazed he keeps trying. He must truly love you."

"I doubt if Henry knows the meaning of the word *love*. I'm just a challenge to him because I keep putting him off. The more I resist, the more persistent he becomes." She cocked her head and pulled on a glove. "I know it isn't fair to keep him dangling, and I do find him attractive. He's the only man of all my old friends who is still single. If it were not for Henry's owning slaves—"

"Laurel, I forbid you to consider marriage to a man you don't love."

She was startled at the vehemence in her mother's tone. "I would like to fall in love, truly I would. But how does one go about it? Wonderful, eligible men don't fall in a girl's apron like apples from a tree. If I married Henry, he would invest in Caldwell Shipping. I'm sure I could eventually persuade him to free his slaves and provide a living for those willing to work at Magnolia Plantation."

"Don't be too sure, Laurel. Henry might promise you anything to get you to the altar, then ignore your pleas ever after. He's nearly thirty now, and he makes all the decisions at Magnolia since his parents passed away last year. In my opinion, his whole world centers on increasing the Beauregard wealth."

Laurel was surprisingly gratified to hear her mother's words. Her deepest feelings were justified. "I do believe you're right, Mother. That's been my impression all along. If Henry mentions his offer again today I will tell him he must absolutely find another woman to marry."

"A fine idea. Now, hurry along, honey. Your father has ordered the carriage around, and the weather is ideal for a picnic. It's a shame the Mackinnons aren't able to attend."

Laurel slipped her hand through her mother's arm and followed her through the door into the upper hallway. "Isn't that shocking? To think Henry's royal guest is a bitter enemy of our cousins. I assume that means the earl is our enemy, too."

"What the earl did was unbelievable, but I know it's true. If we must meet this devil, I'll be polite for Mr. Beauregard's sake, but I won't engage Lord Trowbridge in conversation. Nor will your father. If you must visit with him, you should avoid mentioning you are the new owner of Strathmor Castle. It appears we'll be ducking plenty of folks today, and doing very little socializing."

"Oh? Whom else must we avoid?"

"Shannon is bringing a friend who arrived in New Orleans a few days ago. The gentleman is staying at her hotel."

Laurel was instantly fascinated. "Shannon has a friend? A man? Mother, maybe she's found love at last."

"She assures me that is not the case, though he's quite attractive, she says."

"But why must we avoid him?"

"We'll be polite, of course, but the man is a shipbuilder from Newport. He's gotten rich off building slavers, and he's here meeting **with** his partners in that dreadful business."

"Then I despise him already," Laurel snapped as they reached the entry hall downstairs. "I will tell Shannon she keeps poor company. Really, I'm surprised at my sister. I thought she had higher standards."

Rebecca leaned close to her ear. "I'm sure she does, so I suspect there's a cat in the hen house."

"You mean there's subterfuge afoot?" Laurel asked breathlessly.

"Shannon is as much an abolitionist as we are, but must keep her opinions to herself or her business would be ruined. Personally, I think she's after information from the scoundrel. Maybe she hopes to find proof of some illegal doings that could put him in prison."

"She would do it, I know she would," Laurel exclaimed. She had always idolized her older sister, and she could easily envision Shannon bringing some outlaw to justice.

"The afternoon should be plenty interesting," noted Rebecca. "Like a divided war camp, with the planters on one side and the abolitionists, what few there are of us, on the other. I just hope the food is good and we can excuse ourselves early."

"What's the man's name? Shannon's friend, I mean."

"Hammond Brown. There's your father with the carriage. Bring your parasol, darling." Rebecca gave her a sly wink. "Remember the crow's feet."

Laurel's mind was spinning. It was all she could do to conceal how the name *Hammond Brown* affected her. She had met this man two years ago at a masked ball at Shannon's hotel. He had appeared from nowhere, and seemed to be acquainted with Kyle Wyndford. He was tall and had a commanding presence, even though she could see only his eyes and lower jaw beneath the mask he was wearing. He had danced with her, taking her breath with some mysterious magic she couldn't describe. Something strong and unforgettable had passed between them. She had felt it with every fiber of her being. Her heart had raced, her cheeks had burned, her palms had turned clammy. He'd whispered that his name was Hammond Brown, and after one dance, he had promptly disappeared. She had never seen or heard from him again, and her inquiries about him to Mr. Wyndford revealed only that the man had a ship that stopped occasionally in New Orleans on business.

Today, she would once again see this stranger whose image had seeped into her thoughts for two years. How tragic that he had turned out to be such an evil person. But at least the mystery was solved. She settled in the carriage and accepted a kiss on her cheek from her father. No doubt, she would find Hammond Brown quite unattractive now that he was not so intriguingly disguised.

Cheyne left Shannon Kildaire to visit with her friends beneath a spreading oak, then made his way toward the group of men surrounding the earl of Croydon. He was prepared to present himself as Hammond Brown from Rhode Island. For years, the New Englanders had built ships, shipped their superior rum abroad, then transported slaves on their return trips to America, secretly, of course. Cheyne had learned from his spies that Trowbridge financed such expeditions, although many Englishmen were crusading to suppress the slave traffic entirely. If the earl was secretly engaging in the slave trade, the man would leap at the chance to meet with a Rhode Islander who had connections in the South.

The May afternoon was truly ideal, with a benign sun and a soft breeze wafting from the Mississippi a hundred yards away. On a knoll above the oak grove, a magnificent house in the popular Greek Revival style sat in creamy white elegance backed by the turquoise sky. Close by were peach orchards in full bloom. Beyond the gardens and orchards stretched endless fields of cotton as far as the eye could see. The atmosphere of serenity, gracious living, and ageless beauty was the perfect setting in which to host the first families of a city with as rich a history as any in America.

The first to greet Cheyne was Henry Beauregard. "Welcome to my party. I understand you're with Shannon Kildaire."

"Aye. I'm Hammond Brown. The lady kindly asked me to escort her to your party. Naturally I was delighted." Cheyne was pleased at the way he easily dropped into the cultured style of speech he'd admired as a boy, then disparaged as he'd grown older. He needed his best manners if he was to pull off his disguise as a cultured and sophisticated gentleman. What made it more difficult was that he would be obligated to make conversation with the two people he hated most in the world.

When he'd heard Trowbridge was in New Orleans, he couldn't resist coming face to face with the man who had long ago condemned Jean Lafitte and his entire crew, in absentia, at their trial in London. Trowbridge had once had a ship raided by Lafitte, and the vessel had been relieved of its enormous treasure just stolen from a hapless Spanish galleon on its way to Spain with booty from South America. A predator chain, Sinclair had mused. Thirty years ago, the best captained ship with the most firepower had ruled the seas of the world. Ships were fair game on the unprotected oceans. But Trowbridge didn't see it that way, and had vowed vengeance on Lafitte and his followers. Of course, Lafitte thumbed his nose, but Cheyne had been forced to live with the knowledge that he could never set foot on the British Isles without great risk to his life. He had tried not to care, but if he had any roots at all, they were Scottish. Often he had wondered about his father, and what life might have been like with a home and security and respectability of sorts in his father's land.

Franklin Trowbridge, earl of Croydon, had effectively

blocked any hope Cheyne might have of discovering that life.

While shaking hands with Beauregard, he gave him a close look. Here was the second man he detested above all others: Henry Beauregard, one of the largest slave owners in the States. A man of great wealth and education who would stoop to treating human beings as chattel, beasts of burden, and mere assets in one's list of possessions. It hardly seemed fair the man should be so youthful and handsome. Why didn't evil and greed show in one's face?

"May I introduce my guest of honor," Beauregard said. "Lord Trowbridge, earl of Croydon. Unfortunately her ladyship, the earl's lovely wife, is not with him on his visit to New Orleans. The earl has come in search of a horse, as a matter of fact. Isn't that so, my lord?"

Cheyne quelled his disgust and made a brief bow to the earl. At least in this case, the man was not handsome, but showed unmistakable signs of years of decadent living and overindulgence in food and spirits. Heavy jowled, balding, and paunchy, with sallow skin and yellow teeth, Trowbridge made a poor impression despite his superb suit cut in the latest fashion.

"A pleasure, my lord," muttered Cheyne. The moment was made endurable by the knowledge that he would soon glean the information he needed regarding the slave ships' routes between Europe and Africa and the Americas. "I'm sure you've come to the right place to find the horse you seek."

"We'll see," responded Trowbridge, giving Cheyne a condescending glance. "Your name again? I didn't quite catch it."

"Hammond Brown, from Rhode Island. I have shipping interests there."

The earl cocked an eyebrow and leaned forward. "Rhode Island. Very interesting. Yes, we must speak privately this afternoon. I have business there, you see."

Cheyne was delighted the earl had taken his bait. "Aye. We must do that," he said. He was about to arrange the meeting when from the corner of his eye, he saw a sight that instantly erased everything else from his mind.

Laurel Caldwell had just entered the grove on the arm of her father.

·4·

Ah, I see you've noticed the Caldwells' arrival, Mr. Brown," Beauregard commented. "That is Blaine Caldwell and his wife, Rebecca. On Mr. Caldwell's arm is his youngest daughter, Laurel."

Focusing his attention on Beauregard, Cheyne managed an air of nonchalance. "Shannon Kildaire's adopted parents?"

"Yes. Miss Kildaire was adopted as a child right from the gutter. Most peculiar in my opinion, but charitable, I suppose. She has certainly done well for herself." He leaned forward and said above a whisper, "I'll share a secret with you, Mr. Brown, since you're not a member of our New Orleans set. Miss Laurel Caldwell and I are about to become engaged. If I have my way, we will announce our forthcoming nuptials today. Quite a catch, don't you agree? Too bad the family has fallen on hard times, but I can change all that once I marry the lady. I'll put a few hundred darkies to work planting cotton at Highgrove, and the Caldwells can forget their shipping enterprise." He swelled his chest. "Miss Caldwell and I have been very close since cradle days. Laurel's paternal grandmother was French Creole and a founding member of our most elite New Orleans society." He stroked one sideburn. "Yes indeed, Mr. Brown, keep right on building those slavers I've heard about. Never you mind the idiot U.S. Congress. In a year or two, I may need your ships to provide a labor force at my wife's plantation."

Throughout Beauregard's dialogue, Cheyne stood unmoving, not wishing to speak for fear of betraying his disappointment and disgust. So Laurel Caldwell would marry this pompous slave owner, despite her father's feelings about slavery. The girl must be as empty-headed as she was beautiful. Or else she loved Beauregard, despite his immoral views. When he looked again, she was approaching Shannon Kildaire. Did his friend, Miss Kildaire, know about the engagement? She hadn't mentioned it today when he escorted her here, but why would she think he would be interested?

"Congratulations," he said to Beauregard, more curtly than he intended. Then he faced the earl. He would arrange his tête-à-tête, then leave the company of these charlatans before he revealed his true feelings. Perhaps he would engage Laurel Caldwell in conversation. If she was as vacuous as he now suspected, he could remove her once and for all from his romantic fantasies.

Laurel had expected to see Hammond Brown, take a cursory look, then dismiss him forever from her thoughts.

Her plan failed instantly.

She spotted him the moment she walked into the sun-dappled oak grove. Even with two dozen elegantly dressed ladies and gentlemen enjoying a picnic *al fresco* under the trees, Hammond Brown drew her eye like a magnet, and it was all she could do to keep from staring at him. She saw only his profile where he stood in conversation with Henry Beauregard and two other men, one, no doubt, the dreaded earl of Croydon. She could have recognized Brown in a crowd of hundreds.

His impressive physique and impeccable attire were not the only reasons. There was something else about the man, some indefinable presence that was bound to capture attention, especially that of admiring females. Maybe it was the confident way he stood with one hand knotted behind his back or the way he gestured with the other or the tilt of his wide-brimmed felt hat. Whatever it was, Laurel continued to see him in her mind's eye, long after she forced herself to pay attention to her father, who was speaking to her.

"Laurel, darling, there is Shannon. Why don't you greet her while I join several of the gentlemen. I do have a few friends left among the old-timers." Blaine Caldwell gave her his usual warm, fatherly smile, then ambled off to join the men.

Laurel noticed that her mother was similarly engaged and enjoying herself thoroughly. She was only too happy to follow her father's suggestion. Shannon, at least, might enlighten her about the mysterious Hammond Brown.

"Why, Laurel, honey, how nice to see you." Shannon gave Laurel a broad grin and embraced her. "You're pretty as a picture like always, pumpkin."

"You, too, Shannon. My, just look at that bonnet. The feathers are absolutely glorious."

"The latest from Paris," Shannon effused. "The new shipment of garments I ordered arrived yesterday."

"Shannon, could we speak privately for a moment?" Laurel gave an apologetic smile to Shannon's gathering of acquaintances. "I promise I won't take long, but it's a family matter I need to discuss."

"Of course, dear." Shannon slipped her plump arm around Laurel's waist and guided her to a nearby alcove where chairs had been arranged on a carpet of emerald grass. "Is everything all right, darling? Blaine and Rebecca?"

"They're fine. Working hard, as you can imagine."

Shannon twirled a brass-colored ringlet with one finger. "You know, the rascals won't let me help a bit. Not financially, I mean. After all they did for me, taking me off the streets and doing what they could to stuff a bit of worldly knowledge and manners into my resisting soul. I owe them everything, along with Miss Josephine who left me her *hotel*." She gave Laurel a wink, a reminder that the hotel had once been the most lavish brothel in New Orleans.

"They are independent, Shannon. I can't deny it. But our parents have pride and staunch moral values, which I admire more than anything. I want to be just like them—and just like you."

Shannon guffawed, causing her feathers to shimmer in the sunshine. "I'm mighty complimented, little sister. But I wouldn't wish that on the likes of you. No, chicken, you must take your place in society, marry a dashing gent with a mountain of money, and have lots of beautiful grandchildren for our folks to spoil." She shook her head. "I failed them there, you see. You've got to have double the offspring to make up for my single blessedness."

Laurel nodded. "I'd like to have several children, but the *dashing gent* must appear first. I only know one rich gentleman who is eligible and interested, and for some reason, I can't find the courage to say yes."

"Then don't say it. Just wait and see what turns up."

"Shannon—"

"Yes?"

"I'm curious about your escort today. I wonder if you've found a gentleman that might change your independent ways."

"Mr. Brown? How did you know he escorted me?"

"Mother told me he was staying at your hotel and bringing you to the party. She said he builds ships for use in the slave trade, secretly, of course."

Laurel had the feeling a mask had fallen across Shannon's normally open face. She whispered, "Shannon, you can tell me if you're spying on the man. You know

I'd be in favor of anything you could do to interfere with slavery."

"Laurel, honey, we've shared many secrets over the years. I would trust you with my life. But my lips are sealed regarding Mr. Brown."

Laurel's curiosity knew no bounds. "But Shannon, I wouldn't tell, truly I wouldn't. You see, I met Hammond Brown years ago, at your hotel, actually, at a masked ball. He danced with me, and I must say I found him rather attractive. So you see, I have some right to know who he is and what he's doing here."

A rare furtiveness came into Shannon's eyes. "He is tolerably handsome, I'll agree. But he was wrong to dance with you. He is not a man who should interest you, sweetheart. Believe me, I know what I'm talking about."

"Then Mother was right. Mr. Brown is a greedy scoundrel who would stop at nothing to profit from the slave trade. Wouldn't you just know," she agonized, "and he's the most attractive man I've met in years."

Shannon studied her, almost as if she wanted to reveal something, but then decided against it. Laurel wouldn't ask again. If Shannon implied the man was no good, then she would have to accept that.

"I won't ask any more questions, Shannon. But do be careful. Where there's money to be made, some people can be quite dangerous, no matter how attractive and charming they appear."

Shannon stood and adjusted her befeathered hat. "I suppose I'll have to meet the earl. Haven't met any real royalty before. I wouldn't bother, except I can name-drop to some of my high-toned clientele at the hotel."

Laurel rose to face her. "Speaking of scoundrels, Lord Trowbridge is one of the worst. In fact, none of the family plans to do more than say a polite hello, for Henry's sake. I'll tell you the story when I get the chance, and explain why the Mackinnons aren't here today."

Shannon grinned, obviously hungry for the gossip, but she turned toward her companions under the oak tree.

Alone, Laurel sat again on the bench. She snapped open her fan and gazed through the shrubbery at the colorful gathering. Several of her girlfriends were here, all with their husbands and a few with young children. One was pregnant and starting to show her increased weight. This picnic would be that lady's last for a time, Laurel thought, with a surge of envy.

"Excuse me, Miss Caldwell."

She turned to look into a face she hadn't seen, but had imagined these past two years in her deepest dreams. Her heart nearly stopped. To her dismay, Mr. Hammond Brown was ruggedly handsome, stunning, with his chiseled features, his shock of well groomed sable hair with a hint of silver at the temples, and with eyes as wise as a priest's. He was more astonishingly attractive than in her wildest fantasies. Not smooth and youthful and vapid like Henry. Quite the opposite. Mr. Brown looked like a man who had seen a great deal of life, endured hardship and danger, fought dragons and villains, and come away a wounded but heroic victor.

Stop it, Laurel stormed at herself. *You're conjuring up someone who doesn't exist. And the man hasn't even said hello.*

"You've asked to be excused, sir," she said with barely a trace of nerves, "but I'm not sure why."

"For disturbing the reverie of such a lovely lady. If your thoughts are as exquisite as your person, I am a villain for interrupting them."

Glib. Smooth as silk, she thought. It's what she would have expected of him. "I don't believe we've been introduced," she said, an edge to her tone.

"Not exactly. But we danced together years ago. Not that you'd remember, since I wore a mask at the time. Or that you would have cause to remember, at any rate. My name is Hammond Brown. And you are Miss Laurel

Caldwell. I have the pleasure of escorting your sister, Miss Kildaire, today. I would have waited for her to introduce us, but I don't expect to be here long. I was afraid I might miss the opportunity to speak to you."

Laurel raised her fan and fluttered it beneath her chin. "Then good afternoon, Mr. Brown. I fear I don't recall our dance together. It's been some time."

"Two years, during my last visit to your fair city. I would be happy to bring you a glass of punch. I believe that's the primary refreshment at these afternoon occasions."

"You needn't bother. My sister will expect you to serve her, however."

"I have just delivered a cup to Miss Kildaire. She's engrossed in private conversation with her friends at the moment. I have a meeting with the earl of Croydon shortly. I stole this opportunity to introduce myself and see if I could be of service. It hardly seemed fitting for you to be alone."

"Your concern is unnecessary, Mr. Brown. Actually—"

"Laurel! There you are."

She turned to see Henry Beauregard entering the bower. Why his sudden appearance angered her, she couldn't say, but it definitely was an annoyance.

"Mr. Beauregard," muttered Mr. Brown, his voice distinctly cool.

"I didn't see you slip away, my dear." Henry's tone was mildly chastising. "I was visiting with the earl, I suppose." He reached for her gloved hand and brushed it with his lips. Then he said, "So you've met Mr. Brown."

"We met years ago, Henry, at a party given by Shannon." She was annoyed at herself for feeling obligated to explain her previous introduction. Why did Henry invariably raise her defenses?"

Henry looked directly at Hammond Brown. "The earl will see you now, in private, sir. I hope your chat will be brief, since I have a surprise planned. I have a special charity in New Orleans. The Society for the Care of Unfortunate Orphans. We're having a small fund-raising today—an auction. I've collected some wonderful items for the block." One side of his mouth curled in a smile. He said in a low tone, "A quadroon woman of remarkable beauty will be offered to the gentlemen only."

Overcome with disgust, Laurel pretended not to hear.

"Excellent," Cheyne said vigorously. "If I find her appealing, I'll test the depths of your guests' pockets." Barely within his vision, Laurel's reaction caught Cheyne's eye. He didn't need to look directly at her to feel her shock and seething anger. At least, she was decent enough to find fault with the sale of a human being at an afternoon picnic. On the other hand, she had better know now what sort of man she was about to marry. When she started to rise, he reached for her hand before Beauregard could offer his. *"Mademoiselle, s'il vous plaît."*

She kept her hands at her sides. Slowly she raised her eyes to stare at him, her expression stunned. He had to wonder why *he* was receiving the brunt of her anger. After all, it was her fiancé who had announced the auction.

"Laurel, my dear, allow *me.*" Beauregard extended his elbow and placed her hand on it. She moved mechanically, as if she had no will of her own. She did truly appear half-witted at the moment. Perhaps she had gone the way of other Southern belles when it came to political and economic matters. The ladies were rumored to be ruled by father or brother or husband, whichever male she was most indebted to at the time.

Cheyne removed his hat and bowed as the couple turned to go. "Good afternoon, Miss Caldwell. Or perhaps I should say a final *adieu.* I sail tomorrow. We may not meet again."

With one hand clutching Beauregard's sleeve, the other holding the closed fan pressed to her bosom,

Laurel answered tightly, "Farewell, Mr. Brown. No, I don't expect we'll meet."

He watched the two stroll toward the barbecue table where a feast was spread. He had the oddest feeling that a lovely fantasy he'd held for years had just been destroyed. The crushing depression that settled around his heart surprised him. He hadn't thought he was still capable of such feelings. The child-woman he had idolized for so long had plunged from her lofty position. She was like every other woman who had chosen to subjugate herself to the will of a powerful man. He should have expected it, but somehow he had held out hope Laurel Caldwell would be different.

With one more ideal dashed, he could concentrate now on prying information from the infamous earl of Croydon.

· 5 ·

Laurel's shocked horror blazed into flame. "Henry, we must talk. Privately. At once." She pulled her hand from his elbow and planted her feet, forcing him to halt in mid stride to face her.

"Now?" He smiled and nodded at a passing guest. "I thought we would visit after the barbecue—"

"Now, Henry Beauregard!"

"Very well. Don't make a scene. We'll go to the library."

Biting her lip to contain the words simmering on her tongue, she whirled and marched toward the house. She felt the edge of her broad-brimmed skimmer lift in the breeze as she hurried up the path.

Once inside the library, she faced a perplexed Henry. "I must tell you, sir, I am completely appalled at the idea of your selling a woman to the highest bidder. It's a travesty at any time, but at a *party*—well, really. It smacks of some pagan orgy and is in the worst possible taste, to say the least."

Henry looked relieved. "Oh, is that what has you in such a dither, my sweet? I thought I had done something dreadful to offend you."

"But I am offended. You know I detest slavery. Especially the buying and selling of women and children. What will the ladies think if you sell a beautiful woman—perhaps to someone's husband—here, at your party?"

He gave her a smile of long-suffering patience. "First of all, dear Laurel, every one of the ladies, with two or three exceptions, has just such a slave tending to her needs every day, provided by a husband who wishes to relieve her of mundane chores beneath her class. Where do you think the dark-skinned servants come from? Or the mammies who look after the children? From the slave market, that's where."

"Originally, yes," she stormed. "But now, most of the house slaves are born on the plantations. You, yourself, have sworn you treat your slaves like valued members of the family. Where did you acquire this poor woman? Doesn't she have any family?" Laurel paced before him, hating the arrogant way he spoke to her as if she had the mind of a child.

"As a matter of fact, I'm doing the wench a great favor. She's young and unusually attractive, that cream color I like best. She grew up in a hovel in St. John's Bayou, illegitimate, and raised like a mongrel pup. I saw her a few days ago and arranged the purchase from her guardian, who said she had agreed to do anything to escape her miserable surroundings. With her looks and her surprising education—she speaks French and swears she can read—she will be accepted into a secure position in a fine home in New Orleans. I brought her here to keep her from public auction, and, if you'll recall, the money goes to a good cause. Naturally I will hold the sale while the ladies are taking their afternoon rest. Any of them should be delighted when they reappear to find their husband has surprised them with an exceptional new maid as a gift."

Laurel stopped her pacing to stare at him. Henry really believed he was doing something wonderful for all concerned. *How blind he was. How blind they all were.* She controlled herself and tried to think more clearly. In analyzing her reaction, she admitted that part of her uncontrollable anger had been caused by the absolute proof of Hammond Brown's plunge from his pedestal. The man had practically licked his chops at the chance to buy a beautiful mulatto, and he had no wife who needed a serving girl. She felt as if she had witnessed the wolf finding Little Red Riding Hood on his doorstep. Since Mr. Brown was almost a stranger, she could hardly have spoken her mind to him, even if she had not been too shocked to speak at all. All her disgust and disappointment had been directed at Henry Beauregard. Furthermore, she had been diverted from what she really intended to say to Henry today.

Taking a deep breath, she began more calmly. "I did lose my temper, Henry. But this matter of your owning slaves is only one more deterrent to a union of our families. You've been patient with me, more so than I deserve."

"Laurel, darling—"

She stepped away as he moved near. "No, Henry. I must tell you once and for all, I will not marry you. Not ever. Perhaps I am fated to be a spinster like my sister, as you've suggested. So be it. You must be free to search for a suitable wife. I must be free to follow whatever course my life will take."

His brow furrowed as if he hadn't heard or didn't comprehend her words. After several seconds when the only sounds were the ticking of the wall clock and the chattering of sparrows outside the open window, his expression cleared, and he gazed at her in resignation. "You're making a mistake. You'll see that someday, Laurel, but then it will be too late."

"Perhaps," she said magnanimously.

"I will ask one favor of you. Don't speak to anyone today of your refusal. I don't wish to be a source of gossip or pity at my own celebration."

She almost smiled at how little fuss he made, now that she'd convinced him her rejection was final. She would bet he already had a new conquest in mind. "I quite understand. In fact, I expect to leave shortly with my parents. Our guests, the Mackinnons were unable to attend, so we must return to Highgrove before dinner."

"The Mackinnons? Oh yes, the half-breed. Why didn't they come?" he asked idly.

"It seems the former lord of the Mackinnon Clan is no friend to the earl of Croydon. They're sworn enemies, in fact. Mr. Mackinnon didn't wish to confront the earl and cause you any possible embarrassment. I will do as you ask by not mentioning my refusal of your hand. You can return that favor by making no mention to the earl that the Mackinnons are guests at Highgrove."

Henry was beginning to act bored. "Done. I dislike conflict of any kind. The earl is heading for Virginia in a few days to continue his search for a horse." His eyes wandered toward the window. "I must return to my guests."

"By all means."

"No one need know of our discussion, Laurel. We can allow our acquaintances to assume we merely drifted apart by mutual agreement."

"That's fine with me." As she left the library, she felt fatigued and strangely depressed. Relieved, of course, to be rid of Henry Beauregard's courtship. But the depression was more difficult to understand. Was it because she suddenly had no suitor, at all? She had told her family she wanted nothing more than to stand on her own two feet, to be her own person, and do what she pleased. Now, at age twenty-six, she would have a chance to live up to her words. She had been right to end Henry's hopes, but she felt a bit adrift in uncertain waters. Henry had been an option that had existed for years and was now gone for good.

Maybe her sadness was because of a growing disillusionment with men in general, and with Hammond Brown, in particular. To give up a long-time suitor was unsettling at best, but to lose a fantasy was dreary indeed.

Reaching the garden, she spotted her parents chatting with Shannon. They appeared to have finished their luncheon and might be ready to leave. She was ready. More than ready.

Two days following Henry's picnic, Laurel took one last ride across the hills and fields of Highgrove Plantation. For the next week, she would be busy packing, and then she would move onboard the *Star,* the aging Caldwell frigate moored at the port of New Orleans. She would oversee the loading of her shipment of rice and sugar cane, as well as several barrels of rare indigo. She also planned to sell one hundred exquisite cotton quilts, handmade by some of her Arcadian friends, through a dealer in London. Every bit of merchandise on board was precious and should bring a solid profit. If anything went wrong, if her buyers in Gibraltar, Spain, or the British Isles failed her, she would have to close the doors of Caldwell Shipping. How tragic that would be after so much effort by her grandfather and her father these past sixty years. She felt the past and the future resting squarely on her shoulders, but she was full of confidence, and her spirits restored after the unpleasantness at Magnolia Plantation.

As she topped a hill and halted to enjoy one last look from above her gracious home on the bend of the Mississippi, she saw a rider coming toward her. Fletcher Mackinnon. No one she knew rode with such amazing skill and ease, with or without a proper saddle and tack. Today the half Lakota Sioux wore his buckskins, and his long hair blew free in the wind. The forty-three-year-old Fletcher looked as fit as a young warrior.

She waved as he urged his mount up the slope. "Hello, Fletcher. Isn't it a glorious day?"

He reined in and controlled his fractious mount. "Your horses are second to none, Laurel. This stallion is a handful."

"You have yet to encounter the horse you can't handle, Fletcher Mackinnon. But thank you. We've been breeding with great care for several generations."

Patting the animal's shoulder, Fletcher gazed at the lush scenery spread below them. "I wanted a moment alone with you to wish you good luck on your journey to Skye. I pray you won't be disappointed when you reach the island and inspect our old castle there. For all I know, it could be a crumbling ruin by now."

"I doubt it. You've only been away two years, and Strathmor was standing for nearly a hundred years before that. Your daughter described it to me in detail. She truly loved the place, you know."

"Aye. At first Skye found it hard to believe we were selling the place. But with England ruling Scotland and taxing the people to death, our pleasures were meager. There is no glory in starving, I can tell you."

"I understand. But Aunt Elizabeth's novels are selling well. Wouldn't her income have saved the property? Or do I presume too much to inquire into your private affairs?"

"Not at all, lass. We're family, after all, and you have

bought the place for a fair price. Aye, my Beth's writing brings in money, but as long as I have life, I will not be dependent on her income. She is free to do whatever she likes with her earnings, but as her husband, I provide financial security for her."

Laurel smiled inwardly at Fletcher's proud stand. She had enormous respect for this man who had endured so much. "Well, you're doing very well for yourself, Fletcher. From all reports, your cattle are thriving in Dakota, after only a short time. And Skye is married to one of the wealthiest and most powerful men in the area. You should be a happy man."

"Indeed I am. And I wish you happiness with my island home. I wanted to ask you to give my warmest regards to my old friends, the MacCraes. Kenneth MacCrae is a crofter nearby, and he'll welcome news from me. Tell him, if he isn't satisfied with how things are going, he must come to America. I'll see to it he establishes his family as my neighbors in Dakota."

"I'll be sure to do that."

"Be sure to meet Rosie MacCrae. She's Kenneth's second wife and a bonnie lady. She was Skye's playmate since they were wee sprites. If you need help with the house, she would be a good choice."

"I will be looking for help, Fletcher. My plan is to spend next winter and spring making the castle comfortable, though I won't have much money to spend on it right away. While I'm there, I'll explore the possibilities of making a shipping port of Kylerhae village. I hope to off-load goods from New Orleans and sell to Scotland just as easily as to England. I'd be delighted to do business with Scottish relatives, if possible. Mother's family were Sutherlands, you know."

"Aye. I remember your family's visits to our shores when you were a child. We had some fine times at clan gatherings in those days. Your family has been very good to me, Laurel. You made us feel at home in New Orleans before we went west, and then you bought the castle. I'll never forget all you've done for me and my sweet Beth, and for my daughter, too."

"I hope a year from this fall I'll be able to visit both families in Dakota. Let's see, Skye's twins will be eighteen months old by then. I'm just dying to see them."

"They're wonderful bairns. Our new house should be finished by then, and I ordered furniture yesterday in New Orleans. I want Beth to have the best, even in our western land."

Her attention turned back to the awesome landscape, then focused on the paddock where Badger Wyndford was now working with Desert Mirage. "Mirage is adjusting well to Louisiana."

"Aye. We'll miss Mirage and Badger in Dakota this winter, but the two will flourish at Highgrove, I'm certain."

"She's a remarkable filly. Our horses are fine, but I've never seen such a creature as your half Arab. I would put her up against any horse in the world for sheer beauty and grace." She had no sooner spoken, when the most astonishing idea crept into her thoughts. For several seconds, she stared at the filly prancing and tossing its mane, then she fixed her gaze on Fletcher. "I had the most amazing idea just now."

"What's that?"

"I learned from Henry Beauregard about a contest being held in London a year from this July. Prince Albert is quite a sportsman, and he is sponsoring the competition himself. He's offering a hundred thousand pounds to the horse that is judged the most beautiful in the world. But the animal must have great stamina, since a cross-country race is involved. Didn't you tell me these Arab horses can run forever?"

"Over long distances, they're incomparable. The Berbers have trusted their lives to their mounts for centuries, bred them for stamina, even sometimes kept them inside their tents on the desert. And Mirage's dam was pure Indian pony, with a heart the size of a mountain.

43

That filly carries the best of two great civilizations in her bloodlines. Are you suggesting what I think you are?"

"Why not, Fletcher? Do you think Mirage would be mature enough to compete by that time."

"Aye, a well trained two-year-old will be able to hold her own. And her beauty is evident."

"Then it's a perfect plan," Laurel said happily. "You and Elizabeth and my parents are coming to Skye next spring. You must bring Badger and Desert Mirage. We won't have to decide about the contest until we see how the mare endures the voyage. It is lengthy, after all. But if she does well, you can enter her in the competition. You could win a fortune to lay at Beth's feet."

He grinned at the prospect. "Aye. That I would love to do. But there's one matter we must clear up from the start. Not all the prize money would be mine."

"Oh? Then whose would it be?"

"Half must go to your father, Laurel."

"Oh? Why so? You found the Arab stallion and bred him to your pony."

"I would have died in Tangier if not for special arrangements by your father that led to my rescue. He was out a large sum of money on my behalf. I'm in his debt, and I've been searching for a way to repay him."

Laurel knew Fletcher was well aware of the Caldwell's financial dilemma. "Naturally he could use the extra funds, but that would be between you and my father. I didn't realize he was instrumental in your escape."

"He was, along with one other person whom I cannot name."

There it was again. That mystery that no one would talk about. Something had happened two years ago when the Mackinnons had first arrived in New Orleans. That was about the time when Hammond Brown had appeared at the masked ball. *No,* she told herself, there couldn't possibly be any connection between that scoundrel and Fletcher's rescue with his stallion from Tangier.

At the time she had been too absorbed at Caldwell Shipping to question the events.

She leaned forward in her saddle. "I've heard tantalizing hints about your rescue, Fletcher, but never any details. Doesn't anyone trust me to know the truth, not even my own relatives?"

Fletcher looked thoughtful for a time. "Very well. I'll tell you what I know. Have you heard of the Sea Falcon?"

"Of course. Who hasn't? I admire him greatly, but he's hated by the planters. I've heard the slave owners have put a price on his head of twenty thousand dollars, but no one has a chance to collect. His identity is unknown and he sails from foreign ports, well out of everyone's reach."

"Aye. I'll tell you if you promise to keep it a secret."

Her pulse was pounding. "You don't mean—"

"The Sea Falcon came to my rescue. Your father paid him well, I'm certain."

She caught her breath. Her father? The hardworking, conservative businessman, the former war hero, Blaine Caldwell, had had dealings with this infamous outlaw? How thrilling! "I'm delighted, Fletcher. I wish I had known. But why didn't Father tell me?"

"Secrecy is life and death to the Falcon, you see. All of us who know him have taken a sacred oath not to reveal his identity."

"Really?" She was absolutely breathless at the tale. "Is he an American?"

"I'm not free to say, but I wouldn't consider him such, if I were you. He is a man without a country, as they say."

"And you know him? But you won't tell me who he is?" Her curiosity was on fire.

"I've said too much already. But I would like my horse to win the prize. I could repay your father for helping me."

Laurel was about to plead, beg, cajole—anything to learn the secret, but Badger shouted at them. Frustrated, she waved back. "What is it, Badger?"

His voice was barely audible. "Come see what Mirage can do."

"We must go, I suppose," she said to Fletcher. "Thank you for sharing as much as you have. And I won't breathe a word to Father."

"Thank *you* for your idea about the horse competition. We'll have to discuss the prospects over dinner."

Riding down the hill in the spring sunshine, Laurel was elated. She was free of any ties to Henry Beauregard, and she had so much to look forward to, so many adventures in store when she sailed next week toward the Mediterranean.

·6·

Shannon! Welcome aboard the *Star!*" Laurel jumped from behind her desk in the captain's cabin and embraced her sister. "I'm surprised to see you. Please sit down." She shifted a stack of papers from a chair.

Three days before, Laurel had moved into a room at Shannon's hotel in the French Quarter. Her parents had arrived yesterday, and tomorrow night a farewell dinner was planned at Miss Delphine's Restaurant with all the family in attendance.

"I do love ships," Shannon said, glancing about. "Especially when they're anchored in a safe harbor."

"We'll be sailing in two days. On our way at last. I'm going over my supply list this morning."

"I don't want to tarry too long since I can see you're mighty busy."

Laurel leaned on the edge of her desk. "I do have a stack of things waiting for my attention. The last of the crates will be loaded today; tomorrow, we'll take on the supplies for the galley."

"You had already gone when I stopped by your room, but I'm glad for an excuse to see the *Star* again. Looks like you'll be comfy and cozy on your voyage."

"I left the hotel this morning at the crack of dawn. So much to do, you know. I can't believe I'm occupying the captain's cabin. Father always used it when we traveled together. His charts and books are here. I must admit I feel quite important taking over this space for myself," she added grinning.

Shannon appeared to glow as she sat in the sun streaming from the bank of broad windows at the ship's stern. Her fuchsia dress and oversized hat with matching pink feathers took on a life of their own. "I wanted to ask a favor of you, dear."

"Anything, Shannon, just name it."

"I don't want to impose."

"Goodness, we're sisters, aren't we? You couldn't impose, no matter what."

Shannon nodded and returned Laurel's smile. "Well, I've been wondering if you have a traveling companion, a lady's maid, you know, for your trip." She appeared hesitant, unusual for her.

"A companion? Don't tell me you agree with my mother on that. She's been after me for weeks, but I don't need any help. Besides, I wouldn't want to drag some poor soul away from home for a year just so I could have someone to chat with over supper."

"Maybe I can solve the problem to everyone's satisfaction."

"I don't understand."

"I have someone in mind who would very much like to go with you—as your lady's maid, or in whatever capacity you'd choose."

"Really?"

"She's a quadroon girl, about seventeen, I reckon. She's from the bayou and wants to escape New Orleans. She's a good girl, never been loose with men, if you don't mind my speaking plainly. But she's too pretty to be safe in this town, or anywhere where her kind are considered slaves."

"Goodness. In that case, I'd be delighted to have her. Does she understand we'll be at sea for weeks and then in Scotland until next summer?"

"I don't believe she'll ever want to come back. You see, she was born under questionable circumstances in St. John's. She's illegitimate, or she wouldn't have been sold as a slave." Her voice dropped to a whisper. "She says her grandmother is Marie Laveau."

"Laveau, the voodoo witch?"

"A good witch, mostly, by all reports, with plenty of friends in New Orleans—some in high society."

"Shannon, is this the slave girl who was auctioned at Henry's party?"

"Yes, that very one."

"You mean *you* bought her?"

"No. Ladies weren't allowed at the auction. She was given to me afterwards. I had to keep it a secret until I could find a way to get her out of New Orleans. I was told several men at the sale were panting for the girl, but they couldn't top the high bidder. If they knew he had given her to me, they'd be tearing down my front door to find her."

Laurel absorbed this carefully. Then she asked quietly, "And who, may I ask, was the high bidder?"

"Mr. Hammond Brown. Guess he's got more money than a king. I heard that his first bid caused everyone else to shut their mouths and put their money clips back in their pockets. It was over in the wink of an eye, and the girl was his."

She wasn't surprised. "So, when did Mr. Brown give her to you?"

"Right after the sale. I was having a sherry under a tree during that siesta nonsense, and he marched up with the girl and said we must leave the party. I wasn't in a hurry, since I was expecting to finagle a dance with the earl, but Mr. Brown insisted he had to go at once. He said I could stay, if I liked, but I decided I'd had enough of royalty. The earl's sure no prize to look at. So I went on along with Mr. Brown. It was kinda peculiar, bounding along the river road with that dapper gentleman and this good-looking gal in a makeshift dress who'd just been sold at auction. She looked miserable, thin and delicate with big sad eyes like brown saucers. I think she was mostly scared, and I wanted to tell her she was not so unlucky to be bought by a handsome man like Mr. Brown. Could've been worse."

Laurel was utterly fascinated. She had known Hammond Brown would buy the girl, but why would he pay a fortune, then give her away? He'd made a killing from slavery, and could profit handsomely from selling a beautiful Negro. On the other hand, she had assumed he wanted the girl for himself. "And then what happened?" she asked breathlessly.

"We were almost back to the hotel when he told me he was sailing for Newport the next day. He said he was having second thoughts about the girl, and would I look after her, find her a safe place, a proper position somewhere. I said sure. She could work at the hotel as a chambermaid. But he said no, that wasn't safe enough, that she needed to get away from the men who had oogled her at the sale."

"Mr. Brown said that?"

"He surely did. I figured *him* for an oogler as good as the next, but guess he had other things on his mind. So, I told him I would take her in and keep it a secret until I could figure out what to do with her. Then he really surprised me."

Laurel was spellbound. "What did he do?"

"He took out her legal title and a pen and used his knee as a table. He wrote the word *emancipated* in big letters beneath her name."

"He did? After paying all that money for her?"

"Here it is." Shannon opened her string purse and produced the document. Under the girl's name, Nicole Petit, was inscribed *Emancipated* in bold print. "I was mighty impressed with what he'd done."

"Fancy that," sighed Laurel. Her villainous Mr. Brown had just risen a notch from the bottom of his pedestal. "I really am astonished, considering he builds ships for use in the slave trade."

Shannon paused and touched her gloved fingers to her lips. "Oh, he must have his reasons. I didn't ask what they were."

"So Nicole Petit is prepared to go with me to the Isle of Skye."

"I talked to her about it, offered a few other options like going West, but she said she'd prefer to leave the American continent as soon as possible. Can't say that I blame her."

"You say she's pleasant, with some education?"

"Sweet as honey. No temperament I can see. Smart too, and speaks French like a lady. Learned it as a child, she said, between cleaning and cooking and scrubbing for years. She said her greatest fear always had been getting caught and sold into slavery, and sure enough, Mr. Beauregard saw her and kidnapped her from the bayou. Your old friend, Henry, knows a prize when he sees one. I bet he made a bundle at the auction, and he will give a mere pittance to the charity he was touting."

Laurel didn't care about Henry. To take Nicole Petit as her maid and companion needed no further consideration. What did tug at her was why a slave-trading scoundrel, a lustful man like Hammond Brown, would do such a thing: spend all that money to help a woman of color find a better life. He must have had some ulterior reason, she mused. How titillating, and just when she thought she had put the mystery of Hammond Brown to rest, once and for all. She handed the paper back to Shannon. "I'm truly pleased to have her travel with me. I'll pay her, of course, and I'll certainly enjoy her company. I only hope she won't be seasick."

Shannon rose, smiling broadly. "I appreciate it, Laurel. Nicole will, too, and Mother will be satisfied you're not alone with all those lusty seamen." She shook her finger under Laurel's nose. "This time I agree with Mother. A young lady needs a female helpmate when she travels abroad."

"I suppose so. When will I meet Nicole? I want to be sure she has all she needs for the journey. Plenty of warm, useful clothing."

"I'll take care of all that and have her here before you sail on Tuesday."

"Good. Actually, I'm very pleased. You have done me a favor, not the reverse."

After Shannon left the ship, Laurel found herself in a contemplative mood. She couldn't take her mind off Hammond Brown. The more she heard about him, the more enigmatic he became. She was sorry, now, she hadn't had time to talk with him at Magnolia Plantation.

With her thoughts drifting, she opened her trunk and peered inside. She wanted to be sure she had packed the special items of clothing her seamstress had made for her for the trip. Three pairs of plain cotton ankle-length pants, almost like men's breeches, but cut much looser so curves were not revealed. Also a similar pair made from heavy wool. Skirts could be a nuisance on a ship at sea, especially in a storm. While she was all feminine frills and lace in New Orleans society, her place on the *Star* would require an entirely different wardrobe. She would work closely with Captain Harding, as her father had always done. She had great confidence in Captain Harding's abilities, but she herself was capable of taking command of the frigate and guiding them to a safe port, if that became necessary. The crew were seasoned professionals, mostly family men with high moral standards who had known her since she was a child. Not that they wouldn't tip a tankard or two if they had the chance.

Laurel closed the trunk and went back to her desk. Staring at her checklist where it lay in shards of sunlight that rocked gently with the movement of the ship, she felt a rush of excitement. She concluded that one's anticipation on the eve of an adventure was the best part of it. She had a good feeling about the upcoming voyage. Everything was in perfect order, and she was eager to get under way.

· 7 ·

Tangier, Morocco, June 1842

Cheyne stared in disbelief at the scene before him. Here in this dark, squalid hut on the outskirts of Tangier, a woman sat hunched like a mound of clay, shackled to a corpse.

"God in heaven," he mumbled. "Now I've seen it all."

He knelt beside the woman and tried to see her face. Only her eyes were visible above the dark veil, and they were tightly closed. It was as if she were sculpted from the earthen floor, draped with dirty cloth, unmoving, and unseeing. Yet she lived. He could detect the flutter of an eyelash, the slight sound of her breath as she inhaled and exhaled.

"You'll be all right now, madam." He whipped a blade from beneath his burnoose and cut the thick rope binding the ankle of the dead body to the wrists of the living female.

"There, you've nothing to fear," he soothed.

Gradually the eyelids lifted to reveal eyes almost as lifeless as those of the corpse.

"I'm Cheyne Sinclair. My servant suspected there was trouble and brought me at once. Your captors have fled. Unfortunately your friend here has no need of my help, but has gone to meet Allah. Carry her home, Rafi." Cheyne said. "We'll revive her first and ask questions later."

Rafi scooped up the woman, who slumped against him and closed her eyes. "How long do you suppose she's been like this?" he asked angrily. "Who would leave a woman tied to a rotting body?"

"Saad, the slave-trader, would do such a thing if he thought he was suddenly in danger." Cheyne followed Rafi into the heat of the noonday Moroccan sun. "Saad is moving up my list of jackals I'd like to eliminate from this earth." A sudden wind whipped his robes, and he pulled his cowl around his head. Dust and trash from the alley swirled around him as he turned to his left. "Take her to the palace and give her to Fatima. I'll be along later. I want to tell one of the locals to take care of the body in the hut."

After a brief explanation to a vender at a nearby stall, Cheyne hugged his cloak around him and made his way toward home. The wind had been blowing fiercely across the straits for six days, ever since he'd returned from his last voyage to New Orleans. Now it filled his nostrils with rank odors and clogged his teeth with dirt and grit.

Walking along the narrow streets of the medina, he cursed the slave trade once again. It was the sin of Africa and a blight on the New World. When would it end? he wondered as he increased his pace. He had been disappointed to see the practice flourishing in the American South. Ever since cotton had become king, slavery had become a seemingly indispensable way of life. He had tried hard after he left New Orleans to forget about

Laurel Caldwell marrying a rich slave-owner, but despite his deep disappointment over the woman, he couldn't forget how lovely she looked the afternoon he'd seen her in the shady bower at Magnolia Plantation. If only they could have talked awhile, but that ass, Beauregard, had interrupted them. Then, after the auction, Cheyne knew he should get the quadroon girl off the premises as soon as possible. He had obtained all the information he needed anyway, but he would have given a great deal for a last farewell to the enchanting Miss Caldwell. The next time he was in New Orleans, she would be Mrs. Henry Beauregard, heading down the perfumed path followed by all the wives of wealthy Southern gentlemen.

He spat in the dirt and cursed himself for thinking of her. She was dead to him, as sure as if she were in her coffin. And he had work to do. The frigate was being outfitted for battle even now. Soon he would be prowling the Atlantic sea lanes, on the lookout for slaving ships.

He cut across an alley, shielding his face as he went, then hurried up the steps of his palace and entered the sheltered veranda with its arched columns framing the ocean. He signaled his return to the guard and pushed back the hood of his burnoose. His lips tasted of sand and grit and sweat.

Passing quickly through the main salon, he tossed aside his cloak and headed toward Fatima's quarters, where Rafi would have left the woman to be cared for. He would see to it that she returned to her home, wherever that was, as soon as she could travel. He entered the women's quarters and strode across the marble floor toward the inner courtyard.

"Fatima?" he called.

A plump, doe-eyed woman in a colorful caftan hurried to greet him. "Captain Sinclair, what a terrible thing, such mistreatment of a poor lady."

"Slavery is always terrible, Fatima. Is she going to be all right? Does she need a physican?"

"No, I don't need a physcian," came a surprisingly strong female voice from the next room.

Cheyne stopped and gazed quizzically at Fatima. "Is that the voice of our prostrate captive?"

A woman strolled into the courtyard and paused by the fountain. No longer a lump beneath a dusty cloak, she stood like a vision of loveliness beside the sparkling water in the play of light and shadow. She wore a diaphanous silk robe that lifted in the breeze. Her sleek black hair, still damp from a recent washing, hung below her hips and was held in place at her forehead by a rope of gold. She was young, but her eyes were wise and seductively slanted with a hint of amber in their brown depths. The robe did little to conceal her perfect figure, full breasts and well rounded hips and narrow waist.

Cheyne could hardly believe this was the half-dead creature he had rescued less than an hour ago. For once, he was totally at a loss for words, but could only stare in amazement.

"I bathed her, as you can see," explained Fatima, obviously pleased with the miracle she had produced. "She must have been meant for the sultan's harem."

Collecting himself, Cheyne studied the lady. "Ahem, aye, well, what is your name, madam? I'm pleased you've recovered so rapidly from your ordeal."

She lifted a feathery eyebrow. "Shazade Amin, from Ketema. You are Cheyne Sinclair, the man to whom I owe my life."

"Aye, I'm Sinclair, but you owe me nothing. Have you had something to eat?" he thought suddenly to ask.

"Your servant brought me juice and a biscuit. It's enough for now."

"You speak excellent English."

"Yes, and French and Spanish and Berber. I was born in Spain, but I came to Morocco with my father a few years ago."

"And where is your father now?"

For the first time, the lady appeared uncertain. "Gone. With the Bedouins, I suppose."

"And your mother? Will she be concerned for you?"

"She died in Spain when I was a child. My father kept me with his women until I came of age. A few months ago, Saad, the slave merchant, offered him a very handsome sum for me."

"I thought so. Then where am I to send you, now that you're free?"

"I would like to stay here, if I could be of some use." Her slow suggestive smile left no doubt of her meaning.

"Mistress Shazade, I will be happy for you to stay, but only as my guest until we locate some family member who will make a home for you. Maybe you'd like to return to your mother's people in Spain. My household staff is complete, and since I have no wife, Fatima manages the women's quarters."

"You have no wife? Not even one?"

"I'm a Scotsman, lass, and despite appearances, I have a few scruples remaining from my days among Christian pirates."

She looked perplexed. "But you must have women, unless . . . unless . . ."

"I'm no eunuch, if that's what you're asking. I don't find it appropriate for us to stand here before Fatima discussing my personal affairs. Now, if you'll excuse me, I have work to do. Make yourself at home, Mistress. Fatima will see to your needs." He was speaking gruffly, but making things clear right away was the best course with women, his experience had proven. As alluring as Shazade was, he was not going to tumble a strange lady who had arrived under his roof in such peculiar circumstances. He had enemies on several continents and spies were everywhere. The woman's quick recovery after being hauled across Morocco to the coastal slave market was decidedly suspicious. "Fatima," he said, tearing his eyes from the luscious Shazade, "I'll be sailing within the week. See that this lady is well cared for." Later he would instruct Fatima to keep a close eye on the woman. He didn't want Shazade to feel like a prisoner, since he'd just promised her freedom, but while she was in his home, her activities would have to be watched.

·8·

Pull! Pull! Pull!"

Laurel planted her boots against the planks and pulled hard on the rigging. Behind her, Nicole Petit grunted and tugged with all her might.

Gradually the sail was hoisted overhead and secured.

Captain Harding stood beside the ladies as the canvas billowed to catch the shifting wind. Smiling indulgently, several of the ship's crew observed the women's lesson in sailing. "Well done," said the captain. "You'd better take a rest now. We'll hold this position till the wind shifts back to the northwest."

"Aren't we going in the wrong direction? Spain is to our north," said Laurel.

"We're only tacking," explained Harding. "We're fighting a stiff wind coming through the straits, so we're slowed a bit."

With a satisfied smile, Laurel motioned to Nicole to follow her below into the airy captain's cabin. Once inside, she pulled off her cap and leather gloves and wiped the sweat from her forehead and throat. "We're learning, Nicole," she observed happily. "I hope that wasn't too tiring for you."

"No, miss. I feel right starched after all that effort. Working in the brisk sea air must be a healthy thing to do." Nicole slipped off her sturdy gloves and pushed back damp midnight-black curls from her temples.

"Pour us cups of water, please Nicole. I'm terribly thirsty." Laurel took a close look at her rumpled blouse and breeches. She and Nicole had washed their clothes as best they could since they left Bermuda almost a month before. Life aboard ship on a lengthy voyage was geared to practicalities, not luxurious living. She inspected her palms. The calluses were growing, but she was determined to experience every aspect of sailing a ship. In the weeks they'd been at sea, she had tried her hand at everything except sleeping in a hammock and firing one of the ten antique cannon lined up on the gun deck. So far, the journey had been routine to the point of boring: no equipment failures, no bad weather, no illnesses, and no threats from enemy vessels.

Not that she had expected any threats like those in the old days, when pirates roamed these waters. Now, modern navies plied the oceans in enormous man-of-wars and ships of the line. The Barbary pirates along the African coast had been the last diehards, but had finally given up their evil ways and gone into hiding or retirement. She was confident that the Atlantic was safe for legitimate shipping. The only vessels stopped and boarded lately were slavers, and they deserved whatever fate should befall them. To her the infamous Sea Falcon was a hero for saving the Negroes, though he was quite the opposite to her Southern planter friends.

Nicole handed her a drink and poured a cup for herself. "There, miss. Would you like to bathe before dinner arrives?"

"No, thank you, dear. I'll wait till after we've eaten, then sponge off before bed. You're free to rest in your quarters, if you like."

Laurel took a large swallow from the tin cup as Nicole let herself out the door. She thought again how ideal Nicole was as both servant and companion. Shannon hadn't exaggerated one bit about the pretty quadroon's special qualities. Not only had the girl not been seasick, but she had adapted to life on the ship as if born to the waves. She was intelligent and eager to try any new task asked of her. Laurel thought with gratitude how much Nicole had helped to ease the loneliness of the journey, though the girl wasn't much of a talker. Nicole probably didn't want to say much about her unfortunate beginnings in the swamps, even though Laurel encouraged her to speak freely of those days, especially regarding any secrets Nicole had learned from her grandmother, Marie Laveau. Nicole had explained that her mother had been close to one of Marie's sons, and thus Nicole was conceived. Laurel was as fascinated as anyone with the legendary Marie Leaveau, who had magical powers, was quite a beauty, and was the mother of fifteen children. Yes, it was plain Nicole took pride in her grandmother, even though she herself had been born out of wedlock.

Laurel had urged her to tell her about voodoo, but Nicole had politely declined. If Nicole had learned any voodoo magic, good or bad, she was keeping that knowledge to herself. But the girl had been happy to share secret family recipes in exchange for instruction in crocheting.

Laurel stretched out on the narrow bed and closed her eyes. Two days until landfall, Captain Harding had predicted. A few clouds had gathered late this afternoon, but they weren't especially threatening. She was thinking how she would wring a good price for her cargo from the Spanish tradesmen along the coast, when Nicole came back into the room.

"Pardon, miss. I wanted you to see how well the dress you gave me fits. I'll only have to stitch it up here and there. I think the crocheted scarf we've been working on looks mighty pretty with it."

Sitting up, Laurel gazed at Nicole. The shadows had grown long and a light mist was penetrating the open windows. "My, you are lovely, Nicole. *C'est parfait. Je l'aime bien.*" She laughed pleasantly. "And look at me. I could pass as a deck hand, smell and all."

The ship's timbers creaked as it listed to port. "I think

we're in for a squall," Laurel commented, getting off the bed and closing the window. "I'll go topside and consult our captain."

The words were no sooner spoken when a shout reached them from the lookout. "Sail ho! Off starboard bow!"

Laurel grabbed her cap. "A sail. Wait here, Nicole. I'll be right back." She hurried up to the wheel deck and found Captain Harding standing beside the helmsman. A stiff wind raked her skin and she pulled the cap down around her ears. "What is it, Captain? Can you see her flag?"

"No, ma'am. But she's headed our way. The fog keeps blocking my view." Harding raised his spyglass and studied the approaching vessel.

Laurel waited, squinting through the mist. The dying rays of the sun filtered through the moisture, giving her a sense of floating through a swirling cloud of gray and gold. She could see the frigate now. It was a large ship, though not as large as the navy's ships of the line. It was rapidly closing the gap between them, coming toward them at full sail. Couldn't their captain see the *Star?* Maybe the fog and deepening twilight blocked his view.

"There," said Harding. "Their flag is hoisted. My God—"

"What's wrong, Captain?" She shaded her eyes, but couldn't make out the banner floating atop the mainmast.

"The flag is black and white."

"What? Surely not a pirate's skull and crossbones?"

"No, not a skull. Something else. I can't see it clearly, but I don't like it. Barbary pirates used to regularly prowl these waters. Helmsman!" he yelled. "Hard to port!"

As the helmsman leaned into the wheel, a thunderous noise split the air. It was immediately followed by a whooshing sound and a loud splash on the port side of the ship.

"What was that?" Laurel cried, hurrying to the rail to peer at the green swells below.

"Damned if it wasn't a cannon ball. You'd better go below, Miss Caldwell."

"A cannon ball?" she shouted. "Captain, prepare *our* cannons." She was more angry than frightened. The explosion had been dangerously close to the *Star*. "If that's a pirate ship, we must defend ourselves."

A second salvo roared from the frigate closing in on them. This round splashed into their path, forcing the helmsman to frantically reverse the wheel in an attempt to change course.

Laurel was thrown against the rail as the *Star* slowed and shuddered in confusion like a blind horse pulled this way and that.

Captain Harding grasped her arm. "Are you all right, miss? I insist you go below. We may have to stop and allow them to board."

"Board!" she cried. "But they might be planning to steal my cargo."

"The only other choice is to turn and run with the wind, try to lose them in the fog."

"Do you think we can?"

"I fear it's too late. They're under full sail and coming hard."

"How dare they!" she screamed. "They *must* be pirates with that black and white flag. They want my ship and my goods and maybe our lives. They'll find they've met their match." Her voice rose in furious indignation as she stared across the water. "We can try to outrun them, Captain, but in case that's impossible, order the men to prepare our weapons. I won't be taken without a fight."

"Very well, Miss Caldwell, but if we fire on them, we could be in real trouble."

"The entire future of Caldwell Shipping depends on this enterprise, Captain Harding." She glared at the sleek modern ship, its gunports bristling with cannons. The vessel had lowered its mainsail and was maneuvering as if it intended to fire a broadside. "If the pirates board the ship, we'll lose not only the cargo, but possibly our lives. We could be captured, tortured, all manner of terrible things."

He gave her a solemn look. "I understand." Staring back at the looming ship, he shook his head. "I never thought this could happen. I fear we're not battle ready. But they're upon us. We can't outrun them."

"Then we have no choice. We must fire, Captain, at once!"

Harding yelled at his astonished crew. "Five of you, cast loose the guns! The rest stand by to lower sail."

A balding sailor called back, "But Cap'n, we haven't fired those things in years."

"Do as I say," ordered Harding.

"What's wrong with the crew?" Laurel demanded. "We do have weapons, after all. I assume the cannons are in good working order. You did promise me that, didn't you?"

"Aye, they work. Or they did four or five years ago."

"Four or five—" she sputtered. "They haven't been tested since then?"

"I'll do my best," Harding said and hurried down the steps.

She heard him shout his order. "Run out the guns. Prime and fire when ready!" He paused as some protest drifted upward. "Where do you think, Smith?" he answered loudly. "Aim at their cannons, you idiot. Maybe we can hit one and blow them out of the water."

Laurel's knuckles were white as she clung to the rail, her heart racing. She was furious at this threat to her beloved ship and precious cargo. She worried about what might befall her sailors, and she had no doubt that she and Nicole were doomed to a terrible fate if the pirates took them captive.

Two cannons fired from the port bow of the *Star*, then two more.

She snatched up the spyglass left behind by the captain and searched for the results of her counterattack. She saw four small eruptions at sea, nowhere near the looming pirate ship. Apparently her beloved old crew was terribly out of practice in the art of self-defense. Almost as if in embarrassment, a fifth cannon lobbed its missile into the water a few yards beyond the side of the *Star*.

A sudden explosion came from the gun deck. Men shouted and scrambled upward.

The captain intercepted a crewman, questioned him, and then hurried toward Laurel. "I'm sorry, Miss Caldwell, one of our cannons has blown up."

"Oh," she gasped, "is anyone injured?"

"No, luckily, but we've got a dangerous fire burning down below. We'll try to get the pumps going."

She nodded as Harding rushed away to take charge of the pump brigade. The pirates were upon them, slowing, maneuvering into position as if they planned to board. She looked at the stunned helmsman whose arms hung as limp as his lower jaw. Too late, she realized she had allowed her fondness for her crew to blind her to their dearth of rigorous training. She realized now they had never been in battle. They seemed utterly confused and helpless.

She had to do something. Flames were suddenly leaping along the fo'c'sle. For the first time, fear penetrated her anger. Were they really being attacked by pirates—in this day and age? Was it possible her ship might sink? She looked up at her ship's canvas flapping ineffectively in the shifting wind. The *Star* was beginning to revolve slowly, with no direction, no firm hand at the wheel.

Laurel shouted at the helmsman. "Hold her steady as she goes! I'll see about the fire." She rushed down the steps and found the captain directing several men dragging hoses, which were attached to the pump. To her horror she could see the fire was spreading rapidly. She screamed, "The quilts are burning!" Picking up a section of hose, she placed herself between two straining crewmen and held on to it as water began spurting from the nozzle.

Cheyne was taken completely by surprise. The outdated frigate he'd spotted through the mist was American built and appeared to be heading southwest. It was exactly where he would expect a slaver to be. If the ship had been an innocent merchant vessel, it would have halted at the first salvo, endured his inspection, than gone its way. Once the captain recognized the Sea Falcon's flag, he should have known he had nothing to fear. But if it was indeed a slaver, it would have tried to outrun him or given up without a fight, considering it was outmanuevered and outgunned by his intimidating ship, the *Monsoon*. Leaning against the rail with his spyglass, he almost laughed at the absurd cannon rounds plopping into the water far beyond his warship. The sight brought to mind a small boy tripping over his own feet and tossing pebbles toward a giant animal bearing down on him.

"Rafi," he shouted. "Let's end this quickly. We'll move in and board. Be prepared for small arms fire. That feisty little craft is putting up a fight."

"But look, *Capitaine*. The ship is on fire."

"Bloody saints, did we hit the thing?"

"No, sir. We didn't come near it. We fired our shots well beyond the bow to get them to stop so we could board."

"Maneuver closer and we'll survey the situation. I've heard of slavers tossing their human cargo overboard, but never have I heard of anyone burning his own ship. If the fire looks bad, we'll rescue whoever's aboard, unless they keep shooting at us." Cheyne checked his pistols and fingered the knife at his belt. He was dressed like one of his Turks, complete with turban, but he wore a Colt revolver at each hip, gifts from his American friend, Kyle Wyndford. Shaking his head, he watched his men prepare for boarding. He didn't like this kind of nasty business. Whoever had ordered the frigate to return fire must be desperate or suicidal. He would lead the boarding party and pray the captain of the strange little frigate would come to his senses before someone was killed.

· 9 ·

Within minutes of picking up the water hose, Laurel realized their efforts to douse the fire were hopeless. The flames were leaping from below where the cannon had plunged into the midst of the cargo. The puny flow of water from the nozzle was turning into sizzling steam and ash, making her eyes sting and her lungs ache.

Dropping the hose, she looked for Captain Harding, but he was nowhere to be seen. Momentary panic gripped her, but she calmed herself and yelled at the men struggling to put out the fire. "We must abandon ship! Go topside at once and uncover the lifeboats. Find Captain Harding."

The men responded quickly. Sloshing through ankle deep water, she headed for her cabin, where she hoped to salvage a few personal items. Surely by now, Nicole had gone to the main deck.

A nightmare. This was her worst nightmare coming true. She didn't have time to think about all that was lost, but concentrated on everyone's safety. Deep in her mind, she cursed the dreadful pirates who had caused this tragedy.

Quickly, she snatched up her jewel case, then removed the pearl-handled derringer from the desk drawer. Beside it was the bill of lading listing her cargo. She stuffed it in her pocket, trying not to think of all the people in Louisiana who had entrusted her with their livelihood.

The ship lurched as something bumped along its length. The pirate ship. From the Barbary coast, no doubt. Would these beasts allow her crew to escape in the longboats or would they murder and rape and steal whatever they could find?

Rape. She clenched her teeth and hid the pistol in the pocket of her breeches. Then she shoved her hair up under her cap. With her mannish attire and her face smeared with dirt and ashes, she would be unlikely to attract lustful attention.

She coughed in the acrid smoke as she climbed the steps to the upper deck. Arriving topside, she encountered total chaos.

Men in turbans, brandishing swords and pistols, were boarding the *Star*. Her men attempting to lower the lifeboats were being stopped and forced to hold their hands above their heads. Other members of her crew were running to and fro, shouting to each other, making no effort to defend the ship.

Tongues of flame were creeping along the foremast and bowsprit, whipped by strong winds. The *Star* was doomed, no doubt about it.

Looming beside the *Star,* the pirate ship seemed like a giant bird of prey with its victim firmly clutched in its talons. Several grappling hooks held the smaller frigate captive, while the pirates leaped onto its deck.

Laurel stayed out of sight in the shadows, searching desperately for any sign of Captain Harding.

Finally, she saw him standing near the wheel, almost obscured by wind and smoke. Several feet behind him crouched Nicole, still dressed in her pretty satin gown, the crocheted shawl draped over her shoulders. Nicole's eyes were sweeping across the ship, no doubt in search of her mistress. If only the girl didn't look so feminine and pretty. If these bandits were bent on rape, they would eventually discover they had a lovely victim.

A tall muscular man climbed up the steps to confront Harding. He carried a sword and what appeared to be a quilt over one arm.

Laurel held her breath. What would Captain Harding do in these terrible circumstances? He was courageous, she was certain. But he was hardly in a position to make demands when he was completely outnumbered and his ship was sinking. Her heart thudded mercilessly, and she was beginning to regret she'd insisted they fire on the pirate ship. She had been far too confident of their means of self-defense. Maybe they should have tried to negotiate, but could one ever negotiate with pirates bent on thievery and murder? She watched closely. If the pirate killed Harding, they were all doomed.

She couldn't hear the conversation, but the turbaned pirate captain was pointing to the fire with the tip of his sword. Then he listened intently to Captain Harding. Suddenly he raised his arm toward heaven and shouted a word that sounded a lot like *godalmightydamn*. Something Captain Harding said had upset the pirate terribly. Whatever the villain's feelings were at this moment, they were nothing compared to her own outrage.

The pirate barely glanced at Nicole, then handed the quilt to Harding and crossed to the rail and surveyed the turmoil below. Harding passed the quilt to Nicole who quickly wrapped it around her.

The pirate captain drew his pistol and fired it into the air. Stepping back in the sudden silence, he indicated that Harding would speak.

Captain Harding stepped forward. "Men of the *Star*, our ship is sinking. The captain of the *Monsoon* will take us to Tangier, our nearest port. Time is short, so we must abandon ship and board his frigate with all speed. Make certain none of your comrades are left below. Make a quick sweep below decks, Mr. Smith. I'll remain on the *Star* until everyone is accounted for."

So they were not to die just yet, Laurel thought grimly. Tangier. An evil den of iniquity, so she'd heard. She would continue in the disguise of a crewman and pray Nicole would escape a fate worse than death. Somehow, she must signal Captain Harding she was safe and would look out for herself.

She slipped from her hiding place and moved alongside several burly crewmen who were headed for the plank joining the *Star* to the *Monsoon*. Keeping her head down, she saw that the pirate captain was gathering his brigands into some sort of order, commanding them to return to their own ship. It gave her some limited satisfaction to know that although she had lost her ship and cargo, the pirate would have nothing to enrich his coffers. On the other hand, he would have twenty American seamen and two females to do with as he wished. She knew she couldn't possibly keep her identity a secret forever.

Captain Harding was assisting Nicole to the main deck when Laurel reached them. For one second, she had them to herself, and she seized the opportunity to tug on Harding's sleeve. In a low tone, she whispered, "I'm all right. I'll stay with the crew. Tell Nicole." After that brief message, she hurried to join the group of men going over to the *Monsoon*. Once on board the massive pirate ship, she glanced back and caught a furtive nod from her captain, then lingered near the rail to watch what would happen next.

Captain Harding scooped up Nicole, still wrapped in the quilt, and handed her to the second mate of the *Star*. That crewman carried her to the pirate ship and kept her close to him. Then Harding placed himself near the gangplank where he could count his men as they left the burning ship. The pirate captain joined him and waited by his side until everyone was off the *Star*.

Harding looked one last time across the deck, which was beginning to list toward the bow, then saluted smartly before he left the vessel to its fate. With surprising gallantry, the pirate bowed the captain of the *Star* toward the *Monsoon* and followed him on board.

Jumping atop a hatch cover, the pirate shouted to his crew. "Cut the ropes unless you want to go down with the frigate. Mr. Rafi, take command of the ship. Omar, once the *Star* is gone, show her crew below. Captain Harding, I'll entertain you in my cabin, along with the lady."

Laurel was astonished. This was no Turk barking orders, nor even an Englishman. That voice was distinctly American. And she could swear it had a familiar ring.

Her attention was drawn back to the terrible sight of the *Star* sinking by its bow in a roar of sizzle and steam. Tears filled her eyes as she watched all her hopes and dreams disappear under the dark swells of the Atlantic. This was the end of Caldwell Shipping. After the indifferent sea had covered every sign of her ship, her pain turned rapidly into hatred. Fingering the tiny pistol, she swore revenge for her lost vessel, for its precious cargo, and for the loss of her family's fortune. A diabolical thought entered her mind. Perhaps the pirate would try to rape her, once he discovered she was a woman. She would put a bullet into his black heart. After that, she really didn't care what happened to her, now that all was lost to her and to her family.

Cheyne was livid. The problem was, he had mostly himself to blame. Storming into his cabin, he tossed his sword onto his cot and spewed curses in three languages.

He had been responsible for sinking Blaine Caldwell's ship!

Not directly or intentionally, but the results were the same. The irony of his mistake was impossible to believe, but it had happened. To make sure the captain wasn't lying, Cheyne had made a quick inspection below decks before the *Star* had gone down. Stacked neatly in the hold was the shipment of goods from New Orleans, including crates of exquisite quilts, no doubt handmade by Arcadian ladies during hours of tedious work by flickering candlelight. He had saved one quilt and given it to the captain. Later he had seen Captain Harding carrying a woman aboard the *Monsoon* wrapped in the quilt. A woman! Hell, he could have sent an innocent lady to her death if the ship had sunk rapidly. Not to mention killing twenty aging seamen and their courageous captain.

He thought of the woman and wondered what she was doing on the voyage. He hadn't gotten a good look at her, but he would guess she was Harding's wife or daughter. Many captain's wives sailed with their husbands on a regular basis. Better than all those months alone, they argued.

He yanked open his locker and pulled out a bottle of brandy, but he doubted if all the brandy in France would stop the pain he was feeling now. He had just sunk the ship of his dear friend and partner, a fine gentleman who was known to be in financial distress.

Rafi entered the cabin. "The *Star*'s crew is in their quarters where we usually put the slaves. I've ordered rum for the lot."

"Did you reassure them, explain they're quite safe, that this whole unfortunate event was an accident?

"I did, sir. I pointed out it was their own cannon that exploded. We never intended to sink them."

"No one protested?"

"One fellow wanted to know what in hell we stopped them for. Said it was an act of piracy, in his opinion."

Cheyne took a long draught straight from the bottle. Wiping his lips with the back of his hand, he grunted, "It sure looks like it."

"Excuse me, *Capitaine,* but we could explain our true purpose. Tell them you're the Sea Falcon."

"No! We can't take that risk. The *Star's* owner is an old friend, so I'm praying he will understand what happened today. We're in luck, after all, that no one recognized our flag. I don't want anyone knowing I'm the Sea Falcon or our true purpose."

"Then what will we say, sir?"

"Hell, tell them we *are* pirates. Why not? We'll take them to Tangier and find them decent quarters until the next available ship sailing for New Orleans. We'll send them home with tales of how they were captured by brigands, then well treated and released. We'll give privateering an entirely new reputation."

Rafi shifted his weight and cleared his throat.

"What else, Rafi? My mood is black as midnight."

"Captain Harding is with his men, but he will be here to meet with you shortly."

"Good. I suppose my first apology will be to that gentleman."

"And the woman—"

"Aye. The woman will need her privacy. If she's the captain's wife, we'll arrange a cabin for them." He glanced around his spacious quarters. "I suppose I could give them mine. It's the least I can do after this fiasco." He took another drink.

"I don't believe the two are together, *Capitaine.* Once she was safely aboard the *Monsoon,* she—she, ah—"

"What, Rafi?"

"She became a tiger, *Capitaine.* I've never seen a woman behave like that. She said she'd put a curse on all of us, and sounded like she meant it."

"Can you blame her? So she's not the captain's wife. You don't suppose—"

"That she's his mistress? *Oui,* that would be my guess. She's very beautiful."

Cheyne cocked an eyebrow at Rafi's tone. "You're not easily impressed, *mon ami.*"

"Her temper was magnificent. She cursed me in French as well as English."

"Maybe she's a foreigner. Traveling to Spain in the captain's care. Did you invite her to come here with Harding?"

"Oui. I was most humble and courteous, I assure you. She calmed herself and I took her to the guest cabin."

"Then we'll get to the bottom of the mystery soon." Cheyne unwound his turban and tossed it next to his sword. "Do you know what it means to *eat crow,* Rafi?"

"No, sir. A crow is a bird."

"It means I'll be crawling on my belly to these people, and I've had little practice at it. Go to the galley and arrange the best meal possible, and send a bottle of wine. I'll try to soothe them with refreshment and apologies."

Rafi smiled sympathetically and left the cabin.

· 10 ·

In the dim light of the *Monsoon's* cannon deck, Laurel pulled herself together and took time to reassure her dismayed crew. She pointed out they had survived the attack and were not clapped in irons. There was hope, and they must all keep up their courage. The men nodded and smiled and she felt their admiration like a gift to soothe her broken heart.

"Excuse me, Miss Caldwell," said a graying seaman, his cap in his hand.

"What is it, Mr. Smith?"

"I know everyone agrees with me that you're the bravest and best ship owner's daughter any of us ever knew."

"Thank you, Mr. Smith," she answered graciously, knowing full well she was the only ship owner's daughter any of them knew. "You all have been extremely faithful to me and to my father for many years. Don't despair. I expect to get to the bottom of this, and I'm sure my father will compensate you for your inconvenience. Captain Harding will speak to the pirate captain and do his best to insure our safety. I'll continue in my disguise for a time, until I feel it's safe to reveal who I am."

"Begging your pardon, ma'am," murmured a shy crewman, "but you're the prettiest gal who ever served aboard a frigate, even in that getup."

Enthusiastic applause from the men sent roses to her cheeks.

Turning away, she crooked her finger toward Captain Harding and drew him aside. "Captain, I'm going to find out what's happened to Nicole. Mr. Smith said one of the pirates took her somewhere."

"I spoke with the pirate. He said his name is Rafi Hamid, and he was taking her to a cabin next to Captain Sinclair."

"Sinclair! So that's the brute's name. Obviously he wants Nicole conveniently on hand. I'm going to find her at once."

"I'll come with you."

"No, Captain. I'll be much less noticeable alone. I'll size up the situation, then decide what to do. If this Captain Sinclair has one bit of honor, which I doubt, I'll reveal I'm a woman and demand Nicole and I are treated properly until we are set free."

"I'd prefer to come with you."

"No. That's an order. If something happens to me, the crew will need your help. Their lives might depend on your experience and cool head."

"Yes, ma'am." Harding touched the bill of his cap with one finger. "Good luck. I'll be within earshot, at any rate."

Laurel felt the ship dipping into the swells. Outside, night had fallen, and only the occasional torch lighted the companionway. Moving silently except for the squashing of her soaked boots, she inched toward the usual location of the captain's quarters. The *Monsoon* was an impressively large frigate, but its cabin arrangement was much the same as the *Star's*.

The sound of sobbing caught her ear. Not likely to be Captain Sinclair, she thought angrily. Turning a doorknob, she poked her head into a small, well lit room. Sure enough, Nicole was sitting on a wooden chair, her head buried in her hands.

"Nicole," she called in a loud whisper.

The girl jumped and gaped at her with tear-filled eyes. "Miss Caldwell. I prayed you'd come."

Laurel hurried to embrace her, caring not in the least that she was smearing dirt and ash across Nicole's badly rumpled pink satin dress. "Are you all right, dear? They haven't hurt you, have they?"

The girl was trembling and her eyes swollen from crying. "I'm so frightened. I know what they'll do. I just know." She swallowed more sobs.

"No, that won't happen, Nicole. I promise. We won't be raped as long as I have one breath left in me. Captain Harding and the crew are being well treated, so far, so we mustn't give up hope."

"I'm a good girl, Miss Caldwell. I don't want to be ruined. It hasn't been easy in the swamps, but—"

Laurel hugged her again. The seventeen-year-old seemed like a frightened child at this moment. But who wouldn't be frightened after having a ship burned around her and being kidnapped by wicked pirates?

Footsteps sounded in the companionway.

Laurel placed a finger over her lips and gazed around the room. Spotting a closet, she squeezed inside. If the person approaching was Sinclair, and if he tried anything with Nicole, she could shoot him at close range. She was an excellent shot, but the derringer was so small she would need to be close to be sure of killing the man.

Otherwise, she might only turn him into a murderous beast.

Someone knocked on the door. "Madam, the captain requests the honor of your presence in his cabin. He offers dinner and wine, along with his apologies."

Peeking through the slats fronting the closet door, Laurel tried to see what was happening. Nicole stood in the center of the room, tongue-tied and frozen.

"May I enter?" came the low-pitched voice with a slight French accent.

Nicole didn't respond.

The door was pushed opened slowly. "Are you well, madam?"

"Ye—yes," Nicole stammered. "But I'm not hungry. I'll stay here."

"The captain is most insistent. In fact, he's also expecting Captain Harding. He wishes to meet with the two of you to determine what's best to be done after this unfortunate accident."

Laurel pursed her lips. Accident? The *Star* had been doing just fine, minding its own business while engaged in legitimate enterprise, until the devil ship caused its demise.

Nicole had sense enough not to look toward the closet. She clutched the shawl around her and exited the cabin escorted by the man called Rafi Hamid, a very exotic looking creature with hawk-like features, white turban, and ballooning breeches tucked into red boots with curved, pointed toes.

Laurel waited until their footsteps died away, then left her hiding place and slipped into the companionway. The two had apparently entered the adjoining cabin. The door was ajar and voices reached her.

She removed the derringer. Moving as stealthily as possible, she backed along the wall. Not for a minute did she believe the pirate planned to wine and dine Nicole and Captain Harding. It didn't make sense that he would force the *Star* into exchanging cannon fire, thus causing it to sink, then treat his victims to a repast as they cruised toward Tangier. She knew all about pirates, their cruelty and complete lack of moral character. Laurel had promised Nicole she would protect her from rape, and if that meant shooting a man, she was prepared to do it.

She heard Nicole cry out. With her pistol cocked, she jumped into the lighted doorway.

The tall pirate captain had his hands on Nicole's shoulders. Rafi Hamid stood at one side watching.

Nicole cried again, "You! It can't be. No!"

Without another thought, Laurel fired at the villain's head. The man jerked back and bumped against the desk behind him, blood running down his forehead and across his nose.

Rafi leaped toward her and knocked the gun from her hand.

Instantly, the captain was upon her. He grasped her upper arms and held her in a painful grip.

Laurel's heart raced wildly. The bullet had only grazed him, though his face was streaked with blood. She could count the rest of her life in seconds.

He shook her till her teeth rattled and she had to bite her lip to keep from screaming. "What's wrong with you, lad? No one's harmed you, have they?"

Planting her feet, she tried to pull away. The man's grip was like steel. His blood dripped onto his flowing white shirt.

Abruptly he released her. She kicked him as hard as she could in the shin.

He slapped her sharply across her cheek. "Stop fighting, boy, or I'll have to lock you up. I swear to you there's nothing to—"

Her cap was knocked to the floor. She heard the captain's words stop short. She took a quick look at Nicole, who was gripping a post and appeared about to faint. All she felt was white-hot anger at the captain, at herself because she hadn't killed him, and at God, who had let her fall into such terrible circumstances.

"A woman!" Rafi exclaimed.

"Hell fire, another female," spat the captain. "And more of a tigress than Nicole."

The captain's odd tone penetrated Laurel's brain. He had said Nicole as if knew the girl.

Suddenly Nicole rushed to her side. "He's Mr. Brown. The man who bought me in New Orleans."

This information took several seconds to register in Laurel's frenzied brain. She couldn't have heard correctly. Looking from Nicole to the captain, she tried to sort things out. "Brown?" she choked. "But Captain Harding told me his name is Sinclair."

The captain took the cloth Rafi was holding and wiped some of the blood from his face. "One and the same. I recognized Nicole Petit a minute ago, and of course, she recognized me. But who the hell are you, madam?"

Laurel stumbled backward. Her knees were shaking and she couldn't force a sensible thought into her head. Mr. Brown? *Her* Mr. Brown? Mr. Brown, the ship builder and slave owner from Newport? As he cleaned blood from his face and held the towel against his forehead to stem the flow, she indeed recognized him. Handsome as ever, even more so, with his hair damply curling and his tanned skin accented by the white towel and open-necked shirt. He didn't recognize her in her dirty clothes with her face streaked with grime. Frantically she tried to think of some way to continue her subterfuge.

"I don't think he'll rape us, Miss Laurel," said Nicole with deep concern.

"What did you say?" bellowed Mr. Brown. "Rape? Of course not. I—" He paused and stared at the two of them. "What name was that?"

Nicole moaned and covered her lips. "I'm sorry, miss. Forgive me, I forgot."

Laurel took a deep breath and glared at the man studying her intently. "So we meet again, Mr. Brown. This time, you've outdone yourself in your attempt to gain my attention."

Cheyne was thunderstruck. This filthy ragamuffin who had just tried to kill him and whom he'd cuffed briskly in the face was none other than Laurel Caldwell. He prayed it wasn't so. But today was a day his prayers were simply not being answered.

For the first time in his life, he was absolutely lost for words. He handed the bloody rag to Rafi and stood stupidly gaping at the upturned face fixing him with such a heated expression. He saw now the delicate shape of jaw and chin, the aristocratic little nose, the gold in the tangle of sooty curls. God forgive him, he had *slapped* her.

He turned his back and crossed to his desk. Hell, he was feeling dizzy. All he needed to add to this deplorable scene was to pass out in front of everyone.

Rafi stepped near. "I'll get the physician at once, *mon Capitaine*. You've lost a great deal of blood."

Cheyne nodded and sat on the edge of his desk, then dared to look back at the two women, one a slave he'd bought two months ago and given to Shannon Kildaire, the other the woman he had desired beyond all reason for as long as he could remember. He figured he had two choices: he could crawl like a worm and beg forgiveness, or he could assume the role of villain and let them come to their own conclusions. Somehow the latter had greater appeal.

Straightening his spine, he said firmly, "I'm sorry I was rough with you, Miss Caldwell, but that disguise was your choice, and quite effective. If you take on the role of a male, you must be prepared to accept the consequences."

His words sent her eyebrows skyward. "And once I thought you were a gentleman! Granted, I misled you, but now that you know who I am, I would have expected some slight apology, if not for striking me, then for sinking my ship. Shannon warned me you were an evil man, but I was willing to give you the benefit of the doubt—until today."

"I didn't sink your ship. I merely attempted to delay it. Your own poorly maintained cannon sent the *Star* to the bottom."

Her fists were jammed at her waist. "Thanks to *you,* I found it necessary to fire my cannons, sir."

"That was your miscalulation. I thought at the time it was a foolish thing to do."

He watched her control her temper with difficulty. Unfortunately, he found her more fascinating than ever. Had there ever been such a woman? His vision of her was as a beautiful Southern belle in her flowing skirts and bonnet. Long before that, he had seen her as an adorable, though spoiled and pampered, child. He had assumed that by now she was the wife of Henry Beauregard, but here she was, a mischievous imp, helpless, disheveled, at his mercy, and yet untamed and ready to do battle. What would it be like to embrace her, force her to his will, kiss those lips into utter submission?

"How dare you accuse me of being foolish!" she snapped. "I demand an explanation."

Cheyne weighed his answer. He knew he could explain to her father how he had made the mistake of thinking the ship might be a slaver. After fully compensating Caldwell Shipping for its loss, he and Blaine Caldwell could continue as friends and partners in their clandestine business. But Beauregard, the largest supporter of the slave trade in southern Louisiana, had told him Laurel was his fiancée. Cheyne couldn't count on her loyalty, and there was much at risk. If word got back to Beauregard that Cheyne Sinclair was the Sea Falcon, the entire enterprise could be doomed and Blaine Caldwell ruined and possibly imprisoned. Knowing his next words would condemn him to perdition in her eyes, he said calmly, "I'm a privateer. I find it an interesting and lucrative hobby."

He was impressed with the way her face barely changed expression. Only her eyes betrayed the coldness overtaking her heart. If he'd ever thought he could win her respect, all hope was lost. He would have given a tidy sum to be able to turn and walk away from the look she was giving him, but he was trapped here in his own cabin. The burning along his scalp was negligible compared to the ache in his heart.

"A pirate," she said finally, as if she was forced to accept some terrible truth. "I'm not sure which I despise more, pirates or slave traders. Since you embody both vices, I don't suppose it makes any difference."

"Not to me. But in all fairness, I don't build slave ships in Newport, nor do I buy and sell slaves. Mr. Brown is a pseudonym I use when I find it necessary."

"You bought Nicole."

"Aye, but I promptly set her free."

"You know that's the truth, Miss Laurel."

She flicked a glance at Nicole, who was watching with fascination.

"Very well," Laurel said with a lift of her chin. "I withdraw the accusation of slave trader. You're merely a pirate, a thief, a destroyer of innocent merchant ships, and perhaps a murderer."

"I've killed a few men in my time. Oh, you forgot—*rapist.*" He suspected he'd gone too far when he saw her face blanch. He stood abruptly. "I must apologize." His head began swimming. He sat back heavily and touched his scalp. From some distance, he heard voices. Rafi had arrived with the ship's physician.

Rafi was beside him. His voice was far away. "Sit still, *mon ami.* The doctor will tend you. And here is Captain Harding."

Cheyne put his hand down to steady himself, but the desk seemed to tilt toward him. Damned if he wasn't going to pass out, after all.

·11·

Laurel watched as Mr. Brown was tended by his physician. He had nearly fainted, but had recovered sufficiently to sit on his desk and mutter oaths while the doctor washed and treated his wound. She couldn't remember purposely hurting anyone in her entire life, but now she had caused Mr. Brown to suffer. Before her stirrings of guilt could spread, she reminded herself of the man's act of piracy.

Captain Harding entered the cabin. He scrutinized her, then glanced at the proceedings taking place at the captain's desk. "What's going on?" he asked in a low tone.

"I shot the pirate captain, I'm afraid."

"You *shot* him? You shot Captain Sinclair?"

"Yes, Sinclair. And why not?" she said defensively. "After what he did, I'm sorry I didn't take better aim."

Harding gave her a disbelieving smile. "No, ma'am. I'm sure you're mistaken. I've known you since you were a child, and you're not one to enjoy killing a person, not even a pirate."

Laurel gazed back at Sinclair and grudgingly admitted Captain Harding was right. As much as she hated the scoundrel, she was glad she hadn't actually killed him. His grumpy comments to his doctor proved he would live to continue his wicked ways.

Behind them, a voice called, "Dinner is here, Captain."

She and Harding and Nicole turned to see a youth at the door carrying a sizable silver tray.

"Do you suppose we're still invited to dinner?" Harding inquired.

Laurel looked at the physician putting away his bandages.

"I'm not sure what our pirate captain has in mind," she said softly. "He must have ordered dinner before my unsuccessful attempt to kill him."

"Frankly, Miss Caldwell, I don't believe you were included in the invitation to dine," Harding commented. "Just me and Miss Petit. Understandable, since Sinclair didn't know you were aboard."

"Then I believe I'll leave." She spun toward the door.

"One moment, Miss Caldwell!"

Sinclair's voice stopped her, but she didn't turn.

"Doctor, you may go," he said. "Rafi, escort Miss Petit and Captain Harding to the lady's quarters and take the dinner tray with you. I want to speak to Miss Caldwell alone. She will join her friends shortly."

"I don't wish to be alone with you, sir," Laurel said, keeping her back to him.

"Are you afraid of me, my lady?"

The challenge in his voice had to be met. Slowly she revolved to face him. "Should I be?"

"Considering your recent description of my character, you might have good reason."

She frowned at him to hide the uncontrollable flutter of her heart at the sight of his rugged good looks. She found it easier to imagine him a wounded hero than a black-hearted villain. She replied, "I'm sure you're weak from loss of blood, so perhaps it's safe. If you would like to speak with me, I will accommodate you briefly. Captain, escort Nicole to her cabin. Enjoy your dinner. I assure you, I have no appetite whatsoever."

Once they were alone, Sinclair rose and opened his cabinet and removed a bottle of wine. "Personally, I would like a drink. Could I entice you, Miss Caldwell? Perhaps a taste of wine would help restore your flagging appetite, though I realize attempting murder could upset one's digestion."

"Not murder, Captain Sinclair. Revenge."

"Aye. Revenge." He poured wine into silver goblets. "But didn't the Lord say, *Revenge is mine?* Or something to that effect?"

"He also said he would *help those who helped themselves,* or something like that."

"How nice we're both Bible scholars." He held out the drink. "I propose a toast to peace between us. I want to explain what I plan to do to make amends for my blunder today."

She took the goblet. "Then you admit the blunder was yours."

"I instigated the problem, so I must bear most of the blame, but I again point out that when I was below your decks, I saw cannons in such poor condition, 'tis a wonder they didn't blow up of their own accord."

"Well, they didn't. They blew up when I was forced to light their fuses, thanks to you, Captain Sinclair or Mr. Brown—whoever you are."

"I'll accept that if you will adopt my correct name. In New Orleans, I'm Hammond Brown. Everywhere else in the world, I'm Cheyne Sinclair."

She sipped the claret, glad to have something to cool her parched throat. Then she said, "Very well, *Captain Sinclair.* As far as I'm concerned, your name is irrelevant. What does matter is what you intend to do about this atrocity."

His lips twitched. He appeared to be holding back a smile.

"What could you possibly find amusing, sir?"

His expression became solemn, but his eyes held humor. "You. The way you look in those boyish clothes, your face, your hair—"

She had almost forgotten her unladylike garb. "I was taking a lesson in seamanship from my captain. When we were attacked by pirates, I thought I would hide the fact—cover my—pretend I was a lad," she finished lamely, heat rising in her cheeks. She chastised herself for feeling the need to offer an explanation to this man. "Let me assure you, there is nothing even slightly amusing in what has taken place."

His eyes were twinkling. Didn't the idiot realize what he had done? "You spoke of compensation, sir. I'm not sure you have the means to repay me and my family and friends for your evil act. The *Star* was a fine ship, fully loaded with priceless cargo. My crew and I nearly lost our lives, and now we're in a most difficult situation. The cost to you would be enormous."

He drained his goblet and set it aside. "I expected that. Allow me to make you an offer."

"Very well."

"First, you and your crew will be treated with every courtesy until we reach Tangier. At that time, your men will be comfortably housed. You and Miss Petit, of course, will be guests in my home. I assure you the quarters are quite comfortable."

"I hope we won't be there any length of time."

"Only as long as it takes to replace your ship with a new one, a fine craft with every modern amenity. If you'll provide me with a dollar figure equal to your cargo, I will pay you the entire amount without question. As you know, I have made the acquaintance of your father. I will send a letter of explanation to him as soon as possible. You're welcome to add your own description of the events in your personal communication, placing the blame entirely at my doorstep."

She was impressed. A new ship? Monetary compensation for her cargo? That would take a fortune. He was studying her with a veiled expression behind half-lowered lids. He still looked rather pale, and she couldn't help noticing the blood on his bandage and staining his shirt. It occurred to her he didn't have to do any of what

84

he'd just offered. She and her crew were entirely at his mercy. Suddenly she was confused and feeling the onset of fatigue. "Why, may I ask, would you attack my ship, cause it to sink, then give me a new one?"

"I told you I'm a privateer. Have been for many years. I learned my trade from your countryman, Jean Lafitte, and I've been somewhat successful at it. I was returning home from a voyage and saw your ship, alone and unprotected. My intention was to board it and take any valuables, then send you on your way. Naturally I'm sorry to have been the cause of Mr. Caldwell's ship going to the bottom, and I want to make amends. I have enough enemies without making powerful new ones. Also, let me assure you, to replace your ship and cargo will barely dent my bank account."

Laurel turned the goblet in her fingers and considered his words. He was being fair enough, if he was telling the truth. Pirates were infamous liars, she knew, but she supposed she had no choice but to accept his offer and hope for the best. She held out the goblet and said, "Very well, Captain Sinclair, that will have to do for now. But I will hold you to every promise."

He did smile now.

The sight cartwheeled her heart. She said sharply, "If you'll excuse me, I'd like to rejoin my friend, Miss Petit. I'll share quarters with her."

He moved off the desk and stood. She'd forgotten how tall he was.

"Fine," he said. "I'll have hot water sent from the galley. You could do with a good scrubbing."

She almost returned his smile, but caught herself. "I would appreciate that. Unfortunately, all my clothes went down with the *Star*. I'll have to endure these until we reach land."

"That won't be long, but perhaps this will be more comfortable in the meantime." As he spoke, he reached into his wardrobe and removed an exquisite black silk caftan. He exchanged the robe for her goblet. "We'll dock by mid morning tomorrow." He touched the bandage on his forehead for a fleeting second. "Until then, the *Monsoon* is yours to command."

Holding the robe, watching his struggle against pain, she murmured, "I—I'm rather sorry I wounded you. I don't ordinarily lean toward violence."

"Is that a fact?" He retrieved the derringer from the floor. Handing it to her, he said, "I'm uncertain whether you're sorry you shot me, or sorry you didn't kill me. Which is it, Miss Caldwell?"

She took the gun and dropped it into her pocket beside the small jewel box. "I can't honestly answer that yet. We'll have to wait to see if a pirate such as you can keep his word. Your record with me is highly suspect."

"Really?"

"You introduced yourself as Hammond Brown. Now I learn you are Cheyne Sinclair. You said you were a ship builder from Rhode Island. Now you say that isn't so."

"I'm capable of lying when necessary. But that was only false information, not broken promises."

"Honesty is honesty."

"Then question my honesty but not my integrity."

The man's nerve was astounding. "But of course. Why would I question the integrity of a man who tried to rob me, and failing that, caused me the loss of a valuable ship?"

"We've been over that point, Miss Caldwell. Our conversation is going in circles."

"I agree. I'm going to my cabin." She swiftly left the room and marched down the companionway. She knew he followed her, but she ignored his presence.

Nicole's cabin door stood open. Laurel hurried inside and found the girl, alone and glassy eyed, sitting on one of the two narrow beds.

"I'll leave you ladies now," said Captain Sinclair from behind her. "Please let me know if I can be of any service between now and when we disembark. If the voyage was to be lengthy, I would insist you and Miss Petit take my cabin, but under the circumstances—"

"We wouldn't consider it," Laurel snapped.

She kept her back toward the hall until she knew he had returned to his quarters, then she shut the door and sat on the bed with the robe across her lap. For several seconds, she faced Nicole in silence.

Finally, she asked, "Where is Captain Harding?"

"The captain only stayed long enough to make sure I was safe. The other man, Mr. Hamid, said he would be available if we needed anything."

"Goodness. Everyone is suddenly concerned about our welfare." She pushed her hair back with both hands and sighed. "What an adventure! I'm so tired, I feel dizzy."

"Do you think we're safe now?"

"I believe so, though I wouldn't swear to anything." She saw the dinner tray sitting on a table. "Have you eaten yet?"

"A few bites. The food was very strange, and I'm not hungry anyway. The wine tasted good, though."

Laurel spotted a pitcher and bowl and began to rinse her face. Her hands were trembling, probably because of the shock and strain of the ordeal. Noticing that Nicole had stretched out on the bed, she removed her soiled clothing and pulled on the robe. It swallowed her, but was feathery light and luxurious against her skin. The wine must have relaxed her, she thought, as she realized she could barely keep her eyes open. She lay down on her bed, turned down the gas lamp, and settled onto a pillow. In the blue shifting glow, with the sound of waves thudding against the side of the ship, she thought of Captain Sinclair, the former Hammond Brown. Thank heavens she hadn't killed him. She mustn't let her temper blind her to reason ever again. As she drifted into sleep, she was surprisingly content, and vaguely stimulated. She had wanted adventure, and now she had it. Tomorrow she would be in Tangier, the guest of this mysterious and enigmatic man, who kept reappearing in her life in the most extraordinary manner. Rocking gently in her bed, she felt a smile creep across her lips. Yes, indeed, she was anticipating the morrow with far more interest than she'd dreamed possible.

· 12 ·

Cheyne couldn't believe it had happened, that he actually had been responsible for sinking Laurel Caldwell's ship. Regardless of his original intentions or the condition of the *Star's* cannons, he was the guilty culprit in the tragedy. He had spent a sleepless night, not only because of his throbbing head, but because of his staggering misfortune. Every time he tried to lie down and close his eyes, he saw the frigate sinking under the waves, followed by a second vision of a dirty-faced young woman taking close aim at him with her pistol. Following that image was a third one, a sight that he was certain to remember till his dying day: that same defiant woman, her eyes blazing, her gun smoking, facing him with courage and spirit that took his breath away. What a sight she had been! He had admired many beautiful women, but none had compared to Laurel Caldwell when she had scorched him with her fiery temper while he stood stunned and bloody before her.

Hell, she had *shot* him. What had been in her heart when she aimed her derringer at him and pulled the trigger? How much fear or hatred did that take? Later she had calmed down and appeared to regret her action. He couldn't decide which hurt worse: her furious attack or her cold dismissal.

Now, as he leaned on the railing of his captain's walk

and waited for the sun to lift above the blue-green horizon, he vowed to do everything in his power to put things right with Laurel.

Laurel. Her name flowed through his mind and crossed his lips like the soft fragrance of a spring flower. Gentle, feminine, seductive. She was all those things, despite her inner strength and rapier tongue. One thing for certain, she was marrying the wrong man. Henry Beauregard was nowhere near her equal, except where money was concerned.

Cheyne rested his aching forehead on his fingertips and cursed Beauregard from here to Sunday. The man was a fop, an arrogant and cruel dandy, self-centered and cowardly; he didn't deserve a woman like Laurel Caldwell. Standing there as the immense vaulted sky took on an azure glow, he wondered if there was anything he could do to prevent her from making such a terrible mistake. She would be miserable; he was sure of it. He wished with every fiber of his being that he could pay court to her. But he was even more unworthy than Beauregard. He was at least ten years her senior, and those years had been filled with wild adventure and reckless living. Not until this very morning had he longed for respectability. Laurel was not only respectable, she was a paragon of loveliness and virtue in a world that valued such things above all else. What few values his world contained were related to swordplay, thievery, and debauchery. Accumulating wealth? Aye, he had done that, and he was proud of his success, but it was incredibly easy when one didn't care too much about living to a ripe old age.

A glance at the crow's nest showed him his lookout was on duty. Land would be sighted soon. He would address the crew of the *Star* and assign Rafi the task of seeing them safely ashore. He would conduct the women to his palace in his closed carriage so they wouldn't be exposed to curious eyes.

What would Laurel Caldwell think of his enormous

mansion overlooking the sea? He had obtained the structure years ago from the last leader of the Asilah pirates, then filled it with furnishings and treasures from around the world. It was garish, he knew, but the sight of his riches gave him a great deal of satisfaction. He, Cheyne Sinclair, bastard son, abandoned by parents and scorned by proper society, had done quite well for himself. He liked the way he lived, and didn't give a damn about anyone's opinion. That is, he hadn't until yesterday. When he thought of Highgrove Plantation, its elegant charm revealing generations of cultured living, he couldn't help wondering if Laurel might disparage the way he lived in his outlaw fortress. She might turn up that perky nose at his collection of colorful and exotic furnishings, much of it stolen years ago from Spanish and Turkish pirates. And though he didn't have a harem, there were several beautiful women who visited on occasion.

Nonsense. He wouldn't worry about her opinions. Cheyne shook off his gloom and headed for his cabin. He would see to her every comfort and give her the new ship he had under construction at his shipyards at Asilah. If that wasn't satisfactory, it was the best he could do. He had returned her pistol, and she might yet choose to use it on him. Why the hell not? Killed in his prime by a beautiful outraged woman. That seemed as good a way to die as any.

Laurel awakened as the sun peeked through the small window of the cabin. For a second, she thought she was aboard the *Star,* then remembrance flooded back, making her shiver in the coolness of the shadowy room.

"Nicole," she called to her cabin mate. "Wake up. We land in Tangier today."

Nicole stirred, stretched, then, cat-like, rose to a sitting position. "Tangier. Yes, ma'am. I don't know much about the place."

"It's in Morocco, a mysterious country ruled by a

sultan who is Muslim and very rich and powerful. I believe the men keep many slaves and several wives. If the women don't behave, they are beaten, beheaded, or stoned to death. And everyone prays to Allah many times a day."

"Who is Allah?"

"Their god."

"They're not Christians?"

Laurel moved to the wash basin. "Not in the least. But the United States is on friendly terms with the country, just the same. Otherwise, I wouldn't have sailed so close to their coast."

"I don't see how we could be friends with such an evil place."

"Friendliness between countries isn't based on religion anymore, but on economics."

"What's economics?"

"Business enterprise."

"The world is much stranger than I expected. Do you think it's safe to be Christians in Morocco? I wouldn't want to lose my head." Nicole wrapped her hands protectively around her throat.

Laurel dropped her silk caftan to the floor and washed her hands and face with the cool water in the pitcher. Then she was forced to put on the soiled clothing of yesterday. She had no intention of entering Morocco looking like a heathen. "I'm sure it's safe, Nicole. The United States has a consulate there, a large building actually. It was built as a reward to Morocco for being the first country to recognize the independence of the United States. That was when Thomas Jefferson was president. So you see, our countries have been friendly for years. I don't believe we need worry about being beheaded."

"You surely know a lot about such things."

"I have to learn about all the countries we sail near. You never know what might happen when you're at sea," she added pointedly.

A tap came at the door.

Laurel jumped at the sound. Her nerves weren't yet settled, despite her confident speech. "Who's there?"

"The cabin boy. I have tea and biscuits."

She opened the door and accepted the tray. "Thank you. We'll be out soon."

"Captain Sinclair sent his regards, my lady. He said you have the freedom of the ship. We'll make landfall within the hour."

"Thank him for his kindness," she said coolly and shut the door. All things considered, she should be furious and indignant. But her pulse quickened at the thought of arriving in Tangier, seeing this exotic and mysterious land she'd read about in fairy tale books about Arabian nights. And try as she might to deny it, she was titillated by the idea of Captain Sinclair acting as their host. Naturally, if he misbehaved in any way, she could count on help from several quarters: from the United States Consulate, from her crew, and from Captain Harding.

Wearing his usual attire of fitted breeches, a scarlet sash securing the waist of a flowing shirt, and a white turban, Cheyne escorted Laurel and Nicole to the upper deck of the *Monsoon*. Her polite but cool greeting this morning didn't offer promise for good future relations. On the other hand, the summer day was pristine and Tangier beckoned like a waiting jewel on the coast a few hundred yards away. He must anchor in the bay and take his reluctant guests ashore in longboats.

"Allow me, Miss Caldwell." He held out his hand to assist her into the boat. Her fingers were warm, despite her air of arrogant martyrdom. Her expression was pained and obviously intended as a pointed reminder of his terrible crime of yesterday, but she did look adorable in that rumpled mannish clothing, her face freshly scrubbed, and her unconfined hair turning to gold in the morning sun.

Nicole Petit looked equally fetching in her satin dress, he noticed, and his crew had given both women a furtive, but thorough inspection as they disembarked.

"I hope you passed a comfortable night," he commented as the oarsman turned them toward town. A second, larger yawl was loading the crew of the *Star* and would follow in their wake.

"I slept well, thank you," answered Laurel, gazing across the water toward the gleaming whitewashed village nestled along the shore and climbing the hills beyond.

"I appreciate your concern over my wound," Cheyne said sarcastically. For his impertinence, he received a dagger-like glance from exquisite eyes.

"I'd forgotten the incident," Laurel said. "Naturally the damage is hidden by your turban. Are you now a Muslim, Captain Sinclair?"

"No. But I find the traditional Arab headgear practical in this climate. Also it gives me a sense of brotherhood with my neighbors."

"Your neighbors? Oh yes, the Barbary pirates and slave-traders who populate this coastal area."

"The pirates you speak of have long since gone into retirement. As a matter of fact, I helped several of them on their way a few years ago."

"You fought the pirates?"

"Aye, and won. Hence my foothold in Morocco."

"So with the pirates gone, you prey on legitimate shipping."

"I give in to temptation when some foolish craft drifts into my gunsights like a fish wishing to be ensnared."

He controlled his amusement at the sight of her angry glare and the toss of her head. He remembered that toss from her party long ago in New Orleans, the fateful day twenty years ago when she had called him *dirty*. His humor faded, and he turned his attention to the dock and the handful of people gathered there, congregated to see who was arriving with the captain.

At the quay, he hopped ashore and assisted the ladies to alight. Quickly, he motioned to the coach that had been dispatched from his house as soon as his ship had come into view. His staff was well trained and efficient.

Within minutes, the three were making their way from the waterfront, then along a side street and up a hill toward his palace perched on a high point above the city.

After peering in silence for a time at the passing scenery, Laurel leaned back in her seat and said, "Your town appears rather sinister. I must impress upon you, I expect our stay to be brief. How long until we have the ship you promised?"

"I'm not sure until I speak with my shipbuilders at Asilah. A new frigate was under construction before my last voyage. I will assign it to you, and you can aid in the design." For the first time this morning, he saw Laurel's expression become less dour.

"That seems fair," she responded. How far is Asilah from Tangier? I'd like to go there as soon as possible."

"Asilah is down the coast about thirty miles."

"Why is the ship there?"

"It's the safest port in Morocco. Not much of a town, though. It was occupied in the last century by Spanish Muslims escaping from Andalusia. We'll visit there at the proper time, then once your ship is launched, the frigate will sail to Tangier to take you aboard."

"But that means my captain and crew will have to be in Asilah."

"Aye. In fact, they're heading there tomorrow. My second-in-command, Rafi Hamid, will take them down the coast at first light."

"You mean, Miss Petit and I will not have my crew at hand in case—in case—"

"In case of what, Miss Caldwell?"

Her eyes became veiled, but she had already betrayed her fears. Cheyne knew he had made the right decision by sending her crew beyond her reach. Not that she would need them to defend her, but because too many people in Tangier knew he was the Sea Falcon. Once her captain and crew were safely in Asilah, they would be much less likely to learn the truth of his identity and reveal it to their mistress. If Laurel discovered he was the infamous Falcon, she could pass on the news to her fiancé, Henry Beauregard. While at his palace in Tangier, he could keep the lady under close surveillance, watched by his staff, and sequestered from the world outside.

· 13 ·

Laurel was unable to conceal her fascination with Tangier: the narrow streets, the open bazaars, the dark-skinned people in robes and turbans and fezzes, whose eyes stared back at her with such depths of mystery. Even in the coach, she was assailed with odors of exotic spices, and from a minaret came a husky call to prayer. The whine of a stringed instrument accompanied by the rhythmical beat of an African drum drifted from some hidden recess, adding to her sense of unreality.

Captain Sinclair's announcement that she was to be separated from Harding and his crew was extremely unsettling. She must meet with Harding before he left for Asilah. She would instruct him to make a full report to the American consul regarding the sinking of the *Star*. She would also send a letter at once to her father in New Orleans. Sinclair had promised to arrange immediate correspondence, and she intended to hold him to his pledge.

The coach climbed a steep hill and pulled up in front of a massive stucco wall with an arched entrance sealed by a carved metallic door. As they approached, the door slowly swung open and the carriage rolled inside.

"Welcome to my humble cottage," murmured the captain, stepping down from the carriage. "I named it Tamerlane in honor of a Mongol conqueror whose exploits I admired as a boy."

Laurel's disparaging response died in her throat as she allowed him to assist her from the coach. Surrounding her was the Arabian palace of her dreams: a spacious flagstone courtyard centered by a spraying fountain, fruit trees, and a profusion of flowers, with a stone balustrade fronting on the expanse of limitless sea. The air was soft, caressing, perfumed, and from a distance came the sound of a lute. In contrast to this serene vista sat six life-size lions, their teeth bared as they ruled in gilded splendor, guarding both sides of the doorway to the main structure.

Captain Sinclair extended his elbow as if they were about to enter the parlor of a New Orleans home.

She rested her hand on his sleeve, aware of how foolish the feminine gesture appeared when she was dressed like an untidy cabin boy. But her enchantment with his palace erased every thought as they strolled inside the cool interior, followed by an open-mouthed Nicole.

"Would you care for tea or orange juice, or something stronger?" Sinclair asked the two of them.

Laurel was so overwhelmed by the lavishness of the octagonal room where they were standing that she barely heard him. The floor was covered by plush Persian carpets in hues of ruby red and sapphire blue. Low divans were arranged in groups with cushioned chairs and matching ottomans; small brass tables displayed porcelain bowls of flowers and fresh fruit. On one wall stood an immense ebony cabinet inlaid with mother-of-pearl. A tall grandfather clock, fit for the entryway of an English baron, dominated another section of wall. The room had no exterior windows, but was lighted from above by soaring glass panes. A sizable orange tree, dripping with fruit, grew in one corner as if believing it was truly outdoors.

Laurel gazed in awe, then said, "My, this is quite impressive."

"I warned you I was a successful pirate," answered Sinclair. "Can you imagine how many innocent men died to provide me with such luxury?"

His reminder brought her back to earth. "Indeed, I can." She dared look closely at him, vexed at the way his exotic appearance in his Moroccan garb intrigued her. "I compliment you on your honesty, sir. At least, you're truthful about your own lack of scruples."

A half smile was his response to her insult. "May I direct you to your private quarters? I'll have my housekeeper, Fatima, supervise your bath and provide suitable garments for you and Miss Petit."

"Yes, I would appreciate that."

"I'll wait in my office. Luncheon will be a light repast served on the veranda, if that pleases you."

"My, my, my," muttered Nicole, rolling her eyes upward.

"Of course. Then we can discuss my ship," said Laurel. "Also, I want to visit the American Consulate as soon as possible."

"I'll send a message at once. More than likely, the consul will send an envoy here to greet you. It's not customary for foreign women to be seen in the streets."

She must remember she was a foreigner and should adhere to the traditions of this strange land. On the other hand, she was an American and would demand her rights. "Very well, but I will not be kept in confinement. I expect to go out whenever I please."

A shadow passed his eyes. "I understand your feelings, Miss Caldwell, but even in New Orleans, ladies travel with some protection, a gentleman or a chaperone. Since you're unfamiliar with Tangier, and your unusual looks are sure to draw attention, I must insist you never leave this house without my permission."

"I agree to inform you when I want to go out, but your permission will not be required."

He frowned. "Call it what you wish. I think we're clear on the matter."

A middle-aged woman wearing a blue caftan and a silk veil concealing her hair entered the room and bowed. "The rooms are ready, Captain."

"Thank you. Miss Caldwell, this is Fatima, head of my household staff. She was educated in London and I'm sure you'll find her quite helpful. She'll show you to your suite."

"And Nicole?"

"Miss Petit will go with Fatima to the women's quarters. She'll be comfortable there and will be close by to attend to your needs. Is this agreeable?"

Laurel was reluctant to be separated from Nicole, but decided to accept the arrangement for now. She returned Fatima's shy polite smile. "We are in need of refreshing, as you can see."

"Then come, please, mistress."

With Nicole beside her, she followed Fatima's silent padded footsteps through another arched doorway and down a tiled hall into a suite of rooms as luxuriously appointed as the grand salon where they had first arrived.

"If you please, my lady, here we have a sleeping chamber and a solarium. Towels and soap have been provided for your bath, as well as perfumes and oils. Now that I have an idea of your size, I will bring clothing within the hour."

It was all Laurel could do not to gape like a simpleton at the extravagance of the rooms. The furnishings were French, with gilded chairs and tables in the style of Louis XIV. Hand-woven tapestries graced the walls and the Aubusson rug was the largest and loveliest she had ever seen. Greek and Roman statues encircled a raised tile tub in the bathing room, and one entire wall was hidden by an intricate Chinese screen of exquisite color and delicacy. Again, light was provided by overhead skylights, but the abundance of Venetian glass sconces would easily turn darkness to daylight. It occurred to her that Captain Sinclair must have stolen these luxuries from his victims from around the world.

With a speechless Nicole in her wake, Laurel walked into the bedroom and caught her breath. A massive mahogany four-poster bed with a rich canopy, ornately carved in the Spanish style, dominated the room. A dressing table laden with silver and gold toilet articles sat near a mirrored wardrobe, competing for space with a chaise longue and several tables and more scattered ottomans.

"It's fit for a queen," sighed Nicole.

"Yes, but the queen must have questionable taste and a penchant for thievery."

"Will that be all, mistress?" Fatima asked.

"Yes, thank you. I believe I'll begin with a bath since I see water is available in the tub."

"The sun has warmed it. I've placed a robe nearby."

"You're very kind, Fatima. I appreciate your help."

"If Miss Petit will come with me, I'll show her to her quarters."

As soon as the two had gone, Laurel headed for the tub, which was large enough for several bathers and would better be described as a pool.

Alone in the spacious sunny bathing room, surrounded by ferns and exotic plants like a tropical grotto, Laurel removed her shirt and breeches, her chemise and underdrawers, and stepped gingerly into the water, finding it warmed as promised by the sun's rays slanting from the skylight. She felt sinfully wonderful as she sank to her neck in the sweetly scented liquid. Laying back her head, she let her hair float free, and then she herself floated just below the surface, the tips of her well-formed breasts occasionally breaking through the crystal water.

Envisioning Cheyne Sinclair sent a flurry of conflicting emotions racing through her. He must be fabulously wealthy, but how dreadful to think how his riches had been obtained. It was peculiar she hadn't heard that a pirate still roved these waters. To the best of her knowledge, the Atlantic route to Spain and Gibraltar had been safe for years. Nor had her father ever mentioned this rogue privateer, and he had known every pirate in the business since he took over Caldwell Shipping thirty years ago. Sinclair had said he ousted the Barbary pirates and acquired this stronghold. He must be a fierce fighter, as ruthless as he was handsome, and incredibly bold to slip in and out of New Orleans from time to time.

There was no question, he was absolutely the most attractive man she'd ever met. His magnetism had captivated her from their first meeting in New Orleans two years ago. At Henry Beauregard's picnic the then Mr. Brown had dominated the gathering with the power of his presence. And now, as a pirate and a blackguard in Persian attire, he was more fascinating than ever.

She splashed the water until it boiled around her. She mustn't be such a silly fool over a man's looks. Hadn't she learned anything in twenty-six years? But one other matter continued to disturb her. If he was so evil, why had he paid a hugely inflated price for Nicole, then given the girl her freedom and placed her safely with Shannon? That was the act of a gentleman. In fact, very few Southern gentlemen would have been so magnanimous.

"Excuse me, may I offer my services?"

Laurel squeaked and covered her breasts. From nowhere, a woman had appeared and was staring down at her, allowing her no modesty at all.

"Please turn your back," Laurel sputtered and reached for the towel beside the pool. She stepped out and wrapped it around her. "Who are you, may I ask?"

"I am Shazade Amin, a friend of Captain Sinclair's."

"A friend?" She pushed the dripping hair from her eyes and took a close look at the intruder. The woman was a raven-haired beauty, and her gossamer blouse and ballooning pantaloons revealed a stunning figure. Her eyes were outlined with kohl and a golden chain encircled her forehead. On her feet, she wore silver embroidered slippers with turned up toes. Her bare forearms were encircled with golden bracelets.

"I fill many roles for the captain: friend, servant, others. His wish is my command."

Laurel could well imagine what other roles this gorgeous woman filled. "He sent you to me?" she asked, hugging the towel tightly around her.

"I came when I heard he had a guest. Is there anything you need?"

She could swear hostility gleamed from those seductive eyes. Did the woman think of her as a rival for Captain Sinclair's attention? "I do need clean clothing, but I expect my own servant will bring it soon. Or Fatima."

"Fatima is gathering garments now. Finding Western style clothing at a moment's notice is not easy in Tangier."

"I'm sorry to be so much trouble, but I must have a proper wardrobe. Captain Sinclair sent my ship and all my belongings to the bottom of the Atlantic."

"I see." The woman looked satisfied with that information. Laurel wondered if she had revealed too much, but the truth was out and couldn't be recalled.

"I'm happy to meet you, Shazade. But I have no need for your services."

Shazade smiled coolly, bowed, and hurried from the room.

Under her breath, Laurel mumbled, "Don't they have locks on doors around here?"

Fatima appeared promptly with an armload of clothing. "I did the best I could, mistress. I found several dresses and lingerie, though not the latest fashion, I'm afraid."

"Anything will be fashionable after those rags I wore upon my arrival. I'm deeply grateful for your help, Fatima. I hope we'll be friends during my stay."

"I'm sure we will," the lady said pleasantly. "Your servant, Nicole, is coming soon to help you dress and to arrange your hair. She said you're having luncheon with the master on the terrace."

Laurel inspected the gown Fatima had spread across the bed. Yes, she was having lunch on the terrace, but the man was not her *master* and never would be. No amount of charm would make her forget what he'd done, or what a scoundrel he was. With renewed determination, she began considering the many demands she would make of Captain Sinclair.

Cheyne had changed into a tailored suit, similar to the one he had worn at Beauregard's in New Orleans. He stood on the shaded terrace and watched a servant lay the table for two. The very fact that he was entertaining Laurel Caldwell at luncheon in his own home was like a miracle from heaven. No, he was long past miracles from heaven or anywhere else, he told himself. But he intended to enjoy this sudden gift to the fullest, keeping in mind he must allow her to believe he was truly a villain.

"Pardon, *mon capitaine,* I wish to report that the crew of the *Star* is comfortable in their lodgings." Rafi had come directly to him as instructed.

"Very good, Rafi. Begin preparations at once to transport the lot to Asilah. Tomorrow if possible. I want you to take Captain Harding to the shipyards and determine how long it will be until a ship can be ready for launching."

"There is a frigate set to sail within two or three months. It's very fine. Carries thirty-six guns. The ship will be a great loss to your fleet, sir."

"No matter. It now belongs to Caldwell Shipping."

"This is the same Caldwell who supports us in the fight against slavery?"

"Aye. His daughter was aboard the *Star.*"

"The miss who shot you?"

"Aye, the very one."

"Then she had good reason."

"According to her, she had more than one reason. First, she blames me for sinking her ship, and second, she thought I was about to rape her servant."

"You? Rape! You would never do such an evil thing."

"Thank you, but she doesn't know anything about me, except I'm a fraud and a pirate and a murderer."

"A murderer? You killed only those who deserved to die."

"I repeat, she knows nothing about me."

"But didn't you save a relative of hers from brigands here in Tangier? A man who had come in search of a horse?"

"Fletcher Mackinnon. I did, but that's another well kept secret. Mackinnon is Miss Caldwell's uncle by marriage."

"And Miss Caldwell knows nothing of your involvement with her father all these years? Or of your friendship with Jean Lafitte?"

"I saw her at a ball in New Orleans two years ago, then again at a barbeque two months ago. Her father was present on both occasions, but we made a point not to engage in conversation in public. She has no idea of our secret partnership. I did tell her about my friendship with Lafitte. I figured that information should reinforce my pirate story. Also, more than twenty years ago, she and I met as children, but she wouldn't remember that. That's the extent of it."

"So she has no idea you're the Sea Falcon, that you prey on slave ships and rescue their cargo?"

"That's one secret that *must* be kept, Rafi. She's engaged to marry one of the largest slave-owners in the South. If she finds out the identity of the Sea Falcon, she'll likely tell the bastard all she knows. And he, in turn, is a friend of our old nemesis, the earl of Croydon."

"Franklin Trowbridge? How unfortunate."

"The world's a smaller place than we'd like at times. If the earl found out who I am and where I can be found, he would like nothing better than to bring me to justice in England. Getting rid of me would clear the way for his continuing profits in the slave trade."

"Then we must keep this Caldwell woman under close watch. With her men in Asilah, they will not likely learn you're the Sea Falcon. No one in that ancient pit of intrigue cares about anyone's true identity."

"Exactly my conclusion."

Fatima walked onto the terrace, wearing a smile of immense satisfaction. "The lady, sir. Mistress Caldwell."

Cheyne's heart skipped a beat when Laurel walked into the sunlight, her head high, her chin set in determination, and more lovely, in her outdated gown of powder-blue satin and Spanish lace, than in his wildest fantasies.

·14·

Good afternoon, Captain. Mr. Hamid."

Rafi gave Laurel a traditional salaam as he bowed himself from the terrace.

"Good afternoon, my lady." Sinclair raised her hand to his lips and kissed her fingertips.

She was impressed with the captain's gracious manners and also his change in appearance. He seemed quite at ease with his dual role of pirate and gentleman. The turban was gone, and the wound to his scalp was hidden beneath neatly trimmed hair. His beige suit was impeccably tailored and he sported a dark brown silk cravat. All in all, Captain Sinclair would have looked at home in the finest drawing room in Louisiana.

"I hope you're feeling as refreshed as you appear. I realize you've had quite an ordeal."

Ignoring his honeyed words, Laurel moved toward the table. "I'm quite hungry, actually."

He swiftly pulled out her chair. The enormous ruby ring glinting on his finger was the only sign of his true calling as a thief. The minute the two were seated, she stared unflinchingly into his eyes. "I will come directly to the point, sir. I hold you responsible for my unpleasant circumstances, the loss of my ship and cargo, and the delay in my journey to Scotland."

"Scotland?" His eyebrows arched. "I thought you were bound for Spain?"

"That was an intermediate stop to sell my cargo. Here is the bill of lading." From her pocket, she produced the rumpled paper listing all her trade goods. "I expect to be compensated in full, so that my producers in Louisiana will sustain no loss because of your folly."

"Of course." His tone was reassuring, if one could believe he told the truth. "And then you were going to Scotland? I thought your future husband would be too impatient to allow such a journey."

Husband? What was he talking about? Suddenly she remembered that Captain Sinclair had made the acquaintance of Henry Beauregard. Henry must have told him they were engaged. "You refer to Mr. Beauregard, I assume."

"Aye. He told me you are betrothed and would soon marry."

She kept her expression unchanged as she absorbed this announcement. Henry had lied, but since the captain assumed she was engaged, she decided it was a good idea to carry on the subterfuge. The position of fiancée gave her more protection than that of spinster. "Naturally Mr. Beauregard is impatient. In fact, we argued at length about it the very afternoon you were visiting in New Orleans. But I'm a very persistent woman, sir, and I generally have my way. My fiancé is anxiously awaiting my return next summer. Then we'll be wed."

"Next summer?" He looked astonished. "You weren't planning to return home for a year?"

Had she taken another misstep? If he thought no one was expecting her till next summer, he might use that information to his advantage. She could disappear into the African desert and never be heard from again. "Actually I have two homes now. I have recently purchased a castle on the Isle of Skye in the Hebrides. That will become my second home and a port of call for Caldwell Shipping."

He stroked his chin as if searching for a lost memory. "Aye. I recall now your father mentioned such a purchase. The former property of a relative."

So Captain Sinclair had a closer connection to her father than she was aware of. If he knew about that purchase, what else did he know about her family?

A bare-chested boy in swirling satin pantaloons placed bowls of fresh fruit before them.

She picked up her fork and idly stirred the pieces. "I have many questions, Captain Sinclair. First, when will I have a ship that is ready to sail? I'm dismayed that my crew must leave Tangier to obtain the vessel."

"I realize you find your present accommodations uncomfortable, but you will have to endure them for at least two months, maybe three."

Laurel dropped her fork. "Three months? But that will be September. I find that completely unacceptable."

"A frigate is under construction in Asilah, as I explained. It won't be seaworthy for at least two months. I won't send you abroad in an unfinished craft, no matter how unacceptable you find the delay."

She had been afraid of this. "Why can't you buy a completed ship, one I can leave in immediately?"

"There are none available that are comparable to the *Star*. I'm deeply sorry, but I'm afraid you have no choice. Your new ship will be a thirty-six gun frigate, built by some of the best craftsmen in the world. The wait will be worthwhile, I assure you."

He could be lying again. With her captain and crew gone and no ship in sight, she could be kept here, a virtual prisoner, until this man became tired of his game of cat and mouse. "I'll accept your offer on one condition."

"What is that, may I ask?"

"I must go to Asilah to see the ship." She fixed him with her most determined look.

"That can be arranged."

"Immediately. Tomorrow with my crew."

"No. That's not possible."

So she had called his bluff. "And why not?"

"I have important business here in Tangier. I cannot leave on such short notice."

"I didn't say you must accompany me. I'll be with Captain Harding, and someone to guide us, I suppose."

She saw clouds of anger fill his eyes, but for some reason, he didn't frighten her. Despite his harsh words and arrogance, she sensed she had some hold on him; for some reason, oddly enough, he wanted to please her.

"You have demanded a ship, and you shall have a fine one. You have asked to see it, and so you shall. But not tomorrow. Rafi Hamid will conduct your crew there, then return with a report. That should take a week or ten days. At that time, we will schedule a visit to Asilah. I give you my word."

"The word of a pirate?"

"It's the best I can do."

Laurel cut into a melon and took a bite. She really had no choice. She hated to believe she was a prisoner of this man, but she was feeling more like one every minute. She took a sip of orange juice, then dabbed her lips with her linen napkin. "Very well. I will wait. But in the meantime, I want to contact the American Consulate."

"I have already done so. The consul is in France and will return in a fortnight. A courier from his office will arrive tomorrow afternoon to take letters for mailing abroad. You will compose something suitable, I assume."

"A full description of the events of yesterday. It's possible my father will send a ship immediately to bring me home," she fabricated. She well knew Caldwell Shipping was presently without any ship at all. "I had some difficulty convincing him I could manage this journey without him. It appears he was wiser than I thought when he warned me of danger."

"I've always admired his wisdom."

There it was again—a hint that he knew her father very well. "Tell me, Captain Sinclair, when did you first meet my father?"

She held his gaze as he considered her question. She would have given a great deal to know what was going on behind those mysterious green eyes.

"Since you've asked, I will surprise you a bit, I think."

"Nothing you do would surprise me, sir. Not after yesterday."

"Would it surprise you to know I've been acquainted with your family for twenty years?"

She was not only surprised, she was astonished. "Twenty years! But I never saw you before the ball at Shannon's hotel. I know all my father's acquaintances."

"You have seen me. At a party at your home when you were five, and I was fifteen."

"What? Five?"

"Aye. I was a lad serving Jean Lafitte in those days. I never knew my parents, but I was born and raised on Barataria. Jean was my idol, my mentor, and sponsored my first ventures as a privateer."

"My goodness." She was at a loss for words. This man had been living on the invisible fringes of her life for years, and she'd never known it.

"You mustn't think ill of your father for keeping me a secret. I'm not someone he would welcome into his social circle. But you know what great friends he was with Lafitte, that Jean saved his life during the Battle of New Orleans."

"Yes, of course, I knew that. My father always defended Lafitte, even when the man was forced to leave the United States."

"Because of his loyalty to Lafitte, your father accepted me on the few occasions I appeared in New Orleans. One more thing: like Lafitte, I have never sunk an American ship engaged in *legitimate* enterprise. Until yesterday."

"But you've sunk many others."

"In the old days I preyed on Spanish looters like an alligator on a rabbit. They were thieves, and enemies of England and the United States. I spared lives, but I stripped the ships bare. I also raided the Sales pirates and plundered their stolen goods with a completely clear conscience. I might add I have never sunk an English ship, unless it flew the skull and crossbones, despite the claims of your friend, Trowbridge, the earl of Croydon."

"The earl is not my friend. As a matter of fact, he's an enemy of my relatives, the Mackinnons. What does he claim about you?"

"He knows I sailed with Lafitte. Lafitte had no reservations about attacking English ships since the United States was at war with England. Trowbridge has made a personal vendetta of finding and prosecuting any of Lafitte's followers, no matter how many years has passed since they were privateering."

"I'm intrigued that you would dare socialize with your enemy. But then, that wasn't you; that was Hammond Brown."

"Aye. I rather enjoyed the situation. I gather the earl is a friend of your fiancé, Mr. Beauregard."

A servant removed the fruit and set plates of cold chicken and rice on the table. Laurel said, "My fiancé has many friends who call on occasion. I don't know them all, and he doesn't ask my approval. He may be on friendly terms with the earl, but I am not. Trowbridge tried to have my uncle, Fletcher Mackinnon, executed for a crime he didn't commit. That was the reason the Mackinnons didn't appear at Henry's picnic."

The captain ignored his plate. "I'm glad to know we're in agreement on at least one important question." His eyes held hers for such a long time, she became uneasy. Then abruptly he said, "I suggest you write to Mr. Beauregard promptly. This may be the only correspondence you'll have with him before you sail for Scotland."

"I will, I assure you," she snapped, and dug into her chicken. For the next several minutes, she ate with gusto, avoiding looking at the captain. Everything was clear now. As a friend of Jean Lafitte, he would always be welcomed at her father's home. In fact, she might be able to forgive him for sinking the *Star*, considering her cannon did explode and he was trying to make amends. And if she forgave him for that, maybe she could forgive him for being a pirate. The thought made her lay down her fork and gaze across at him. He hadn't eaten, but was studying her with the oddest expression, almost as if he had special feelings for her. Surely that was impossible. In a heartbeat, his expression changed to one of cool regard.

The next moment, a willowy figure drifted onto the terrace; a curvaceous woman in filmy attire appeared at the captain's elbow, then sank to her knees before him.

Laurel stared at the subservient display by Shazade Amin. She had never seen a woman kneel to a man. The sight was shocking.

"Forgive me, Captain Sinclair, but I must beg your attention," Shazade murmured.

The captain looked casually at Shazade, as if a woman rushing to kneel at his feet was a commonplace occurrence.

"The horse you ordered for me has arrived and has

become uncontrollable in the stable. I fear she will injure herself without your skilled hand."

Sinclair laid aside his napkin and stood, then assisted Shazade to her feet. "I'll come at once. Shazade, have you met my guest, Miss Caldwell, from the United States?"

"Yes, we have met," answered Shazade with scarcely a glance toward Laurel. "Please hurry, sir."

"Will you excuse me, Miss Caldwell. This appears to be something of an emergency."

"Of course. I myself know the value of horses."

As she sat watching the captain walk away behind Shazade, the most bizarre feeling sifted through her. Something akin to jealousy, which she hadn't experienced since she was eighteen and her favorite beau had asked her best friend for the last dance at the ball. Whatever had made her think Captain Sinclair might care for her? And why should that matter? Perhaps this beautiful woman was the love of his life. She herself was only a duty and an obligation. Probably his concern was based on his connection with her father. Her confidence dipped, and she began to feel uncomfortable and out of place sitting alone on the terrace. She supposed she should leave, but she didn't know exactly where to go.

Fatima rushed from inside, carrying a leather notebook. "The master sent me to bring you this. Paper and pen for writing. There is a desk in your room, or you may stay here, if you like."

"I'll go to my room, thank you, Fatima. Is there anything planned for the balance of the day?"

"Only the usual dinner at eight. The captain will attend, along with you and Miss Petit, Mr. Hamid, Captain Harding, and, of course, Miss Amin. I believe there will be musical entertainment."

"Very well. I'll occupy myself until then with my letters." Laurel strolled back to her room, but felt herself slipping into depression. As long as she had considered the captain her adversary, she had been filled with high spirits and ready to do battle. But now that matters seemed settled and he had left her to her own amusement, she felt the wind was gone from her sails, and she was lonely and neglected. She couldn't deny she was enormously attracted to Cheyne Sinclair. But she must realize she meant nothing to him. He was a prince in Tangier, a mature man with a full life and a beautiful woman kowtowing to him. Maybe there were other women; probably so, if he followed the customs of the Arabs.

Her rooms no longer seemed fascinating and inviting. As she pulled up the chair at the desk, she felt the walls closing in like a prison. Here she was, a captive bird in a cage of gold. If only she could travel to Skye at once, or even return to New Orleans. *Dear Mother and Father,* she began in bold script. *The most amazing thing has occurred. . . .*

· 15 ·

The dingy, smoke-filled room at the back of Abou's Antique Shop glowed in the shimmering light of a dozen candles. Seated on a cushion, Shazade waited for Saad, the slave merchant, to react to her news.

"So Captain Sinclair fell for our little trick," Saad commented.

"I'm sure of it. He was convinced you kidnapped me. The corpse bound to my ankle was a most convincing touch." She shivered at the memory, but grinned nervously at Saad. The man's harsh expression, along with his swarthy skin, his beak-like nose and piercing ebony eyes, reminded her of his treacherous nature. She feared and disliked this man who made his living from selling humans into bondage, but he was powerful, and she needed a powerful ally if she was to accumulate wealth in this land of her father. She would stop at nothing to achieve her goal.

"And you've been accepted in the captain's home since that day?"

"Yes. Treated royally."

"You have been to his bed?"

She was silent for several seconds. This was one part of her story she hated to reveal. For weeks, she had tried to seduce the captain. She knew he admired her beauty, and several times he had been forced to leave the room to control his arousal. He wanted her, but he hadn't taken her to bed. "Not yet," she answered. "But he will come to me soon. Unless . . ."

"Unless what?"

"As I told you, he sank an American ship yesterday. He rescued a woman, a beautiful woman with golden hair. Her body is in full bloom."

"You've seen her?"

"In her bath. I made a point to inspect her, and she is exceptional for a white woman."

"So you think this woman may win him although *you* have failed?"

She pursed her lips, then snapped, "I don't know. I saw him gazing at her with great interest at luncheon today. I interrupted, and he was easily drawn from her side, but I fear he is attracted by her beauty."

Saad took a puff on his slender cigar and blew the smoke toward the swagged cloth ceiling. "I won't concern myself with her. I can arrange her disappearance if I find that necessary. What is disturbing is that you haven't gotten the proof I need for my employer to make an arrest. When I took you from the brothel in Casablanca, I expected you to use your beauty and experience to get necessary information from Cheyne Sinclair. I'm certain Sinclair is the right man, but I need proof he is the Sea Falcon if my employer is to pay me what he promised."

This was the opening she'd been waiting for. "But I do have proof."

Saad put down his cigar and leaned forward. "Is that so?"

She pulled out a small bundle. "I found the key to the chest in his bedroom. Inside the chest was this." She unfolded a black and white flag displaying a bird of prey with wings outspread.

Saad snatched it from her hands. "His flag. I've heard of this. The Sea Falcon. You say you found this with Captain Sinclair's personal belongings?"

"In the trunk in his private bedroom," she answered proudly. "I took great risk by going there."

"Excellent. This will help immensely, but I'll need more than this to convince the powerful man I'm dealing with that we have our culprit."

"Why does the man suspect Captain Sinclair?"

"He's been pursuing this information for years. He is extremely eager to bring an end to the Sea Falcon's activities.

"Because the Falcon preys on slavers?"

"That's one reason. My employer is making a fortune by secretly sponsoring illegal American slave ships. But he will gain in two ways if he captures Cheyne Sinclair. He will rid himself of the man causing him to lose slave-trade profits, and he will also be rewarded handsomely for capturing a pirate. A price was put on Sinclair's head years ago when he was privateering with Lafitte. He was a ruthless and dangerous fighter."

Shazade lifted her veil across her face. "I mustn't stay longer. A banquet is being held tonight in honor of the woman from America."

"Your news is most interesting. If the Falcon sank an innocent American ship, he is becoming careless. He must have thought the ship was a slaver."

"What is your plan, Saad? Captain Sinclair has told me I must leave his home. I explained I have no safe place to go, but he insists he will help me find one."

"I'm extremely disappointed you haven't lured him to bed, Shazade. That is where a man's tongue loosens and his secrets can be learned."

"I'm sure I will soon be successful."

"Good. If you fail, you'll go back to Casablanca."

"Perhaps not. I still have family in Spain."

"Suit yourself."

"One more thing of interest. The captain may be going to Asilah next week. I overheard him talking to his friend, Rafi Hamid, about inspecting a ship under construction."

Saad almost smiled. "This is good news. If he goes there, I'll follow him. I've heard Sinclair often delivers the blacks to Asilah so they can return to their homes. If we could capture him there, we might find someone to recognize him, someone who for a handful of silver would swear the Sea Falcon is actually Cheyne Sinclair."

"If I'm forced to leave Tamerlane, I'll accompany you. I would be happy to see the haughty Sea Falcon dragged from his golden perch."

Saad removed a pouch and handed her several coins. "Despite your failure as a seductress, you've brought valuable information. Don't get caught, Shazade. I have no interest in risking my neck to help you."

"I'm very careful around the servants. I speak mostly French, and few of the servants understand the language. The captain prefers an English-speaking staff."

He waved her away. "Go to your banquet and report to me any new information, especially if Sinclair is going to Asilah. When he does, I'll put a plan into action. Without his palace guards and his friends in Tangier, Captain Sinclair will be a much easier target."

Wearing her outdated but elegant Spanish gown created from yards of silk brocade, Laurel followed Rafi

Hamid into the banquet hall of Sinclair's Tamerlane Palace. At her side walked Nicole, attired in a modest dress, suitable for a lady's maid in the style of ten years past. Laurel was certain the clothing had been stolen from Spaniards and had been hastily assembled for this emergency.

The dining room was brightly lit with crystal chandeliers and torches blazing from the surrounding walls. A long table, set with gold and silver plates and goblets, stood at one end of the room. Sofas piled with brightly embroidered cushions flanked the table. Already, a dozen men in traditional Arab garb had taken seats and were lounging on the pillows. Near the center of the room, musicians with stringed instruments, flutes, and muted drums played haunting Arabic melodies.

Cheyne Sinclair left his chair at the center of the table and came to greet the new arrivals. He was stunning in his ankle-length white satin coat embroidered with swirls of golden thread. His indigo-blue pants were flared at the hips and tapered to fit snugly along his muscular calves. Tonight he had on white kid-skin boots with curving toes. Unlike his male guests who wore turbans, his head was bare. Most titillating of all was the way his silk shirt was open to his waist, giving enticing glimpses of his deeply tanned chest with its clearly visible dark thatch of hair. Around his neck hung a massive chain supporting a sizable golden ingot. His ruby ring caught the light as he reached for her hand and bowed. It was obvious that Captain Sinclair enjoyed displaying his wealth like a youngster with a roomful of expensive toys.

"Welcome, Miss Caldwell. Allow me to escort you to the place of honor at my table."

"At the master's side," she noted crisply.

He cocked an eyebrow. "I am the master in my own house. Would you have it otherwise?"

Laurel slipped her arm through his elbow and strolled beside him. "Do I have a choice?"

"Probably not. But I'm willing to discuss the matter."

He seated her, then nodded toward Rafi, who was guiding Nicole to a chair next to his at the far end of the table. Laurel could see Nicole was overwhelmed by the magnificent setting, by the treatment she was receiving, and perhaps by Rafi Hamid, as well.

No sooner was she seated than Captain Harding entered the room. He came directly to the table and gave her a reassuring smile.

"Good evening, Miss Caldwell. I'm happy to see you looking well."

She felt extraordinary relief at the sight of his familiar face. "I'm so glad you're here, Captain. How are the men?"

"Very well, indeed. Their quarters are excellent and they've received all the food and drink they can handle." He faced Sinclair. "The men's only complaint is that they're not allowed beyond the boundaries of their quarters. Are we prisoners, sir?"

"Not prisoners," Sinclair said. "Only confined for this one night for your protection. Tomorrow you leave for Asilah down the coast. Once there, you will be completely free to go wherever you please. I myself will visit there later next week to see how work on the frigate is proceeding. At that time, we'll be able to determine when you will depart for Scotland."

Harding looked satisfied. "Is that agreeable with you, Miss Caldwell?"

She looked from one man to the other. "I suppose so. I plan to visit Asilah with Captain Sinclair. He has offered to hear my suggestions for the design of the ship."

"Seems fair. Certainly the least he can do," Harding added pointedly.

"Take a seat, Captain Harding," invited Sinclair. "We'll have a feast and some traditional Middle Eastern entertainment."

Laurel purposely kept her attention on Harding to the exclusion of her host. She hated the way her heart leaped when she looked at Captain Sinclair, and she feared her eyes would betray her uncontrollable attraction. She wondered where the alluring Shazade was this evening. She had expected to see her seated next to the captain.

Servants delivered trays laden with pungent dishes. Goblets were filled with wine for those whose religious beliefs allowed alcohol to be consumed.

She was studying the fragrant pastries on her plate when Sinclair leaned near and broke the silence that had separated them for several minutes.

"Bstila," he said.

"It smells delicious. What's inside?"

"It's my chef's masterpiece. I understand he uses ten pigeons, forty eggs, four pounds of butter, sugar, almonds, saffron, and several other secret ingredients. I'd like your opinion of the flavor."

She cut into the delicate pastry and took a bite. It melted in her mouth and the taste was pure heaven. She was forced to look at him. His smile was relaxed, open, and unassuming. "Wonderful," she said, licking her lips. "My compliments."

"I'll tell the cooks. The preparation is an all-day process."

The sudden ring of tiny cymbals drew her attention. A woman completely covered from head to toe in scarlet and turquoise veils swirled into the center of the room near the musicians. Her feet were bare and bells encircled her ankles, keeping time with the steady ringing of the cymbals she wore on her fingers.

Fascinated, Laurel watched the woman's graceful swaying as she raised her arms and began a dance of unmistakable feminine enticement. As she moved, the woman tossed aside one veil after another. Her slender body was revealed from her satin halter to just below her navel where a filmy skirt clung precariously to her hips. Laurel stared in amazement as the woman eased the fluttering fabric from her face.

Shazade Amin.

Shazade's dark eyes flashed at Captain Sinclair as she

revolved before him, only the table and a small space separating her abundant charms from his solemn gaze.

Laurel lowered her eyes, but peeked at the the captain. He was intent on Shazade's undulations, as was every other man in the room. She turned toward Rafi Hamid and Nicole, but to her dismay, they had disappeared. Where in heaven's name was Nicole? Would the girl leave her mistress unattended? With a flood of embarrassment, Laurel realized she was the only female in a roomful of lusty men who were aroused to heights of passion by Shazade's alluring performance.

Shazade turned her back toward the table and firmly set her feet, then started to sway in time to the drumbeat. She picked up a tiny plate holding a lighted candle. Raising it aloft, she arched her body backward and balanced her weight between spread legs. The gossamer panels falling from her hip bones to her ankles emphasized every curve, every female contour as if she were totally uncovered. With the burning candle aloft in her palm, the flame seemed to erupt from her flesh. In this impossible configuration, she bent her spine and lowered her head until her hair created an ebony waterfall as it brushed the floor.

The music softened, but the drum beat intensified. Laurel couldn't tear her eyes from the sight of that expanse of smooth skin, the rib cage, the slightly rounded belly, and lower, the suggestion of a soft mound beneath the sheer fabric. Her hand fluttered to her own bare neck. Earlier tonight the scooped neckline with its lace edges had worried her because of its daring decolletage. But now she felt like the most modest of matrons. What would her mother say to the shocking sight of this nearly naked woman? Laurel was certain Rebecca Caldwell would be horrified, but she would conceal her thoughts behind her charming Tennessee chuckle.

With that inspiration, Laurel straightened her shoulders and kept a tight smile on her lips.

The top of Shazade's head was inches from the floor,

her stomach a level surface. Her upside-down eyes were focused on Captain Sinclair. With great care, she lowered the plate with the candle to her stomach and placed it on her navel.

Laurel became aware of the audience clapping in time with the drums. The men must have seen this demonstration before and knew what to expect; their anticipation swept around the room like an approaching wind. She stared at the tiny candle flame moving up and down, ever so slightly, in time with Shazade's breathing. Then Shazade's stomach muscles began to ripple like gentle waves on a golden sea. The flame danced; the men's clapping intensified. With great skill, Shazade revolved, until her bare knees and thinly draped pelvis faced the captain.

Laurel's forehead burned with embarrassment. What could she do? She knew her parish priest would insist she leave the room without delay. On the other hand, she had a personal rule when in foreign countries to respect the local customs as much as possible. To interrupt the proceedings with a flamboyant exit would only call attention to herself, make her look foolish and uppity. Maybe that's exactly what Shazade hoped she would do. That thought settled her in her chair.

The music swelled. Shazade took the candle from her stomach and rose to face Captain Sinclair. With a seductive smile, she placed the candle on the table before him, as blatant a symbolic gesture as Laurel had ever seen. The music ended and applause exploded. Shazade bowed humbly toward the captain, her palms touching, then she scurried from the room.

Laurel was too shocked to move or speak. She stared at her plate and tried to sort out the wild emotions coursing through her. She wouldn't blame Captain Sinclair if he left immediately to go in pursuit of the luscious creature who had welcomed him.

A hand came into view. Captain Sinclair placed the

candle on her plate, then leaned near to blow out the flame.

She looked up at him. His face remained solemn, but his eyes were intense with heat and something else that resembled a mixture of anger and concern. Was his snuffing of the candle also symbolic? What a romantic fantasy, she thought, her heart pounding.

"Come with me, *cherie*," he whispered.

·16·

Cherie. A French term of endearment. "No, I'd rather not leave," Laurel said flatly, proud of the firmness in her tone.

"You need a breath of air—and you must allow me to apologize."

"Apologize? For what?"

"For Shazade's dance. Lovely, but inappropriate for mixed company—and certainly unexpected."

She did her best to appear nonchalant. "It's finished. I don't need to go outside."

He pushed back his chair and extended his hand. "I believe you do."

She could hardly refuse. Everyone was staring, including Captain Harding. She didn't know why she must leave the room, or where the captain was taking her, or what might happen when they got there, but she could not refuse his forceful invitation. She stood, rested her hand on his sleeve, then fixed her sight directly before her as they strode side by side through French doors leading to a veranda beyond the dining room.

A brisk salt-scented sea breeze ruffled her hair and

caught at the lace trim along her bodice. Pulling her hand from the captain's arm, she marched to the low wall surrounding the veranda and stared into the darkness. From below came the sound of surf crashing on invisible rocks. To her left, a stone pillar soared upward, supporting the overhanging roof. A climbing rose bush twined around the pillar to the ceiling, then erupted in a cascade of crimson blooms. On the far wall, a torch produced a flame that struggled in the wind, sending light dancing across the dark masonry.

"I had no idea Shazade intended such a display," Captain Sinclair said. "I'm sorry if you were embarrassed."

Laurel spoke without turning. "Where is Nicole?"

"She's gone for a stroll with Hamid. He told me before the banquet he intended to ask her to walk in the garden. She's quite lovely, you know."

She shifted her eyes toward him. "Indeed she is. That's part of my concern. She's also very young and not very worldly, although wise for her years."

"I assure you she's safe with Hamid. He has great respect for women and maintains high moral standards."

"An odd description of a pirate."

"Nevertheless, 'tis true."

"I hope you're right. I've grown very fond of Nicole since I hired her to be my maid. She's become a companion, a friend. Her well being is extremely important to me."

"I understand, and I promise you she's in good hands."

She was unnerved by his presence, confused by her rush of feeling. She felt safer going on the offensive. "At least she won't ever be a slave. Unlike you and your countrymen of Morocco, I am absolutely opposed to slavery."

"I don't support slavery, nor am I responsible for the Moroccans and their practices."

"Practices? Such as the dance by Shazade?"

"As I explained, I was as surprised as you. I had invited her to join us for dinner. I didn't expect her stunning performance. I guarantee, she will be severely reprimanded. I suppose she was driven by jealousy."

"She was jealous?"

"Of you."

"Why would such a beautiful woman be jealous of me?"

"She's accustomed to sitting by my side at dinner. I suppose she felt replaced."

"Please assure her she may take her rightful seat from this day forward." She turned away, but a thorn snagged her skirt. She reached to pull it free and stabbed a second thorn into her finger. "Ouch." She pressed the wound to her lips.

"Allow me," he said gently.

Her finger was stinging, but her heart was doing cartwheels when he held her hand up to the torchlight. His grasp was firm and rough, not soft like Henry Beauregard's. His touch was gentle as he stroked the wound with his thumb.

"The thorn's impaled, I fear."

"I will survive." Her voice was unnecessarily harsh. "I'll go to my room and have Nicole extract it—once she reappears from her stroll."

"Laurel, you're a very strong woman, the bravest I've ever known. Your father was a hero in the last war. Your mother is a spunky lady. I believe you're a great deal like them."

She was totally disarmed by his comments, and acutely aware of his use of her Christian name. "You appear well acquainted with my family, Captain Sinclair. I know you were a friend of Lafitte's, but I'm curious about your connection with my parents, beginning with the party you attended when I was a child."

He continued to hold her hand, but gazed beyond her. "That was long ago, in another time, another world."

"I realize that. Would you tell me about it?" She had no will to withdraw her hand, nor could she find the strength to take her eyes from his face with its strong angles softened in the flickering glow from the torch.

Without looking at her, he spoke in a low tone. "It was summer. As I said, I was a callow youth of fifteen, full of vinegar and proud of the fact I was a favorite of Jean Lafitte. Jean told me to tidy myself, wear clean clothing, and we would go to a picnic at Highgrove Plantation, the country home of the Caldwells, one of the most prestigious families in New Orleans. We took a boat upriver from Barataria. When I secured the boat at the landing, I got mud on my hands and clothes, but I was never one to worry about such matters."

"I can imagine."

He flicked her a glance, then looked back toward the sea. "When we arrived at Highgrove, the party was in progress. I admit I was dazzled by it all: the music, the grand ladies and gents, and especially the food."

"Did we meet?"

Turning, he looked closely at her, then leaned against the low wall while continuing to hold her hand. "You were a cherub in ruffles and ribbons, with a halo of golden curls."

"I was five. It was my birthday."

"I know. Before leaving, I glimpsed your cake."

"I do remember that cake. It was in the shape of a lamb reclining in grass, all covered with white icing and coconut. It had large brown eyes made from pecans, and it was smiling. When it was time to cut the cake, I threw quite a tantrum. I wouldn't let my lamb be eaten and insisted on taking it to my room. My parents were forced to give in to my wishes since it was, after all, my birthday, and the guests had to settle for ices and pralines rushed from the kitchen."

He smiled down at her. "Spoiled. I knew it. What happened to the cake?"

She couldn't help smiling back at him. "The cake

became even more spoiled than I. It stayed in my room until it turned green and developed an odor. To this day, I refuse to eat lamb. I can't bear to think of the little darlings going under the knife to satisfy my appetite."

"I'll remember that. Mutton is a staple of the Moroccan table."

"Did we speak to each other at the party?"

His smile faded. "We did."

"What did we say? Or do you recall?"

"I recall." His eyes clouded. "Nothing really. Just a passing comment."

Laurel sensed there was more to it than that. "Tell me. I want to know, or you'll have this advantage over me."

"You were playing with a red ball, with the other children. I was watching from beside a gardenia bush. Never in my life had I possessed the slightest touch of shyness until that afternoon. I'm afraid my enormous self-esteem took a beating."

"You didn't join in the games?"

"I wasn't truly a guest. Just an outsider."

Something about the way he said outsider tugged at her heart. She began to understand what he must have felt that day. "Go on."

"The ball rolled to my feet and I picked it up. You ran to get it and saw me for the first time. You said—"

"What did I say?"

"Unfortunately, I got dirt on your white sleeve. You said . . ."

She relived that painful moment with him. "Please tell me?" she murmured.

He released her hand and grinned at her. "Very amusing," he quipped. "You brushed at the spot and told me I was dirty. You suggested I should bathe more often. Something like that."

He was chuckling, but she was heartsick. How cruel children could be. He must have hated her from that day to this.

"Then I owe you an apology for my rudeness."

"Aye, I believe you do. I've been waiting more than twenty years for you to apologize."

"Better late than never," she intoned.

"Too bad I had to sink your ship to receive it." His remark was accompanied by a teasing smile.

Something very powerful was happening inside her. Her heart was engulfed with tender affection like the onset of a spring storm. "But I must apologize, not just for my childish words of long ago, but also for shooting you yesterday. I know now you wouldn't have hurt Nicole. I made a mistake, but I was extremely upset. That's my only excuse."

"I'll accept your excuse—and your apology, Laurel. 'Tis not the first wound I've received, and not likely to be the last," he said lightly.

She found it natural and pleasant for him to speak her name with such intimacy. She felt they had a common bond, shared memories, mutual acquaintances. "I have one more regret," she heard herself saying. "I am sorry you're a pirate."

He studied her for a time, then a smile played around his lips. "At this moment, so am I. Shall we return to dinner?"

"I don't think so. I'll go to my room to remove the thorn."

"Nay, it would be better if you made one more appearance with me at the banquet. Otherwise, every man present will assume we're involved in a serious liaison."

"You mean—"

"Aye."

"Very well." Pulling herself together, she walked with him along the veranda and into the banquet hall. The music had resumed, and the two received only a few curious glances when they entered.

Once seated, he snapped his fingers to a servant who rushed to fill their goblets. Then he reached for her hand and took a close look. "I believe I can get that thorn out with the tip of a knife, if you're feeling courageous enough to allow me to try."

She wouldn't have complained if he'd sliced off her finger. "Go right ahead."

From inside his coat, he withdrew a savage-looking curved dagger with a jeweled handle. Grasping her finger tightly, he squeezed, pressing the end of the thorn into view. "Roses exact their price," he said, "like many other beautiful things in life." With that, he placed the point of the knife against the thorn and lifted it from her flesh.

Laurel barely felt the sting, but was aware of the strength of Sinclair's hand and the care he used in removing the thorn. She focused on the gleam of his hair as he bent near, the way a strand fell over his forehead, the glimpse of stitches in his scalp almost hidden by a thick shock. How kind he seemed, how amazingly forgiving, after she had nearly killed him. He had not once berated her for her act. She couldn't believe this fairminded man could actually attack innocent ships and steal other men's possessions. If he had only preyed on other pirates, she could understand his motives. But, if that were so, why had he attacked the *Star*? Suddenly she wanted desperately to believe in his innocence. Surely there was some reasonable explanation for what he had done.

With the thorn gone, he touched his napkin to her finger to absorb one tiny drop of blood. When he looked up at her, she saw a fleeting look of pain behind his eyes. She was jolted by the sight, and wondered if he was feeling more than just compassion for her small discomfort. Why? Why would her presence cause him such distress? Suddenly, he set his jaw, then released her hand.

"Thank you," she said softly.

He leaned back in his chair.

She felt a door slam shut between them. What had she done?

"You may go now, if you like," he said sharply. "Your reputation is quite safe."

Astonished at the change in him, she tried to think clearly. "Go? Yes, perhaps I should."

He turned to her, and his expression was as cold as the marble floor and pillars of the banquet hall. "I won't see you again until we go to Asilah. Next week, I expect. I've arranged for you and Nicole to sightsee and shop, if you like. Mention my name at any bazaar and the items you choose will be yours. Tomorrow at noon, the official from the U.S. consulate will call. Fatima will provide luncheon. I have much business to attend to in the north. I'll send word when I'm ready to inspect your ship."

Feeling totally rejected, Laurel matched his coolness. "Fine. I'm eager to see the ship, as you know. Now, if you'll excuse me."

He crooked a finger toward Captain Harding, who promptly rose and rushed over to them. "Escort Miss Caldwell to her suite, sir. Then take your leave of her. Your crew will be expecting you back in your quarters by now."

She could see Harding was annoyed by Captain Sinclair's imperious manner. What had become of Cheyne Sinclair's warmth and boyish charm? What had happened to his calling her Laurel? "Good evening, Captain Sinclair," she said, rising to take Harding's arm. "It's been most entertaining."

As she reached the doorway, she took one last look over her shoulder. Cheyne Sinclair was exiting across the way. Where was he going, now that they had finished their brief tête-à-tête? As soon as he had won her trust and admiration, he had tossed her aside like an unwanted scrap from his table. Did he go to a rendezvous with Shazade? Very likely, she thought, as annoyance and jealousy vied for position inside her. Crushed and hurt, she chastised herself for nearly making a terrible mistake. She had been about to forgive Captain Sinclair for his evil past and his decadent present. Very well, she would forgive him. But she wouldn't forget again they lived in two different worlds, worlds which could never be reconciled, not in this lifetime, or ever, as far as she was concerned.

Silently, she walked along the hall, oblivious of Harding at her side. When she arrived at her suite, she waited while he opened the door, then she bid him a quick goodnight and farewell. They would meet again at Asilah.

Entering her rooms, she was startled when Nicole rushed up to her.

"I've been waiting," Nicole effused. "I wanted to share something with you, mistress, something wonderful."

"I'm happy to see you're safely here," said Laurel, crisply. "I was worried about you."

Nicole rolled her eyes toward the ceiling and clasped her hands. "No need to worry, miss. I am happy beyond words."

"Really? Why is that?"

Nicole fluttered her eyelashes and grinned sheepishly. "I believe I'm in love, Miss Laurel. *Oui,* I'm sure I am."

His mind in a turmoil, Cheyne hurried to the servants' quarters and pounded on the door of Shazade's private suite. He was annoyed with himself for falling further under Laurel Caldwell's spell, and he was ready to direct his anger at Shazade Amin. If not for Shazade, he wouldn't have felt compelled to escort Laurel to the veranda. Nor would he have had the opportunity to tell that inane story about his wounded ego at Laurel's fifth birthday party. He had made a fool of himself, but it wouldn't happen again.

Picturing Shazade's wildly erotic dance, he felt his temper flame. His instincts had been correct when he'd wanted the woman to leave his home soon after her arrival. Instead, he had given her courtesy and respect. But his sympathy had been stretched to the breaking point, and now he was determined she must go. She had disgraced herself in front of all his guests. If she had hoped to lure him to her bed by her scandalous conduct, she had made a mistake. He was not an Arab, and her dance, while skillful and alluring, was inappropriate and insulting to his American guests. The girl must vacate his house.

Shazade flung open the door, her face alight with a smile of satisfaction "I knew you'd come," she cried.

He pushed inside. "Miss Amin, you must leave my house. I only allow you to stay a day or two more so you may secure a safe residence elsewhere. I'll provide you with funds for a month. Or you may use the money to travel wherever you like. The important thing is, you must make a new life for yourself. I can no longer be responsible for you."

During his pronouncement, her face fell, then tears pooled in her eyes. He hated that, but his anger and frustration left no room for sympathy. "Your dance was beautiful," he said more gently, "but you know as well as I that it was a ploy to embarrass Miss Caldwell and draw my attention to yourself and away from her."

Shazade pouted and wiped her eyes. "You've never looked at me, not really. I admit I wanted your attention, or if not yours, then attention from some other man in the room. A woman has few choices in Morocco. I need the support of a man of means."

"You shouldn't have any problem. You are indeed very attractive, and obviously intelligent. I'll give you the address of an innkeeper who keeps an expensive establishment near the American consulate. If you are employed there, you will come in contact with wealthy travelers from around the world. You'll find a rich husband easily enough. Are we in agreement?"

"Yes. I'll go," she said, flipping her hair across her shoulder.

"I'm leaving in the morning. Fatima will take care that my instructions are carried out. Good-bye Miss Amin, and Allah go with you." He touched his heart and his forehead as he bowed in the traditional way, then left the room.

"Dammit," he muttered as he headed back to the banquet hall. "The little vixen." He had planned a special occasion for Laurel, something to show her the flavor of life in Morocco. And then Shazade had flaunted herself in the most scandalous dance he'd seen since he arrived in this country. Even so, he had nearly fallen into his own deadly trap this evening. Laurel Caldwell hypnotized him with her grace and spirit and loveliness. He had idolized the memory of her for so long, that to be near her sent his senses reeling. He had sounded like a whining imbecile. Amazingly, she hadn't ridiculed him, but appeared to understand his long-ago pain. He had felt her compassion reach out to him. Bloody saints, if he wasn't careful, he could fall in love with the woman. That would be a damned stupid thing to do. She was a fantasy, a fantasy who belonged to another world, and to another man.

But tonight it had taken every ounce of strength he had to keep from taking her in his arms and kissing those inviting lips. What would she have done? Slapped him? Probably. He would have risked that, but he couldn't risk the kiss, not because of her, but because of himself. One kiss and he could be lost forever. One kiss could break his heart and leave him empty for the rest of his life. No, space was what he needed, distance from Miss Caldwell. He could avoid her for a week or so and give his emotions time to cool off, but there was nothing he could do about the upcoming journey to Asilah. He had promised her she could see the ship, and he was a man of his word. After they completed their investigations in Asilah, he would send her back to Tangier with Captain Harding, while he himself stayed in the village with the crew to implement her instructions. After that, he didn't know what excuse he'd find for staying away from her until she sailed, but he would come up with something. Let her go to Scotland, let her marry Beauregard, let her forget Cheyne Sinclair existed. She would be happy in her own world, even if Beauregard was a cruel villain and a pompous ass rolled into one.

He entered the dining hall and slumped into his chair. Draining his goblet, he cursed himself for a fool. How he would get through the next two months he couldn't guess. But somehow he must.

· 17 ·

Laurel was certain Nicole was merely swept up in the magic of the moment, the girl's head turned by the attention of a handsome and exotic man who was a Berber and a pirate. During Laurel's first restless night under Cheyne Sinclair's roof, she decided both she and Nicole must pull themselves together and concentrate on escaping the lure of Morocco and continuing their journey to the Isle of Skye.

She had dreaded spending a boring week at Tamerlane, with Captain Sinclair gone and nothing to do but play the part of tourist and reluctant guest. To her surprise, the days flew by under the guidance of Rafi Hamid and Fatima. Laurel wondered if her restlessness had diminished because of the balmy sea air, the frequent baths in the sunny solarium, the constant pampering by countless servants, and the steady supply of fine wine and delicious food. She had Nicole's company much of the time, but she found she enjoyed being alone in the perfumed splendor of Tamerlane. She spent hours on her private veranda, reading books from the captain's extensive library, or just gazing at the ever-changing seascape beyond the fortress walls.

Her visit with the emissary from the consulate's office was brief and businesslike. She reported her ship's sinking and the exact circumstances of the event. Stopping short of accusing Captain Sinclair of evil intent, she merely described the tragedy and asked for the report to be made to the proper officials of her govenment.

Her letter to her parents was completed and mailed the second day of her stay. She also wrote to Shannon Kildaire, informing her that their acquaintance, one Mr. Hammond Brown, was none other than Cheyne Sinclair, the last of the Barbary Coast pirates. She felt that Shannon had a right to know the man's true identity, and also that Nicole was doing well and making an excellent companion. Naturally, she didn't mention Nicole's sudden fascination with Rafi Hamid, nor did she write to Henry Beauregard.

During a succession of brilliant days, she and Nicole accompanied Fatima on tours of the ancient town, its bazaar, the old medina, the villas of the wealthy, and the historical sites where Phoenicians and Romans had occupied the area long before the Arabs. She was impressed with the verdant fields, the citrus orchards, and the pine and cedar forests occupying the land between the coast and the distant Rif Mountains with their barren and forbidding peaks.

She heard nothing from Captain Sinclair, nor did she glimpse his exquisite dancing girl. It occurred to her he might have taken the woman with him on a journey. She did her best to put him from her mind, but discovered this was impossible during the long balmy evenings in his palace.

One late afternoon, she was lounging on her veranda, engrossed in a Jane Austen novel, when footsteps echoed across the flagstones.

Cheyne Sinclair had returned.

Dressed casually in belted shirt and snug pants tucked into his boots, he presented her with a distant smile. "I hope you're well, Miss Caldwell. Fatima assures me she has done a proper job of showing you the sights."

Closing her book, Laurel responded with an equally cool tone. "She's done wonderfully, thank you. Tangier has much to recommend it. Not that I would want to take up permanent residence, of course."

He accepted her barb without flinching. "Actually that's why I've come to offer you a change of scene."

She sat up. "Really? We're going to see my new ship?"

"We leave at dawn tomorrow. Will the early start inconvenience you greatly?"

"Not at all. I've always been an early riser. What must I do to prepare?"

"Fatima will help you choose suitable clothing for yourself and Nicole. We're going overland by the coast road. The caravan is being readied even as we speak."

"Caravan? What sort of caravan?"

"A substantial entourage. Camels, wagons, horses. We'll camp overnight near the coastal dunes, then arrive in Asilah before nightfall the following day. I've arranged for private quarters inside the walls of the village. When you've rested, you will see the progress of your ship."

Her enthusiasm was fired, despite the captain's less than gracious manner. "I'm looking forward to it." She started to rise, but he suddenly nodded and spun on his heel and left her. His coldness settled in her bones, a new reminder of the differences between them. He must have overcome any sense of guilt over the sinking and was now mired in resentment at having to spend time and money to placate her. That realization started a dull ache in the pit of her stomach. She shouldn't have expected special treatment from the captain, but that night on his terrace, he had been so friendly, so warm and open, as if he really cared about her.

Shaking her head, she rose and walked into her boudoir. Whatever illusions she had about Cheyne Sinclair must be quickly destroyed. He didn't care for her, and what difference would it make if he did? Was she so desperate for love that she would be attracted to a pirate? A *pirate?*

She pulled open the wardrobe; informal clothing should be ideal for the journey. Perhaps her depression was caused by witnessing Nicole's glow of happiness that was growing with each passing day. She knew Nicole spent time with Rafi Hamid when she wasn't mingling with the servants in their quarters. Laurel would have worried more, but she was inclined to accept Sinclair's testimony of the man's character. She had warned Nicole to be cautious, and that was all she could do. After she had pointed out the dangers of their position, she had allowed Nicole to come to her own conclusions. As a matter of fact, she had given some thought to what Nicole's life would be like if she were to marry Rafi Hamid. Perhaps the lovely quadroon would have a wonderful time here in Morocco. She had some distant roots in Africa, after all.

Nicole rushed into the room. "Miss Laurel, Miss Laurel!" She was breathless and appeared concerned.

"What's wrong, Nicole?"

"I must tell you something I just overheard in the kitchen."

"Oh? What's that?"

"Shazade was in the kitchen today."

"But I thought she had gone, maybe with the captain."

"No, but she's left Tamerlane. She has a friend in the kitchen, a French girl who helps with the cooking. She came to see her friend today and they sat in the corner speaking in French."

"You eavesdropped on their conversation?"

"I did, I admit. They didn't know I could understand them, of course."

"What were they talking about?"

"Shazade said she had moved into a fine hotel near the American consulate. She showed the French girl a pocketful of coins and said she was doing very well, even though Captain Sinclair had sent her away."

Despite herself, Laurel couldn't help feeling pleased that the captain had dismissed Shazade. Admittedly, a very uncharitable attitude. "I'm glad she's thriving," she murmured in an attempt to be fair. "I don't see the problem."

"It was the other thing she said, the part about an employer of hers laying a trap for Captain Sinclair."

"A trap? What sort of trap?"

"I didn't hear much more, but she said her employer intended to capture him and send him to England. Then she would be rich from sharing in the reward."

"You're sure she didn't mention a name? Her employer's name?"

"No. My ears pricked up, but she was speaking so low, I missed most of it. I'm worried for the captain, and for Rafi Hamid, too. If Captain Sinclair is captured, what will become of Rafi?"

Laurel sat on the bed. Were the men in danger, or was Nicole overreacting to kitchen gossip? "I suppose I should warn him, but this could be a common occurrence, considering he's a pirate, after all. Most pirates live with a price on their head. They must take danger for granted. No doubt, the captain has enemies here in Tangier. That's why his palace is well guarded. Still . . ."

"Is it all right if I tell Rafi? I believe Shazade is evil, even if she is very beautiful." She tapped her cheek. "I could put a spell on her, you know. I could make a charm, a powerful gris-gris I learned from my grandmother."

"My goodness, Nicole, you mean Marie Laveau?"

Nicole tucked her head. "Yes, ma'am. I didn't want to tell you, but I have the power. Do you think I should do something against Shazade?"

"No, I'm sure that isn't neccessary. But I have news as well. We're going to Asilah tomorrow."

"Tomorrow? Oh, I hadn't heard about that."

"Captain Sinclair just informed me that we leave Tangier at sunup. We must pack our things."

"Of course, right away."

"But when you see Rafi, tell him what you've heard. When we return, he may want to confront Shazade and force her to explain what she's up to."

Nicole nodded. "Very well. I'm plenty glad we're going away from here. Rafi says we'll have a fine time traveling down the coast, riding camels and meeting more Berbers like him. I do like these people in Morocco. I might be kin to some of them—ancient ancestors, you know."

"I expect you're right. Now, open the chests and let's select some clothing. What does one wear to ride a camel, do you suppose?"

Laurel was not to learn the fine points of camel riding. Instead she was given an exquisite small bay mare as a mount, which reminded her a great deal of the beautiful Desert Mirage in training at Highgrove.

Dawn was breaking over the rolling hills south of Tangier as the caravan left the city. Rafi Hamid was plainly in charge of the expedition as he galloped his stallion between the lead horses and the camels and wagons at the rear.

Riding beside Laurel, Nicole's head was continually twisting to keep Hamid in view.

"He is wonderful, isn't he?" Nicole whispered. Her voice was breathy through the yashmak, the double veil covering her face.

Laurel felt foolish in the tent-like clothing Fatima insisted they wear in public. But the garb did have some advantages. She could cast her eyes in any direction without anyone knowing where she looked. And she was looking anxiously for Cheyne Sinclair.

"Yes, Mr. Hamid cuts quite a fine figure," she noted.

"But do be practical, Nicole. Don't let romance blind you to reality."

She could tell her words fell on deaf ears as Nicole turned in her saddle to watch Rafi Hamid flash by, his robes flowing, his horsemanship superb.

The day was soon beastly hot, the only respite an occasional breeze off the sea when they rounded hills and the ocean came into view. Their pace was surprisingly brisk, and when they stopped for a rest at high noon in a shady orange grove, Hamid came to report they were making good progress.

Laurel spoke to Rafi. "The scenery is quite spectacular, Mr. Hamid." With an air of indifference she asked, "Is Captain Sinclair accompanying us? I haven't seen him, and I do want his assistance tomorrow when we view the ship."

"He rode ahead last night, madam. He wished to make certain our camp for tonight is in readiness."

"I assume I'll see Captain Harding and my crew when we reach Asilah."

"Unfortunately, they're occupied elsewhere. They've gone—ah, sightseeing in the mountains this week."

"Sightseeing? You can't be serious? My crew is *sightseeing?*"

"Yes, madam. That is my understanding."

Laurel put down the cheese-stuffed pita she'd been nibbling and stared at Hamid. "I find this hard to believe, though I'm sure you wouldn't lie to me. Captain Harding knew I'd be coming to see the ship. Surely he wouldn't leave the town during my visit, along with my entire crew."

Hamid dropped his eyes. "The timing of your inspection was not known. The men were bored and restless, so I've heard. Excuse me, I must see to the caravan." He hurried away after a glance at Nicole who was gazing at him as if he were a god fallen to earth.

Laurel was more than annoyed; she was angry. Cheyne Sinclair had no right to take control of her captain and crew. Was there some reason he wanted to keep her apart from her own employees? The thought made her uneasy.

Nicole was replacing her veils and heading for her horse. Laurel decided there was nothing to be done but follow and make the best of things. She knew from her map the location of Asilah, and they were indeed headed toward it. When next she saw Captain Sinclair, she would give him a piece of her mind, and insist that Captain Harding be produced.

The steamy afternoon seemed endless. Late in the day, as the caravan plodded into a large palm grove, centered by several brightly striped tents near a well, Laurel felt ready to fall off her horse and melt into a sodden puddle.

Rafi appeared and assisted her and Nicole to alight, then bowed them toward the tents. "Please refresh yourself, madams. I'll have food and drink provided shortly. But first, I must see to the beasts."

Although Rafi treated Laurel with great courtesy, she had the distinct feeling his attentions were focused on Nicole. He must be as smitten with the girl as Nicole was with him.

"Thank you, Rafi. Would it be too much to ask for me to meet with Captain Sinclair?" she asked curtly. "I thought he would be here to receive us."

"He may come later. His men who set up the camp reported he had ridden to the next village to get supplies."

Supplies, she thought in annoyance. They had a dozen camels loaded with supplies they brought from Tangier. Too exhausted to question further, she entered her tent and began stripping out of her robes. Her nose felt hot, and she was certain it was burned by the sun, despite her efforts to protect her skin. She washed from a large bowl and took a moment to admire the beauty of the tent's interior, the silken drapery, the gleaming copper utensils, the pillowed bed arranged on Persian rugs covering the floor.

For more than an hour, she stretched out on the bed and rested her aching body. Then Nicole arrived from the adjoining tent and they enjoyed a supper of sliced meats, cheeses, fresh fruit, bread, and red wine, followed by tiny cups of rich coffee. Laurel suspected the meat was mutton, but she was too hungry to stick to her pledge not to eat the "darlings." Their serving boy said nothing, then cleared the dishes and left them in peace.

"Would you excuse me, Miss Laurel?" Nicole asked with a somewhat guilty smile. "I wish to visit with Rafi, now that his duties are complete."

Laurel sighed, understanding completely. "Of course, dear. I believe I'll take a stroll myself. If I'm not mistaken, I hear the surf beyond that row of sand dunes. A cooling walk at sundown is just what I need."

Nicole hurried away, and Laurel drifted outside and toward the sandy rise between the camp and the ocean. On the far side of the oasis, the camel drivers had gathered and begun to sing softly, accompanied by stringed instuments and a muffled drum.

Laurel was feeling vaguely depressed. The captain had abandoned her to his underling, a Berber, who was infatuated with Nicole. The couple's attraction was quite natural, but she suddenly felt friendless and alone. She thought of Highgrove and her parents and Shannon. Well, she had wanted adventure and here she was in the midst of the greatest adventure of her life. But she wasn't enjoying herself, not since Cheyne Sinclair had become an indifferent stranger.

She climbed to the top of the dune and paused to admire the expanse of sea, blue-black now in the early evening, with the sun's last glow fading on the far horizon. The surf had grown calm, and she suddenly had an irresistible desire to feel the water on her warm flesh.

Without hesitating, she went down to the beach, then stopped to pull off her slippers and stockings. Holding these aloft in one hand, she gathered her skirts above her ankles and waded into the water's edge. She stepped gingerly along the bubbling foam, relishing the cool liquid around her ankles and the soft mud between her toes. She shook her head until her hair pins scattered and her hair drifted loosely around her shoulders. Turning her back to the land, she closed her eyes, lifted her chin and inhaled the invigorating breeze off the Atlantic.

Suddenly something heavy struck her in the middle of her back, almost sending her into the waves. She dropped her shoes and stockings and desperately fought for her balance.

· 18 ·

Laurel whirled and came face to nose with a riderless white horse. The animal tossed its head. She stumbled again and grabbed for the reins flapping near her hand. Her skirts were soaked below her knees and twisted around her calves. Using the horse to steady herself, she wondered what had happened to its rider. "For heaven's sake! Easy, boy."

A man's laughter drifted from atop the sand dune.

Still clinging to the horse's reins, she stared through the approaching darkness toward the mound. Outlined by bonfires blazing behind him, wearing a turban and a wind-whipped cape, his booted legs apart and his hands on his hips, stood Cheyne Sinclair. No Arabian sheik had ever looked more commanding or more excitingly romantic.

"Is this your horse?" she shouted. "The beast nearly knocked me into the sea."

Cheyne marched down from the dune and stopped several yards away. "You deserved a dunking after such rash behavior."

"Rash? What's rash about wading through an inch of calm tide?"

"Nothing, unless you're wandering alone in the night on a beach in Morocco. I thought you deserved a lesson, with the help of my stallion, Caliph."

"You ordered the horse to—to attack me?"

Cheyne laughed again. The sound was hearty and contagious.

She felt herself responding to his merriment. "This is not amusing," she said sharply. "I've lost my shoes and my dress is ruined." A wave stuck her legs from behind and she held more tightly to the horse. "A gentleman would offer some assistance," she said.

"Since no gentleman is present, you'll have to rely on Caliph. Besides I'm wearing my favorite new boots."

She grasped the stallion's bridle firmly. He whinnied and grew still beside her. She was thinking of mounting, when Cheyne whistled softly.

Caliph tossed his head, jerking her sideways. She screeched as she was pulled from the surf and dumped on the sand at the feet of Cheyne Sinclair.

Her cheeks flamed as Cheyne placed his hands under her arms and raised her to her feet. She found herself gripping his upper arms, but hastily released them and stepped back. Acutely aware of his marvelous physique and potent masculinity, she pushed back her hair and turned to walk down the beach.

At once, he fell into step beside her. Caliph trailed behind.

She refused to look at the captain. She was bedraggled and shoeless, and he looked breathtakingly like the hero of one of Elizabeth's romantic novels.

"Where are you going?" he asked in a low voice.

"Away from you, Captain."

"I wouldn't go too far, if I were you. You're wet and the night is cooling rapidly. There are broken shells about and you're barefooted."

"All this because of you. And your undisciplined stallion."

"Undisciplined? Caliph?" He chuckled again.

"You taught him that trick?"

"Arabian horses are smarter than most people. He always obeys me instantly."

She threw him a glance. This was a mistake since the sight of his deeply tanned face accentuated by the white turban, his eyes and lips reflecting humor, sent sudden waves of pleasure to every part of her.

"I see I must come to the rescue after all." He scooped her into his arms and walked to a large flat boulder. Placing her carefully on it, he sat beside her. "We should return to camp. On the other hand, the moon is rising. A beautiful sight." He continued to look at her.

"Captain Sinclair—"

"Why not call me Cheyne? After all, we met twenty years ago. We're hardly strangers."

She drew up her knees and did her best to cover her ankles and feet with the wet fabric. "I do have some questions, Cheyne."

"Not tonight. We'll have time for questions when we reach Asilah."

She knew she had some important matters to discuss, but she couldn't recall exactly what they were. His overwhelming presence was destroying the normal processes of her mind. "Very well, but I will expect a complete explanation of what's going on." She felt his gaze on her and kept her eyes determinedly on the trail of moonlight wafting across the undulating waves.

"Always in command," he muttered. "I thought Southern ladies were helpless and sweet and compliant."

She shifted to face him. "Not all. I suppose you're used to compliant women, women who kneel at your feet and call you *master.*"

His white grin sent tingles along her spine. "This is Morocco, after all. Men and women have a somewhat

143

different relationship than in other countries. But the end result is the same."

"I see." She thought better of pursuing this line of conversation. "So you like Morocco. How long have you made it your home?"

"About ten years. I left Lafitte and sailed my own ship for a time. I gave the Spanish plenty of reason to hate me."

"You have no family at all?"

"None. Lafitte was my surrogate father, and since we parted, I've made my way alone."

"You don't miss having a wife, children?"

He gazed toward the sea. "I've thought of marriage. I'm very fond of children. Perhaps before long . . ." His voice fell and he looked back at her. "I suppose you and Beauregard are planning to have several."

"Uh—Henry, yes. I love children. I'd like to begin right away. After all, I'm twenty-six. I believe Henry would like a large brood."

He stiffened and his face clouded. "Twenty-six. A good age to be," he said absently. "You're shivering. We'd better go."

"One minute, Cheyne. I do have something important to tell you."

"What's that?"

"Nicole saw Shazade in your kitchen yesterday. She overheard the woman speaking in French to her friend. Shazade said her employer planned to capture you and send you to England. There is a great reward for you."

His mouth crooked at one corner. "'Tis nothing new in this, and nothing to fear. Shazade is angry because I sent her away. And there's been a price on my head in England for twenty years." He stood and called to Caliph. The horse trotted at once to his side. "But I appreciate the warning. I do have enemies."

He swung easily into the saddle and held out his hand toward her. "Come," he said softly.

Entranced, she took his hand, then allowed him to lift her across the saddle in front of him. His arm curled protectively around her waist. She felt his muscles contract and the warmth of his chest against her back.

Caliph cantered along the surf scattering the moon-splashed tide. For one enchanting moment, Laurel relaxed in Cheyne's embrace and allowed herself to dissolve into her magical surroundings. Yes, this was the fantasy, the adventure, the romance she had dreamed of. How incredibly delightful it was to experience it at last.

The ride was brief, and in minutes she was deposited at the flap of her tent.

"Au revoir, mademoiselle," said Cheyne. "I will see you tomorrow in Asilah."

"Yes," she whispered, hating to think of anything beyond this instant in time. "In Asilah."

"Sleep well." He pivoted Caliph and rode into the shadows.

With a sigh, Laurel noticed a light in Nicole's tent and heard movement. Nicole had returned from her own tryst and was safe and sound. She considered saying goodnight to the girl, but then decided she didn't want to break the spell of her own romantic interlude. She went into her tent and began removing her dripping skirts.

Compared to Tangier, Asilah was crude and dusty and a remnant from the ancient past. The caravan arrived at dusk and passed beneath one of the two arched gates to enter a place forgotten by time.

Laurel was an experienced rider, but she didn't remember ever being so saddle weary. She dropped her reins before a two-story stucco structure and allowed Hamid to ease her to the ground. Swathed in her robe and veils, she followed him into the poorly lit entryway, barely aware that Nicole stumbled along beside her. At this point, she had not the slightest interest in seeing Cheyne Sinclair, or anyone else, for that matter. She dreamed of the luxurious tub at Tamerlane, and wondered if there was any possibility of a bath in this rustic dwelling.

A woman bowed low and indicated tile steps leading up from the courtyard. "This way, señoritas, *por favor*," the lady murmured. "My casa is yours to command."

Hamid led the way, carrying the ladies' small traveling trunks. Arriving at an open doorway, he bowed. "Asilah has a Spanish history, but the proprietress speaks passable English. I assume Captain Sinclair has taken rooms for himself on the opposite side of the courtyard. That is his usual arrangement. A guard will be on duty for your protection. If you need anything, ask for Francesca."

"Yes, thank you, Mr. Hamid," Laurel responded wearily. "We'll rest well, I'm sure."

The two-room suite was shabby, but spacious. There was no bathing tub, but large pitchers of water and clean towels were provided in each bedroom. Also a bowl of tempting fruit and a decanter of almond milk, a favorite drink of the Muslims, were placed on a low table surrounded by bright cushions.

Laurel moved, trance like, to refresh herself, and made a satisfying meal of an orange and slices of cantaloupe. The almond milk, created from diluted almond paste, sugar, and orange extract, was a heavenly drink after the day's hot journey. Barely murmuring good night to Nicole, she fell into bed and was asleep in minutes.

Morning came all too soon as roosters greeted the sun rising above the Atlantic's eastern horizon.

Laurel's thigh muscles ached, but she left her bed and strolled to the balcony to gaze across flat roofs toward the sea. A few deep breaths, laced with clean salt air, cleared her head.

"Good morning, Miss Laurel."

She turned to see Nicole, dressed in an attractive riding habit with her blue caftan over her arm, standing in the middle of the bedroom.

"My goodness, you look ready to go out."

"I wanted to see to your toilette, miss, but when I peeked in, you were deeply asleep. You see, I arranged to meet Rafi for an early morning ride beyond the city. But I can delay if you need me."

"No, by all means, go on your ride. But I stand in awe of your willingness to climb aboard a horse today. I'm stiff as a plank."

"Then excuse me. Rafi sent word he's waiting."

"Please tell Francesca I'd like coffee or tea, as soon as it's convenient. And my stomach is reminding me of the sparse dinner we had last night."

"Yes, ma'am. When we're together, I'll tell Rafi what Shazade said in the kitchen."

"Yes, that's a good idea."

Nicole rushed out the door, her mind obviously on her romantic rendezvous.

Laurel pulled on her robe over her filmy gown and began to peel an orange. Within minutes, a knock sounded, and Francesca entered with a carafe of steaming coffee that made Laurel's mouth water.

"Thank you, Francesca. That should help my eyes to focus. Could you tell me if Mr. Sinclair is about? We have urgent business in Asilah and I'd like an early start."

"He left a few minutes ago, but sent this to you." The dark-eyed Francesca pulled a note from her sash and handed it to Laurel. "He said to tell you he would return at mid morning to escort you to the harbor."

After Francesca left, Laurel eagerly opened the note.

Miss Caldwell, I hope you have rested well after your journey. I have ordered a carriage for 10:00 and we will inspect your new frigate. Following that, you might enjoy a stroll through the medina of the town and a late luncheon at a quaint bazaar and orchard near the seawall. I understand Rafi and Nicole have plans of their own for the day. Tomorrow a sloop will take you

*back up the coast to Tangier. An easier passage than
the one on horseback. Cheyne Sinclair.*

So she would be spending time with Cheyne. The
thought fluttered inside her. What would his mood be
after their recent encounter on the beach?

She ate her breakfast, then dressed in a simple skirt
and blouse, brushed her hair and pinned it as best she
could without benefit of a lady's maid. How titillating to
be going out alone with a man who was almost a
stranger. Her mother, independent as she was, would
have the vapors if she knew. Not to mention that the
man was an infamous privateer, a freebooter who had
caused the sinking of the *Star*.

On the other hand, she would wear the concealing
djellaba and veils, so who would be the wiser? Perhaps
the locals felt that a woman draped like a tent had no
need for a chaperone and could go out freely with
whomever she pleased.

When she heard the clip-clop of a horse's hooves on
the cobbles below, she leaned over her balcony to see if
Cheyne had arrived.

To her chagrin, he looked up and spotted her from the
open conveyance. He lifted his hand in greeting. Had she
seemed too eager? She wasn't a schoolgirl, after all.

"Good day, Miss Caldwell," he called as he stepped
from the carriage. "I'll be at your door in minutes. No
need for robes today. Asilah is mostly Spanish and
Christian. Ladies go forth with their faces exposed." He
disappeared under the arch before she could respond.

After pulling on a jacket, she descended into the
courtyard where he was waiting by the fountain. In the
morning light, wearing a wide-brimmed hat, open-neck
shirt, snug pants, and knee-high boots, he looked as
casually self-assured as he was handsome. Her own
confidence wavered briefly, but then she lifted her head
and approached with a firm step.

"I'm happy to see you, Cheyne, but I must question the whereabouts of Captain Harding and my crew."

His eyes narrowed, but he gave her a crooked smile and offered his arm. "Touring in the West," he said flatly. "They've gone to Fez, I believe, to visit the Rif Mountains."

Taking his arm, she frowned up at him. "This is absurd. I've come to see my ship, and my captain isn't here to meet me. Captain Harding didn't come to Morocco to see the sights, Mr. Sinclair."

"Your captain will have plenty of time to make suggestions as the building progresses. You'll find there isn't much to see yet of the frigate, at any rate."

Laurel smelled a rat. Something in Cheyne's words and manner didn't ring true. She had a sneaking suspicion that he was deliberately preventing her from meeting with her captain. And perhaps the crew, as well. What was he hiding, and why?

Silently she climbed aboard the carriage and took a seat.

Cheyne sat beside her and retrieved something from the floor. A parasol.

"It took some doing, but I found this for you. I know what store you Southern ladies put in your complexion. The sun can be scalding during the Moroccan summer."

He was smiling, gazing at her as if he couldn't help himself. At this close range, she saw lines at the corners of his eyes and a scar cutting though his left eyebrow. A previous calculation of his age indicated he was about thirty-six. What adventures he must have had in his lifetime. What tales he could tell. Curiosity consumed her, but she merely opened the parasol, turned her head and watched the passing low-slung brown buildings lining the street.

In minutes they were at the waterfront. There, near a jetty extending into the tiny harbor, stood her unfinished frigate. The hull was complete, but no masts were set.

The ship was impressively large, but beyond that she saw little on which to make any judgment.

"Oh dear. It's not very far along, is it."

"I've hired a dozen extra workmen. I hadn't realized the necessity for speed until last week."

She was deeply disappointed. She had come all this way for nothing, it appeared. She stayed in the carriage since little could be gained by walking around the hull sitting in its frame.

"I do have blueprints with me. You could inspect them and recommend changes. I assure you, your every request will be carried out."

Laurel believed he was being absolutely honest with her. His hat shadowed his eyes, but his lips were highlighted, and she found herself fascinating by them. Quickly she turned away. What was it about this man that confounded her? Maybe, despite his wicked past and lack of any sort of proper upbringing, she detected sensitivity and thoughtfulness, and oddly, his barely concealed desire to please her. It was as if his mask of cynicism slipped on occasion, and he unwittingly granted her some power over him she couldn't understand. He did have a sense of humor, she thought, remembering the way he teased her on the beach two nights ago. Did she have power over him? If so, how could she use it to get her way in these strange circumstances? And most unsettling of all, what did she truly want from him? A ship, of course. And the freedom to continue her journey. But there was something else, something profound and emotional that teased her from some hidden place beyond her comprehension.

Nonsense. Here in the bright light of day, she had her feelings well under control. She faced him again and said coolly, "I've seen enough. The blueprints should be helpful, though."

"Very well. Shall we tour the village, since the day is ours?"

"Indeed, I would like that. It's quite different from Tangier."

"That's because the Spanish have occupied it for many years. It's a blend of Arab, Christian, and Jew. All living peaceably for generations. There is the mosque; there is the cathedral." As he pointed out the most prominent structures of the town, a single bell began to sound from the church tower. A flock of blackbirds rose in a swoosh and headed out to sea.

Laurel noticed that the women walking the streets were mostly unveiled, although hooded Muslims moved among them. As the carriage approached the main plaza, the driver drew up and halted.

"We must walk from here," explained Sinclair. "Only foot traffic allowed."

She took Cheyne's hand and stepped to the cobbles. His touch was cool and firm. She had the distinct sensation that she walked in a dream, that she would suddenly awaken and find herself back aboard her ship or even in her bedroom at Highgrove.

Strolling under her parasol, she moved in silence, gazing into alleys and stopping occasionally to inspect a merchant's display of trinkets and clothing and handmade furnishings. The streets were crowded and she felt more than one furtive glance from passersby. Did anyone recognize Captain Sinclair? He must be known here if he had ships built and hired local residents to work for him.

Suddenly he stopped and stared through an open doorway.

"Dammit," he muttered.

"Is something wrong?"

"A slave bazaar. I can't stop the practice nationwide, but it's a rarity here in Asilah."

Laurel was startled by his comment. "Then you do disapprove of slavery?"

"Aye, as I've said before. Wait here. On second

thought, you'd better step inside. Just stay in the shadows. They've got a child no more than five on the auction block. I can't permit that."

She slipped in after him, wondering why he thought he could take charge of the proceedings. Perhaps he welded more influence than she realized.

Watching from beneath the doorway, she heard him confront the auctioneer, speaking Arabic in a harsh voice.

The auctioneer argued loudly, pointing at several buyers who had been bidding on the child.

Laurel's heart ached for the young boy who stood on a dais and stared stoically at the proceedings. He was light skinned and had blue eyes, but his hair was dark and curling. How could he be here, lost and alone and certainly frightened? Where were his parents? Even in America, she had never seen a child being sold alone.

Cheyne pulled coins from his pocket and forced them into the hand of the slave dealer. He spoke angrily to the man, then took the boy's hand and walked toward her.

"Let's get out of here," he snapped.

·19·

Laurel was deeply moved by Cheyne's actions. Here was proof of his compassion and anti-slavery sentiments. "You bought the boy?" she asked.

"I did."

"But doesn't he have parents?" She looked into the child's upturned face. The poor lad was almost in tears, no doubt completely terrified and confused. She smiled at him, wishing she could speak to him and reassure him that he was now safe.

"Of course. All children have parents. His have just enriched themselves with my coin."

She shook her head as they walked across the plaza toward the cathedral. She understood forced slavery, but this was the first she'd seen of the voluntary sale of children. The idea was dreadful beyond belief.

"This is appalling," she said. "I'm so happy you intervened."

"It's rare to see one so young for sale. Especially a boy. Young girls are more in demand."

She was shocked into silence.

"I'll leave him with the nuns at the church. He's probably Muslim, but they'll know where he can best be sheltered." Suddenly he swung the youngster up on his hip and grinned at him. He said something pleasant in the native tongue and was rewarded by a shy smile for his effort.

Laurel felt her heart melt at the warmth in Cheyne's smile. He couldn't be entirely evil, not if he held such concern for a ragged little boy.

Inside the cool sanctuary, small and simply embellished, a Catholic sister was soon located and the boy placed in her care. Cheyne left more money and then guided Laurel back into the sunny plaza.

"Would you like some lunch? I've a friend whose shop provides snacks and orange juice, freshly squeezed from his own orchards, just outside the town. Simple fare, but refreshing."

"I'd be delighted," she said gaily, her wall of resistance to Cheyne Sinclair no longer in place.

Cheyne had given up trying to keep his heart from being broken by Laurel Caldwell. When he had seen her wading in the shallows under the stars, balancing her shoes and stockings, with her hair floating free around her shoulders, he had lost his battle once and for all. He adored her, and the fact she was another man's fiancée was something he would have to deal with the best way he could. Later, he might be able to avoid her, but for this one day, she would be his.

Only one day. He would allow himself the pleasure of her company, show her the frigate, escort her around the village, then entertain her over an informal meal. Tomorrow he would see her off to Tangier on the sloop with Nicole and Rafi, and he would spend the next month or so supervising the ship's construction and continue his efforts to stop slavers whenever he could. Rafi was dependable and would see to Laurel's safety while she was in Tangier.

The carriage rattled out of the walled town and through a mile of verdant wooded countryside. Citrus groves were interspersed among the woods, and the air was balmy and sweet with the breeze from the nearby ocean.

Cheyne made small talk as they rode, becoming increasingly aware of the change in Laurel's mood. She was animated, interested in their surroundings, and often gave him her undivided attention and numerous warm smiles. He supposed she was impressed by his purchase of the boy, but winning her admiration and affection was the last thing he desired. God knew, he had affection enough for both of them. He had overstepped the bounds of propriety on the beach. Now he must make certain their relationship was pleasant and businesslike and nothing more. But it was bloody difficult when she was so lovely and engaging.

"We'll stop here. There's Felipe's citrus stand. It's a short walk through the orange trees to the beach. Would you like to picnic there?"

Her eyes glowed. "Yes, very much."

He helped her from the carriage and they walked to the rustic hut offering refreshment to travelers.

Leaving her at a table in the shade, he purchased cups of sweetened orange juice, a bottle of the local wine, and fresh-baked bread with slices of goat cheese. He was pleased to find freshly prepared baklava, a sticky sweet cake with sugar and crushed almonds layered between paper-thin pastry.

Balancing his purchases, he led her several yards to a sandy beach fronting a small cove. "I don't have a blanket, so I suppose we'll have to sit on the sand."

She grinned at him. "My clothing is so rumpled, a little sand won't be noticed. This is a lovely spot to dine."

He found a spot in the shade of a gnarled cedar and spread out the lunch on a rock. "There. This will have to do."

She settled beside the makeshift table and removed her hat. Her golden hair caught the light as it wafted around her neck and shoulders. He had never seen anything so lovely, so soft and appealing. Kneeling in the sand, he poured the wine into small glasses and offered her a drink.

"I thought we should toast your new ship. What will you name it?" He watched her sip the liquid, then run her tongue over her lips. His loins tightened at the innocently sensuous sight.

"I suppose I'll just call it the *Star* like the ship that was lost."

"Perhaps *The Star of Tangier*. A reminder of the vessel's beginnings."

"Yes, I like that." She sighed and smoothed back her hair. He noticed that her fingers were delicate and tapered, like those of a lady of fine breeding, and yet they were strong enough to pull a ship's rigging into place. His thoughts were getting away from him. *Remember she's engaged to Henry Beauregard,* he told himself. Clamping his teeth, he looked toward the gentle surf a few yards away. The idea of that arrogant bastard bedding this woman, fathering her children, pierced him like Toledo steel.

"I want to tell you again, Cheyne, how pleased I am

you freed the boy today. That's the second time you've done such a generous act for someone less fortunate. You paid a high price for Nicole, then gave her to my sister. An extraordinary gesture. And you proved your fairness by saving that poor lad."

When he looked back at her, her face was alight with admiration. He had to stop this at once. "As I've said, I don't condone slavery. Piracy is vice enough, don't you agree?"

Her smile faded and she nibbled on a piece of cheese. "Yes, of course. I'd almost forgotten."

"We mustn't forget anything, Laurel. Especially not who we are and where we've come from. I told you I have no family. The fact is, I never met my father, and my mother disappeared soon after I was born. I was left in Lafitte's camp to be raised by anyone who wanted the task. In short, Laurel, I'm illegitimate. Not that it bothers me, of course. I've had a grand time in my life. I wouldn't trade it for all the fancy titles in the world."

Her hazel eyes had green flecks, he noticed, as she gazed solemnly at him. Was she shocked he was so outspoken about his birth? On the contrary, she looked completely sympathetic. Hell, he didn't want to inspire her pity any more than he wanted to encourage her affection. "In other words, I enjoy being a pirate. It's what I do best and I'm proud of my success."

Her eyes became bleak. "Yes, you're right. But you have been fair about the *Star*, and I thought—well, perhaps we could be friends, after all."

"Friends? For today, I suppose. Once your ship sails, we can forget each other exist."

He had wounded her, and he felt her pain and embarrassment like hot coals in his belly.

She put down her cup and rose. He could swear tears were sparkling in the corners of her eyes. If she wept, he would be undone.

She walked away from their rock and toward the edge

of the oncoming tide. The wind caught her hair, lifting it from her neck and tossing it around her forehead and cheeks. Like a man caught in an undertow, he followed her.

She was unreal, a goddess of love like Aphrodite, a temptress rising from the sea. Time stood still and he lost all sense of reality. When he saw moisture on her cheeks, his heart was completely enslaved.

"Laurel," he whispered. "My darling girl—" Without rational thought, he grasped her shoulders and turned her toward him. Her eyes widened, her lips parted, but she didn't resist him. Tenderly he wiped the moisture from her cheeks, then bent to press his lips to their damp coolness.

He felt her arms slide upward along his shoulders and linger there. Her fair beauty, her trust, her acquiescence were irresistible. He slid an arm around her and tilted her chin with his forefinger. Such exquisite lips, lips that had scorned him and now invited his kiss. With a low moan, he covered them, pressed them apart, tried to hold back, then crushed her to him with a passion that couldn't be restrained.

She clung to him, trapped by his embrace, and returned his kiss with a woman's unleashed desire. The feel of her, the taste of her, her silken female body in his arms, set fire to his very core. After the kiss ended, he held her close, allowing their bodies to meld into one, sculptured by the wind, heated by the sun, and anointed by the spray from the surf.

"Cheyne," she whispered, her lips so near the opening of his shirt that he could feel her soft breath on his skin. "Cheyne, it is madness to feel what I'm feeling."

He couldn't look at her. To do so would have destroyed him. Fighting for control, he said, "Madness. Aye, lass, I agree. I ask your forgiveness for what just happened. It will never happen again."

She was trembling. She should have slapped him, but

instead, she encircled his waist and rested her head against his chest. This was a woman who needed love, needed a man to fulfill her needs. He couldn't be that man and he had no right to her sweetness.

Taking her elbow, he guided her off the beach and back to their carriage. He couldn't guess what she was thinking, what she was feeling, but she strode silently beside him. Shock, dismay, alarm, anger. Whatever it was, it couldn't match the misery in his own heart. He placed her in the carriage and signaled the startled driver.

"We're going back to town," he called. "Quickly. The lady isn't feeling well." Climbing in beside her, he kept his eyes averted as if watching the passing scenery. But he saw nothing but Laurel Caldwell walking down the aisle at the cathedral in New Orleans, smiling behind her veil at her incredibly fortunate husband-to-be, giving herself and all her loveliness and intelligence and spirit to that simpering idiot slave owner, Beauregard. She would be miserable. If only he could save her from a life of regret and unhappiness, he would gladly die in the process.

For hours, Laurel was numb with shock. As soon as she regained the privacy of her suite, after barely acknowledging Cheyne Sinclair's mumbled apologies and farewell, she paced the floor like a caged animal. Her emotions were in turmoil and her brain simply wouldn't function. Time after time, she touched her lips, wondering if she could ever forget what had happened this afternoon. First, Cheyne had broken through her defenses, won her admiration and respect, then kissed her into mindless ecstasy. Then he had stupefied her with his cold reaction and hauled her home like an unwanted sack of flour. Why he had kissed her she couldn't fathom. If only she had struggled, or demanded an apology, or even slapped him for his bold disregard of propriety. Once she had hated and feared him enough to shoot him. Hate, fear, love: fierce emotions that could tear one apart in seconds. All three possessed her now. She was afraid she could easily fall in love with Cheyne Sinclair and she hated him for causing her such agony.

After what seemed like hours of feverish pacing, she threw herself on her bed and started to cry. Her body had betrayed her today. Her longing for love in all its forms had overcome her good sense. After sobbing brokenly into her pillow, she began to realize she was completely exhausted. Night had fallen, and she pulled the embroidered cotton spread over her knees and began to doze.

Sometime later, she heard a noise. Was it Nicole arriving? Or Francesca looking in on her? Anticipating Nicole's return, she hadn't locked her door.

Footsteps sounded on the tile. She rolled over. Suddenly a heavy fabric was thrown over her and her arms pinned to her sides.

Desperately she tried to scream, but her voice was muffled and she gasped for air. She felt herself hoisted upward, then slung over someone's shoulder. Her bare feet were exposed, and a rope was tied around her ankles. She thrashed in her smothering cocoon, but to no avail. As she was carried out of the room and down the steps by her silent invisible abductor, she felt faint from terror and lack of oxygen. Her lips formed the name *Cheyne* before she lost consciousness.

·20·

The heat of the day lingered in the Bedouin encampment on the outskirts of Asilah long after the sun disappeared beyond Mount Tisouka in the west. A dozen robed men finished their evening meal and quietly began putting out their cooking fires and preparing the camels for travel. With luck, they would soon ride south down the rugged coast toward Sale where a ship was waiting to take their leader and his prize across the sea. Their departure from Asilah would be sudden and swift, if all went according to plan.

In his tent, which was small and meant for travel, Saad Terraf sat cross-legged on a goat skin and sipped tea from a metal cup.

Shazade knelt opposite him. "They should be here soon, Saad. Surely four men can quickly overpower one female."

"Yes, but their task is not simple. They must wait until the woman is alone in her room, then capture her guard and secure him, while letting the knowledge of her destination slip out in his hearing. Once Sinclair discovers the woman's whereabouts, he'll come in quick pursuit."

"Just as you planned."

"My employer wants the man alive. A confession is the surest way to prove Cheyne Sinclair is the Falcon. The English are as skilled in obtaining confessions as the Spanish and the Arabs."

"You speak of your employer, but the time has come, master, to reveal his identity to me. Suppose something should go wrong tonight. If we should become separated, I'll need to know who to contact for help. If you should be captured and imprisoned, I'll need money to buy your freedom."

Saad put down his cup and stroked his pointed beard. "I believe I can trust you, now that you're no longer closely connected to Sinclair."

"I despise him," she said, tossing her head. "He is a bastard and a filthy dog who deserves a cruel fate."

"You sound like a woman scorned."

"I care nothing for him. I want to see him crawl in a camel's dung heap."

"Calm yourself, my pet. You'll soon have your revenge for his rejection."

"Where is the Falcon's flag I stole for you?"

Saad patted the front of his flowing shirt. "In a safe place. Once we have him bound and helpless, I will flaunt it in his face. Then we sail for England."

Shazade leaned forward. "You haven't yet told me who pays you."

"An English nobleman. Franklin Trowbridge, earl of Croydon. He secured my services two years ago in his search for the man raiding his slave ships. You know the name of my intermediary in Cadiz. If anything should happen to me, contact him immediately. He will know how to get in touch with the earl."

Shazade smiled and sat back on her heels. "I'm sure nothing will happen, Saad. But if it should, I'll quickly take steps to secure your freedom."

Saad reached out and placed his palm on her cheek. "I'm sure you will, my dear, because without me, you will return to the gutter where I found you. Even from a prison cell, I have power in this land. Don't fail. You are the only person who knows the identity of the man who pays me. If you don't do as I command, I can arrange to have that pretty throat sliced to the bone." He encircled her neck and squeezed it before releasing her.

The tent flap flew open. "They're back!" announced a dark-faced Bedouin. "They're putting the woman in the main tent."

Laurel regained consciousness in a dim light, surrounded by a conical enclosure and assailed with mixed odors of incense, cooking oil, and animal dung. She was lying on a rug, and when she tried to move, she discovered her wrists were bound behind her and her ankles firmly tied. At least she wasn't gagged and she could breathe freely.

She gazed around as her vision cleared, and found she wasn't alone. Across from her sat a swarthy male in Arab robes, his owlish eyes fixed on her, a slight smile playing around his lips, which were barely visible between black mustache and beard.

"Where am I?" she demanded hoarsely. "Who are you?"

The man leaned forward, then snapped his fingers. From the shadows, a veiled woman stepped forward and held out a cup of water. Laurel coughed and rose to a sitting position, then drank greedily, not minding that water dribbled down her chin and spilled across her bodice. She still wore yesterday's clothing, which was now stained and dirty and ripped along one sleeve and across the outer skirt. Squinting through the murky half light of a flickering oil lamp, she studied the man opposite her. A shiver ran through her as she realized he had all the warmth and compassion of a coiled cobra.

"What are you going to do with me?" she managed through lips already dry again, this time from fear.

"Allow me to introduce myself. I am Saad Terraf, the slave dealer. No harm will come to you if you obey my instructions."

Slave dealer. Was this a nightmare? Mustering her courage, she said, "I've already been harmed. I nearly smothered to death and have been dragged God knows where and trussed like a goat. I'm an American citizen with important connections. I'll be quickly missed and you'll be hunted down and arrested."

"Is that so? We shall see, Miss Caldwell."

The use of her name caught her off guard. "How do you know who I am?"

"How I know is of no importance. What *is* important is that you now belong to me. If you cooperate, I won't kill you."

Panic raced through her like lightning. Fleetingly she felt dizzy again, but forced herself to think clearly and regain control. "I don't wish to die, Mr. Terraf, but I will not be your slave. That I promise."

"Nor do I desire you as my slave, madam. If I sell you, your new master will pay me a fortune. I don't want *you*, American lady; I want your weight in gold."

So that was it. If she disappeared into the Sahara or beyond, she wouldn't be the first white woman to do so. She knew a search would be mounted, if not by Cheyne Sinclair, then at least by her family. But by then, it could be too late. She would die before she would submit to these beasts. How long would it take for Cheyne to discover she had been abducted? How would he know where to find her? "Where are we?" she ventured.

"In a camp outside the town of Asilah. I'm awaiting contact from a possible buyer. You may as well get some sleep. This could take several hours."

Approaching hysteria, she actually felt like laughing. So this was how it felt to be sold as a slave. How ironic that she, who had always abhorred slavery, was now about to become a slave. Well, she wouldn't do it. Whoever bought her would regret it to his dying day; she'd make sure of that.

Saad rose and ducked out of the tent without a backward glance.

For a time, she worked on her bonds, desperately trying to loosen the knot at her wrists. She was considering knocking over the lamp and attempting to burn the ropes when a draped figure entered, the same person who had given her water a short time before.

"Help me," she pleaded. "Set me free and you'll be richly rewarded. *S'il vous plaît.* Do you speak French?"

"Oui. But with you I speak English." The woman lowered her veil and squatted beside her.

"Shazade! What are you doing here?"

"I've come to take my revenge."

"Revenge for what?" Laurel didn't know if she was relieved or alarmed to see Shazade's familiar face. At least this was someone she knew. Unfortunately the *someone* was hardly her friend. "I've done nothing to harm you. You know who I am. And you know Captain Sinclair. He was good to you, and I thought you were prospering." She heard desperation in her voice, but couldn't prevent it.

"Prospering, but not in the way I would like. I wanted the captain, but he refused me. Now I want money, and Saad will help me get it."

"By selling me? So you told him I was coming to Asilah. You suggested I be captured and sold as a slave. Is that it?"

"I told him about you, but the capture was his idea. Actually I doubt if you'll be sold."

Hope leaped inside her. "You do? Then what will he do with me?"

"Use you as bait."

"What? Bait? For what purpose?"

"Saad has important connections in England. He works for a powerful nobleman who will make him very rich."

"Englishman? You mean, that dreadful man who had me dragged from my bed tonight works for the British? I can't believe it."

"He works for anyone who pays well. A certain nobleman has offered a fortune for the capture of Captain Cheyne Sinclair."

The pieces fell instantly into place. Cheyne had told her he was wanted by the British, by the earl of Croydon in particular. The earl must be the villain behind all this. She thought of Nicole's warning. Shazade must be employed by Saad to spy on Cheyne's household. Saad would be rewarded by Lord Trowbridge for turning over the pirate to British authorities.

And she was the bait that would lure Cheyne Sinclair to his doom.

She faced Shazade. "Don't do this, I beg of you. The captain is a wealthy man. We'll go together and ask him to reward you for setting me free. I'm sure he'll be generous. You can't want his death. Surely not after he was good to you. I thought you cared for him."

Shazade's cat-like eyes glittered in the lamplight. "That is what I meant by revenge. I offered to be his woman and he refused me. I didn't expect to be his wife, but I wanted to share his bed. That he is not celibate is a well known fact among his household. But he refused to sleep with me. If he had given me love, I would never have sold his secrets to Saad. Now, I must do whatever Saad asks of me."

Laurel thought Shazade's sense of honor entirely twisted. But learning that Cheyne had enough character to resist Shazade's advances gave her the first bit of pleasure she'd felt in several hours. "Shazade, I myself have wealth and important friends. Return with me to Tangier. I promise you protection and safe passage on my ship anywhere you care to go. You'll be a rich woman."

Shazade stood and replaced her veil. "I'll be rich. And the insulting and arrogant Captain Sinclair will be hanged from the gallows in London. Your burden will be to live with the knowledge you brought him to this end." Laughing, she hurried from the tent.

Laurel sagged to the carpet. How could this be happening? No doubt Cheyne would come in search of her. No doubt Saad had left a clear trail.

An hour passed, then another. She had no thought of sleep, but lay quietly, listening to the night breeze brushing the sides of her prison.

All at once, she heard a new sound not far from where she lay. Straining her ears, she listened. The canvas was being cut. Sitting up, she saw a curved knife blade jutting through the side of the tent. Paralyzed with indecision, she watched the slit grow larger. Should she scream a warning that this was a trap? Or would her cry alert guards who would swoop in for the attack?

A man pushed inside. He wore the robes of an Arab.

His mouth was hidden, but his green eyes were unmistakably Cheyne Sinclair's.

"Cheyne, it's a trap," she said in a loud whisper. "They've used me to capture you. Saad—"

"Shh. I know." He sliced at the ropes around her ankles.

"You know?" she rasped under her breath. "Then why—"

He put his fingers over her lips. "Don't speak. We have perhaps only seconds." Then he went back to work on her bonds. "I know 'tis me they're after," he murmured, reaching for her wrists. "You warned me, and I stupidly ignored you. The important thing now is to get you out of here. Help is coming. If I—"

Suddenly the tent flap was thrown open and half a dozen turbaned Bedouins swarmed inside.

Laurel screamed and scooted against the canvas behind her. Her feet were free, but her wrists still tied.

In horror she watched as four men grabbed Cheyne and wrestled him to the floor. Saad Terraf stood by and watched, a gleam of victory in his eyes. Saad leaned over Cheyne and ripped the cloth from his face, then punched him hard across the jaw. Held down by four men, Cheyne was helpless, as Saad kicked him viciously in the side time after time, then knelt beside him to press a dagger to his throat.

Laurel screamed again.

"I'm not going to kill you," snarled Saad. "I want you alive."

Shazade hurried into the tent. She held a lighted torch above Cheyne's inert body.

Laurel thought Cheyne might be unconscious until she heard his voice.

"You have the upper hand, Saad. You and Shazade. I'm the one you want. Let the lady go."

Laurel was paralyzed with fear. She felt cool air from the jagged tear in the canvas close by, but she couldn't make herself move toward the opening. Cheyne could die at any second or be dragged away and she would never see him again. He had said help was coming. Pray God, where was it?

"The American woman will come with us for now," Saad said. "We'll dispose of her somewhere along the way."

The sound of horses' hooves came from outside.

"What's that?" Saad asked in alarm. "Get Sinclair and let's go! Forget the woman."

Shots rang out from beyond the tent. A man's cry split the air.

Rafi Hamid pushed inside, pistols in both hands. More shots and screams echoed through the night.

"Rafi! Help!" Laurel yelled.

The four Bedouins who had been holding Cheyne were on their feet. A handful of men in shabby western garb, carrying guns and swords, charged into the tent.

As Laurel watched the confrontation from her place on the floor, Shazade dropped her torch and threw herself against Saad's chest, then fell to her knees and crawled around the edge of the tent while more shots were fired and two of the Bedouins were pierced by the newcomers' flashing blades.

In frantic haste, Shazade pushed through the opening Cheyne had made with his dagger and disappeared into the night.

Laurel looked up just in time to see Saad Terraf grab his face and reel backward, then slide down the canvas to the floor. She got to her feet, though her knees were weak as butter. Stepping past a twitching body, she got to Cheyne and dropped down beside him.

Rafi bent over them. "Are you all right, Miss Caldwell?" Behind him, the last of the Bedouins was being marched from the tent.

"I'm fine. But Cheyne is hurt. Please untie me."

She leaned over Cheyne while Rafi freed her wrists. Cheyne's eyes were closed and his lip was bleeding and starting to swell. His burnoose was torn apart and his shirt ripped and bloody.

"Cheyne, how badly are you hurt?"

He flinched and opened his eyes to gaze up at her.

She studied his bruised face as blood seeped from his lip. "What can I do?" she said, her voice heavy with anguish.

Rafi knelt beside them. "Your plan worked perfectly, *mon ami*. At least they didn't kill you."

"I'm all right," Cheyne said, casting a quick glance at Laurel. "You'd better go check the camp, Rafi. Saad may have friends nearby."

Rafi nodded. "I'll send someone to help you. A carriage is coming. We'll take you and Miss Caldwell back to Asilah."

After Rafi left, Cheyne pushed to one elbow, but grimaced and gripped his ribcage.

"Cheyne, I'm so sorry. So very—"

"My fault entirely," he said through clenched teeth. "I came as fast as I could. I was afraid they would— Tell me, Laurel, did they harm you in any way? You know what I'm talking about. Only I will ever know the truth, but I must know." He grasped her wrist. "Terraf will burn in hell forever," he rasped, his eyes feverish with blazing hatred.

"I expect he will, for any number of reasons. But not for raping me."

"Then he didn't—" His expression held such concern, she wanted to weep, but she controlled her emotions and answered him. "I swear he didn't touch me. I was only the bait to lure you here. Saad is dead, and I don't care. Shazade was here with him, but she escaped. And Cheyne, she said an Englishman hired Saad to capture you."

He relaxed, but kept his hand pressed to his side. "You're not harmed. That's all I care about. You wouldn't be here at all if not for my blundering. Then tonight I left you unguarded while I walked the streets of the town. Rafi was careless, too, but he's in love. Love is a powerful distraction."

She felt tears forcing their way into her eyes. Was there any chance Cheyne Sinclair was truly in love with her? After all, he had risked his life to save her. He must have known when he rushed alone into the tent that he was likely to be killed or captured. Was it because he loved her? Or was it merely duty? Something in his expression at this moment made her think he cared deeply for her. As for herself, she had lost her heart to him—absolutely. "What you did tonight was heroic, Cheyne," she said softly as she lowered her eyes. "I'll never forget it," she murmured. "In fact, I think I've fallen quite in love with you." The words slipped out without warning.

She looked up quickly and saw he had closed his eyes. She wondered if he had heard her. He looked very pale in the glow from the lantern and the dying fire of Shazade's discarded torch. "Cheyne," she whispered. "Is the pain great?"

Without opening his eyes, he found her hand and pressed his lips against her palm. The kiss filled her with indescribable delight. Then he looked at her. "Nothing to compare with the pain I felt when I discovered you had been kidnapped." The slight curve of his battered lips melted her heart.

Rafi entered the tent. "The carriage is here. Several of the Bedouins escaped in the dark. I understand a woman went with them."

Laurel got to her feet and watched as Rafi assisted Cheyne to stand. Walking beside them, she left the tent and crossed to the waiting carriage.

Someone held open the door, and she climbed inside. Without looking toward her, Cheyne extricated himself from Rafi's arm and straightened. He was ragged and bloodied. The thought of his courage and all that he'd endured for her took her breath away.

"I can ride," he said. "Get me a horse and a pistol."

"Cheyne, please ride in the coach," she insisted. "You took a terrible beating!"

He walked over to the carriage and slammed the door, remaining outside. He stared at her through the window, his face suddenly a frozen mask. "No, thank you. I'll ride guard with the others. It's only a few miles back to Asilah."

Stunned at his cold look and behavior, she leaned back in the darkness. She heard him speak to Rafi.

"Get her on the sloop tomorrow as soon as she's rested. I want her safely back at Tamerlane."

She couldn't believe her ears. Peeking through the glazing, she saw him ease himself into the saddle of a waiting horse. Even in the dim light of a half moon, she could see how much pain he was in. A few minutes before, he had kissed her hand, gazed at her as if he had deep feelings for her, told her how much he had worried about her.

And she had told him she loved him. He must not have heard her. Otherwise why would he send her away so abruptly? These sudden mood changes of his were terribly upsetting and extremely confusing. This was the third time he had appeared close to an emotional attachment and had then slammed the door between them. Another glance outside revealed he was mounted and directing his men toward the road.

The carriage jolted away. Pounding in her ears were the hoofbeats of her mounted escort. Oddly, she didn't weep. She wanted to, but her eyes were dry and she felt a creeping numbness inside. One rational thought occurred to her as they traveled back to Asilah. Cheyne might be shutting her out because of her betrothal to Henry Beauregard. That made sense. She was inclined to forget she was supposed to be an engaged woman. Maybe if she told Cheyne the truth about that, he would be honest with her. Did Cheyne care for her, or did he not?

Until she knew the answer, she was bound to be completely miserable.

After a brief journey, the carriage halted at the inn. As soon as the coach door was open, she was embraced by a nearly hysterical Nicole. As if in a trance, she made her way to her room. With effort, she began to tell Nicole about the awful experience. But there was no way she could describe the ache in her heart.

·21·

Cheyne sat in the dark on his balcony and stared out to sea. Despite his aching ribs and the painful cuts on his neck and chest, he refused to take a drink from the decanter at his elbow. He wanted to suffer. He deserved it. And he wanted to think clearly about what he must do about Laurel Caldwell.

He could no longer avoid the truth. He was in love with the lady, and worse, she believed she was in love with him. He had heard her murmured words last night. But he couldn't let her throw away the life she had planned, her future, all she knew and loved, because of a fleeting infatuation. She didn't know him. Not really. He was a cynic with few illusions left. He had vowed never to give his heart to a woman, and so he had never given a woman his name. He had lived life at the fastest pace possible, defying death to take him, not really caring, as long as he was free to enjoy all life's pleasures to the fullest.

Rather a selfish way to live, he thought, watching the first azure glow of the new day appear on the distant horizon. His only regret was that he had no children of his own. Not that he had wanted the responsibility of raising a child, but he had a soft spot for youngsters, a tenderness that could grow into something he feared most: love. Love beyond his control. Only true love could cut a man down, bring him to his knees, destroy any hope for personal happiness. He had never wanted to risk that happening to him, but dammit to hell, it had happened now.

He thought of Laurel smiling at him, her lips welcoming his kiss. He thought of her innocence and her courage. When he believed she had been kidnapped, he had lived with all the demons from hell writhing inside him. Rafi had wanted to storm the tent, take the villains by surprise, thereby putting no one at special risk, but Cheyne had insisted on slipping inside alone to make sure Laurel was protected. He had hoped to get her out before confronting the kidnappers, but if that didn't happen, he had expected to take the brunt of their assault until his men arrived. He would not allow her to be slaughtered like a sacrificial lamb, not while he lived. All things considered, the plan had worked well. Saad deserved to die, and Shazade was out of his life for good. She wouldn't dare return to Tangier after what she'd done. As for Franklin Trowbridge, the obvious instigator of the plot, Cheyne had lived with his threats for years. He would just be more careful in the future.

But when Laurel Caldwell had said she loved him, he knew he was a hopelessly lost soul. One moment more, and he would have held her in his arms, proclaimed his love for her, completely disregarding the lady's best interests and claiming her as his own. How could he, Cheyne Sinclair, a bastard, a pirate, a wanted man, have anything to offer? She was young, with her whole life ahead, a life that should include a respectable husband, financial security, and children. She could have all that with Henry Beauregard.

His stomach turned. Beauregard would never make her happy. Never. If she had ever loved Beauregard, she didn't love him now. Cheyne felt he must somehow save her from that fate.

He moved, groaning from sharp pains where Saad had landed blow upon blow. Probably cracked a rib, but it could have been worse. Much worse. He guessed the bastard hadn't cut his throat because the earl wanted him alive.

He shivered in the ocean breeze. He needed to sleep, but his whirling thoughts wouldn't let him relax. Today Laurel had sailed to Tamerlane, where she would be safe. He would stay in Asilah and supervise the building of her ship. She must be heartbroken over his rejection and neglect, but what else could he do?

As he watched the sky lighten into pink and listened to the crash of the rising surf beyond the village, punctuated by the sleepy crowing of a rooster, the strangest idea formed in his mind. Strange, impossible, outrageous—but perhaps this was one way out of this dilemma, not necessarily for him, but for his darling Laurel.

She must be marrying Beauregard to get money to help Caldwell Shipping. Her father wouldn't permit it if he knew, but Cheyne could imagine her sacrificing herself for just such a cause. If she was going to marry Beauregard for money, why not marry *him* instead? He figured he could buy and sell Beauregard ten times over. She wanted children. Cheyne was certain he could take care of that request with enthusiasm. Laurel had said she loved him, even though she believed him to be a pirate. She might be willing to change the course of her life if he offered her the two things she wanted most: money and a child. As a bonus, he would give her the freedom to go anywhere, do anything she wanted. Naturally, she would expect to be his legal wife. But if she eventually became dissatistfied, the marriage could be ended without much difficulty. He would agree to a divorce any time she asked for one.

He was stunned at the idea. Was he an idiot to consider making such a proposal? She would surely

think he was insane and ridicule him mercilessly. So
what if she did? If she would agree, he could lay his
fortune at her feet, give her a child, then set her free. As a
wanted man, he wouldn't be able to live with her
anywhere but in Morocco, but she would be extremely
rich and free to make her home anywhere she pleased.
She was a smart businesswoman and certainly ambi-
tious. She might like the arrangement.

As for him, he would have the memory of possessing
the only woman he would ever love, even if only for a
short time. And he would have a child by Laurel Caldwell.

He thought about that. A boy or girl to live after him,
but who would move in a world he could never enter. A
child who would be far superior to his father and who
would lift the name Sinclair from a questionable past to
a legitimate and respected future, a child who would
benefit from a father's vast wealth and a mother's
prestigious family. The more he considered it, the more
he liked the idea. Hell, it was worth a try.

For a week following her kidnapping, Laurel moved as
if in a dream. The cruise back to Tangier was brief and
uneventful, except for Nicole's joyful and not too surprising announcement that she had accepted Rafi
Hamid's proposal of marriage. After searching the port
at Asilah for any sign of Cheyne, Laurel gave up hope
and sank into a depression that she couldn't overcome.

Nicole fussed over her, trying to get her to eat and take
some interest in her surroundings, but Laurel felt dead
inside. How terrible that she had reached the age of
twenty-six without knowing the slightest thing about
love, then to discover that incomparable feeling, only to
learn that her love wasn't returned.

In contrast, Nicole floated through the days on a cloud
of happiness. Laurel did her best to put on a happy face
for Nicole's sake. The day before the wedding, Nicole

attended the mosque and officially adopted the Muslim faith of her husband-to-be.

It was at the small celebration following a private Muslim ceremony that Laurel once again encountered Cheyne.

The party was held in the guest parlor of Rafi's home inside the walls of the Tamerlane compound. The house was whitewashed stucco, spotless and airy, with a view of the sea from a small private courtyard. Laurel could imagine how happy Nicole, or any woman, would be to share such a pleasant setting with the man she loved.

Nicole's replacement, a doe-eyed young French girl who spoke four languages, accompanied Laurel to the house. Rafi's mother and three sisters were acting as hostesses and the feast was impressive indeed. But the joy of the occasion, seeing Nicole and Rafi so happy and in love, only deepened Laurel's depression. She hated being so self-centered, but without Nicole, without her own captain and crew, without any American to converse with, she felt loneliness settle over her like a dulling fog.

Leaving her shoes outside and wearing the traditional babouches, she sat alone on a low divan and watched the revelers. The scent of orange and thyme and bay leaf and mint filled the air. Nibbling at the succulent dishes, smiling in response to the curious glances of strangers, she listened to the exotic music and wished desperately she could go home.

When Cheyne entered, dressed like a sultan in a white satin shirt and breeches, a turban and flowing cape embroidered with gold thread and encrusted with jewels, the gathering hushed and bowed in obeisance. He was a great hero to these people, akin to a god. His large frame, coupled with his grace and self-assurance, added to that illusion.

As she watched from her corner, he presented an extravagantly large golden necklace to Nicole. This would serve as her dowry since she had no family here to do the honors. Following the presentation, Cheyne motioned for the music to continue, then moved out of the limelight and made his way in her direction.

Laurel held her breath. Her hands were clammy while her mouth was dry. Her nerves were at the breaking point. She doubted if any man had ever looked so magnificent.

His smile for her was slight, but inviting. "Will you accompany me outside, Miss Caldwell? I wish to speak alone with you, if I have your permission."

His air of a Southern gentleman, while dressed in the garb of an Arabian prince, was peculiarly incongruous. Still, she gave him her hand and walked with him to the deserted courtyard. Birds were rioting overhead in the late afternoon sun. Here, under the gnarled branches of an ancient olive tree, with a white diamond sky and endless indigo sea as a background, and roses perfuming the air, Cheyne Sinclair asked her to become his wife.

· 22 ·

Excuse me. What did you say?" Laurel was positive she had misunderstood Cheyne.

"I said, this is a nice place for a marriage proposal. I hope you won't be too startled if I ask you to become my wife."

She was leaning back against the concrete wall surrounding the courtyard, gazing up at him. After her heart skipped several beats, it began thudding frantically, sending heat to her cheeks and a wavy sensation inside her stomach.

Straightening, she stared at him in shocked silence.

"I realize this is sudden," he said, "but I've thought it over this past week and believe it's a wise move for both of us." He spoke calmly and appeared to be sober.

She hadn't misunderstood. Cheyne Sinclair was suggesting marriage in the same tone as if he were asking her to take a stroll in the marketplace. Surely this meant he loved her. Hope flowed into her heart.

Finding her voice, she said, "Why do you think it's a wise move?"

"For several good reasons. First, 'tis time you were wed. You're a fine woman and should not be wasted."

Was this supposed to be a compliment? She found his reason totally inadequate for considering such a serious step. What about loving her?

"Second, you plan to marry Henry Beauregard. I don't like the man, and feel he's a poor choice as a husband."

Her hopes of a moment ago, her first seeds of joy, were rapidly disappearing. His second reason for marrying her was as foolish as the first. She couldn't restrain her biting response. "Oh, really? I'm afraid I find your opinion of Mr. Beauregard irrelevant. Please continue. This is very amusing."

"Third, I am filthy rich. I could lay the world at your feet, give you and your family security and wealth beyond your dreams. As I said, I've done very well at the business of pirating."

This reason was truly an insult. "I'm touched by your modest opinion of yourself. I am not for sale, however. Nor are any of the Caldwells."

"Of course not, but I thought I'd mention my money as a possible benefit. One more thing. I could give you a child."

This observation sent her eyebrows vaulting. "Well, Mr. Sinclair, that doesn't distinguish you from any number of men I might consider for matrimony."

"Aye, but here's the best part of my proposal."

"I can't wait to hear it."

"I will provide you with a fortune, get you with child, then set you free to live your life anywhere you please. I understand your need to pursue your own interests. I have important interests of my own."

This suggestion sent her reeling. She studied him, wondering if the beating he had taken from Saad had relieved him of his senses. "I beg your pardon?"

"I know it sounds very odd, but before you decline, consider the possibilities. I believe I know what you want from life. I think I can fulfill all those necessities. The arrangement needn't be permanent. We can always get a divorce later, if you like. Or there's the chance I'll be killed while engaged in my various business enterprises. I do have several enemies, as you know. What could be nicer than to be a fabulously rich young widow, with your only responsibility a small child to raise? I realize this is sudden and that I should be asking your father for your hand, but under the circumstances I cannot, and time is of the essence."

"Time is of the essence," Laurel muttered incredulously. "Why is that?"

"Because you wish to continue your voyage as soon as possible. I wouldn't want to delay your journey."

Laying her hand over her breast, she gaped at him. The man must be insane. "Are you suggesting that we marry at once, that you—you impregnate me as if I were a prize mare in the stable, then send me on my way to Skye?"

"Exactly. Well, not the *mare* part. Naturally, you would be treated with every consideration and with deep respect regarding the matter of begetting a child."

She shook her head. "Forgive me if I am completely astonished."

"Of course. I expected you to be. Just give yourself time to consider my suggestion."

"I thought time was of the essence."

"It is. But we have the entire afternoon here at Rafi's wedding feast. You can give me your answer later today."

Laurel began laughing for some strange reason and turned away, but she wasn't amused, and to her surprise, she discovered her lashes were damp with tears. She would give anything to be loved by Cheyne Sinclair, to be his wife. She had told him she loved him, but he must not have heard her, or else he simply didn't care. This was a business proposition, one that would lead only to a broken heart. Hers. Looking back at him, she dabbed at her eyes. "I can't believe you're serious. What could you possibly gain from such an arrangement?"

"Quite a lot. A child to carry my name. A child who will be raised by the finest family I've ever known. A child who will live the life I could never have."

He *was* serious. Completely serious. He didn't love her, didn't want her, didn't want to be tied to her, but he wanted a child by her. Or rather, he wanted a child who would hold a place in upper-class society, a child who carried his blood and his name. How much egotism could a man have? He wanted to reproduce himself for posterity, but he wanted no part of love, companionship, or child rearing.

"No," she said sharply. "I won't be a broodmare for you. I find your proposal totally outrageous and out of the question."

"I explained it wouldn't be like that. We'll have a quiet Christian ceremony at the local chapel. I'll give you jewels that will make Nicole's gift look like a pittance. I'll open an enormous bank account in France in your name, and yours alone. We'll take a honeymoon cruise, if you like. I assure you I'm a skillful lover. I will give you pleasure, I guarantee. Then, when your ship is ready, you will sail to Skye as planned. Hopefully, you will be with child. After that, I will stay out of your life."

She gasped. Her cheeks flamed. She struggled for words.

At last, he reached out to touch her shoulder. "Laurel, there is affection between us. I'm sure of it. You enjoyed our kiss. So did I."

She started to pull away, but he wouldn't release her. Instead he drew her close and put one arm around her shoulders, while with the other hand he tilted her chin. His touch fired her, sending hot waves through the center of her being.

"I want you, Laurel Anne Caldwell, and that's the truth of it." He crushed her lips, lifting her into his embrace, forcing her into mindless submission as the kiss lingered until she couldn't breathe. Then his lips moved to the hollow of her exposed throat. She clung to him, her eyes closed, her body craving more of him, needing him, her woman's passion no longer permitting her to deny its existence.

He released her slowly, his hands caressing her arms, lightly brushing her wrists and fingers before drawing away. "Allow me to help you, Laurel. I—do care for you."

Gazing into his eyes, she tried desperately to see through to his soul. She knew little about this man, but she knew she loved him. He inflamed her beyond all reason. She cared nothing for his money, but she longed to lie in his bed, to be possessed by him, to give him pleasure, if she could, after all he had suffered in his lifetime. She sensed that beneath his self-assured, flamboyant exterior lay suffering, loneliness, and frustration. She wanted to help him find happiness. "I have a question to ask before I can consider your offer."

"Ask. I'll answer truthfully, I give you my word, even if it damns me to hell in your sight."

"Have you loved someone else? Have you loved a woman and lost her? After all, you're somewhat older than I, and without a wife."

His eyelids lowered, but didn't quite close. She couldn't be sure if he still saw her or had moved into some distant memory. "I loved once," he said finally. "I adored a girl when I was too young to know the meaning of the word *love.*"

"And you lost her?"

"Let's just say she was very young. She grew up and so did I. We went our separate ways."

"You never went in search of her?"

"Never. I saw her once, but she was engaged to someone else."

"Did you tell her you loved her?"

"No. Why should I allow my pride to be dragged in the dirt along with my heart?"

"Do you still love her?"

"Does it matter?"

"I'd rather not give myself fully to someone who loves another woman. I would find that too degrading."

"I assure you that is not the case."

"Then I'll think about it." This was crazy. She was out of her mind to consider such a proposal. But she couldn't find it in her power when she looked at him, felt his awesome presence, knew full well her heart belonged to him, to say the word no.

"Then let's go inside. I need to toast the newlyweds. We'll meet again at Tamerlane on the terrace after the feast. Agreed?"

"Yes," she whispered, unable to hide the tremor in her voice.

The remainder of the afternoon passed in a blur. Laurel smiled and nodded and congratulated the happy couple, but her mind was elsewhere and her emotions were seesawing within her. She needed time to think. Or did she?

At the close of the afternoon, the bride asked her to accompany her to her wedding bower for a private farewell.

Laurel hugged Nicole warmly and tried to concentrate on saying something meaningful. "I'll miss you terribly, dear, but I'm so happy for you. Rafi will make you a good husband. You'll have a long life together."

"I hope so, Miss Laurel, but if we had only this one night, I would gladly die in his arms tomorrow."

"You love him that much?"

"I do."

"Then you don't think giving up your home in America, all that you know and care for, is too much to sacrifice for love?"

"If I were the queen of the world, I'd leave it all behind to lie with him just once, to give myself to him, to give him all the pleasure I can, to make my body one with his."

"I do believe you truly love him, Nicole. And you have a man who will return your feelings. I envy you. More than I can say."

Nicole smiled shyly. "You'll find love one day, miss. If not Mr. Beauregard, someone else."

Henry's name sent chills along her spine. To think she had once considered marrying Henry Beauregard. The thought of him taking her to bed, of how close she had come to giving him her virginity and her life, was exactly what she needed to make her decision. "Nicole, when you return from your honeymoon in the mountains, I may have a surprise for you. Go now with my blessing and with God's. Enjoy your happiness."

Nicole gave her a squeeze and giggled. "Thank you. I'm surely glad I came along with you on your ship, even if it did sink. Oh, and I guess it's Allah now who's blessing me. But I don't think there's much difference."

Laurel laughed. "Probably not. But be careful practicing the gris-gris you learned from Marie Leaveau. Allah might not approve."

She left Nicole so the bride could begin the traditional disrobing ceremony supervised by her new female in-laws. Her step was light and her head was clear. She had made her decision.

·23·

Cheyne felt like a man awaiting the outcome of a murder trial. Would he live or die? While keeping a cool facade, laughing and visiting with the guests at the wedding, he was drowning with anxiety.

At least Laurel hadn't completely rejected his offer. She had been astonished, had even laughed at him, but she hadn't said no. Not yet, anyway. He dared not look at her during the festivities. What if he saw ridicule and rejection in her face? He had been a fool to put himself through this. He should have taken what few scraps of pleasure he could from this entire incident, then sent her away and gone on with his life.

He thought the celebration would never end, but at last he was able to say his farewells, kiss the bride, and return to Tamerlane. The palace was deserted, with everyone still at the wedding feast. He went to the kitchen and found a bottle of French wine, then picked up two crystal goblets and strolled onto the terrace. She might join him in a drink or she might not. If she merely refused his proposal and left, he would drink the entire bottle himself. He would need it, for certain.

He sat on the chaise for a while, trying to appear more relaxed than he felt. Finally his nerves forced him to move about the terrace in random pacing.

"Hello, Cheyne."

He spun to face her. The slight smile she wore sent hope skyrocketing inside him.

"Good evening, Laurel. Would you join me in a glass of wine?"

"I'd be pleased," she said.

This was another good sign. Dare he hope she would accept his astonishing offer? He filled the goblets and handed her one. It took every ounce of his will to stand quietly while she sipped the liquid. Finally, he plunged in. "Have you reached a decision? You may have more time, if you like—"

"No."

"What?"

"I mean, *no,* I don't need more time. As you pointed out, time is crucial. I've decided to accept your offer."

His heart contracted. He was flooded with joy; he couldn't speak for several seconds. "I'm delighted," he finally said without betraying his rampant emotions. "Tomorrow we'll meet with the priest. The next day we'll be married. Is that agreeable?"

"If you like." Her smile had faded.

Reaching in his pocket, he removed a velvet pouch. "You'll have a proper ring, but for our brief engagement, perhaps this will do as a gift." Opening the pouch, he removed a necklace fit for a queen. The antique golden chain held dozens of filigreed rosettes set with precious jewels: rubies, diamonds and emeralds. "Allow me."

She turned her back and lifted her hair while he fastened the clasp.

"Lovely," he murmured as she revolved slowly to look up at him. Her eyes were veiled, almost sad. "Doesn't it please you? I have dozens more necklaces to choose from. But this was a gift on its way from the king of Spain to the wife of the viceroy of Peru. Created from Inca gold, I assume, three hundred years ago."

"And stolen by you from a Spanish ship."

"Aye. I risked my life to get it. Any man can *purchase* a necklace for his bride-to-be."

"I see. Thank you. It is extraordinary."

He heard bitterness in her tone. She didn't look happy. What had he done wrong? Maybe he shouldn't worry, since, after all, she had agreed to become his wife.

"Is that all you want from me?" she asked wearily.

"If you're tired, don't let me detain you." He couldn't understand why the camaraderie they had enjoyed last week had disappeared, especially since they were now engaged. She looked more like a woman on her way to a funeral than one anticipating her wedding. Had he been mistaken to think she cared for him, found him attractive? She had said she loved him the night he had saved her life. Had she merely been swept away by overwhelming gratitude and the drama of the moment?

"Laurel, if you're not satisfied with our arrangement, please say so."

"I'm satisfied or I wouldn't have accepted. I have much to gain, as you pointed out."

So the money was what had won her over. He should have guessed. She had been willing to marry Beauregard for a small fortune. His own much larger fortune had carried the day. Ignoring the growing ache deep inside, he smiled and raised her hand to his lips. After kissing her cold fingertips, he said, "You've made me very happy, Miss Laurel Caldwell. I'll escort you to your room. The new maid will come soon to serve you for the evening. Tomorrow we'll visit the priest."

Her amber eyes flicked across his face. He had a sense that something was missing, that somehow he had disappointed her, but he couldn't figure out how that was possible. He would have loved to sweep her into his arms, to kiss her again as he had before, to tell her how much he adored her, how he had loved her for years. But she was his fiancée now, his future wife. She must be treated with respect, as he had promised.

In silence, they walked to her door. Bowing again, he left her for the night. On the way back to the terrace, he wondered why he wasn't brimming with joy. His wildest dream was about to come true. But he wasn't brimming with anything. He felt empty, depressed, confused. *Who could figure out a woman anyway?*

* * *

The wedding took less than an hour. The priest appeared uncomfortable as he conducted the holy rites over Cheyne Sinclair, a man with questionable religious connections, but he was warm and kind to Laurel, helping her to make it through the ceremony with a semblance of normality and a pretense of pleasure.

She wore a wedding dress of antique white satin and a veil flowing to her hem created from yards of French lace. The gown didn't fit very well, and had a slightly musty odor that she attempted to overcome with a liberal sprinkling of fine perfume. Her new maid had done a passable job of helping her bathe and arrange her freshly washed hair atop her head, leaving a few delicate curls around her ears and the nape of her neck. She didn't wear the necklace, since it was not at all appropriate for the occasion.

Laurel had slept little the past two nights and moved as if in a trance through the daylight hours. Vaguely aware of the excitement in the palace, she had done her best to respond pleasantly to Fatima's excited scurrying to and fro. During the morning, she had supervised the packing of numerous dresses and the lingerie sewn for her since her arrival in Tangier. At least these personal items were not stolen or borrowed from someone else.

The wedding was planned for four o'clock, to be followed by a private formal dinner in the small banquet hall of the palace. Tomorrow the newlyweds would leave on the captain's sloop for a cruise through the straits and along the Spanish coast. How long this would last was anyone's guess.

The morning of the wedding, she had such an attack of nerves, she almost called the whole thing off. What would her mother think of this sudden marriage? What would her father say when he found out? Cheyne didn't love her, so why should she give herself to him in marriage. He was attracted to her in the usual way a man was attracted to a woman. But the word love had never crossed his lips. Not once. Even Nicole had received a declaration of love, but there was nothing from Cheyne but a businesslike proposal and stolen jewelry. She was about to send for him and tell him she'd changed her mind, when a guest was announced.

The maid curtsied as Captain Harding strode into the room carrying a large bouquet created of white roses and orange blossoms.

Her relief at seeing a friendly face almost made her weep. Through the years, Harding had been like a surrogate father, and his presence today was strengthening.

"Captain, I'm so pleased to see you."

Grinning, he held out the flowers. "Congratulations, Miss Caldwell. A messenger arrived in Asilah yesterday informing me of the wedding. I rode through the night to get here. Here's a bouquet from me and the crew. I must say, you look beautiful in your wedding dress. I'll be proud to represent your father and give your hand in marriage."

"I'm so happy you came." She took the flowers. "I suppose you were quite surprised when you heard the news."

The captain looked thoughtful for several seconds. "Not too surprised, actually. Captain Sinclair is respected by everyone I've met. I believe he's sincere when he says he regrets the sinking of the *Star,* and we all heard how he saved you from the slave trader at the risk of his life. Not to mention, he's good-looking and wealthy enough to turn most ladies' heads with ease."

"But I will be his *wife.*"

"Aye. In fact, the crew and I were wondering when we would be allowed to return home, considering this new turn of events. Will you still need the new frigate?"

"Oh yes. We'll be sailing to Skye as soon as the ship is ready."

"I assume Captain Sinclair will accompany us."

"I'm not sure he will, though he may travel there later.

You see, he has powerful enemies in England. He could be in danger in the British Isles."

"Then you could stay here." He glanced about. "This place is not exactly a mud hovel, you know."

She wanted to say that she had not been asked to stay. Cheyne had never once raised the possibility. Instead she murmured, "Captain Sinclair understands how important it is that I go to Skye to claim my property. I'll return here later."

"Whatever suits you. But let me say, I believe you're marrying a good man. He's building you a fine ship and that speaks well of his character."

Fatima rushed into the room. "The carriage is here. Come along, both of you. We don't want to keep the master waiting."

The master. Laurel cringed at the title, but grasped Captain Harding's arm and went outside. She would simply have to see it through. If she was sorry afterward, she would deal with the problem then.

·24·

Between the time Laurel walked down the aisle on Captain Harding's arm, and the token kiss given her by her new husband at the close of the ceremony, Laurel slipped into a state of absolute unreality. She said the words, moved where she was directed, and managed a smile or two. But she had the sensation of sleepwalking, and felt nothing inside but the tiniest flutter when she looked closely into Cheyne's searching eyes.

A closed carriage whisked the wedding party, which included the bride and groom, Captain Harding, and a beaming Fatima, back to Tamerlane. Here a sumptuous feast awaited them, served on a table laden with golden dishes and silver goblets arranged atop an exquisite white damask tablecloth.

Laurel discovered, without surprise, that she was the only female seated at the table. Fatima had hurried off to the kitchen to supervise the parade of fragrant dishes, each one a culinary masterpiece of French, Arabian, or Spanish creation.

She sat next to Cheyne, but they spoke not a word other than an occasional polite *would you care for more wine* or *please pass the butter*. She felt his eyes on her from time to time, but for the life of her, she couldn't believe this was anything other than a midsummer night's dream. She kept thinking about Nicole's happiness, which had been the inspiration for her own plunge into matrimony. Why didn't she feel as joyful as Nicole? Had she been far too hasty? Perspiration dampened her nape and trickled down the back of her satin dress.

Besides Captain Harding, the guests were acquaintances of Cheyne's, several of his high-ranking seamen, a trader or two from the town, and the same emissary from the Consulate who had earlier made Laurel's acquaintance. The dozen men enjoyed themselves, becoming more raucous as the evening progressed and goblets were refilled. Their increased hilarity finally drowned out the music of lute and drum. Even Harding took full advantage of the occasion to indulge his appetites.

Laurel pecked at her food, occasionally studying the enormous diamond set in a wide embossed gold band that covered the upper half of her finger. Cheyne's taste in jewels ran to *the bigger the better*. She wondered if she could eventually request something less gaudy and more comfortable.

Eventually. She reminded herself there would be no *eventually* in her relationship with Cheyne Sinclair. They would have a few weeks together as man and wife, then she would go her way. What had she been thinking of to strike such a bargain? What would everyone say? And what would happen if she failed to become pregnant in the short time Cheyne had allotted for that feat? They hadn't discussed that eventuality. In fact, they hadn't discussed much of anything.

Laurel looked at her husband from beneath lowered lashes. He was busy rehashing the story of how the dey of Algeria had struck the French ambassador with a fly-swatter, thereby providing King Charles of France an excuse to invade Africa. It was unanimously agreed that Sultan Abd-al-Rahman was leading Morocco into inevitable war with France.

As if he felt her growing unease, Cheyne suddenly turned and leaned near. "We can leave now. Everyone will understand. Are you ready?"

Her mouth went dry. So it was off to the bedroom, just like that. "I suppose so," she murmured.

When he pushed back his chair, wild applause broke out, glasses were lifted and cheers echoed around the room.

"Madam Sinclair," he said, giving her an inviting smile. "Allow me."

She took his hand, offered a nervous thank you to the guests, and walked with as much dignity as possible from the banquet hall.

They entered Cheyne's office, a place that had been off limits till now. Closing the doors behind them, he crossed to his desk and unfolded a document. "I wanted to show you this, Laurel. 'Tis very important."

Trying to think with a clear head, she looked at the paper spread before her.

"This is the title to Tamerlane. I've had you named as joint owner with the right of inheritance. You'll have no trouble if something happens to me, since women's legal rights to property are respected here. Later, if there's a child, his name will be placed there."

"Or *her* name," she pointed out. *"If* we're successful," she couldn't resist adding.

"Naturally," he mumbled. "At any rate, I wanted you to know Tamerlane is yours as much as it mine. Here's something else, something entirely your own."

She stared absently at the document. She found the interjection of business at this particular time extremely unromantic. But then, she shouldn't have expected romance from a man who viewed their marriage as merely a practical arrangement to suit the two of them.

"This is an account book from my Paris bank," Cheyne explained. "I've deposited a hundred thousand pounds into an account in the name of Laurel Anne Sinclair. More will come later."

The sum was staggering. She looked closely at the figures.

"I thought you would prefer pounds so you could use the funds to begin restoring Strathmor Castle immediately. Just notify any Scottish bank. Later, if you prefer American dollars, they'll be made available. I expect to place half a million dollars in this account before spring. Is this agreeable?" He looked at her, waiting for her response.

Suddenly, she felt sick through and through. She felt she had sold herself into servitude, regardless of the immense figures involved in the transaction. She had sold her body to be used to breed this man's yet-to-be conceived offspring. Where was love? Where was commitment? Where was happiness?

"Laurel? Are you all right, lass?" It was the first note of tenderness she'd heard all day.

Her knees were weak. "I don't know. I'm not sure." Her voice sounded as if it didn't belong to her.

" 'Tis a great deal of money. But I can give you more. I will make certain you have everything you need, no matter the cost. I assure you—"

"No. No. No."

"What's wrong? You look very pale, Laurel." He hesitated. "God, I wasn't thinking. I'm an ass. This could have waited, but I thought you'd like to know everything is in order. Would you like some wine? Here, I'll get you a chair. I only planned to stop here for a minute, then take you to your room."

"I don't want to sit. And yes, I'd like to go to my room. I'm suffocating in this dress and—and I'm very tired." She knew it wasn't the dress. She was suffocating in shame and remorse.

He leaped to open the door, then before she could protest, he lifted her in his arms and marched with her down the hall, his boots echoing on the mosaic tile.

Once in her room, he placed her in a chair. "Everyone has left the palace except Fatima. She'll attend you." His voice became low. "Laurel, my darling girl. Have no fear. I won't approach you until you are ready, entirely ready. Forget about having a child. Perhaps that isn't meant to be. The important thing is you have my name and the security of my fortune. I wouldn't have suggested this unless I believed you cared for me. Surely you know how much—how much I care for you. I'll find Fatima." He grasped her hand and raised it to his lips. "Rest, Laurel. Call for me if you care to see me." He spun and left the room.

Sitting there, she took several deep breaths, then tugged off the veil and let it fall to the floor. She couldn't seem to move. She merely stared at the closed door and listened to the distant pounding of the surf beyond the breakwater. Gradually her pulse returned to normal. The breeze cooled the sweat from her brow and she realized the shadows were lengthening.

The door creaked open. Fatima entered with her arms laden with blood-red roses. Her smile was much more tentative than it had been at the ceremony. "Madam Sinclair, the master sent these." She brought the roses to Laurel and placed them in her arms.

Rising slowly, Laurel crossed to the terrace and stared at the gathering dusk. She smelled rain in the air, and glimpsed a storm moving across the channel. The sails of a small craft caught the dying light as it made for the harbor. She had no safe harbor, she thought, with a swelling of self-pity. She had only herself in this strange exotic place, ruled by a man who was half gentleman, half pirate. A man whom she had sworn before God to love and obey until death.

She tossed one rose over the wall and watched it fall to the courtyard below. The simple act was somehow comforting. She threw another and then another.

"What are you doing, ma'am?" asked Fatima at her elbow.

"I don't know, Fatima," she responded softly. "I have not the slightest idea."

From his private quarters, Cheyne saw something fall from the upper terrace to his private courtyard. He had just entered the suite and removed his coat and tossed it over a chair. For the wedding, he had worn his best western style trousers, his tobacco brown frock coat and fawn brocade waistcoat. He had wanted Laurel to feel as much at home as possible by attempting to make everything, from the ceremony to the last course of the banquet, resemble a traditional wedding in New Orleans.

He was confused and deeply disturbed by Laurel's actions. She had looked as lovely as an angel from heaven, but she was equally distant and untouchable. He hadn't forced her to accept his proposal. She had done so of her own free will. But today she acted like a lamb going under the knife, like the lamb she had said she pitied.

He saw another object fall from above and walked over to pick it up. A rose. One of the red roses he'd sent to Laurel. Another fell and another. Hell, she was throwing them over her balcony. Did she find him so distasteful that she didn't even want flowers from him? He'd misjudged her entirely. Sunk in gloom, he reentered his room and dropped into a chair.

A knock interrupted his dark thoughts.

"Who is it?"

"Fatima, sir. Your wife said she has no need of me this evening."

"My wife," he grumbled under his breath. "Very well, Fatima. You may go to your quarters. Have all the other guests gone?"

"Yes, Captain. The palace is deserted."

"Very well. Remember, Madam Sinclair and I will leave on my ship tomorrow morning. We'll return within a week, I expect."

"Have a nice voyage, sir." Her voice was decidedly suspicious.

"Thank you. Good evening." He stared outside as more roses plunged to the tiles of his veranda.

Laurel studied the remaining long-stemmed red rose. The bloom was full and fragrant. Was it the color that annoyed her, or the thought of her obligation to the sender. The rose was innocent, despite its flaming scarlet petals. Was Cheyne Sinclair innocent? He had simply made her an offer, and she had accepted. He had fulfilled his part, there was no denying that. And here she was, hiding from him, failing to carry out her end of their bargain. He had said they could forget having a child. Now that she thought about it, his suggestion had been very magnanimous, considering a child was the reason he made the offer in the first place. She placed the last rose on the balcony railing.

She removed her dress and put on the filmy silk gown and negligee Fatima had left on the bed for her. She hadn't wanted Fatima's help tonight. The effort to pretend to be happy was just too much of a struggle.

The sound of a guitar drifted upward. She knew Cheyne's suite was somewhere below hers. Was that he playing? The melody was Spanish or Moorish, not played with great skill, but very haunting and rather sad.

Walking barefooted onto her terrace, she looked down. There, with his boot on a stool and strumming a slightly out of tune guitar, stood Cheyne. She could barely see him in the darkness, but she noticed he had removed his coat and cravat and was standing amidst her scattered discarded roses. The moon hadn't yet risen, so the only light was from a row of flickering candles encased in bulbous glass vases along the veranda wall.

He was unaware of her presence, but perhaps he knew she could hear his playing. The sight of his head bowed over the instrument, his shoulders broad beneath the crisp white linen shirt, stirred her emotions to life. Her memories of him came flooding back—of the way he looked behind his mask when they first met, of the way he'd quickly forgiven her for shooting him, of the way he'd risked his life to save her from the slave trader.

Without a second thought, she tossed the last rose at his feet.

He stopped playing and looked up at her.

"I'm coming down."

He paused only briefly before speaking. "I'll meet you halfway."

· 25 ·

Cheyne waited at the foot of the broad stone stairway leading to the second level. Torches lighted the area. The night air was thick and humid, and scented with the heady fragrance of honeysuckle, jasmine, and roses in full summer bloom.

Laurel descended the steps toward him. He was surprised and amused to see she was swathed from head to toe in the quilt rescued from the *Star*. He glimpsed delicate ankles and small bare feet beneath the dragging quilt. She had taken the pins from her hair and it fell around her shoulders, lifting in the soft breeze from the ocean. No bride had ever approached her husband looking more charmingly seductive.

He climbed the steps toward her. "The quilt is most becoming, lass."

"It's all I had of my very own. I didn't want to come to you in borrowed attire."

He picked her up in his arms, carrying her in her quilt like a precious bundle waiting to be unwrapped. He didn't go directly to his suite, but strolled about the expansive plaza, relishing the feel of her slight body against him, her arms now resting around his neck.

"Look around you, Laurel. Nothing here is borrowed. 'Tis yours as surely as it is mine. You are mistress of Tamerlane now. I want you to feel at home." He passed the fountain splashing in the center of the walled enclosure.

She moved in his arms. The quilt fell away from one shoulder, revealing she did indeed wear something underneath: the sheer gown and negligee provided by Fatima. He forced himself to walk slowly, though the pressure in his groin was growing with each passing second.

"I appreciate your generosity, Cheyne. You've been very fair."

"No more than you, Laurel Anne."

His path took him toward his quarters. Opening the carved door with his shoulder, he entered the airy room and carried her to the chaise beneath the overhanging roof of the open veranda. Gently, he eased her down. "I'm happy to know you're pleased, but I meant what I said. Your body belongs only to you. If you've decided not to bear a child, I will respect your wishes, and your privacy."

She gazed at him, her face partially obscured in shadow. "I do want a child. You are my husband, and I think we should seal our bargain as we discussed."

His throat tightened. His love for this woman, and his spiraling passion, became one, filling him with such emotion, he was consumed beyond anything he'd ever experienced.

She curled her knees under her. The quilt fell across her lap. Beyond her, the moon was making an appearance above the sea, shedding light across her pale figure. He could see the outline of her breasts, the tips barely visible under the thin fabric. He sat beside her on the satin brocade chaise, slipped one hand around her shoulders and drew her to him. Covering her lips, he kissed her tenderly, then with increasing intensity.

He heard her low moan, felt the tension in her body. She had put up a brave front, but she was a virgin after all, with no experience in the art of love.

On the other hand, he knew exactly what he was doing. And he had the patience and skill of many years to help him guide her into this new world of desire.

With his lips near her temple, he whispered, "Relax my sweet girl. Let me show you what love can do."

She opened her eyes.

He closed them with kisses.

His lips lingered near her ear as he loosened the tiny bows of her negligee. With his fingers entwined in her hair, he lowered her head back and nuzzled the vein beneath her ear, then charted a moist trail across the hollow of her throat and along the edge of the low-cut bodice of her gown.

She sighed and relaxed against his arm.

He eased her against the back of the chaise and opened the fabric of the negligee and gown, luxuriating in the sight of her exquisitely formed body. When she placed an arm over her breast, he gently moved it aside and bent to kiss the rosebud nipple revealed there. She tensed for one second, then relaxed again and made a purring sound in her throat. He moved to the other nipple and teased it with his tongue, then covered it with his lips and suckled until he felt her tremble in response.

"You're perfect, my darling. Made for this." Holding his desire in check, he caressed the swell of her breasts, her stomach, her hips. Then he rose to quickly strip off his confining garments. He hadn't expected to make love on the chaise, but he saw no reason not to continue. Straddling it, he parted her thighs. Not daring to look yet at the dark triangle, he put his hands on her waist and slid her toward him, then pressed her legs apart and massaged her until all tension left her. Then he inched forward and balanced his weight over her.

"Laurel, Laurel, my sweet lass . . ."

Her hands moved along his bare shoulders, then encircled his neck. He felt her eyes on him and believed she would find him acceptable. His body was as sturdy as a youth's, muscular and fit from his vigorous life. He kissed the soft flesh between her breasts and moved downward, skimming over her heart and lingering on the tender rise of her stomach. He stroked the silken slopes of her hips, then pressed her thighs with his palm before cupping her calf. Her breath was coming in ragged gasps. Her body was responding willingly, eagerly. But there was time, worlds of time, to make this first experience for her magical and unforgettable.

Taking one small foot in each hand, he bent her knees. She was prone now on the chaise, her head back, her eyes closed, her body pliant and willing. He nuzzled her softness, then explored her moist femininity. Again, she moaned and writhed under this first invasion.

"'Tis all right, sweetheart. Your beauty humbles me, Laurel." The tide was building in him; his fierce control wavered. Finding her bud with his fingertips, he circled it until he knew her lovely body was ready, then he suspended his weight over her, teasing the secret place with his maleness until she was gasping and quivering, her back arched, her fingers digging into the fabric at her side.

Aye, this was a woman of passion, latent and hidden, waiting for this very moment to be stoked into life. With a groan of surrender, he entered her to complete the journey created by nature to bond man and woman in body and spirit. Driving past her veil of innocence, he felt her stiffen, but she made no sound of protest. His heart turned to liquid as he forced himself to hold back, easing away, then piercing once more as he began the rhythm older than man's memory.

Taking time to kiss each breast once again, he felt the answering storm building within her.

"I love you, Laurel. God knows, I love you." His voice was breathy with the pain of restraint.

"Cheyne," she gasped. "My love."

With every sense and sensation centered, he sank into the depths of her, devouring her, taking her with him toward the peak of fulfillment. He heard her cries and knew they were of delight, not pain. His last rational thought was a silent prayer for her pleasure, then he gave himself to the aching, searing, shattering release of his male hunger.

Mindless, every part of her crying out for an answer to her desperate longing, Laurel groaned in ecstasy as Cheyne carried her to heights she'd never known existed. With the darkness clothing her with modesty, with only her husband to see her nakedness, she had no thought of hesitation, but was aware only of the feel of him, the taste of him, his touch, his expert ministrations, his murmured words of encouragement and caring.

Love. Oh yes, he loved her. He had said so at last. No man could share so much intimate joy unless his heart was overflowing with that intense emotion.

Her own turbulent release matched his, and when his possession ended, she lay panting, exhausted, tingling from her head to her toes.

"My precious Laurel." He stretched out beside her and drew her head against his chest. He was damp and had a slightly pungent aroma, very masculine, very stirring, and remarkably satisfying. She had made him her own, and she was thoroughly content. His hard muscles rippled under her cheek. One hand cupped her buttocks and turned her toward him. As a sea breeze feathered across her skin, she was overcome with a serene languor. She shivered in his embrace and wrapped her arm around his waist.

Lifting a portion of the quilt, he pulled it over them. "I pray I didn't hurt you, my darling. At least, not too much."

His voice was distant. She couldn't hold her eyes open. "No. Only a moment, but no longer." She wanted to speak her deepest feelings, but she was too sleepy to search for words. "I love you," she murmured. Heaven help her, she knew it was true.

Sometime during the night, the squall hit, splattering the veranda with large raindrops and rapidly cooling the air. Laurel moved in Cheyne's embrace. Her back was curved against his naked body. Feeling his arousal along her spine, she smiled and laid one hand over his, which rested on her breast.

Getting up from the chaise, he gathered her into his arms.

"Cheyne?" she murmured sleepily.

"Shh, lass. We're going to bed. 'Tis warm and cozy there."

The satin sheets of his sinfully large bed felt cool to her skin. Cheyne was invisible in the darkness, but he was there, close and protective and needful of her.

She felt slightly wanton as she ran her hand along the hard planes of his stomach and hips. Finding him ready, she shyly encircled him with her fingers.

"Christ, Laurel," he said huskily. "Do you want—"

"Yes," she whispered and pressed her pelvis against his thigh.

With a groan, he put his hands around her waist and raised her above him, then showed her the way to astonishing new delights.

* * *

200

Laurel slept late. The morning was overcast for a time, and she felt safe and warm, lazy and lethargic, and most definitely fulfilled. Cheyne had whispered to her hours before that he was leaving to prepare the sloop for their honeymoon trip. He would return before noon, and with good weather, they would sail for the Mediterranean.

Finally she forced herself to rise and ring for Fatima. When the woman bustled in with a tray of fruit and coffee, Laurel handed her the quilt with a slightly embarrassed grin. "This needs washing, I fear."

Fatima beamed knowingly.

Laurel assumed she had gained status in Fatima's eyes, and no doubt the stains on the quilt would be the talk of the servant's quarters within the hour.

By the time Cheyne returned at noon, the sun had broken through the clouds and the air was fresh and invigorating. Laurel's carrying cases were packed, and she wore a simple dress and her hair tied in a bright blue ribbon.

When he stood staring at her in undisguised admiration, she felt their new intimacy like a living thing.

"The boat is waiting and we must go with the tide. Otherwise—" He grinned at her, then took her hand and led her down the steps.

Laurel was sure she had never been happier in her entire life.

· 26 ·

Day after golden day followed in succession, like the priceless links of a queen's jeweled necklace. Even more spectacular were the nights at sea, the gentle rocking of the boat gliding across velvet water, and overhead the heavens sprinkled with diamonds from one horizon to the other, dominated by an ever-blossoming moon as July spilled into August.

Cheyne had a crew of four quiet, disciplined seamen who did their best not to intrude on the privacy of the newlyweds. Often Laurel and Cheyne manned the ship themselves, Cheyne showing off his strength and muscular physique, Laurel proudly displaying her own skill with both navigation and rigging.

Barefooted and wearing a minimum of clothing, they played like children, laughing, teasing, embracing at every opportunity. The world was theirs, and nothing intruded to mar their joy.

For both, time meant nothing, their only reality the sun and waves and bracing sea winds. Often they tied up at some deserted beach along Africa's north shore and swam in the sun-warmed water or strolled in the sand, searching for shells or trinkets washed ashore from some distant land.

And they made love. Every night and frequently in the day, if privacy could be found beneath the trees along the beach. They anchored twice near villages in the south of France and once in southern Spain, walking through the narrow streets, holding hands and shopping for souvenirs like the summer tourists.

Finally, after nearly three idyllic weeks, Cheyne announced they must return to Tangier. He had business matters and he wanted to check on the progress of Laurel's ship.

Only then did Laurel feel a darkening of her mood, a hint that time was moving on, and the real world was waiting for her.

They weighed anchor at the port near Tamerlane on a cloudless day in mid August. Waiting for them on the pier stood Rafi Hamid and Nicole.

"Nicole!" cried Laurel, hurrying along the gangplank, then hugging the girl warmly. "I'm so glad to see you."

Nicole stood back and grinned. "So we're both married ladies. I was sure surprised at the news when we got back from our wedding trip."

"I knew you would be." Laurel put her arm around Nicole and they walked arm in arm to a waiting carriage. Behind them came their husbands, deep in conversation.

"You didn't say you were in love with Captain Sinclair," Nicole said. "You just let me babble on and on about my own love without saying a word."

"My decision was rather sudden, I admit. But I do love him, Nicole. More than I can ever say."

When the four entered the courtyard at Tamerlane, they were met by a row of servants who directed them to a welcoming feast. They dined like equals in the small banquet hall, talking and laughing and sharing tales of their recent travels.

Afterwards, Nicole and Rafi hurried away to their own quarters, and Cheyne strolled with his arm around Laurel to his suite.

She had thought they might make love there in the slanted beams of the afternoon sun, but Cheyne only embraced her. "I must leave at once for Asilah," he said, matter-of-factly. "There's some problem with the setting of the masts on your ship. Minor, I hope, but I may be gone a week."

"I'll go with you."

"Nay, this is man's work. I'll need to take charge and solve several disputes. There would be nothing for you to do."

Flooded with disappointment, she moved away from his arms. "Nothing?"

"Trust me, Laurel. I need to give my undivided attention to this project. You do want your ship on schedule, do you not?"

Her schedule? She had forgotten she had a schedule. She hadn't wanted to think of the bargain she had with Cheyne, but only of the indescribable joy of the past few weeks. "Oh yes, naturally. I want my ship as soon as possible."

He studied her as if searching for a reason for her suddenly brusque tone. "I assumed so. I'll have a report for you when I return. In the meantime, enjoy the palace. Spend time with Nicole." He tweaked her cheek. "You girls will have a lot to talk about, I'm sure. Go shopping. Buy out the bazaar. You'll want to take gifts home, I presume."

Home. Didn't he realize her home was now with him? He had told her to make herself at home at Tamerlane. At the time, she hadn't expected she would, but things were different now. Or were they?

She moved to the table and traced its surface with her finger. "Yes, girl talk and shopping. That sounds very nice. Maybe I could redecorate the palace. Some of your furnishings are not exactly to my taste."

He didn't appear to catch her barb, or else he was indifferent to her suggestion. "I'm taking the sloop down the coast. I'll see you soon." Without a bow, or a kiss, or a hint of regret at leaving her, he strode from the room.

Standing there, watching the door close behind him, Laurel knotted her hands and heaved a sigh. He had enjoyed himself on their honeymoon, she was certain. But men had a way of keeping everything in its proper place: love, work, play. Each had a slot and an allotted time. He was now off to work without a backward glance. She must remember their idyllic journey and try not to be possessive of him. He loved her. He had told her so on their wedding night. And he showed his love in so many ways, she couldn't count them. Especially with his body. Unless of course, he was also able to separate the desires of his body from the desires of his heart. Was it possible Cheyne had *pretended* to love her just to keep things pleasant while he planted his seed? The thought was abhorrent. If so, she had been completely fooled.

Unsettled and all of a sudden lonely and depressed, she pulled up a chair and gazed out to sea. Men were such strange and confusing creatures. Nicole was obviously happy with Rafi, and from all reports, her cousin Skye was absolutely adored by her husband, Kyle. She had been so certain Cheyne had come to truly love her, but perhaps she had only wanted that so much, she had believed it to be true. She wished fervently Shannon was here. That wise lady would know how to advise her, even if she was a spinster.

Fatima entered bringing a glass of orange tea.

Grateful for the distraction, Laurel smiled warmly. "The captain is off to Asilah. I suppose I'll browse in the library this afternoon."

"This came yesterday, ma'am. News from home, I expect."

A letter from home. Eagerly Laurel took it and tore it open as Fatima slipped out of the room.

My darling Laurel. Your mother and I pray this finds you safe and happy. We received your letter this morning, along with the official report of the Star's sinking. What a tragedy, but thank God you and the crew are all safe. I do believe the sinking was an accident, and I ask you to place yourself in Captain Sinclair's hands. I've known the man for a number of years and am certain he is reliable. If he promises you a new ship, he will fulfill his promise. I first met him when he was a boy under the command of my old friend, Jean Lafitte. As you know, Jean was a privateer, some say a pirate, but I knew him as a bold friend to whom I owed my life. Whatever course Cheyne Sinclair follows, he cannot be entirely blamed, since he grew up with Lafitte as his idol. I know personally that Sinclair has much to recommend him. On the other hand, I will be glad to hear that you and Captain Harding and the others are safely in Scotland. Write to us as soon as you've taken up residence there. You'll be glad to know Desert Mirage is doing well with her lessons. Our plans are to travel to Scotland in late May and bring the horse. We miss you terribly and have lighted candles at the cathedral in thanks for your being spared from the shipwreck. Your mother sends her love and Shannon as well. I am mailing a letter to Captain Sinclair under separate cover. With all our love and affection, Mother and Father.

Laurel reread the letter three times before she laid it aside. The encouraging remarks about Cheyne were comforting. At least he hadn't lied about his connections to her family. But now she must write her parents and tell them about her marriage. How could she begin? What could she say? If she had decided to marry Cheyne and live with him in Tangier, her marriage would make some sense. But how could she explain she had married him, then intended to sail to Scotland without him?

Forced to consider the prospect, she didn't see how she could leave him at all. She rested a hand on her stomach. Even now, she could be carrying his child. Would he change his mind about sending her away if she were pregnant? Or would he be more likely to keep her close if she were not? The urgency of claiming her property in Scotland no longer existed, as far as she was concerned. She wanted to stay at Tamerlane, or anywhere, as long as Cheyne was with her. But that wasn't their arrangement. He wanted a child, and he wanted the child raised elsewhere. He had made that perfectly plain.

In the hour that followed, Laurel began four letters to her parents, then crushed the papers and tossed them aside. Finally she decided she would simply have to await developments. They had suggested she write to them from Scotland, so there wasn't any hurry to correspond.

Crossing to her balcony wall, she looked down, remembering how she'd tossed the roses, then made the fateful decision to consummate her marriage. She thought of Nicole's words that nothing was more important than sharing love, if only for one night of bliss. Laurel contemplated the many nights and the glorious days she'd spent with Cheyne Sinclair. Soon he would return and they might continue to share love and laughter. But deep inside, she had a deadly feeling that things would never be the same again. She had experienced the greatest joy imaginable. But now the honeymoon was over.

· 27 ·

Cheyne was in his cups and he knew it. He had spent the past few weeks pushing his ship builders to the limit. He had even done manual labor himself in order to speed the project. In hard, physical, sweat-inducing work, he had found some relief from the pain in his heart. Tonight, he had searched for solace with a bottle of Spanish brandy.

Cheyne had always been a private person, keeping his deepest feelings to himself, but he had just told Rafi the whole story while pacing back and fourth like a madman in the middle of the night.

In his simple hut in Asilah, Rafi was reclining on a couch, eating from a plate of dates. But during the telling, he had stopped chewing and listened intently.

"Hell, I don't know why I did it," Cheyne stormed. "I'd give anything if I had stayed in Asilah and concentrated on her ship, instead of going to Tangier and losing my concentration altogether. I ought to be horsewhipped."

Rafi sat up and crossed his legs. "I don't understand why you have such a problem, *mon ami*. You love this

207

woman; she loves you. You're married. You're both healthy and rich. What else is there?"

"Honor, Rafi. Honor."

"I fail to see dishonor in what you've done."

"I've taken advantage of her, in the worst possible way. It's one thing to take a woman's body, but I've taken her heart. I knew she was attracted to me physically, attracted enough to enjoy sleeping with me and possibly bear my child. But she's given me something even more profound than her innocence and her body."

"More profound than that?" Rafi's voice held disbelief.

"Her love, you bloody idiot."

Rafi shook his head and bit into the date.

Cheyne stopped pacing. "I'm sorry. You're not an idiot. I'm the one who's the biggest fool in Morocco. Or any other place. I made a bargain with the lady. I had no intention of destroying her life and her happiness. I was so intent on keeping her from Beauregard and providing her with financial security, that I encouraged her love. And by all that's holy, she believes I'm in love with her. I even slipped the night I first possessed her and told her I loved her."

"It's true, isn't it?"

"Aye, but I'd like to cut my tongue out for saying it."

"Then rescind your bargain. Keep her in Tangier. Have children with her and live a happy life."

"I can't. She would be willing enough right now, but what about later, when she has children and should take her rightful place in society."

"Society? What do you mean *society?*"

"Look at it this way, Rafi. You're a Berber. You visit your people and they visit you. Is that important to you?"

"Of course. It defines who I am as a man."

"Exactly. Laurel comes from a society in New Orleans where heritage and breeding and respectability are essential to fulfillment in life. 'Tis like British royalty, a closed group of elite families who own and manage everything. She is part of that. I've met her parents and I know what I'm talking about. My idea was for her to become my wife, then return to her own world to raise our child. If I stayed out of the way, no one would know she's married to the Sea Falcon, a man who's not only a bastard, but who has a price on his head. She could explain that her husband is a successful shipping tycoon she met on her travels, a man who dislikes America. And she'd have so much money, no one would dare question her story. I don't expect to live to a ripe old age, considering my clandestine activities at sea against the slavers. She could become a widow, or she could divorce me and marry a man from her own class. I never intended to break her heart or ruin her life. I swear it." He reached for the brandy flask.

"And what about *your* heart, *mon capitaine?*"

"I thought I could keep my emotions under control, though I expected to pay a high price in misery. The thought of holding her in my arms, making her mine, was so great a temptation I couldn't resist it. I just hadn't expected—"

"Expected what?"

His voice fell. "To lose myself completely. To love so deeply that I'm consumed with her. To not want to draw another breath unless she's beside me, or somewhere within reach."

"How did this happen? It's not good for a woman to have such power."

"Don't you think I know that! I've never let it happen before. Never, in all these years. Maybe I should have taken a wife long ago. Some docile pretty little wench to satisfy my needs and give me children."

"No, my friend, that isn't your way. You've a passionate nature, not just about women, but about everything: your friends, your clothes, great causes, even the color of the roses in your garden. There is nothing gray about you—only whitest white and reddest red and blackest black."

"Well, I've done myself in this time. I have to let her go. I have to *make* her go. I can't have the marriage annulled after what's happened. But I can suggest a divorce once she's settled in Skye. Distance will help her forget. And at least, she'll have the money."

"And what if she's pregnant?"

Cheyne felt the blood rush from his head. "She could be. I suppose she'll know before long. Pray she isn't, Rafi. Ask Allah to spare me that torture."

"Torture?"

"The torture of knowing she has my child and I can be no part of her life or the child's. I didn't think this would be a problem, but now I'm haunted by the prospect." He banged his metal tankard on the table, splashing the contents. "I can't make a home in New Orleans, not while I continue to sabotage the slave trade. I take a chance now and then of appearing there as Hammond Brown, but even that is dangerous. I can't afford to risk the lives of everyone involved with me. I sure as hell can't go to Scotland or England. The earl of Croydon would pounce like a wolf. You know he was behind Saad's plot in Asilah. I'd have my neck stretched at Tyburn, for sure. That would make a fine legacy for my wife and child."

"And she won't live in Morocco?"

"She doesn't belong in our world, Rafi. A world of conflict, with war imminent, and a way of life completely foreign to anything she's ever known. She should have pretty dresses and bonnets and attend church socials and barbeques. She will want her parents to be near her and her friends and gossip and green lawns and magnolias. I won't cause her to be banished from all that."

"Maybe you underestimate her strength, and her love for you."

"Not her strength. I stand in awe of her courage. But her love for me is new and like a blazing fire that will soon die without fuel to keep it alive. I'm not going to give her that fuel."

"You'll offer her no choice?"

"She's young and in love. She might choose to stay now, then live to regret it. No, I made a firm arrangement with her. She understood fully. I must send her to Skye, as we agreed. In the meantime, I'll just stay away from her. When I'm with her, I inevitably betray my true feelings. The ship will be ready in two weeks and I'll sail to Tangier and load it for the journey to Scotland. You'll have to take a message to her right away, Rafi. Tell her I'm not coming."

"In some places, such a messenger can be beheaded."

"Nevertheless, you'll have to go. Tell her I'm detained because of her ship. Christ, tell her I'm detained because of some woman. Maybe she'll start to hate me right away." He threw his tankard viciously against the wall, where it clanged and crashed to the earthen floor. "I'm going to the ship."

"It's after midnight, sir. The workmen are sleeping."

"Then I'll wake them," he shouted. "The sooner we get this over with, the sooner I can get back to the business of freeing slaves." He knew he was acting like a fool, but he didn't give a damn. The agony in his heart was more than he could bear tonight. And he saw no help for it.

Ten days after returning from her honeymoon, Laurel suspected she was pregnant.

"Are you sure, Miss Laurel?"

"No, but it's very likely, Nicole."

"Maybe it's worry. About the ship and the voyage. Worry can delay your time."

"It's possible, but I doubt it." Laurel fingered the glass of sweetened citrus juice and gazed around Nicole's tiny garden. "It's ironic, Nicole. A few months ago, you were a slave being sold at auction. Now I envy you more than I can say. You have a husband who loves you, a charming house, a new family who come to call. You'll have children soon, I expect. And I am being sent away by the only man I will ever love." This was the first time she could say the words out loud. She had secluded herself for days, ever since word came from Cheyne announcing he would stay in Asilah until the ship was ready. He told her to prepare for sailing, that *The Star of Tangier* would leave for Scotland the first week in September. Captain Harding would be in charge and her crew was eager for the voyage.

Not a word of affection. Not a question about her well being. Just a curt message and nothing more. Her worst fears were confirmed. He'd charmed her, seduced her, and impregnated her. Then abandoned her. Well, not entirely. He had made her very rich.

"I'm not taking the money, Nicole. I've made up my mind about that. All I'm taking is funds equal to what I lost when the ship sank. That should be enough to modernize Strathmor Castle and survive until spring. If we're lucky, and Desert Mirage wins the competition, my parents will have no money worries after that."

Nicole started to sniffle.

Laurel was long past tears. "The baby will be born in May, I expect. Shortly before my parents arrive in Scotland. That will be nice." Her voice was hollow and tinged with bitterness."

Nicole hiccuped to cover a sob. "What about the captain? Mr. Sinclair? It's his baby, too."

"I've thought of that. Naturally I'll send word after the child is born. Before then, I don't want Cheyne to know. He has no real interest in the baby. All he wants is to have a child of his raised in elite society."

"I don't understand."

"From what he's told me, I'm guessing the problem

goes back to his own boyhood. He was an outcast then, so now he will make sure his offspring is accepted. He made his objective perfectly clear when he proposed to me."

"He's going to a lot of trouble, seems to me." Nicole shook her head. "I thought he was kinder than that, a fair man who truly cares for folks."

"That's part of the problem, Nicole. He changes like a day in spring. He once said he loved me, but he must have been lying or he wouldn't neglect me and send me away. I don't want to use the excuse of pregnancy to force him to remain at my side. Not that I could, considering he has no interest in raising the child."

"This is all very strange to me, if I do say so."

"And to me. The whole episode is peculiar beyond belief. I've thought a great deal about it, though, and I've made up my mind. If he has no affection for the baby we have created together, then he will know nothing of the child, except for the most obligatory information. I do have my pride, after all." She leaned forward. "Nicole, you must swear on the Bible not to tell him. I've been good to you, haven't I? Now you must repay me by promising not to tell Cheyne."

"I don't have a Bible anymore. Just the Koran."

"Then get it. That will do nicely."

Nicole stepped into her cottage and quickly returned. "I don't know if Muslims swear on the Koran, but I can do it anyway, if you truly want me to."

"I do. Swear now. You won't tell Cheyne I believe I carry his child."

"I swear."

"Thank you. Besides, if it turns out I have his baby, I will certainly inform him. I'll send him the news once it's here."

Nicole began weeping into her handkerchief. "I'm going to miss you something awful, Miss Laurel."

She patted Nicole's hand. "Let's dispense with *Miss*

Laurel. We're equals, as far as I'm concerned, and anyway, I'm not a *miss* anymore. I'd better go home now. I'm still trying to decide what things to take. Oh, I almost forgot." She reached in her pocket and removed the enormous blue-white diamond wedding ring she'd worn only once, then put away for safekeeping. Cheyne had promptly replaced it with a simpler antique Persian ring made of gold, set with rubies and pearls.

"Take the diamond, Nicole, and hide it until I'm gone. I never cared for it, but its worth a fortune. Return it to Captain Sinclair after I sail."

Tears were streaking Nicole's cheeks as she took the ring. "I hope you come back to Tangier, Miss—I mean, Laurel. You're the best friend I ever had. The people here are nice, but you're a wonderful lady."

Feeling desperately tired, and slightly woozy, Laurel stood and hugged Nicole. "I'll see you again before we sail. Provisioning the ship will take a few days."

Nicole shook her head. She wore native dress most of the time, but unless she was going out, she didn't wear a veil. "Rafi and I are going to the mountains tomorrow, right after the ship arrives from Asilah. His parents are having a feast day and we must attend."

Laurel took this news as one more disappointment. But sooner or later she knew she had to part with Nicole. She embraced her, fighting back her own tears. "God be with you, dear. Or Allah, whichever gives you comfort. I will write to you, I promise. One more thing, Nicole. I want you to know you were right. Despite everything, I would do it again. The time Cheyne and I were together was paradise; it must last me a lifetime. The memory of those days and nights will be my greatest joy until I draw my last breath." After one last hug, she pulled her chador around her head, then hurried back through the compound to her own quarters.

·28·

The Star of Tangier was a shipowner's dream: full rigged, sleek, and graceful, mounting thirty cannon and carrying the latest of navigational aids.

Laurel stood gazing across the bay where the ship had weighed anchor and lowered canvas while provisions were transported in numerous small craft from the quay. She would be sailing within the hour. Her meeting last night with Captain Harding had been reassuring, but she hadn't set eyes on her husband in almost three weeks. He had not even bothered to come to her when the ship arrived, but had sent Harding instead. He was on board the new *Star,* but he had elected to stay away from her during her last night in Tangier. His excuse was he had last minute checking to do of supplies. At least, that's what he told Harding to say. Nothing could be plainer. Cheyne was finished with her, once and for all.

Her trunks were stacked beside her as the yawl made its way from the ship. She had said her good-byes to Fatima and assured her she would be all right waiting alone on the dock.

The wind ruffled her hair and tugged at her traveling cloak. The sun was warm again today, and she detected the scent of citrus drifting on the wind from the fields near the town. Her time in Morocco had been both terrifying and idyllic. Would she ever return? She had no idea.

When the boat pulled alongside the quay, Cheyne jumped out and walked toward her. The sight of him tore through her like a dozen heated needles and her mouth went dry as the Sahara.

He swept his buccaneer's hat from his head and made a slight bow. "Your ship, Laurel. As promised."

His face was unreadable. He wasn't smiling, but appeared distracted and very businesslike. She had the feeling he looked right through her, as if this parting was something to be gotten over with quickly so he could get on with more pressing matters.

"It's magnificent," she managed through the knot in her throat. "Captain Harding tells me it's stable and seaworthy and my every request has been carried out. I'm grateful for your generosity." Could he hear the strain in her voice? Could he detect her agony? If so, he didn't show any emotion.

"She's the finest frigate ever built in Morocco. The cruise along the coast from Asilah proved it without a doubt. You should be arriving in Scotland in two weeks if the currents are favorable. 'Tis easy to see why your family puts such store by Captain Harding."

She couldn't end it like this. She just couldn't. "Cheyne," she said above a whisper. "We are man and wife. I think you must have forgotten."

His jaw set. At last he looked directly into her eyes. "Nay. I haven't forgotten. But I've decided our decision to marry was a mistake. You're a lovely lady, Laurel. I've carried a boyish fantasy of you for years. But I'm not a man who likes being tied down, bound to one woman. I've avoided it for thirty-six years, and I was simply swept away by your abundant charms."

She gasped. She had thought she was prepared for the worst, but Cheyne's blunt remarks cut her to the depths of her soul. "You mean—you're sorry for what happened between us? Sorry?" To keep her hands from shaking, she clasped them in front of her.

"Sorry? Not entirely." He gazed past her shoulder. "We had a fine time together, did we not? No lasting harm done, I suppose." His eyes snapped back to search her face.

She knew he was asking if she were pregnant. After his cruel comment, she was desperately glad he didn't know the truth. Almost unable to speak because of the agony welling inside her, she cleared her throat and blinked back tears. "No, no lasting harm. None at all." She watched him closely, hoping, praying for some reaction, some hint of disappointment, but his face remained unchanged. If he had truly wanted her to have his child, he might have suggested she linger awhile in Tangier, or he might have sailed with her to Scotland. But he appeared not to care in the least, but only to be eager to be rid of her.

Anger and damaged pride penetrated her heartbreak. "Actually I enjoyed myself in your country," she said with intended sarcasm. "Especially our honeymoon. I've always wanted a private tour of the villages and beaches along the coasts. You made an excellent guide." At last she had jarred his icy facade.

"I—I'm glad you see it that way. I admit I enjoyed it myself."

"Was it worth the cost?" she asked sharply. "I fear your bank account has suffered greatly. Perhaps you would like your money back?"

"Of course not. I'm a man of my word. You married me and I'm deeply appreciative. Besides, some poorly protected ship will pass this way soon. I'll ransack it and quickly refill my coffers."

His businesslike indifference to her feelings inflicted more wounds. "Then you intend to continue pirating? Isn't that profession old-fashioned and dangerous, considering warships of most civilized nations are determined to end it?"

"Aye, but 'tis in my blood, you see. 'Tis all I know to do with the skills I learned from Lafitte."

She was feeling sick. Not only because of her condition, but because she loved Cheyne, despite everything, and he was throwing away his life and any chance for happiness, his and hers. The lump in her throat was growing larger. "I'm sorry for you, Cheyne," she said softly. "I fear you'll end your days alone and unhappy."

"Happiness isn't in my stars, Laurel. Not lasting happiness, anyway. I take it in bits and pieces, wherever I can find it. To your credit, I found it for a time with you."

His first kind words were almost her undoing. After a pause to collect herself, she murmured, "And now we move on."

"It's best this way. I hope you're not greatly disappointed. After all, our arrangement was clear from the beginning."

"But since there isn't a child—" She stumbled over the lie, and stared at his tanned throat above the crisp whiteness of his open-neck shirt.

"Just as well," he said quickly. "I had illusions of immortality, but only briefly. You're certainly better off without the burden, and we can part without this obligation between us."

Laurel swallowed her despair. Time later for tears. Not now, when all she had left was her pride. She actually found the courage to force a lopsided smile to her lips. "Perhaps we should find a way to end our marriage. It does seem a rather unnecessary connection."

"Perhaps we should. Why don't you speak to a solicitor in Scotland? I'll sign whatever papers you send."

His words ripped her apart. Her smile disappeared. She hadn't expected him to agree so quickly and with such ease. "I'll think about it. Maybe next summer after I've renovated my castle on Skye."

"You needn't worry about the money. The account is yours forever. I'll keep it supplied as long as I live, and afterwards as well."

For a fleeting second, she thought she heard some hint of caring in his voice. She held his eyes, making him look at her. "Why would you do that? If we're not married and there isn't a child—"

"Consider it the payment of a debt to my dear friend, your father. Maybe it will keep him from coming after me with all guns blazing for—for what I've done to his daughter."

"A bribe to my father? I see." So Cheyne's friendship with her father, or fear of him, was his primary concern. She lifted her chin. "You haven't forced me against my will. Surely you know I wouldn't malign you to my parents. I intend to tell them exactly what happened. That we were caught up in the romance of Morocco and the bizarre circumstances of our adventure. We were attracted to each other, we married, then decided to go our separate ways. The decision at every step was entirely mutual. You didn't mislead me, or trick me into occupying your bed. Whatever happened, we are both responsible."

His lips tightened. He turned his back and walked to the edge of the dock.

He was moved at last, she knew it. She followed him and touched his arm.

"Laurel, you'd better get in the boat." His voice was low and laden with tension.

"Cheyne," she choked out his name. "Cheyne, come with me to Scotland. The Isle of Skye is remote and you can use a disguise, as you do in New Orleans. We need more time. We can talk things over. I—I do care for you." Frantically she struggled to hold on to the last vestige of her dignity.

He squared his shoulders and faced her. "And I care for you, Laurel. But there's nothing more to say. I cannot go, and you must try to forget me. There are things about me you don't know. Things I've done, am still doing, that might bring you harm and embarrassment. 'Tis finished between us; there's an end to it." His eyes scoured her face. Then he stared over her toward the cloudless sky.

He had shut her out, this time for good. She could see he was adamant. "I married you, Cheyne, knowing you're a privateer and a wanted man. But I love you and believe there's much good in you. I also believed you loved me. I see now I was wrong."

"Laurel, for God's sake, don't say that." For the first time, she saw raw emotion etched in his face. He reached for her, drew her to him, and covered her lips with a kiss so filled with desire and regret, her knees nearly buckled. She embraced him, opening her lips to him, lost in a whirlpool of desperate longing.

When he released her, he gazed back at her, his expression extraordinarily tender and heavy with feeling. He did care. She saw it in his face. It was enough to keep her from dying.

"Never doubt my deep feelings for you, Laurel. Whatever else happens to you in life, you can always know you have been loved."

"Then why—" She forced the words from her lips. "Why must we part?" An uncontrollable sob wracked her body. *No. No, I can't stand to lose you,* burned through her brain.

He placed his hands on her shoulders. "For that very reason. Because I do care about your happiness and your future. Trust me in this, lass. 'Tis the last thing I will ask of you."

"No—"

He kissed her again, crushing her lips, taking her breath, drawing the life from her body.

Clinging to him, she returned the kiss with every ounce of love she owned, not caring if she lived one split second after the kiss ended. A distant echo of Nicole's words sifted through her mind. *I would gladly die in his arms to gain one night of love.*

When he withdrew his mouth and released her, she realized there were worse things in life than death.

"Farewell, Laurel. God bless you. You're an angel far too good for this old pirate."

Blinded by tears, she whirled and found her way to the

yawl waiting down the quay. Where was a veil when she needed it? The oarsman reached up to assist her and she sank to a seat in the bow. She mustn't disgrace herself by breaking down completely in front of one of her English crewmen. Wives were supposed to be strong and collected when they were parted from their husbands. Only young lovers and mistresses were allowed to suffer like heroines in a romantic novel. She wiped her eyes and tried to focus on her ship, waiting for her in the shimmering water under a noonday sun.

She couldn't bear it. She had to look back, just once.

He was gone.

· 29 ·

Franklin Trowbridge waited impatiently in the back room of a pub in a district of London he rarely frequented. The place smelled of whiskey and cheap wine and he was disgusted by the dirt in the corners and cobwebs near the ceiling. He had tossed his heavy cloak over the single chair in the room and now began to walk restlessly in a circle. With every passing minute, he became more agitated and annoyed.

Where was the woman? Mingling with commoners was bad enough without being kept waiting by some mongrel whore from Spain. Only the importance of the meeting kept him from grabbing his coat and leaving the stinking place.

When footsteps sounded outside in the hall, he stiffened.

A knock came on the door and a hushed voice said, "Monsieur? Your Lordship?"

"Yes, come in." He stayed in the shadows as a woman wearing a floor-length cape with enveloping hood slipped inside.

She pushed back the hood, scattering raindrops around her.

He was surprised at her youth and seductive beauty. "Shazade Amin?"

"Oui. I am Shazade Amin. I've come a very long way."

"Yes, at my expense. It had better be worth it."

"I assure you, you will be more than pleased."

"The letter from your man in Cadiz said you had enough proof for me to capture and convict the Sea Falcon. Since I find such clandestine meetings in a place like this extremely distasteful, I hope you'll produce your proof at once, so I can be on my way."

"Do you have the money we asked for?"

"I have it. Enough to pay you well and provide your passage back to Spain."

She studied him with her owl-like onyx eyes.

"Show me your proof immediately, or I'm leaving."

"I was trying to decide if I could trust you."

"Good Lord, woman, I'm a peer of the British realm. You have the gall to question my word? Someone like *you?*"

She reached inside her cloak and pulled out a cloth bundle. She shook it open, revealing a sizable white flag with a black falcon in full flight displayed on the surface.

Trowbridge grabbed it from her hand and held it in the light. Yes, he'd heard the Sea Falcon's flag described. Several surviving captains of his slavers had seen it clearly, to their dismay. "Where did you get this? How do I know it was actually the Falcon's?"

"I myself stole it from Cheyne Sinclair's private suite in Tangier. I have a sworn affidavit to that effect. With this testament in your possession, you won't need me to stay in England for the trial. I don't like it here."

He gave her a look of grudging admiration. Whatever else the woman was, she was not stupid. She wanted to deliver her proof, collect her reward, and leave the country before she could be implicated in any wrongdoing herself. "I understand Saad Terraf is dead. What happened?"

"When he tried to capture Sinclair, he was killed by Sinclair's men."

"Blast it! The Falcon is a slippery villain."

"You must increase your reward to me, sir, for I bring more news, this time news of great importance."

"Speak, woman. If what you offer is worthy, I'll double your reward."

With a smile, she said, "I have reason to believe Cheyne Sinclair may soon travel to the Isle of Skye in the Scottish Hebrides."

"What's this? He wouldn't dare."

"Before I left Morocco for Spain, I learned the captain had married an American woman. Her name is Laurel Caldwell. I saw her at his palace in Tangier."

Trowbridge whistled under his breath. "Caldwell! I met Caldwell in New Orleans. In fact, I met the woman. Married, you say?"

"Oui. But Sinclair sent her away a few weeks after the wedding. He built her a fabulous ship and sent her to Skye. I saw the ship myself. It sailed in early September."

"Wasn't Sinclair with her?"

"No, which is odd I admit, but surely he will soon follow."

"No doubt he will, the fool." He pulled his money pouch from his coat and counted out several gold coins. "Here's the gold you requested. You've done well, Miss Amin. I will triple this if you can accomplish one more feat?"

"I will try."

"I want to know when Cheyne Sinclair travels to Scotland. He may sail or he may go by way of France and England. The important thing is, I must know when he departs his stronghold. Can you or your spies provide me with this knowledge?"

"Easily. I cannot return to Tangier since Sinclair knows I had a hand in his kidnapping, but I have friends in his palace. They will send word to me in Cadiz, and I will let you know immediately."

"Excellent. Excellent. Once the Falcon is in prison, I'm sure he can be forced to confess to his many crimes. Go now. You must travel quickly back to Spain and contact your friends in Tangier. We don't want our bird to escape the trap."

Shazade smiled a dazzling smile. Then she pulled the hood back over her head and let herself out of the room.

Trowbridge stared at the flag, then folded it tightly and stuffed it, along with the affidavit, into his coat. The discomfort of his surroundings was forgotten.

"There it is, Captain Harding. The village of Kylerhae. It's just as my cousin described. My cousin, Skye, is named after this island, you know." Laurel lowered her spyglass and handed it to the captain. The voyage had gone smoothly and they had arrived in the Hebrides two days ahead of schedule. She was extremely grateful since, despite her luxurious new ship, she had been deathly ill much of the time. She had especially missed Nicole when the young kitchen mate had been forced to look after her and balance a bowl beneath her mouth. For certain, the lad would hold a disparaging view of women and their distressing weaknesses. Seasick, she had explained. The boy had believed her, though Laurel doubted if many of the crew did. After all, she had sailed with them on numerous occasions and had as reliable sea legs as any of them. There was no reason on earth for her to stay sick during the comparatively easy voyage around the coast of Portugal, past England, to the Scottish Hebrides. None, except early pregnancy.

Laurel gazed toward the rocky shore and deep green hills rising above the cerulean water of the bay.

The Isle of Skye. Where land and sea, moors and

mountains, merged into gentle camaraderie under a flawless northern sky.

The sight was comforting, Laurel mused, like receiving the welcoming embrace of a close relative one hadn't seen in many years, but remembered as warm and safe and caring. She inhaled deeply, breathing the fragrance of the earth, and smoothed the folds of her shimmering gold-threaded caftan. When she had boarded *The Star of Tangier,* she had discovered a lavish wardrobe installed in her cabin: dresses, evening gowns, robes, even matching accessories and jewelry. These were provided, of course, by a well meaning and possibly guilt-ridden Cheyne Sinclair. None of it was in the least suitable for her new life in Scotland. She wished for the simple cottons and practical woolens she had packed in New Orleans. But those were at the bottom of the sea.

Gazing at Kylerhae, she thought the village had the unreal look of a painting in a picture book. Low, whitewashed cottages hugged the shore. The land sloped upward toward the snow-crowned Cuillin Mountains that centered the island and divided this area from the northern highlands. For the next year, this would be home, this ancestral land of the Clan Mackinnon. For the first time in days, she felt the quickening of her heartbeat and the stirring of her natural optimism.

A cloud lifted and she caught her breath. There, a short distance along the shore on a high bluff stood the massive stone structure she had purchased. Strathmor Castle, the Mackinnon estate and her home until next summer. It loomed in majestic splendor, square and bold and sturdy like its builders. The froth from the waves at its boulder-strewn base ornamented it like ruffles at the bottom of a plain workaday frock.

Captain Harding touched her elbow. "Look there. That must be your welcoming committee."

Sure enough, a rowboat was approaching from Kylerhae carrying a man in a dark suit and a woman wearing a straw bonnet with ribbons rippling in the breeze. The sight of a female after two weeks at sea surrounded by men flooded Laurel with relief.

The boat pulled alongside and Harding crossed to assist the couple to the deck of the *Star*. The man who had been rowing stayed below to secure the small craft.

The captain escorted a middle-aged man and considerably younger woman to where Laurel stood waiting.

The woman curtseyed and handed Laurel a bouquet of purple flowers. "Welcome, Miss Caldwell."

The stocky gentleman pulled his cap from his balding head and gave her a timid grin. "Welcome to Scotland, ma'am. I'm the mayor of Kylerhae, Kenneth MacCrae. And this here's my wife, Rosie."

"I'm very pleased to meet you. Thank you, Mrs. MacCrae, for the lovely flowers."

"They be heather, ma'am," said Rosie. " 'Tis an abundant wild flower from our isle, ye know."

"Yes, so I heard from my cousin, Skye Mackinnon. Or course, she's now Mrs. Wyndford."

The slender young woman with faded red hair bound into a bun, smiled pleasantly. "How is my dear friend, Skye? She wrote to me about the bairns, twin boy and girl, she said."

"She's wonderful, and the babies are adorable. She must have written to you soon after they were born at my home in Louisiana."

"Aye. She did that. And she said ye would be coming soon. We expected ye some months ago."

"Then you didn't know my ship sank off the coast near Tangier?"

The couple looked shocked. "Nay," said Mr. MacCrae. "We haven't had a word lately. Just Mrs. Wyndford's letter saying the new owner of Strathmor, her cousin, would be coming to take possession of the property."

"Then I have much news to share with you."

"Would ye like to go ashore now, ma'am?" inquired Mr. MacCrae.

Laurel looked at Captain Harding. "I'm eager to see the castle, Captain. And I need to have a good visit with the MacCraes."

"Then, by all means, go along. Since you'll be in safe hands, I'll stay aboard for now. But I will need to begin unloading supplies, and the men will want some shore leave ere long."

"Naturally. Make those arrangements as you usually do. As we planned, I'll want the *Star* here for a week or so until we determine what's needed to establish a port of trade. Before winter, the *Star* must return to New Orleans with trade goods, then sail with my family back to Scotland in the spring." She nodded toward the couple. "I'll go with you. I've heard about both of you from Skye. She said she played with you, Rosie, when you were children, that you were best friends."

"Aye. It near broke my heart when the Mackinnons left for America. But I didn't blame them a bit. Things are in a poor state here, with the English taxing us out of house and home, and the crops doing so poorly."

Laurel leaned near Rosie as they made their way to the ladder. "Do you have a dress shop or seamstress in Kylerhae, Mrs. MacCrae? I'm in desperate need of a proper wardrobe. You see, I lost all my clothing when my ship went down, and these fancy robes are all I was able to acquire. I do feel extremely overdressed and uncomfortable."

Rosie looked pleased at the shared confidence. "Still, that's a mighty pretty frock. But I can see 'tis not too practical. Allow Mr. MacCrae to assist you into the boat."

Grasping Rosie's hand and that of her husband, Laurel felt her spirits take a large leap upward. With such pleasant new friends, she might yet survive the ordeal that lay before her.

She was so absorbed in studying her surroundings, she

barely heard Rosie's chatter about crops and weather and the drop in population. She couldn't help noticing the age difference in the couple, and remembered something about Rosie being the second wife of Kenneth MacCrae. His first wife, Ruthie, had died years ago shortly after the birth of their third child. The choice of a mate was certain to be limited in the sparsely populated village, but Mr. MacCrae appeared to be in vigorous good health and a suitable husband for Rosie.

Laurel turned to address him. "I'm honored to meet the mayor of Kylerhae. I will count on you to offer me advice on restoring Strathmor."

"I'd be happy to do that, Miss Caldwell. But ye'll find the castle is much the same as the day the Mackinnons left. My wife and I have been caretakers, ye see. The laird paid us in advance to look after the place until the new owner arrived."

"Wonderful. But, the first thing I must tell you is that I am no longer Miss Caldwell. Since I sailed from New Orleans, I've had quite an adventure, not the least of which includes my marrying a sea captain, Mr. Cheyne Sinclair."

Rosie gaped at her. "Ye're a married lady? Then where is your husband?"

Laurel swallowed as she prepared to tell her story for the first time. Gripping the gunwhale of the bobbing rowboat, she firmly held Rosie's eye. "He's at sea, doing what all sea captains must do, making a living. He sails out of Tangier and is extremely busy delivering goods and fulfilling his contracts to manufacturers in the Mediterranean and the West Indies. Naturally it was hard to part so soon after our wedding, but we had no choice. I'm afraid he will be terribly busy for several more months."

Rosie patted Laurel's knee, her face awash with sympathy. "Ye're a brave woman to come alone, to carry on without your man beside you. But Skye wrote me that ye were a very smart lady and a good businesswoman. Rest assured, the folks from Kylerhae will do all they can to ease your loneliness and make ye feel at home."

Laurel sighed in relief. Telling her tale hadn't been as difficult as she had thought, but there was one more thing she needed to say. She leaned near Rosie's ear and whispered, "And I'm expecting a baby in May." Her smile quivered a bit, but she was pleased at Rosie's round-eyed approval.

Again, Rosie patted her knee. "That's grand, Miss— Mrs. Sinclair. Just grand. Just what we need on Skye. A new bairn to bring us good luck in the future."

With her secret out, Laurel felt a load lift from her shoulders. She would get through this with Rosie and Kenneth to help her. She must concentrate now on getting acquainted with her neighbors and putting her new home in order. Then she could relax and look forward to the arrival of her parents—and her child. She had wept oceans over Cheyne Sinclair, and might do so again. But since he didn't want her, she must find some way to accept what couldn't be changed and go on with her life.

·30·

Laurel threw herself into the challenges before her with the same determination and single-mindedness she had always used in running Caldwell Shipping.

Her first inspection of the castle built of gray whinstone on a jut of land above the sea had fired her imagination and captivated her interest beyond her expectations. She had found the structure run down, but terribly romantic, with its massive baronial hall furnished with family antiques. The upstairs private rooms would be charming and livable once the furniture was dusted and the narrow window panes shining. Soon she and Rosie and Kenneth MacCrae were on a first-name basis, and serious cleaning and polishing were under way.

Laurel selected for her own the bedroom with an expansive view of the sea, then persuaded the MacCraes to occupy the downstairs quarters, which were spacious and comfortable. Also she was quick to employ the MacCrae's three teenage children, their two lively girls as housekeepers, and their son, Bruce, as stable manager. She toured the village, introducing herself to the locals and invited them all to visit any time they could. Though they were bashful and hesitant at first, she was sure she would soon win them over. She arranged for permanent docking for the *Star* at Kylerhae. From here, Captain Harding could begin exploring the possibilities of buying goods to trade in New Orleans. Later he would sail to London and take on additional merchandise before he returned across the Atlantic.

In late September, the mild weather took a sudden turn for the worse. A cold rain raked the island, a sure portent of things to come.

Laurel decided it was time for her first soirée. She had Kenneth post a general invitation to the townspeople, and she herself personally called on the dressmaker and the baker and the resident midwife to request their attendance.

On the eve of the occasion, as the chilly day turned into an even colder night, she strolled around the vaulted banquet hall and checked the table to make certain the feast was ample and attractive. Unfortunately she had found a scant variety of foodstuffs on the island. How she longed for the many delicacies available at her New Orleans market. She would make a point to import some of her favorites to share with her new Scots friends and neighbors.

On the other hand, beef, pork, lamb, fish, and freshly baked bread and pastries were readily obtainable. Regardless of the simplicity of the fare, there was at least plenty to eat at her first party on Skye. One notable addition was a quantity of excellent Scots whisky brought over from the mainland.

Dressed in her newly created forest green woolen frock, she stood by the carved double front doors and greeted her guests personally as they arrived. After a word of welcome to each, she directed them into the hall warmed by a blazing fire near the center of the room. Soon the party of over sixty guests was in full swing and pipes and fiddles began to fill the air with song. Chairs were pushed back and dances began as the wine and whisky helped everyone to relax in their impressive surroundings.

Laurel slipped away and slowly climbed the stairs. She would get a fine view of the proceedings from the second-story landing, then return later when tankards would be hoisted in tribute to the new owner of Strathmor Castle.

Gazing down, she thought of what it must have been like for Skye Mackinnon to grow up in such a place. She knew her cousin had been happy here, surrounded by her family and many friends in the village. She sensed these were good people, austere perhaps, even narrow in their views, but they deserved better than they were getting from their English overlords. No wonder Skye's mother, Elizabeth, had made her special cause helping the poor. They did indeed need a champion in this changing world.

A vision of Cheyne Sinclair pushed itself into her mind. What was he doing this very instant? Did he ever think of her? She had received one letter from him since her arrival. It had been polite, distant, and contained a generous draft from his French bank account. She had sent him a thank-you note, not at all convinced her letter would find its way to Tangier anytime in the near future. He seemed so far away, in another world, a place that only existed in her dreams. But reality was growing inside her, making its small presence known. She questioned again if she should have told Cheyne about the baby. No, her decision had been the correct one. Cheyne wanted a child, an heir, not a wife or the burden of child rearing. His admission that he treasured his freedom and his way of life above everything made that perfectly clear.

Her husband was a pirate to the marrow of his bones. And she was desperately in love with him.

"To Mrs. Sinclair!" came a voice from below.

She ended her unhappy musing and lifted her hand in response.

The cries multiplied and echoed around the walls. "Here, here. To Mrs. Sinclair, the lady of Strathmor Castle."

A lady with no lord, she thought bitterly. Then she smiled and descended the stairs. The last thing she wanted was to be put on a pedestal and worshipped from afar. She was already fond of the people of Skye. She was searching for ways to help them economically, so they wouldn't be forced to emigrate or starve. The ladies did exquisite needlework. She was devising a plan to import cotton and indigo from Louisiana and set up a cottage industry of sewing and lace making. She needed these people as much as they needed her. They must take the place of her own family and her husband. At least, for the foreseeable future.

March 1843

Cheyne lifted the young African girl in his arms and slogged through the surf to the shore. All around him, the freed slaves were shouting and laughing and splashing through the waves to the sandy beach. Behind him, the *Monsoon* lay at anchor, awaiting only the return of its captain before returning to its home port in the north.

"There you are, child," he murmured, setting the thin little creature on her feet.

She smiled up at him, then touched her eyes to catch her tears. She spoke to him in her native dialect, but words were not necessary for his heart to be moved by her look of relief and gratitude. He doubted if she would have survived the journey to the Americas. He considered his immense satisfaction at saving even this one life plenty of reward for the expense and danger of his enterprise.

This time he had saved four hundred people from human bondage.

Looking around, he watched as the nearly naked men, women, and older children swarmed ashore, hugging, crying, and collapsing under the trees. They were home, or near enough to make their way if they so desired. Quickly, he spun and started back toward the rowboat where Rafi waited. Once they had regrouped, the natives would likely want to offer him thanks, but he found that awkward and embarrassing. All he wanted now, after the tension of boarding the Spaniard's ship and convincing an irate slave trader that he must either gave up his booty or his life, was his bed, a good meal, and a quick trip back to Morocco.

Rafi gave him a hand climbing into the skiff.

"Well done, *mon capitaine.*"

"Another successful raid, Rafi. Let's go home."

Rafi leaned in to the oars and moved through the swells. Overhead the sun beat upon the men's bare shoulders and dried the sweat from their brows. "We should be in Tangier within five days," Rafi grunted. "You should take a rest, my friend. You've grown thin, and your eyes are sunken like craters. I wonder if you've recovered from the beating you took from Saad's ruffians."

"That was a long time ago," said Cheyne, closing his eyes and wiping salt spray from his cheek.

"But you haven't rested since. This is the sixth expedition in as many months."

"And the most successful."

"True, but you're killing yourself with the strain."

"I can't stomach the thought of a ship slipping by me. Not when I see how the poor devils are treated, bound like dead fish in rows below decks, with not one bit of human compassion to ease their suffering. God will have a special place in hell for slave traders, Rafi. If there is a God," he added bitterly.

"Of course, there is. God. Allah. A supreme lord above all."

"How can you be so sure?" Cheyne squinted at they neared the *Monsoon*.

"I prayed to Allah for a gift. And my prayer has been answered."

This was something new. Cheyne looked at his lieutenant. "What did you pray for?"

"A son. And now he is growing in Nicole's belly."

"Rafi! You rascal, you didn't tell me."

"I wanted to wait until after the expedition. Now that it's done, we both can celebrate."

The boat bumped against the rope ladder at the *Monsoon's* bow.

"Aye. We will indeed. No time like the present." Cheyne climbed aboard, waved to his crew to raise anchor, and headed for his cabin with Rafi close behind.

He poured himself a brandy and Rafi a spiced orange tea. "Here's to four hundred free souls and to the birth of your son in—when will it be?"

"September. Six months hence."

"Excellent. Nicole will make a fine mother."

Rafi quaffed his drink and wiped his lips with the back of his hand. "She's been eager for a babe, especially after—"

Cheyne lounged against the edge of his desk, and ask idly, "After what?"

"Nothing."

The sound in Rafi's voice caught his attention. He was exhausted, but alert to something being withheld from him. "You can tell me, Rafi. We're like brothers, you and I. Did something happen to Nicole I wasn't aware of?"

"No. Only when other women are pregnant, that creates greater desire for a child. If she doesn't have any already, I mean. That's all. I mean, this is what I think."

Cheyne listened to Rafi's muddled explanation. The man was honest to a fault, and now he was lying, or covering up something. Cheyne put down his goblet. "There's something you're not telling me, Rafi, but perhaps 'tis no concern of mine. I must remind you I'm partially responsible for Nicole since I bought her in New Orleans. I've had a feeling, ever since—ever since Laurel left for Scotland, that things haven't been the same between me and Nicole."

"She hasn't been rude to you!" snapped Rafi.

"Of course not. There isn't a rude breath in her body. I've tried to help her forget how we first met, that I bought her and all that. 'Tis past history, and no fault of hers she was in such a plight. She approved of my marrying Laurel. Laurel said Nicole encouraged her from the beginning. But once Laurel was gone, Nicole seemed withdrawn, rather annoyed with me. I suppose she can't understand how I could let my wife go. I suppose she has every right to question the matter."

"She would never question your decisions, *capitaine*. Not after all you've done for us, for everyone. But she does think of Mrs. Sinclair. She misses her, now especially."

Cheyne clenched his teeth. Then he muttered, "So do I. More than I believed possible. Actually, Rafi, I'm thinking of sailing to Scotland."

"What? Oh no, you can't do that. The English would

hang you for certain, if they got their hands on you. The Sea Falcon is more infamous than ever after these last raids. They'd send their fleet to capture the *Monsoon* the minute you were in their waters."

"I wouldn't sail the *Monsoon*. I could find some other way, go in disguise, take one of the smaller vessels. There must be a way a man could sneak into the highlands of Scotland without being discovered."

"You can't be serious."

Cheyne moved to the window and watched the African coastline growing smaller. "Only half serious. I've had just one note from Laurel, thanking me for some funds I sent. She said she's happy and busy. She didn't mention getting a divorce." He breathed deeply. "I can see her face the day we parted. She wanted me to go with her. She asked me, and I coldly refused. I thought my heart would stop at that minute. I hated myself beyond belief."

"You had no choice. But, forgive me if I say you should have explained your decision."

"Then she might have insisted on staying with me. I've told you how I feel about that. I couldn't allow it."

"And now?"

He closed his eyes, but opened them quickly when Laurel's face drifted before him, lovely, disbelieving, agonizing. That look had haunted him every waking and sleeping moment. It would haunt him to his grave. "I don't know. Maybe if I could see her one more time, know she's well and busy and getting on with her life, I would feel better. Before we met, she was planning to get involved in some kind of horse competition in London in July. I think her parents were planning to visit and bring the horse to Scotland. If I could see her before all that, I could part from her knowing all was well. If I don't make the effort, I don't think either of us will be truly free from pain." Under his breath, he added, "I'll never be, but she might find a way."

For a time, Rafi said nothing. Then he spoke. "Perhaps

you're right. It's plain that you're miserable now. You're driving yourself beyond human endurance. Maybe you should go to Laurel in May."

Cheyne didn't turn. "Why May?"

"The seas are free of ice. The Spaniards will have time to cool their tempers over this latest exploit of the Sea Falcon and turn their attention elsewhere. May is a good month to see one's love, and to make decisions. Besides, that's only two months from now. You will need to rest and make arrangements."

Suddenly Cheyne felt his heart lighten as if a stone was lifted off his chest. "You're right. If I go in May, I won't seem impatient, or like I'm intruding on her life. I'll say I had business in Scotland and wanted to see her, to inquire if she is considering the divorce. Aye, 'tis a good plan. I'll surprise her."

With a nod and a grin, Rafi put down his cup and headed above decks.

·31·

Heavy morning fog had just burned away the sun when Laurel heard a commotion outside her study window. Laying aside the bill of lading Captain Harding had posted to her before he left London, she rose awkwardly and moved to peer outside. This view overlooked the mountains and the main causeway leading to Strathmor from the town road. The only access to the castle was along this bridge of land. No doubt a precaution taken by its original builders in case of enemy attack.

Rubbing her back, she was surprised to see a coach pulling away and heading back toward Kylerhae. She could hear voices below, but whomever had arrived was out of sight, moving toward the door off the back hallway. She recognized Rosie's voice, but not the other. It was definitely female.

So she had a guest. Sighing, she settled back into the chair near the peat fire and glanced at the tea tray. It would have to be replenished. She was tired this morning. The active baby inside her had kept her awake much of the night. Two more months and she could hold the little darling in her arms. She would have given much to have blinked and made the time pass in an instant. On the other hand, she still had arrangements to make before she was ready for her lying-in. The midwife in Kylerhae was a dear lady, but Laurel preferred a physician be on hand, just in case. Years ago, Elizabeth Mackinnon had established a clinic on Skye, but in her absence, the place had fallen on hard times like everything else, and now a mainland physician made a stop once a week in the village. Still, he would surely come if the lady of Strathmor Castle sent for him. Also, Laurel had given no attention to preparing the layette for the baby. She had been so busy having gaslights installed in the castle and supervising the rebuilding of the stable and paddock areas that she had almost forgotten the passing of time. Only during the endless winter nights, and especially at Christmas, had she been forced to think about her new status as wife and mother; then, and whenever she was addressed as Mrs. Sinclair. That had taken some getting used to, but she now answered to the name with ease. She had received one more letter from Cheyne, identical to the first, except he included a greater sum of money. She had also received two long letters from her mother, assuring her they would accept her marriage, though everyone was consumed with curiosity over the details, and promising they would sail to Skye as soon as the new ship arrived. Her mother had said the entourage would include herself, Fletcher and Elizabeth Mackinnon, and Badger Wyndford, who would be in charge of the care of Desert Mirage. Unfortunately her father would be forced to stay behind to manage Highgrove Plantation.

Laurel hadn't written her parents about her pregnancy. She figured her sudden marriage to Cheyne Sinclair was enough for them to deal with until they were reunited with her in person. How surprised they would be to arrive on Skye and discover they had a grandchild, as well as a permanently absent son-in-law.

Footsteps sounded on the stairs. Laurel had instructed Rosie to bring visitors to her study. It was much too tiring for her to go downstairs, then climb up them again. Besides, the vaulted main hall was drafty and uncomfortable, not nearly as cozy and welcoming as Elizabeth Mackinnon's former study. Laurel had found much of Elizabeth's reference library intact, and several first drafts of her now famous romantic novels. She left everything untouched, enjoying the connection with her aunt who had given up so much to travel to America with the husband she adored.

She heard Rosie's soft voice, followed by a woman's laughter. So familiar, but surely impossible.

She had started to rise when the door opened to admit a plump woman in deep scarlet traveling attire, wearing a hat with a red plume trailing about her shoulders.

"Shannon!" Laurel leaped to her feet and rushed into her sister's waiting embrace.

When they parted, Shannon's eyes were as wide as silver dollars. "By all the saints, Laurel, child, look at you!"

Laurel was stunned to see Shannon, but Shannon was equally shocked. "Shannon, why didn't you let me know you were coming. Or did you write? The post is so uncertain. My goodness, my goodness," she sputtered, fighting tears of joy.

"No, I didn't write. I didn't want any special preparations. Actually, I just decided on the spur of the moment to take ship to London, then travel here. I thought I might help you do a few things before the rest of the family arrive. But now—why, Laurel, I'm just flabbergasted."

Laurel took Shannon's gloved hand and squeezed it. "I'm so very glad you did. No one could be more welcome. Rosie, fetch tea, will you, dear. And prepare the room next to mine for my sister." She took a deep breath and wiped her eyes. "Do you need to freshen up now, or can you sit first? I have so much to tell you."

Shannon pulled off her gloves and motioned toward the chairs before the fire. "I freshened plenty before I finally caught the ferry to your charming isle. Waited two days while a herd of sheep was being wrestled from the other side of the sound. I declare, this weather is abominable."

"You've seen the worst of it, I suppose. But spring is right around the corner. The creeks are thawing and the roads are passable."

The two settled into armchairs and sat briefly holding hands.

"Laurel, dear. When are you due? Soon, it appears."

"Early May. I've been feeling fine until just lately. Now I'm fat and tired, and my spirits are drooping. But now that you're here, that has changed in a wink. Except being fat," she quipped.

"Mrs. Sinclair." Shannon spoke softly with a touch of awe. "I must say, we were all set on our heels at the news."

"How did our parents take it, Shandy? I've been so worried. Father wrote me an encouraging letter about Cheyne's character, but that didn't mean he would welcome him as a son-in-law. I'm sure many people in New Orleans remember him as a pirate with Jean Lafitte."

Shannon gazed at her for a rather long time. "He *was* a pirate. Our parents know the whole story, and so do I. As for anyone else in New Orleans, I don't think the Caldwells care a flip what they think."

"But they must have said something, to the Beauregards and others. Surely there's been gossip."

"Such a grist of gossip, you wouldn't believe. But father put a piece in the *Picayune* announcing your marriage to the prominent shipping tycoon, Mr. Cheyne Sinclair, of Scotland, Morocco, and Boston. It said the newlyweds would be honeymooning at the bride's private castle and estates on the Isle of Skye, and would likely visit New Orleans in late summer. After that, the busybodies shut their faces and paid their respects. Why, you should see the silver tea set Henry Beauregard sent out as a wedding gift. Just to prove he had no regrets, I suppose."

Laurel laughed, with her hand across her protruding belly. "I love it! Father is a wonder. Mama, too. I'm so relieved they weren't completely mortified."

Shannon grinned back. "You'll never see the day Rebecca Caldwell is mortified. If she was easily upended, I would have been the death of her years ago. No, their only real concern has been about you. Are you happy? Are you well? Just wait till they get *this* news!" She nodded toward Laurel's stomach.

"I know. Oh, Shannon, I've prayed they would understand. It's all really quite complicated. I'm feeling well enough, but I don't think I'll ever be happy again."

"Where is your husband, Laurel, darling?"

"He's in Tangier, I suppose."

"Tangier? With you like this? Isn't he coming for your lying-in? Surely he wants to be with you."

"I don't expect him. I know it looks dreadful that he's not here, but there are reasons."

"I can't think of any reason good enough."

"One that is excellent. He doesn't know I'm having a baby."

"What?"

"I'll start at the beginning."

For once, Shannon looked truly shocked. "Please do, little sister."

"I explained in my first letter home that Cheyne sank the *Star*. Actually, it was an accident. He tried to board us, and when we fought back, one of our old cannons exploded and we went down. He made sure everyone got safely off, but we lost the cargo. Still, he did try to board our ship. That's an act of piracy."

"Normally, yes. But Father said he replaced the ship with a new one and paid you for the lost cargo."

"He did. You probably passed my new ship, *The Star of Tangier,* somewhere on the Atlantic. It should be in New Orleans by now with a load of trade goods from Scotland and England. It should be arriving here with the family around the end of May or the first of June."

"So what happened to bring about the marriage?"

"You remember Nicole?"

"Of course. A beautiful girl. Mr. Sinclair saved her from the auction. Very gallant, I thought."

"The two of us were given quarters in Cheyne's palace in Tangier. You should see it, Shannon. It would take your breath away and suit you to a T. After that, we had to wait for a new ship to be built. Cheyne was . . ." Her voice became dreamy. "Cheyne was a perfect gentleman, incredibly considerate and caring. There was something between us from the beginning. Something drawing me to him." She dropped her eyes to her hands folded across her lap. "I fell in love, Shandy. Really, truly, in love."

Shannon leaned over to pat her hands. "I'm not surprised. Now I have something to tell you. Cheyne Sinclair has loved you for years, worshipped you actually."

Laurel looked up in surprise. "What makes you think that?"

"Remember, I've known him since his days with Lafitte. We're about the same age, and I've kept up with his comings and goings. Two years ago, at my ball at the hotel when you danced with him, I suspected then he was in love with you."

"You did? Why didn't you say something?"

"It didn't seem to matter. He was older, sailing the high seas, dabbling in dangerous matters. I thought you would marry Henry Beauregard and settle down with lots of babies."

Laurel shook her head. "I almost married Henry. That would have been a dreadful mistake, and Cheyne knew it. He saved me from that, at least."

"So why haven't you told him about the baby?"

Laurel bit her lip, then faced Shannon squarely. "The fact is that he doesn't really love me, not with true, lasting love, anyway. It appears you and I were both fooled about that. He wanted me. Maybe he even had strong feelings for me. He made the most outrageous proposal, and then I stunned myself by accepting. He wanted to marry me, and for me to have his child—in exchange for—"

"In exchange for what?"

"My freedom to go and do as I pleased, and a veritable fortune."

Shannon gaped in silence. Then she choked, "I can't believe it. A fortune, you say?"

Laurel pushed up from her chair and picked up a check from her desk. She held it out to Shannon. "This is the second installment; the first deposit was for one hundred thousand pounds."

Shannon's eyes grew wider, if that was possible. "But this is one hundred and fifty thousand—you mean, he's given you *two hundred and fifty thousand pounds?*"

"Indeed he has. Anyway it's in my name in a French bank account. I've barely touched it. I've used an amount equal to my losses caused by the sinking of the *Star* to modernize Strathmor. I don't intend to touch the rest." She resumed her seat. "Once we were wed, he realized he didn't want to lose his freedom. I loved him, and believed I could change him, make him love me as much as I loved him." She rubbed her forehead. Her hand was shaking. "I really don't know what I thought. Maybe I was drugged by the romance of it all. Anyway, I agreed, and for a few weeks I pretended our happiness would last forever. But in the end, he said he'd made a mistake and suggested a divorce."

"But the baby—" Shannon stammered.

"As I said, he doesn't know anything about the baby. I will inform him later, once it's born."

"But he still gave you a fortune? I thought part of your agreement was producing his child, which obviously is taking place."

"I know. I'm not sure I understand either. Maybe he feels guilty because he talked me into marriage. Also he seems to be in awe of Father. He may fear reprisals from him."

Shannon thought for a moment. "Possibly, but I think there's more to it than that. The man is admirable in many ways. I know that for a fact. And my bet is he loves you to distraction."

Laurel felt her heart flutter beneath her ribs. For months she had told herself Cheyne meant nothing to her, but she had to face the truth. She had wanted his love more than anything on earth, and she still did. She had tried desperately to separate *want* from *need*. If she couldn't prevent herself wanting him, at least she could find the strength to rely on herself and live without him. Now Shannon was raising false hopes, touching her most vulnerable depths. "No, I don't think so. Divorce is out of the question now, of course, but I can live independently without his money now that I have a new vessel and can reestablish Caldwell Shipping. I've made contacts with tradesmen in Edinburgh and Glasgow. I hope to put the ladies of Kylerhae to work in some creative way." She cocked her chin. "I don't have to ever see Cheyne again. In fact, I don't expect to. As far as I know, he's continuing as a pirate, which he says suits him nicely."

"He told you he was still a pirate?"

"Yes. He made that very plain. He loves doing it, he said. He wouldn't consider any other occupation."

Shannon gazed at the fire. "Um. Very well, I won't dispute him, but I'd like to speak directly to him. Do you think he'll come to Skye to see you?"

"I wouldn't think so. After all, Cheyne Sinclair is wanted by the English."

"I know he was convicted in England years ago."

"But there is also the earl of Croydon. I can promise you Franklin Trowbridge is after Cheyne. In another wild adventure, I was kidnapped and used as bait to lure Cheyne to his death."

Shannon's eyes were popping. "Kidnapped. My goodness, child, you've had a terrible time."

Laurel rested her hand protectively across her stomach. "He risked his life to save me. That's when I knew for sure I loved him."

"I see. But you won't go back to Tangier?"

"Never. Not after being so rudely sent away."

"Won't he want to see his child, once he learns about it?"

"He may be curious, but he insisted he only wanted a child to bear his name, to be raised in high society in New Orleans. He needs no personal contact with it, he said. I'm convinced now that he has no interest whatsoever in the baby."

Shannon studied her for a time, her expression registering extreme doubt. And no wonder. The tale was like a bizarre fantasy. A cloud passed in front of the sun and the room darkened. Finally, she muttered, "The pieces don't fit. This puzzle isn't solved yet, not by a long shot."

Rosie arrived with a laden tea tray. "I've tidied the bedroom, Laurel. And here's lunch for the two of ye."

"Thank you, Rosie. Though I'm much too excited to eat."

Shannon reached up and pulled a long needle from her

hat, then removed the lavish creation from her head and handed it to Rosie. "You're eating for two, my dear sister," she said firmly. "I can see I've arrived just in the nick of time."

·32·

Easy, boy. Steady now." Cheyne gripped the bridle of his stocky Shetland pony and urged him onto the barge. In front and behind, other passengers were embarking on the ferry for the brief trip to the Isle of Skye. For once, the May rain had quit, and the water was calmer than usual. The crossing would be brief.

Cheyne glanced behind his rickety wagon and saw that Rafi had also come aboard. He had the feeling Rafi was enjoying this adventure, despite his complaints about crude English manners, the constant dampness, and food fit only for camels. As for himself, he thought of nothing but his goal: to see Laurel, to assure himself she was safe and had everything she needed, then to escape back to Morocco.

One thing was certain, no one would recognize him in this shabby garb, posing as a traveling tinker, with his dark-eyed brother as his assistant. The two had sailed to France, then traveled across country to the English Channel. After trading their fashionable clothing for work clothes, they had entered England as itinerant gypsies. They had bypassed London, and headed due north, living simply, rather than spending money that might give them away as people of means. They lied with ease and slept in uncomfortable beds or on the ground under the stars.

Now, they were nearly at their destination. Cheyne's

heart quickened as the ferry left the mainland and moved slowly toward the island rising a short distance away. He was surprised at the height of it, the view of the snow-capped mountain lifting above the rocky shore.

For weeks, he had anticipated his meeting with Laurel. Once he had made his decision to go to Scotland, he found his impatience growing almost beyond control. She hadn't responded to his last note and payment. Maybe she hadn't received it. He must make certain she had the money. The fortune he'd provided her would give her the freedom and kind of life he wanted her to have, the security and comfort she richly deserved. He had even been thinking of telling her he was the Sea Falcon. But the wives of Blaine Caldwell and Kyle Wyndford had not been informed, so he couldn't do so without express permission from Caldwell. He had written asking for that permission, but hadn't yet received an answer. He knew he was giving in to weakness to desire Laurel's high opinion; he should let her continue to think of him as a pirate and a blackguard. But he longed for her to know the truth. Since he wasn't yet able to reveal his identity, he would at least warn her to avoid Franklin Trowbridge. As Mrs. Cheyne Sinclair, she would be open to scorn, considering she was the wife of a man wanted by the authorities.

Arriving at the small waterfront dock at Kylerhae village, he pulled his horse-drawn cart off the ferry and motioned Rafi near. "We'll stable the horse and find an inn. There we can make inquiries, but I'm betting that castle up on the hill is Strathmor."

Rafi shaded his eyes. "Imposing. Do you suppose we could offer to shoe their horses?" His teeth showed white against his dark skin and heavy beard.

"Nay, Rafi. For this one day, I'll put aside my disguise. Remember I'm supposed to tell Laurel I'm on a business trip to Scotland. Just passing through, as it were."

"She'll see through that lie quick enough. No one ever *passes through* this remote spot on earth."

"Perhaps, but I'll try to convince her our visit is merely a side trip. If she learns of our disguise, she might figure out what danger we're in."

"But you told her you were wanted by the English authorities."

"Aye, but not the worst of it. She knows I'm a special target of the earl of Croydon, but not that I'm the Sea Falcon. That's something I must keep to myself for now."

"Whatever you do, at least you have a pleasant day for your reunion. The sun is warm and the breeze caressing as a lover's breath."

"Poetic, as always, Rafi. But this reunion will be strictly business. Or as much as I can make it so."

Rafi's lip curled. "Good luck, my stricken friend. If you can convince her of that, you must switch from pirating to a career on the stage."

Ignoring Rafi, Cheyne located the nearest stable and led his pony and cart inside.

Within the hour, the two men entered a pub on the main street of the village and approached the bartender. Cheyne had put on a decent suit of clothes after sponging off in his room at the Ram's Head Inn. Rafi was similarly dressed and their arrival in the pub drew little attention.

"Excuse me, sir," said Cheyne in a low voice. "I'm inquiring after the new owner of Strathmor Castle. One Mrs. Cheyne Sinclair."

The muscular barkeep continued wiping a pewter mug. "And who be you?" he asked mildly.

"Mr. Hammond Brown. A tourist, you might say."

"Hm. We get more of those nowadays, though why anyone would want to see this isle is odd to me. Can I get you a drink, sir?"

"Nay. I'm rather in a hurry."

"Hurry? To come or go? There willna be another ferry till Tuesday."

Cheyne threw a look at Rafi. "Oh? Three days? I

wasn't aware of that. I assumed they traversed the sound every day. Perhaps several times."

"Nay, sir. Ye're here now, and bound to stay till Tuesday."

"Very well. Now, tell me if that is Strathmor Castle on the hill."

"It is. The lady of the castle is Mrs. Sinclair. A fine lady and fair."

"Ah, so I've heard. I don't know her, of course, but we have some mutual acquaintances in America. They asked me to look in on her if I came this way."

"She's not receiving guests these days. Hasn't since the first of May."

"Is that so? Isn't she well?"

The barkeep finished wiping the mug and turned his back to put it on a shelf. "Well enough for a new mum, I suppose. Just had the wee one two weeks ago. So ye're not likely to see her this visit."

Cheyne grabbed the edge of the bar. Something exploded under his ribs and his throat contracted. "What did you say?"

The man turned. "I said the lady had a bairn. A boy, they say. The doctor came from the mainland and stayed a week at the clinic. Was a boon to everyone since he tended all our ills while he was here. Now if ye——"

Cheyne's ears were ringing. He felt Rafi's hand on his arm, but he heard nothing else the bartender said. Laurel had a baby. His baby. A boy. She must have known all along she was pregnant, but she didn't tell him, not when they parted, and not in her note. Why had she kept this secret? *Why? Why?* The question burned his brain and tore through his heart. Did she hate him so much she would hide this most critical event from him? Shakily, he inquired, "You said Mrs. Sinclair was doing all right? She—she came through the ordeal without difficulty?"

"As far as I know. Haven't seen her about, of course."

"Who was with her? I mean, what about *Mr.* Sinclair?"

"Guess he's an odd bloke. Hasna been here a'tall since the lady arrived. They say he's a rich sea captain, busy sailing the seas. But I say a man's place is with his wife at such a time. The poorest crofter wouldna abandon his lady when she's bearing his first son."

"My God." Cheyne clenched his fists, then slowly looked at Rafi, who was watching closely.

"Let's sit," muttered Rafi. "Mister, bring us two whiskys."

Cheyne moved woodenly to a small round table by the window. Sinking into a chair, he stared into space, trying to recover from the shock of the news. He had a son. Laurel and he had created a child together. His emotions leaped inside him like jagged thunderbolts, thrusting him from the heights to the depths and back again, leaving him in staggering confusion. This changed everything. There could be no divorce now or ever. He must live only for his wife and his child. But how? Where? What was best for them?

A stiff shot of Scottish whisky settled his nerves. He looked across at a silent Rafi. "I don't know what to say. I have to see her. To try to make this up to her. Do you suppose any of her family are here? Hell, I may walk into Strathmor Castle only to encounter a bullet from Blaine Caldwell. One I thoroughly deserve."

"Don't be too hard on yourself, *mon capitaine*. After all, she hid the truth from you. I hardly call that fair."

"Maybe she didn't know she was pregnant when she left. Maybe she—dammit, I don't know what to think." Cheyne put his head in his hands.

"I believe all will be well. Keep in mind an old proverb of the Berber: *A soft tongue can take milk from a lioness.*"

Abruptly suspicious, Cheyne looked up. "Rafi, you don't seem terribly surprised. Did you know anything about this? I remember when I first said I'd come to Scotland. I thought you were hiding something, but I figured it was none of my business. Dammit to bloody hell, Hamid, did you know?" He pinned Rafi's wrist to the table.

"I knew."

Cheyne pushed to his feet, splattering their drinks. "I ought to flog every inch of the hide off you, you conniving Arab. How could you know and not tell me. After we've been like brothers, after—"

"Calm yourself, *mon ami*. I can explain." His voice was controlled and firm. "Besides, you're calling attention to us. That's not very wise."

Cheyne sank back to his chair. "Your explanation had better be good. Also, you discouraged me from coming sooner. I could have been here, been with Laurel." He swallowed another curse and tightened his grip on Rafi.

"My first duty is to my honor and to my wife's honor. Do you agree to that?"

"Perhaps. It depends," he said coldly.

"Mrs. Sinclair told Nicole she believed she might be pregnant. That was the day before she left for Scotland. She made Nicole swear on the Koran not to tell you. She said it might not be so, but she believed she was. Nicole took a solemn oath not to tell you, but she hadn't sworn not to tell *me*. But of course, I was forced to honor my wife's pledge. Also, I had to respect your wife's wishes. I assumed there was some important reason Mrs. Sinclair withheld the news. And I decided it would be wrong for me to interfere. But when you said you would come to Scotland, I believed you should do it, and then you would see for yourself whatever the truth might be. I assumed if Mrs. Sinclair expected a baby and wanted you with her, she would have written asking you to come. If she didn't want you here, I didn't want to be the one to upset her plans."

"You bastard," Cheyne snarled, but his fury was easing. "I suppose it doesn't matter now. She's had the child while I toyed my way across England and Scotland pretending to be a gypsy. "I'll just have to see her and decide what's to be done next." He stood and slapped coins on the table. "Stay here. I don't want to see your face until I'm good and ready. I'm going to Strathmor and I may or may not return. If you don't hear from me in three days, take the bloody ferry back to the mainland and escape to France. Just remember if you get back to Morocco that Tamerlane belongs to my wife—and to my son!" He slammed out the door and strode up the road toward the castle.

Laurel was relaxing in the nursery, writing in a journal she had tried to keep up to date, and glancing often at the sleeping babe in its cradle near the hearth. Her breasts were sore and tender; soon her darling would awaken and be hungry. She anticipated the moment with relish. He was a healthy beautiful boy. Nothing in her life had prepared her for her feelings toward him. He was a part of her, and a part of the man she loved. She thought she would name him Cheyne Dufour Scott Sinclair. Dufour had been her grandfather, though the wealthy New Orleans gentleman had had the bad luck to die before he made her grandmother his legal wife. Her son had been born in Scotland, and of course, she must fulfill her bargain to her husband by giving him the name of Cheyne Sinclair. After all, Cheyne had paid hugely for the privilege of continuing his family name.

Glancing at the window, she was pleased to see the day was a fine one. For the first time since the birth, she felt a return of her energy. Soon she must be out and about, checking on the new stable and preparing rooms for her family, who would arrive in weeks. Shannon had gone to the kitchen to supervise luncheon. My, what would she have done without Shannon. Her sister had been a godsend through it all. She had stayed by her side the night the pains started and made certain both the midwife and the doctor had been promptly summoned. The birth had been quite routine, they had said, and Laurel remembered little of it, except the incredible moment when she heard her baby's first cry.

She began to hum, then rock the crib, admiring once again the innocent little face with its rosebud lips and wisps of dark hair. Oh yes, she saw Cheyne's features there. Perhaps the very best thing Cheyne Sinclair had done was to create this new life for her to love and succor. She had this much of her elusive pirate, and it would be enough.

Cheyne knocked on the huge double doors at the end of the land bridge leading from the road. He didn't know if this was the front or the back of the place, and he didn't care. Nor did he know exactly how he'd present himself to whomever answered. His heart was pounding with anticipation. Laurel was within this structure. And so was his son.

The door was pulled open by Shannon Kildaire.

·33·

Miss Kildaire!"

"Glory be!"

Cheyne removed his hat. "'Tis good to see you, ma'am. Maybe you won't shoot me before I can explain."

"Come in. No, I won't shoot you. In fact, you're the answer to my prayers."

Cheyne was enormously relieved. If Shannon Kildaire was on the premises, not only was Laurel in excellent hands, but he might have a friend in his corner. He and Miss Kildaire had been acquainted for years and had recently worked together to fight the slave trade. She was one of the few who knew he was the Sea Falcon, and she had always offered him her complete support. On the other hand, this business of his marrying her sister and being absent during the birth of their child would naturally cause her deep concern.

Wearing her usual gaudy attire, Shannon led him into a small room off the hallway containing a cluttered desk and two straight-backed chairs. "This is the office. Serves for everyone from the majordomo to the stable manager. Take a seat and let's talk plainly before you see my little sister. I must say, I do have a few questions. Like, how did the two of you get into this mess in the first place?"

"Hasn't Laurel explained?" he asked, taking the chair opposite her.

"She has. But I want to hear your side."

"Let me set one thing straight immediately, Shannon. I love Laurel Caldwell. Always have, always will."

"I thought so."

"I want only the best for her."

"And the best for her is to raise your offspring alone. Right?"

"I can't swear to that. I thought so once, and on a mad impulse, I made her an offer."

"So she said."

"She believed she was in love with me. She sure as hell didn't love Henry Beauregard. But she was engaged to him."

"Not officially."

"What?"

"He wanted her to marry him, but she never said yes to Henry. I know that for a fact."

This was unsettling news. Laurel had told him, or let him assume, she was going to marry Beauregard. "Hm. I had a rather different impression, but maybe I was wrong. Anyway I figured if she was going to marry for money and children, not for love, she might as well marry me. Then she could have what she wanted and not have to put up with—with—"

"With sleeping with a man she didn't care for?"

"I admire your frankness, Shannon. I always have."

"So you offered her a fortune and she accepted. Didn't it occur to you she might fall desperately in love with you? And then you'd break her heart?"

This cut deeply. "I didn't expect it. I knew she was infatuated, but I never expected it to turn to lasting love. When she first told me she loved me, I tried to reverse everything. I was even cold and unkind to her, though it damn near killed me. I thought once we parted, she would pick herself up and go on with her life. But now there's the baby to think about. Laurel deserves better than a jaded old pirate whose future is as uncertain as the wandering wind," he added with a catch in his voice.

"Uncertain because you're the Sea Falcon?"

He stared hard at her. "She doesn't know *that*, does she?"

"No. She thinks you're the pirate you described. You were pretty convincing when you sank the *Star* from under her."

"A terrible accident. I thought it was an American slaver. Anyway, I just planned to board and take a look. Then the blasted antique cannon exploded and down it went."

"I figured that was it. So did my father."

"Mr. Caldwell understood?"

"He's a smart man, Cheyne, and he trusts you completely. He knows what you've risked for the slave enterprise. We all guessed you had mistaken the *Star* for a slave ship."

"That's a relief. I told Laurel I opposed slavery. Otherwise I don't believe she would ever have been friendly to me, much less become my wife. But I couldn't explain about the Falcon without risk to others."

"All this makes sense to me. All except this foolishness about paying Laurel to have your child."

"That was a ploy to get her to marry me and take my fortune. I don't expect to live forever, and I wanted her to have a wonderful life. I did it because I love her, and—truthfully, I wanted her to be mine, if only for a brief time. That's all." He hung his head, feeling like a schoolboy whose mischief has been discovered.

"I declare, Cheyne Sinclair. I thought you had more sense. But love does crazy things to people sometimes."

"So tell me, Shannon, what's the best thing for me now?"

"You're here, and that's what's important. You know, of course, you have a fine son."

"I just learned the news in town at the local pub. I swear I thought I'd pass out right in front of the bar."

"Then you came from Tangier to see Laurel, not knowing about the babe? I find that revealing—very revealing and very touching."

"I had to see her. If only once more. I was going to offer her a divorce if she wanted to be free of our bargain. I've sent the money already; 'tis hers to keep."

"Another display of good character. But isn't it dangerous for you to be in the British Isles? I was in London on my way here, and there was talk of the Sea Falcon. Some think you're a hero. Others want to draw and quarter you."

"Did you see Franklin Trowbridge?"

"No, thank goodness. Why?"

"The scoundrel kidnapped Laurel in a scheme to capture me."

"Laurel told me. Do you think he knows what you're up to?"

"I doubt it. He's been after me ever since my days with Lafitte. But he has no way of knowing I'm the culprit attacking his slavers."

"And what about Laurel?"

"I've kept my true identity a careful secret. In Morocco I kept a close eye on her and separated her from her captain and crew. I moved them out of Tangier right away. I didn't want local gossip about my activities reaching her through them."

"She should be told the truth, Cheyne. Especially under the circumstances."

"I agree. I wrote to Mr. Caldwell asking him if I could tell her. I've not heard back from him yet, and I won't reveal anything until I do."

"So she won't know the risk you've taken coming here."

"I told her there was a price on my head in England. That's true enough."

"But only half the story. How did you get here without getting caught?"

"I traveled in disguise with my lieutenant, who married Nicole, by the way. We've been disguised as gypsies ever since we entered England. 'Tis working so far."

"I'd say you've earned your interview with your wife," Shannon said rising. "She's upstairs with the baby."

A new emotion, much akin to fear, unfurled inside his stomach. "How can I approach her? What can I say?"

"Try *hello*. If she doesn't faint, you'll be off to a good start."

Laurel eased the baby back into its crib. Her nipples still tingled from the gentle tugging as she leaned down and pulled the blanket over the now sleeping child. Her eyes moistened with tender joy as she watched him yawn and then relax into his blue satin pillow. She had started to hum deep in her throat when she sensed she was not alone. She rose, simultaneously splaying her fingers across her breasts. No one was in the castle this morning but Shannon and Rosie and one of Rosie's daughters, assigned to do dusting.

"Hello, Laurel."

Lounging in the shadow of the door frame, his hat in his hand, stood her husband.

For a brief instant, her vision swam crazily. She had dreamed of him for so many months that she doubted her own sanity. "Cheyne?" she whispered.

"I'm afraid so. And let me say I will never again need to admire a painting of the Madonna and Child. My eyes need only remember what I've just witnessed."

Her throat closed. She clamped her lips until she gained a modicum of control. Finally she was able to say, "So you came, after all. You know everything."

"May I come in? Forgive me for observing you, but the door was ajar. I couldn't bring myself to intrude on the vision I was so fortunate to witness."

"Of course." Pulling her plain wool robe together, she motioned him to approach. "As you can see, much has happened since our parting."

He walked into the room. His eyes focused on hers as he walked forward, but when he reached the cradle, he looked down and gazed for several seconds.

She watched him, her heart in her throat. His being here with her, observing their child, was her every wish come true. How thin and tired he looked. Clean-shaven, simply dressed, and more handsome than she'd even remembered. He must have heard somehow about the baby and come to view his child. Perhaps Nicole had let the secret slip. Or maybe news of her pregnancy had leaked all the way to Tangier.

He looked up at her, his eyes heavy with emotion. She would swear he was moved by the sight of his son. If he were not, he would have to be made of stone.

His mouth tilted at one corner. "Darling Laurel. Why didn't you tell me? I would have risked the fires of hell to be with you."

"I wasn't completely sure I was pregnant. And then you said you had changed your mind about our bargain. You said you didn't want to raise the child, at any rate. I wouldn't have wanted to hold you to our arrangement if you were unwilling."

"I had to say something to encourage you to leave. I thought if I was cold and indifferent, you would be more angry than hurt, you might even hate me, then eventually forget about me."

How could he think such a thing? "You believed I was so shallow that I would forget the man I loved? The man who first made love to me? The man I chose to be my husband and the father of my child? You believed I would take your fortune, but forget you existed? Dear heaven, Cheyne, is this the kind of woman you could love?"

He took one step toward her. "I was wrong. I didn't know you well when I made the proposal. I only knew I cared for you and wanted you. I thought you would marry Beauregard for money, so why not me?"

She gasped. "You thought that?"

"I'm sorry, but I did. I couldn't believe you really loved him."

So the lie she had used for protection had caused such great misunderstanding. She had to take some responsibility for creating a wrong impression. "I see. Then I am partly to blame. But I find it appalling you would think I was willing to sell myself to the highest bidder."

"I just admitted I was completely mistaken. I place no guilt whatever on your shoulders, Laurel. I'm the one who must ask your forgiveness." He glanced toward the sleeping infant.

She rested her hand on the edge of the crib. Was she ready to share her child with a man who had treated her so harshly? "So you've come now to see your child."

"I came to see *you*. The baby is a complete surprise,."

She was stunned. "You mean, you didn't know? Nicole didn't tell you?"

"No. She kept her secret, except from Rafi. Neither one said a word."

"Then you came all this way, took such risk, just to see *me?*"

"I did. I've missed you more than I can say. My plan was to merely stop by to see if you were all right, if you had all you needed, and to see if you still wanted a divorce. Now—"

"There will be no divorce. Actually I never wanted one."

He looked at her for a very long time. Then he said, "Nor did I."

"Cheyne—Cheyne, I'm so very glad to see you," she whispered.

"Lass—" He dropped his hat, and in a heartbeat, he moved around the crib and grasped her shoulders. Pulling her to him, he covered her lips, then wrapped her in a fierce embrace.

Fire exploded within her. She flung her arms around him and hungrily received his kiss. Holding him tightly, feeling his arms pressing her body against his, she was consumed with him, his masculine strength, his fresh-scrubbed smell of soap, the roughness of his coat, and most of all, his mouth claiming hers.

With one arm supporting her back, his head fell to her throat, then lowered beneath the open folds of her robe. He brushed her swollen breasts with his lips and his tongue, but didn't touch her nipples. When he raised his head, his own lashes were damp, and he kissed her forehead and one temple before crushing her again in his arms.

"My precious girl. I was a fool to let you go without me. I was afraid our love would destroy your chances for happiness. I continued to believe it until this very second." He tilted her chin. "Whatever else is between us, whatever we are or ever have been, or ever will be, I promise you now and forever, Mrs. Sinclair, you are my dearest, my one and only love."

Laurel sagged against him, feeling tears spilling along her cheeks. After all the months of holding back, burying her deepest feelings, trying to tear her love from her heart, she was free at last to give herself totally to him. Looking up, she memorized his tender expression, the deep emotion shining from his eyes. Nothing could take this moment from her. She would have it forever. "My love," she murmured. "You're home, at last."

"My home has always been with you, Laurel. I suspected it the first time I saw you, remember? But I had challenges to meet, challenges and adventure while you were growing into a wonderful woman. In spite of my efforts to the contrary, you must now accept the burden of owning my heart."

"Never a burden. I've only been waiting for you to realize that."

He eased away, keeping his arm around her shoulders. "I have much to tell you," he said softly.

She started to close her robe, but he stayed her hand. "Allow me the pleasure. I concede a very young lad has first claim now to your lovely breasts, but I will wait. Later, I will return to my rightful place."

She smiled and looked again at the baby who slept peacefully, momentarily satiated, blissfully unaware of his admiring parents. "He is a wonder, isn't he?"

"The most beautiful baby I've ever seen," Cheyne agreed.

"I thought I would name him Cheyne Dufour Scott Sinclair. What do you think?"

"Perfect."

"Cheyne—"

"What is it, lass?"

She edged away. "You do look tired. Have you seen Shannon? How did you first hear about the baby? How did you get here? When—"

"Hold on, my darling. One question at a time." He spoke softly so as not to disturb the baby.

She smiled indulgently. "He won't wake until his next feeding. What about you? Have you eaten today? I'll send for Rosie."

He retrieved his hat from the floor. "Could we have a bite to eat here? I may never leave this room again. Everything that matters to me in the world is in it."

"Of course." She pulled the bell cord she had recently installed, then gave him another hug before they sat on the small sofa near the window.

Rosie appeared almost at once and looked amazed to find a gentleman in residence.

"Rosie, this is my—"

"Excuse me," interjected Cheyne. "Miss, would you come in and close the door behind you."

Rosie did as requested, appearing even more disturbed.

Laurel looked at Cheyne. His manner had changed swiftly from joyful and relaxed to concerned.

He patted her shoulder reassuringly. "I don't want to alarm anyone, but we may as well discuss this together. Rosie, I'm Cheyne Sinclair, Laurel's husband."

Rosie's mouth flew open, then she grinned. "Pleased to meet you, sir."

"Thank you for looking after my wife these past months. I'm deeply grateful."

Rosie tittered.

"The problem is I've just arrived on Skye and I'm on a rather secret mission. I've just introduced myself to the barkeep near The Ram's Head as Hammond Brown."

"Oh, Mr. Brown again?" teased Laurel. "He does make sudden appearances—and disappearances."

Cheyne shook his head. "I know this is a nuisance, but for now I'd prefer no one know I'm here. Do you understand, Laurel, darling?"

Unfortunately she did. Now that he was here, and had pledged his love, it was time to face practical matters. Obviously he was in danger. "I'm sure Rosie will cooperate fully, won't you, Rosie?"

"Mum's the word, ma'am. I'll tell my husband and children, too."

"Thank you," Cheyne responded. "I can't fully explain, but my work is important and secret, and my comings and goings will have to be furtive, I'm afraid. Also, I have a friend with me."

Laurel perked up. "A friend?"

"My second in command. I'm sure you remember him."

"You mean Raf—" She caught herself in the nick of time. "Yes. Your lieutenant. But where is he?"

"At the village inn."

"But he must come here at once. We have dozens of rooms."

"I'll suggest that, but I'm thinking he may return to the mainland for a week or so. That way, if I am caught, he can escape back to Tangier." He gave her a pointed look.

So there was danger. Perhaps grave danger. She stared at Rosie. "Dear, these matters are terribly important. My husband could be trusting you and your family with his life. Do you understand that?"

"Yes'm," Rosie answered solemnly.

"Then go along and bring us something to eat before the baby wakes."

After Rosie was gone, Laurel snuggled into Cheyne's welcoming arms. "In my joy, I forgot about the danger."

" 'Tis an unfortunate fact of life—I am a pirate, after all."

Laurel dreaded her next question. "Does this mean you can't stay?"

For a long while, he didn't answer. Then he said, "I cannot stay. I will have to return to Tangier. I'm afraid I have no choice."

The sun seemed to have left the room. She rested her head on his chest. "Then we'll be parted for a time, but I'll come to Tangier as soon as possible. I won't let anything keep me away from you."

He stroked her hair and kissed the top of her head. "We have much to think about. Perhaps we'll just travel and raise our son as a citizen of the world, at least for the foreseeable future. Later we must consider his place in the scheme of things, his education."

She grinned up at him. "His place in *society*. You see, I haven't forgotten. But now you sound like a doting father. I'd never have believed it."

He glanced at the cradle. "He changed all that."

"I thought I would call him Scott. Scott Sinclair. What do you think? The name has a nice ring to it."

Cheyne leaned near the crib. "He looks awfully small for such a manly title. But, aye, I like it."

She settled against him. "You know I can't leave for Tangier until after my family's visit and the horse competition. Will you be able to stay to greet everyone?" She knew the answer before he spoke.

"Nay, lass. I must be away long before then."

"Then, how long can you stay?"

"Two weeks perhaps. Three at the most. Rafi and I will need to escape back to France as soon as possible."

It wasn't long, but it was like a little piece of paradise laid in her lap. "I see. And how is Rafi? And Nicole?"

He smiled down at her. "Nicole is pregnant. Her baby will be born in the fall."

Laurel grinned. "I'm so pleased to hear it." She took his hand and returned his smile. She should have been completely happy, but she couldn't shake off the feeling that something wasn't right. Cheyne was here and had declared his love. But something was bothering him, something unsaid but hidden beneath his sincere words of love and caring. For the next days they would have together, she would try to ignore the problems they still faced. She mustn't let imagined fears spoil their precious time together.

·34·

Franklin Trowbridge read the letter once more, then crushed it into a ball and tossed it into the fire in his study. Before the coals had time to consume it, he was back at his desk, penning a note to an official in the local sheriff's office asking for an immediate interview.

The earl was extremely pleased. Shazade Amin had

done her work well. The woman had earned every penny she was demanding. Cheyne Sinclair and his lieutenant, Rafi Hamid, were even now in the British Isles. Once Sinclair and his friend were caught and convicted, he would happily send Miss Amin her reward. His only concern was that he must work quickly to capture the two. According to Shazade's letter, the men's plan was to leave Tangier, travel across Spain and France, cross the Channel, and slip into England disguised as gypsy tinkers. Her informer in Tangier said the two would go to the Isle of Skye, then return to Morocco the way they had come. The information also included physical descriptions of both men. Hamid was particularly distinctive with his dark Moorish looks; he would not be hard to spot among Englishmen or Scots.

Trowbridge had his trap well in mind. He would arrange for spies to locate the villains, then the soldiers would swoop in to make the arrest. They would have strict instructions to capture Sinclair alive. Trowbridge knew he might have trouble collecting the reward on the Falcon if there wasn't a confession. The earl smiled to himself. At last, the Sea Falcon had made a fatal mistake.

"Look, Cheyne! Isn't this the perfect place for a pirate to hide his booty?"

Cheyne followed in Laurel's footsteps as she gingerly tiptoed across flat boulders toward a jagged spit of land only a few yards in diameter. The sky overhead was brilliant as polished steel, and for the first time in three weeks, there was no wind at all. The two had spent the day riding the moors and hills beyond the castle, stopping at noon for a picnic provided by Rosie for the occasion. Like children, they played amidst the abundant summer glory, so short-lived, but so spectacular, on this inner island of the Hebrides.

Cheyne laughed as they reached the spit and pulled Laurel against him, as he was inclined to do at every opportunity.

She returned his kiss, then whirled away and climbed the rocks to the far side. "Hurry," she called. "I must show you my secret place before the tide comes in."

He caught up with her and took her hand. "I've seen your secret place, my love. Don't forget that."

Giggling, she raised her eyebrows in mock horror. "So say you. Now duck your head. Just wait till you see what's inside."

Smiling at his exuberant wife, so wonderfully childlike at this moment, he allowed her to lead him under a ledge behind a stunted shrub and into a cave carved into the rock. Indeed, it was an amazing spot. He could stand with only the top of his head brushing the curving stone above and there was room to walk in a large circle. The atmosphere here was cool and pungent, almost like being under water, but with plenty of air to breathe. From some hidden aperture above, light streamed in, giving the enclosure an eerie sort of blue-green sheen.

"What do you think?" Laurel asked excitedly. "Do you have any treasure to hide? You'll need a dead man, though. You know, bones to mark the spot. That's how it's done in all the pirate books."

He pulled her roughly to him. "Aye, my beauty, and you're my victim." He chortled and gave her an evil sneer. Bending one arm behind her back, he kissed her until she struggled for breath. "There, take that. Now beg for mercy, but I will give you no quarter. I have you precisely where I want you."

She jumped away and whipped an imaginary sword from an invisible scabbard at her side. Taking up a defensive stance, she grinned at him. "Ah, ha! You didn't know you would be crossing swords with the infamous Lady Hawk, I reckon. *En garde,* my hotheaded demon. You'll find you've met your fate at last."

He swept out his own pretend sword and circled her. He was so intent on the game, he suddenly banged his head on a jutting rock.

"Oh, my poor pirate," she crooned, rushing to enfold him. "Are you hurt?"

"Only my pride. But as you can see, I've dropped my weapon and am completely at your mercy, Lady Hawk."

She threw her arms around his neck and slowly they sank together to the sandy floor of the cave.

He rolled her atop him and held her there, then trapped her lips and accepted her kiss while her hair made a bower around their heads. He wanted her. The stress in his groin was more demanding than ever. He moved his hands down her spine, feeling her waist, not as narrow as before the baby, but still tantalizing. Then he covered her buttocks, feeling their tension beneath her filmy skirts.

"I'm sure it would be all right to make love now," she whispered. "I asked the doctor yesterday and he said yes. It's been more than a month since the birth, after all."

"You're sure?" he said, feeling his swollen maleness pressed hungrily against the conjunction of her legs. He could still retreat, but he prayed he wouldn't have to. Holding her, caressing her both day and night these past three weeks had been exquisite torture, but he wanted her to know how much he adored her. He was willing to pay any price after what she had been through to present them with their son.

"Yes, my darling. Why do you think I lured you to my hideaway? Mine, and Skye's when she was a child, and her mother, Elizabeth's, many years ago. I wouldn't have known it was here if they hadn't shared their special secret with me."

"They indeed have my gratitude," he murmured, then lifted her and nuzzled the hollow of her throat.

With an impish look, she sat up, straddling him, and began to untie the strings of her bodice. The sight of her full breasts suspended over him sent him spiraling beyond any hope of recovery. He cupped them, raised his head to sweep over them with his tongue, but he did not suckle. The nipples and their life-giving milk was for his son alone.

When he started to roll over, she stopped him. "No, I want to stay like this."

He was amazed at her boldness. Amazed and delighted. "Then I am your willing slave. Do with me as you will."

With her sly smile almost lost in shadow, she unfastened his belt, pulled out his shirttail and opened the buttons of his breeches. She ran her fingers over his chest, massaged his shoulders, and bent occasionally to plant swift kisses on his cheeks and chin and bare body.

Groaning, lifting his hips upward, he wondered how long he could stand this divine torture. "You'd better kill me," he muttered, with his eyes firmly closed. "Otherwise I may revenge this agony by ravishing you, my lady. At any second now."

Her response was to open his breeches and clasp his straining manhood.

He dug his fingers into the sand and groaned. "My God, Laurel."

Then she was over him, accepting him, lowering herself onto him, making soft noises deep in her throat.

He grasped her shoulders and whispered, "You're mine, my darling."

She stopped his words with a kiss and pressed downward.

Some time later, Laurel moved drowsily, aware now of a rising wind beyond their hidden seaside grotto.

"Are you awake?" Cheyne murmured, getting to one elbow and offering her a look that sent warmth to her very soul.

"Did I sleep?"

"Aye, Lady Hawk. For a time."

She sat up abruptly. "My, we must go. Scott will need me."

"The wet nurse is on hand for times like these."

"Yes, but all the same—"

"Of course. I'm only teasing." He helped her to her feet. A cool wind from the cave's aperture caught at her skirts as she fastened her bodice.

As they left, Laurel turned for one last look. "My Aunt Elizabeth told me she once came here to write her romantic tales. I'm glad we made love in this magical place."

Cheyne grasped her hand. "Magic indeed. We'll come again someday."

Once they had hurried across the string of boulders to their waiting horses, they mounted in silence and rode swiftly toward Strathmor. Before they arrived, large raindrops were starting to pummel them.

Shannon met them in the kitchen. "It's about time you scalawags showed up. I was about to send Bruce to scour the island."

Nothing could detract from Laurel's warm glow. "I'm sorry, Shandy. Don't scold us." She threw Cheyne a secret look of pleasure and started toward the stairs as he poured coffee into a cup.

"Laurel!" Shannon's voice stopped her.

She knew instantly something was wrong. "What is it?" she said, spinning on her heel.

"A messenger came from the village. I have bad news."

Laurel rushed back into the kitchen. "What?"

Shannon looked first at her, and then at Cheyne. "The messenger was sent by an innkeeper on the road toward London. It was only a scrap of paper, not even sealed. It was for Cheyne, and I couldn't help reading it." She handed a rumpled piece of paper to Cheyne.

Laurel watched his face and knew something dreadful had happened. Her former euphoria evaporated in an instant.

"It's Rafi," Cheyne said quietly. "He's been caught."

* * *

Laurel watched Cheyne throw several items of clothing into a canvas bag. She hadn't asked him not to go, even though she felt like throwing herself at his feet and begging him to stay, to think only of her and their baby. She knew that would be as useless as it would be unfair.

When he finished, he pulled the bag shut and reached for his hat. He turned to her, and she had never seen his face so stark and so grim. "Looks like I'm Hammond Brown again."

Swallowing her misery, she kept her seat on the edge of the bed, her hands folded in her lap. "What will you do? How will I know what's happening?"

"I'm going first to talk to the innkeeper who sent the message. Rafi was in custody with English soldiers when they stayed at the inn, but still a week's journey from London. Rafi slipped him the note. He must have felt the innkeeper could be trusted."

"Few Scots are sympathetic to British causes. Rafi was very clever."

"In the note, he told me not to come after him, but of course, I must find out what happened. I can't imagine why the English would arrest him. Even if they discovered he was from Morocco, they have no proof he was connected to me, or had ever pirated English ships. It's very mysterious."

"I think it's a trap. It's *you* they want."

He put on his hat. "That may be, but I'm more clever than they think. I won't get caught, but I have to get Rafi out of their clutches."

It was all she could do to hide her panic. "Please come back soon, or let me know where you've gone. I feel it's my fault you lingered here longer than was safe."

He walked over and placed his palm on her cheek. "I and I alone make such decisions for myself, Laurel darling. What we shared today made any risk worthwhile. One thing I must demand of you."

"What's that?" she dragged the words from her throat.

"You mustn't come looking for me if I should disappear, unlikely as that might be."

"How can you ask that of me? Of course——"

"Listen to me. We have not only ourselves, but our child to consider. You know I'm considered a scoundrel and an outlaw in England. I will make sure I'm not arrested, if for no other reason than to spare you and our son the scandal of being connected to a man with such an evil reputation. I will elude capture, or I will die."

A sob escaped her, but she hung on to her emotions. "Cheyne——"

He gave her a half smile. "Nay, don't look so desolate. We'll come through this. God wouldn't be so cruel as to abandon us after we've found such happiness. Farewell, my love. I will make contact again as soon as 'tis safe."

She moved into his arms, but found no comfort, only abject misery. One quick kiss and he was out the door. The squall outside the stone walls halted to gather force, than raged again in renewed fury.

Cheyne traded his pony and cart for the swiftest horse in the stable. He hired a boat to take him to the mainland and rode directly to the inn, ignoring the intermittent rain and the black moonless night. He had gotten Rafi into this mess and he must extricate him at all costs. Not only because he owed that to his friend, but because he well knew the English were capable of torturing information from almost anyone, even a man as courageous as Rafi Hamid. If Rafi were put to the question, he would likely reveal Cheyne's identity as the Sea Falcon. That would mean death for them and exposure of their scheme to all the world. Repercussions could travel all the way to America. At the very least, there would be no more rescues at sea for the poor Africans on their way to the slave markets.

Cheyne's brief rest at the inn and his visit with the innkeeper confirmed that Rafi was indeed being taken to

London. As soon as Cheyne had rested a few hours and purchased a new horse, he headed south. With luck, he could catch up with the soldiers. If his guess was accurate, he would ride into a trap. Laurel had been right about that. Cheyne was positive he was the one the authorities wanted. But how had they known he was in the country? And how had they connected him to Rafi Hamid?

For three days, he kept up a killing pace. Shortly before dusk on the fourth day he spotted a contingent of soldiers jogging along the road ahead of him. Only hours before, they had crossed the border into England. He reined in and trailed them, sizing up the situation.

Gradually, he closed the space between them. When he could hear their voices, he slowed and trailed along until they rounded a turn and he got a good look at them: six uniformed soldiers with a dark-haired, bearded captive in their midst.

Rafi. Cheyne knew he must make his move at once. If he could extricate Rafi, he would send him racing for the Channel and France. As for himself, he would not be taken captive. He would die, here on this deserted road, in a hail of English gunfire. There was no other choice.

He drove his mount into the nearest trees and rode hard until he was certain he was ahead of the soldiers. Then he pulled a scarf over the lower part of his face and retrieved both pistols from his belt. He took up a position before the oncoming contingent. Rafi would know what to do, Cheyne figured.

The lead soldier rode into view.

"Halt!" ordered Cheyne, and aimed both pistols at the man's chest.

The soldier reined up and lifted his arm to stop the others. "What do you want, brigand?"

Cheyne trotted forward. "Move aside. I want a word with your prisoner."

"A visit, eh? Very well, but make it fast." Without

further argument, the soldier guided his horse to the side of the road.

Cheyne knew immediately he had ridden into a trap. Someone knew he and Rafi were in England. How they knew, he had no idea, but he must try to save Rafi. "Order your men out of my way," commanded Cheyne.

"Stand back!" yelled the officer.

Cheyne rode forward, then halted a few feet from Rafi, who was watching with his hands bound before him.

"I told you not to come," Rafi growled. "I can handle this."

"No doubt. But I won't be denied the pleasure of saving your worthless hide one last time."

Rafi leaned forward. "They want *you*," he whispered urgently. "You'll die."

"I know that," answered Cheyne under his breath. Then he shouted. "This man is going free or two of you are dead. Is that understood?"

"Understood," shouted the soldier who faced Cheyne's gun barrel. "He can go, for all we care."

"Get out of here, Rafi. You know where to head."

Rafi snatched his horse's reins. "I'll be back for you."

"Nay," said Cheyne in a low tone. "I won't be waiting. Go to Tamerlane. You have much responsibility now."

For a brief second, he held Rafi's dark gaze. Understanding flowed between them. Rafi knew Cheyne intended to die, here and now. It was Rafi's job to return to Tangier and carry on the work of the Sea Falcon. "Go with Allah," Cheyne muttered.

Rafi dug in his heels and spun the horse off the road and through the trees.

Cheyne waited several heartbeats, then jammed a pistol in his belt and gathered the reins. He backed away, then pivoted his mount. As he had expected, all hell broke loose. In an instant, the soldiers drew their weapons and bore down on him.

But they didn't shoot.

Over his shoulder, he fired at the nearest soldier, hoping to force him to return fire.

The man yelled instead. "Don't try to escape, Sinclair! We have you."

Cheyne knew he had been right. They knew his identity; they had been expecting him. They intended to take him alive.

"Don't kill him!" shouted the officer. "Or Croydon will have every man's skin."

Leaning forward, Cheyne kicked his horse. Shots rang out and the animal stumbled, then fell. Cheyne was thrown to the ground, his breath knocked from him. Before he could clear his head and get to his feet, he was surrounded. A rope went around his neck. Strong hands forced him to his knees as his hands were bound and shackled with chains. His worst nightmare had come true. They had him. He had heard Croydon's name and realized the earl had set this trap. The bastard had his victory at last.

·35·

Laurel stood on the Kylerhae dock, her arms full of wild pink roses and purple heather. Beside her, in his best suit, and wearing a red and green Mackinnon plaid sash and bonnet, stood Kenneth MacCrae. Next to him stood his wife, Rosie, so excited she could hardly contain herself. Surrounding these dignitaries was the entire population of the area: villagers, crofters, the minister, and dozens of children of all ages.

As the two skiffs bringing the guests from *The Star of Tangier,* anchored in the bay, drew near the dock, pipes whined into life and drums rat-a-tatted a welcoming tattoo. "Over the Sea to Skye" was the song of choice to honor the arrival of the former laird of Mackinnon, who had not been replaced since he had left these shores two years earlier.

Laurel was thrilled to see the safe return of her ship, to know at last she would be reunited with her relatives. But her joy was tempered by her deepening worry over Cheyne. Since he'd made his hasty exit three weeks before, there had been no word, directly or indirectly.

She had spent every waking hour in preparations for her family's arrival. Staying extremely busy with the house and the stables had eased her burden a bit. But at night she had tossed and turned, gazed endlessly at the moon-splashed seascape beyond her window, and prayed over and over that Cheyne was safely out of the clutches of the English authorities. Had it not been for the imminent arrival of her mother and family members, she would have gone to London herself to make inquiries. But she dared not leave the island, and there was the baby to consider. If all went as planned, she would be going to London in two weeks, at any rate. The horse competition was scheduled for July twentieth. She no longer had much interest in the race, considering the recent turn of events, but it would give her an excuse to find out if anyone knew anything about her husband.

"Look," cried Shannon. "Mother is in the first boat, next to Fletcher and Elizabeth. What do you suppose the Mackinnons are feeling at this moment?"

Laurel wondered, too. Fletcher had been laird when he left everything behind. Now he was returning as a guest to his own land, to a home and property that had belonged to the Mackinnons for generations. Fletcher's irascible Scottish father had died in a tragic accident at Strathmor, thereby setting off a chain of events that had nearly cost Fletcher his life. Although the blood ties between the Caldwells and the Mackinnons were distant, relatives were relatives. Laurel loved and admired Fletcher and Elizabeth and wanted to make every effort for their comfort and happiness in their former home.

Standing back, she allowed the Kylerhae mayor to exercise his authority by being the first to welcome the Mackinnons ashore. Next to alight from the skiff was Laurel's mother. It was all Laurel could do not to rush forward at once and give her hugs and kisses. This was Rebecca's first visit to her own mother's native land in many years, and her first to Skye. Rebecca was smiling broadly from beneath her wide-brimmed straw hat as she held up her skirts and stepped to the dock.

But dignity must be maintained. As the music of pipe and drum filled the air, Kenneth MacCrae greeted Fletcher with a formal handshake, then the two men embraced. Fletcher looked marvelous. He was a head taller than anyone present and had pulled his long hair back and tied it at the nape of his neck. He also wore the Mackinnon tartan draped over his shoulder and a Glengarry bonnet identical to the mayor's.

The second skiff to arrive brought a beaming Captain Harding and young Badger Wyndford, who leaned precariously against the gunwales in his excitement. Somewhere below decks on *The Star of Tangier* waited the special guest of honor, Desert Mirage.

Laurel could contain herself no longer. Rushing forward, she smiled tearfully and handed her bouquet to Elizabeth Mackinnon, then turned to her mother. Breaking down at last, she wept unashamedly in her mother's close embrace.

"Laurel, darling," Rebecca said, stepping back to study her. "Let me look at you. My goodness, you've filled out. You look marvelous. Is your husband here?"

Laurel shook her head, but found the courage to smile. "Oh Mama, I've so much to tell you."

Shannon approached and received a similar hug from her adopted mother.

Laurel turned to officially greet Fletcher and Elizabeth, who were surrounded by weeping and cheering old friends. "We'll have a reception at the house tomorrow," Laurel called to Elizabeth. "I have carriages waiting."

Elizabeth nodded and grasped Fletcher's arm.

Soon all the family was loaded into two open carriages, heading for the castle under a cloudless blue sky.

Everyone was talking at once. Laurel, her mother, and Shannon were in the lead carriage and in minutes they alighted at the causeway leading to Strathmor. Laurel had just enough time to whisper to her mother that she had a very great secret to share and that she would explain later about Cheyne.

After they paraded inside and were welcomed by the staff, led by Rosie's three offspring in their best bib and tucker, they drifted into the main hall where a feast was spread and a fire blazed, despite the summer warmth outside.

Laurel turned to give Elizabeth and Fletcher her undivided attention. "My darling Mackinnons, consider this your home as it always was. Please don't think of yourselves as guests."

Elizabeth held out her arms and turned in a circle. "But it's marvelous, Laurel. You've managed to keep the gracious and historic feeling of the place, while making it look so comfortable and fashionable. You've done wonders, I must say. Look at the blazing lights! How delightful."

Laurel laughed. "Thank you, Elizabeth. Most of the *wonders* consist of lighting and heating. And there's a new bathing room upstairs. I hope you don't mind that I've prepared the guest suite for you and Fletcher. I've become so attached to your old quarters, I couldn't bring myself to part with them, even for a while."

"Of course not. I wouldn't think of having you do such a thing. No matter what you say, this is your home now, and it's the better for it, I can see. But dear, where is your husband? We're all dying to get reacquainted with Mr. Sinclair. He's quite a hero to us."

Laurel was ready for this. "It's a long story, Elizabeth. He can't be here just now and I'd like to explain in detail later. But first, I have a special presentation to make. There's someone you all must meet without further delay."

This was Rosie's signal to rush upstairs, then return to the waiting assemblage with a bundle in her arms.

Laurel met her at the foot of the curving stairs and took the blanket from her. When she turned, she drew back the edge and said, "Mother, my dear ones, meet the newest addition to our family: Cheyne Dufour Scott Sinclair, my five-week-old son."

Mouths dropped in profound shock. Then, with a cry, Rebecca Caldwell rushed forward to throw her arms around her daughter and her new grandchild.

Laurel experienced the first unrestrained joy since Cheyne had gone. After receiving kisses from her astonished mother, she circled the room to show off her baby. Everyone agreed he was exquisite and the spitting image of his grandfather, Blaine Caldwell.

At last, she was able to sit in a chair by the fire and suggest everyone gather round to hear her story. All except Badger, who had excused himself when Captain Harding arrived leading a disoriented Desert Mirage. Rosie and her daughters passed silver goblets of champagne imported for the occasion.

Holding their breathless attention, Laurel began with the sinking of the *Star* and related every detail of her adventure, up to and including her pirate-husband's dash for safety three weeks before. As she spoke in the hush of the early afternoon, the baby slept soundly in her lap.

When she was finished, Fletcher was the first to react. He jumped to his feet and addressed the group. "I have something to say. First of all, Cheyne Sinclair is no longer a pirate. Whatever he did years ago, is his business. I believe him when he says he never sank an English ship, and if the British are still after his hide, something is amiss. He has an enemy in high places, is my guess. You've married a fine man, Laurel. Your father told me to tell you that. In fact, Blaine asked me to deliver a special message to you, and to the rest of the ladies present, regarding a secret partnership involving Cheyne. Cheyne wrote to him after your wedding. He asked permission to reveal the truth to you about his identity."

"His identity? You mean about his pretending to be Hammond Brown?"

"Not just that. There has been need for secrecy because Cheyne Sinclair, occasionally known as Hammond Brown, is none other than the infamous Sea Falcon."

Gasps echoed around the room.

Laurel was shocked into utter silence.

"Aye, I can see you're surprised, Laurel. He couldn't tell you because he was pledged to secrecy. He feared endangering the lives of his secret partners. I'm proud to say that Shannon is also one of the partners, along with Blaine Caldwell and Kyle Wyndford."

"My husband, too?" said Rebecca. "Well, I'll be!"

"The Sea Falcon?" Laurel managed at last. "The man who has been raiding slave ships for years. Why, the planters just grind their teeth when they hear the name."

Rebecca got to her feet. "I do believe this is the first secret my husband ever kept from me. He should have known I'd totally approve. And Shannon, my own daughter." She wagged her finger. "You're sly as a polecat."

Shannon laughed. "I'm sorry, Mother. I hated not to tell you, but we were all sworn to absolute secrecy. Not that we didn't trust you completely, but we thought it might be a worry to you. Besides the fewer folks aware of our crime, the better."

Clucking to herself, Rebecca resumed her seat. "I'm just tickled pink," she murmured.

Fletcher continued. "As soon as I'm able, I hope to

contribute to the cause myself. You see, I owe my life to Cheyne Sinclair. He saved my neck when I went to Morocco to buy a horse, and he saved the horse in the process. Thanks to him, I'm alive today and here with my Arabian stallion's offspring, Desert Mirage."

Laurel thought her heart would burst with pride and love. Her husband was the Sea Falcon, a man who would risk his life for a great cause. And all the time, he'd let her think he was only a pirate. "I wish I'd known," she said in awed tones. "But I understand his reasons for not telling me."

"He wanted to," Fletcher said, returning to his chair, "but he had given his word to your father not to tell anyone. He was gentleman enough to ask for permission to tell even you. But he didn't want to put anything into writing, so I was asked to bring your father's verbal release of Cheyne's pledge, along with permission to tell Rebecca and my Beth. It might be best not to say anything to young Badger Wyndford. Actually, we expected Cheyne to be here to make the announcement. But in his absence, I've told you everything."

Laurel hugged the baby, who was beginning to awaken. "Thank you, Fletcher. I'm glad to know the truth, but I'm more worried than ever, now that I know he's the Sea Falcon. I can see why he felt he couldn't come to Scotland, and then he did. He took that risk, though he didn't know about the baby." She held her head high. "Somehow all this will come right. I pray we hear something soon."

Elizabeth nodded. "You're a very brave girl, Laurel. All of us want to help in any way we can. Oh, and Skye sent her love. She longed to come, but couldn't, of course."

Laurel lifted the baby to her shoulder. "I haven't had a chance to ask about Skye and her husband and twins. I do hope they fare well."

Elizabeth beamed. "Indeed they do. When we left, Skye and Kyle were headed back to Dakota. A happier, healthier family I never saw. We'll join them there in the fall, once we've won the horse competition in England."

Scott's sudden wails of hunger brought the meeting to a close. Laurel excused herself, and with her mother beside her, climbed the stairs to the nursery. She knew the celebrations would go on for several days, and she was eager for some quiet time with her baby and her mother. If only Cheyne could have been here, her joy would have been total. When she thought of what he'd risked to save the poor souls headed for slavery, she was consumed with love and admiration, and regrets for the harsh things she'd said to him. He would understand, of course, that she had spoken in ignorance, since she didn't know his true cause. Laurel thought it astonishing that her father and Kyle Wyndford and Shannon, too, had been fighting this clandestine battle all these years. She had never been more proud of her family.

·36·

Two rented coaches, flanked by Badger Wyndford and Fletcher Mackinnon on horseback, pulled into the drive at Berkshire Farm near London shortly after noon on July the ninth.

Elizabeth Mackinnon was the first to alight and survey the serene and charming country home where she'd once lived and which had been hers since her uncle's death twenty-two years ago. For years, she had leased the property to her old mentor, Will Cobbett, to be used to benefit the poor from the sprawling city of London ten miles away. After Will's death, she had allowed the tenant farmers on the property to use the house in exchange for looking after the place. Now that her family was situated in America, she had decided to put it on the market.

She reached up to grasp Fletcher's hand as he halted his stocky horse beside her.

"The house looks just the same as always," she observed. "Let's go see the garden where we were wed."

Fletcher leaned over, scooped her up and placed her before him on his saddle. "Aye, let's do. Maybe we should restate our vows for good luck."

Laurel emerged next and shaded her eyes. The square stone house, with its rolling green lawn and enormous oaks, was gracious and inviting. Again she admired the way her Aunt Elizabeth had forsaken her English heritage, along with her Scottish lands, to accompany her half–Lakota Indian warrior back to his roots in the American West. And the lady had done it with confidence and enthusiasm and unqualified love.

Shannon left her coach along with Mary Pickens, the wet nurse engaged for the journey, and Rosie MacCrae, who had volunteered to travel to England to oversee the house while the families were in residence.

Badger had trotted away on the tireless Desert Mirage to inspect the barn and stables at the back of the house.

Laurel gave instructions to the coachman regarding the trunks, then strolled up the front lane toward the door. The house was a quarter the size of her home at Highgrove in Louisiana, but she was impressed with its air of quiet substance.

Fletcher and Elizabeth reappeared, riding at a fast clip. They were laughing gaily at some private joke, and Laurel couldn't help envying their joy. She'd had no news at all from her own husband, and with every passing day, her anxiety grew. At least they were now in London. Elizabeth had several important connections here from her early years, and she was a celebrity because of the popularity of her books. Surely they could learn something about Cheyne, unless, of course, he had been able to rescue Rafi Hamid and slip out of the country undetected. But if that had happened, Laurel was certain he would have sent some word to her by now. Still, she had been on the road for ten days and he wouldn't have known where to find her.

Elizabeth slid from her husband's arms and hurried to unlock the front door. "Forgive me," she said, her cheeks flushed with excitement. "I didn't mean to keep you all waiting, but Fletcher insisted on stealing a kiss at the place we were married. I'm delighted to report my tenants have taken wonderful care of the gardens. The roses are in full bloom and the vegetables are thriving. There's a chapel over there near the family cemetery. I'll give you a tour and tell you all the stories later, but now . . ."

Laurel turned to Mrs. Pickens and took her squirming bundle. "Thank you, Mary. I'll see to his nappies."

By early evening, the travelers had established themselves in their respective rooms, rested a bit, and then gathered in the dining room for a light supper, hastily prepared from the stores on hand. Rosie had collected fresh vegetables from the garden for a salad and had introduced herself to the tenant in charge so that perishables could be acquired and a stable boy employed for the coming days.

Laurel concentrated on tending Scott, then settled him into the small nursery adjoining her room. Mrs. Pickens had a bed there, and between the two of them, and his adoring grandmother and aunts, Scott would have excellent care. The baby had traveled wonderfully, content to be passed from one loving pair of arms to the next as the coaches journeyed along the main road between the Scottish Highlands and London town.

Seated in the last glow of lingering summer twilight, the family lifted their goblets in a toast to their safe arrival at Berkshire.

Fletcher said, "To each of you: Laurel, Rebecca,

Shannon, Badger, Rosie. My wife and I welcome you to Berkshire." Then he offered a brief prayer of thanksgiving.

"Amen," whispered Laurel with the others, then made her own silent prayer for her reunion with Cheyne. It was a prayer she repeated constantly in her mind and heart.

"How does Desert Mirage like his new surroundings?" asked Shannon between spoonfuls of barley soup.

Badger had to finish chewing his mouthful of biscuit before he could reply. "Dandy, Miss Shannon. The stalls are clean as a whistle and the paddock has been raked clear of rocks and the fence painted. Looks like somebody knew the best horse in the world was coming to visit."

Elizabeth said, "My tenants are wonderful people. Excellent farmers and good stockmen as well. I wrote them about our visit before we left New Orleans so they would be ready for us."

Rosie, who was usually included with the family at mealtime, put down her spoon. "I can attest to the fact they're fine folks. Why, the house was dusted and aired, and posies put on the tables. They do speak highly of Miss Elizabeth. They told me how she helped them in the old days and how her friend, Mr. Cobbett, fought with his last breath for the welfare of the poor."

"As you know, I'll soon be selling the property," Elizabeth said. "Fletcher and I no longer want to own real estate abroad, and we can use the money in Dakota. I'll pack up some personal items while I'm here, and some furnishings to be shipped to America. I want Skye to have a few of my mother's things, too. Some of the china and silver—"

A knock at the kitchen door interrupted her. It swung open to reveal a tenant farmer standing with his hat in his hand.

"Come in, Jones," said Fletcher. "What can we do for you?"

"Begging your pardon, sir, but Mrs. MacCrae spread

the word to be on the lookout for any news of a gent called Cheyne Sinclair. I remembered something I heard in town yesterday. I thought I'd better pass it on. Could be a rumor, but my good wife says she read about it in the daily."

Laurel laid down her knife. "By all means, sir, tell us what you've heard."

"The paper said a certain Cheyne Sinclair, a former pirate with Jean Lafitte, had been captured."

With a gasp, Laurel pushed back her chair.

"It said he was found guilty of piracy years ago and was condemned to hang if he was ever caught. And now new charges have been brought. There's to be a hearing right away, it said."

"Oh, no," Laurel said in an anguished voice. "Did the paper say what sort of new charges?"

"No, ma'am."

"I'm afraid I can guess." Logic told Laurel that Trowbridge was behind this. Was it possible the earl knew Cheyne was the Falcon? Was he accusing Cheyne of raiding slave ships? Did he have proof? She gave Fletcher a look of desperation.

Fletcher got to his feet. "Were there any other details?"

"Said he'd probably hang in two weeks at Tyburn. Said the earl of Croydon was bringing the new charges. He being our neighbor, I thought—"

"Trowbridge!" Fletcher shouted. "Trowbridge again!" He left Laurel's side to stare down at the startled man.

"Yessir. His Lordship owns the adjoining estate."

Fletcher looked as if he were near apoplexy. He spun to face his wife. "Did ye hear that, Beth? Curse the devil, Croydon continues to haunt us. I should have killed him when I had the chance. He curses our family like some evil spirit."

Elizabeth rose. "I never expected to cross his path again." She moved around the table and took Laurel's arm. "Trowbridge is as black a villain as they come. But don't despair, dear. We've fought him before, when he schemed and threatened Fletcher's life. His reputation is foul in England, and few of the noble families have anything to do with him or his unpleasant wife. When we attended a ball three years ago in London, we learned he is blacklisted by everyone."

"But Trowbridge's lack of popularity won't help Cheyne," Laurel reasoned.

"It might. After all, we're not sure Trowbridge knows Cheyne is the Falcon. We could try asking the crown for leniency."

"The crown? You mean we could petition Queen Victoria?"

"Why not? If I could take little Scott and visit her, we might make a case for mercy. You know, she's a new mother herself. She wouldn't be eager to take away a baby's father without good cause. But in addition to the queen, there's her consort, Prince Albert. He's an old friend of mine, and believe it or not, a fan of my books."

"You know him personally?" asked Laurel, trying to quiet her racing heart.

"We've met a few times."

Fletcher thanked Jones and excused him. Then he joined the ladies. "The prince is an interesting fellow. He seems fair minded, and he certainly has a great deal of influence on the queen."

Elizabeth looked at her husband. "He admired you, Fletcher. He was fascinated by your Indian background and that you'd become a Scottish laird. I'm sure he would remember us."

"What—what can we do?" asked Laurel.

Fletcher put his arm around her. "We'll go to London tomorrow and request an audience. Pray the royal couple is in residence."

"Where is Cheyne imprisoned? I must see him. Do you think that's possible?"

"Very likely. I know he was condemned in absentia

years ago. A condemned man is allowed to see his family before the execution."

Laurel sagged against Fletcher's broad chest. "Execution. I can't believe it. It's my fault. My fault." She felt hysteria bubbling inside her.

Rebecca hurried to put her arms around Laurel. "Now darling, get hold of yourself. Elizabeth is right. We're here to help you, and surely with three such formidable ladies in the fray and the daring Fletcher Mackinnon on our side we can win Cheyne's freedom."

Laurel looked gratefully into her mother's concerned face. "Thank heavens you're here. All of you," she added, gazing at the others.

Rebecca smiled and nodded. "Not a one of us in this room hasn't faced terrible adversity, Laurel. We're not quitters. We'll find a way."

Elizabeth patted Laurel's arm. "I happen to know that Her Majesty is opposed to slavery. She's very devout, and would hesitate to send a gallant abolitionist such as Cheyne to the gallows. Yes, I think we can make a strong case. Us against Trowbridge." She looked at Fletcher. "Once again."

Two days later, after a frantic flow of correspondence between Berkshire and London, Fletcher escorted Laurel to the formidable Tower of London, while simultaneously, Elizabeth and Rebecca took the baby to visit the queen. Shannon stayed at Berkshire, convinced her lack of refinement would only put a crimp in things. She said the only queen she cared about was one of four in a pat poker hand.

Laurel's eagerness to see Cheyne outweighed her nerves as she walked along the corridor, then climbed down a flight of winding stares to the cells below. Though it was hot and humid outside, here the air was cool and fetid, carrying unpleasant smells she tried to ignore.

The guard leading the way stopped at the end of a hall and slid his key into the lock in a heavy wooden door. "Ten minutes," he growled. "You sir, must wait outside with me."

"I understand." Fletcher gave Laurel an encouraging smile, then moved back as the door grated open.

Laurel blinked in the dimness, then ducked through the doorway and stepped inside.

"Dear God," came the low muffled sound from the dark interior.

She heard his voice before she saw him. "Cheyne," she whispered.

Chains rattled and a figure moved toward her.

She reached out her arms, but he backed away.

"Don't come near me. I'm bloody filthy. Why are you here? I didn't want you to see me like this."

Her lips were trembling and her throat closing. She mustn't give in to her fear and her grief. "You're a fool, Cheyne Sinclair, if you think I give a flip about how you look. I fell in love with your ugly face despite my best efforts not to do it. What's done, is done."

She held her ground as he moved into the light flickering from a candle in a sconce high on the wall.

"I wondered why they lit that candle an hour ago," he muttered.

"You mean, you must stay here in the dark?" Horror clawed at her.

"There was nothing I cared to see, until now."

He was ragged, unshaven, and haggard, but his shoulders were square and his back straight despite the weight of the chains locked to his wrists.

When she saw his eyes, as green as in her dreams, but bleak with worry and fatigue, she moved to him and put her arms around his neck and rested her cheek on his chest.

He couldn't hold her, but she could feel his heart beating and the warmth beneath the thin fabric of his shirt. "Cheyne, my love," she murmured. "We have only a few minutes. Listen to me."

He said nothing. She wondered if he was struggling with his own pain and despair.

"Even now, my mother and Elizabeth are meeting with Queen Victoria. They have little Scottie with them, and hope to touch her heart with our plight."

"Scottie? Here in London?"

Laurel kept her hands on his shoulders. "We came two days ago. Fletcher too. And Badger Wyndford with Desert Mirage."

"Ah, the horse competition. I'd forgotten. Or lost track of time."

"The competition isn't important now."

"I'll warrant 'tis important to Trowbridge, the bloody scoundrel."

"Then you're certain Trowbridge was behind your capture?"

"Aye. The soldiers who captured me dropped his name. At least Rafi got away. He'll continue my work as the Sea Fal—" He stopped and grimaced. "By all that's holy, I'm an idiot. I guess my mind is turning to mush in this place. Forget what I said."

"Cheyne," she said sharply. "I know all about the Sea Falcon. Fletcher told us everything. Father gave his permission, as you requested. Surely you must know how very proud I am of you."

He sighed and shook his head. "Ah, Laurel, my sweet little lass, what misery I've caused you. If only I could undo—"

She cupped one hand over his lips. "Hush. You've given me unbelievable joy and you gave me Scott. Don't forget that. Nicole says one night of love is worth a lifetime of loneliness. We've had much more than one night, and if it's God's will, and I believe it is, we'll have many more."

"Nay, I'll hang as a pirate."

"You won't hang," she said between clenched teeth. "We won't let you. Fletcher outsmarted Trowbridge once before, and Elizabeth has important connections. I told you she's meeting the queen right now."

"I have hopes then. The queen is opposed to slavery, even though many of her subjects still profit from the trade. But Trowbridge might raise such a cry that even the queen would be in the soup. I'm lucky the earl doesn't know I'm the Sea Falcon. He could bring charges that would put me in a noose for certain."

Laurel wondered if she should tell Cheyne about the hint of new accusations. She decided nothing could be gained by upsetting him further at this point. "What if Trowbridge could be persuaded to withdraw the charges?"

"Now why would he do that?" Cheyne raised his hands and rested them above her breasts, fingering the lace and touching her bare flesh above with his fingertips. "Nay, my love, I fear I may have to pay the piper for my evil ways. If it happens, I've no regrets—except leaving you and young Scottie. Rafi will carry on my work, I feel sure. And you will be wealthy and safe in the bosom of your family."

She actually stamped her foot on the hard stone floor. "Cheyne Sinclair, where is your spunk? You're a pirate, a spy, the daring Sea Falcon! Don't you dare give up hope. Not when you've so many completely dedicated and totally unscrupulous people fighting for your life."

He chuckled. "True. With a Lakota warrior, a famous novelist, a Tennessee sharpshooter, and a lady sea captain on my side, I should have a fighting chance."

"Don't forget Shannon Kildaire."

"Shannon, too?"

"Yes indeed. She was a street fighter long before she was an entrepreneur."

He leaned down and touched his lips to hers. His lips were cool, soft, annoyingly evasive, but only briefly teasing. His tongue gently opened her mouth before he claimed her fiercely, lighting fires in every part of her body. Even the chains between them couldn't deter the passion of their hearts and souls.

She wrapped him in an embrace and returned his kiss with every bit of love that was bursting from her deepest being.

When she eased away, she heard the key in the lock behind her. "You won't hang," she murmured. "You'll die a grizzled old grandfather in a feather bed, with me in your arms."

"God willing," he answered. "Go, my darling, before you send me to my knees in an agony of desire for you."

She moved toward the door, then turned. "Enjoy your *agony,* Captain Sinclair. When we meet again, you'll have no time for it."

·37·

Laurel and Fletcher waited in the coach for Elizabeth and Rebecca to reappear. Laurel tried to keep her frayed nerves under control, but every second was like an eternity.

At last the ladies exited the palace and climbed into the carriage.

Searching their faces, Laurel reached for the baby.

Elizabeth leaned forward. "The queen is very sympathetic toward the situation." She smiled a bit. "And she adores Scottie."

Laurel knew the news wasn't good. "What happened?"

Her mother patted her knee. "All is not lost. The

queen listened to all we had to say about how scrupulously Cheyne avoided sacking English ships after the War of 1812. She said she would be willing to give him a full pardon for his crimes—"

"She would! Then why not?"

"Because—because the earl of Croydon has pressed further charges. He says he has proof Cheyne is the Sea Falcon. A hearing has been set for July twenty-first, the day after the horse competition."

"No." Laurel held the baby to her. "The earl has proof? But surely that's impossible."

Fletcher scowled and said, "If Trowbridge has told the authorities he has proof, and word has reached the queen, the man must be plenty sure of himself."

Laurel was sick at heart. Until this moment, she'd been hoping no one knew her husband's identity. "Trowbridge is truly a devil," she murmured. "He has land, family, a title. Why does he do such evil things?"

Fletcher stroked the baby's forehead as the carriage rolled along the street. "We're certain the earl is secretly engaged in the slave trade. After he fell from favor twenty years ago for being suspected of involvement in the death of Queen Caroline, he was stripped of his property except his home near Berkshire. Since then he's been investing in the shipping of slaves. Cheyne uncovered enough information at Beauregard's party in New Orleans to stop several of the earl's ships on the high seas and rescue the Africans. Trowbridge makes no secret of his hatred of the Sea Falcon."

"And now the earl knows the Falcon's identity and has him in prison," Laurel said sadly.

"Trowbridge will rid himself of an enemy and fatten his purse with a reward," Fletcher pointed out.

"A reward, too. So the earl has much to gain," Laurel sighed.

"Aye, there's a sizable reward for the Falcon, though everyone knows 'tis offered to satisfy the demands of a few Englishmen and the Spanish shippers. Now that

Victoria is queen, it is hoped she will push for reform and outlaw the trade entirely."

Laurel sank against the cushion, her spirits as low as they had ever been in her life. When Scottie began to fuss, she lowered him to her lap and stared at his puckish face. She felt suddenly numb, as if she had received a stunning physical blow.

"I know how you feel, my darling," murmured her mother. "But we're not finished yet."

"I'm sorry, Mother. I didn't mean to seem ungrateful." As her mind came back to life, she squeezed her family's hands. "I thank all of you from the bottom of my heart. You did your best. It's just that . . ."

"We understand, Laurel," said Elizabeth. "We had hoped for more, but we'll have to decide what must be done now. I think the queen is on the horns of a dilemma. She's young, you know, and still has to prove herself with the people of her country. I don't believe anyone cares much any more about Cheyne's past association with Lafitte. It's the problem with his being the Sea Falcon that is so difficult."

Laurel gazed at the baby. He was studying her with round curious eyes that were, indeed, much like her father's. But he had Cheyne's mouth and nose and chin, and his hair was dark and growing rapidly. He would be a handsome man some day. She couldn't bear the thought that he would grow up without his father's guidance, knowing that despite high ideals, his father had been hanged as a pirate.

She looked at Fletcher. "There must be something we can do. Something."

The four remained largely silent during the ride back to Berkshire. Laurel's rendezvous with Cheyne and the disappointing results of the ladies' audience with Queen Victoria had left her feeling exhausted and confused.

As they halted before the house, Badger rode up on Desert Mirage. They hadn't told the boy of their critical errand today. They had decided to make his stay here as pleasant as possible and had insisted he focus on the upcoming competition. None of the adults were able to think of anything besides the danger Cheyne was in.

"Hey," Badger shouted, leaning down to peer inside the coach. "Watch this." He pivoted the magnificent mare and pranced in a wide circle across the lawn. The sight was spectacular, but Laurel and the others found their responses forced and lacking in enthusiasm.

"Look!" Badger called again. He reined Mirage in a tight circle, then raced toward them, halting in a swirl of dust.

Fletcher applauded. "Excellent, lad. You'll have the contest in the bag, I'm certain."

"Then we'll all be rich," shouted Badger.

"At least Trowbridge will lose," Fletcher growled. "That's the most important thing to me now."

Badger waved and galloped away toward the stables.

By now, the ladies had left the coach and started toward the front door. Halfway there, still carrying Scottie, Laurel stopped in her tracks. She had the seed of an idea. It was crazy; it was foolish; it was one chance in a million. But at least it was an idea.

"Take Scottie, Mother," she said, handing over the babe. "I want to talk to Elizabeth and Fletcher."

Rebecca went inside as Laurel motioned for the Mackinnons to walk with her toward the gardens.

When they reached the bench amidst the flourishing rose bushes, she sat with the couple beside her.

She began with a question. "How badly do you think Trowbridge wants to win the horse competition?"

"Plenty," said Fletcher. "Prince Albert is giving a prize of a hundred thousand pounds, the largest in history. And of course, the winning horse will certainly be desired by the royal stables as a stud or as a brood mare. There will be balls in honor of the owner and breeder, and to win could assure Trowbridge's reinstatement into London society. The local farmers tell me the earl has a good horse, too. Probably the best stallion in the country. His only competition, so they say, is a French trainer who has brought a mare in for the contest."

"Trowbridge hasn't seen Desert Mirage."

"Aye, that's so."

"Then we must show her to him."

"What?"

"Yes. We must let your neighbor, the illustrious earl, see Mirage. I don't believe any horse on earth is more beautiful or better trained. And she carries the blood of Spirit Dog, your wonderful Indian pony from America. I believe she could plow all day and still win any race she's put to."

Fletcher nodded thoughtfully. "Aye. The second part of the contest is a cross-country race of twenty miles. When she was a filly, she began running across the Dakota grasslands for endless hours. Badger has her in good shape after the sea voyage. You saw how she traveled the Scottish road. She could have continued day and night."

"Exactly," said Laurel. "I realize this would be an enormous sacrifice for our family, but Cheyne's life could be at stake. I'm suggesting we show Mirage to Trowbridge. That should cause him to worry plenty about the outcome of the contest. Then we'll make a private deal."

"I see where you're headed. We'll agree to withdraw Mirage from the contest in exchange for his dropping the charges against Cheyne."

Laurel licked her lips. "What do you think? Am I mad, or is it worth a try?"

Fletcher jumped up and held out his hand. "If I know Trowbridge, he'll go for fortune and fame. The decision may keep him awake a few nights, but I'm betting his greed is greater than his desire to get rid of the Falcon. With a hundred thousand pounds, he can retire from slave trading forever. Plus, if he drops the charges, the royals will secretly applaud the gesture. Some investors in the slave trade may grumble, but they'll have to keep their thoughts to themselves. Laurel, I always knew you were a smart lady. You've just proved it."

·38·

The following day, Laurel set her plan in motion. Luckily the earl was in residence at his estate adjoining Berkshire. A request for a social call by Mrs. Elizabeth Mackinnon was sent by special messenger. As his long absent neighbor, Elizabeth might have good reason to call on Lord Trowbridge. Thank heavens, his acceptance was immediate and positive. The family agreed Laurel should go alone, since she could keep a cool head and negotiate the terms. Her skill at negotiating for Caldwell Shipping was highly respected, and with so much at stake, she would be at her best. Elizabeth and Fletcher wouldn't think of attending, since Trowbridge had, after all, tried to cause their deaths. Fletcher swore he'd had enough of the villain and would be delighted to throttle the man if that would help their cause in any way.

Laurel sat under her parasol in the open carriage rented for the escapade. She was nervous, but confident, and had her plan of attack well in mind. At her side rode Badger on Desert Mirage, who had been expertly brushed and groomed till her rose-tinted coat gleamed in the bright summer sun. Called roan by some, this rare color was described as rose-gray by the Arabians. As Mirage lifted her delicate feet, arched her neck, and trotted beside the carriage, Laurel knew there could not be a more spectacular horse anywhere. She couldn't help regretting that the prince and all the world would miss seeing Mirage, that the mare wouldn't win the prize she so richly deserved. Laurel knew Badger was deeply disappointed, but he had borne the news with courage and understanding. He had spent all morning preparing Mirage for today's outing, and he smiled now and touched his hand to the tip of his broad-brimmed Spanish-style hat.

Laurel kept her parasol shading her face as the carriage rolled up the Croydon drive. She didn't want her subterfuge of switching guests known too soon. The distance to the imposing three-story house was nearly half a furlong. She took a deep breath and lifted her chin, pretending that entering the estate of an English nobleman was an everyday occurrence. From the corner of her eye, she saw Badger putting Mirage through her paces: trotting, cavorting, jogging forward and back along the curving drive. If Trowbridge was at home and glanced from his window, he was certain to be dazzled by the sight.

Her prayers were answered when she saw a lace curtain lift and a man peer at them as they traveled toward the house. She recognized Trowbridge from their brief meeting at Beauregard's party. *So far, so good,* she thought.

When they arrived at the entrance to the house, the door swung open and Croyden himself walked out onto the porch. Laurel saw he had changed little from the pompous, overweight, pale-skinned man she recalled. How she hated him. Disgust filled her throat.

Trowbridge stared at young Badger, who was circling around the drive, pretending to have difficulty controlling his spirited mount.

He tore his eyes from the sight and approached her carriage. "Good day, Mrs.——" He stopped on the bottom step and stared at her. "Pardon, but I was expecting Mrs. Mackinnon."

"Good afternoon, My Lord," Laurel held out her hand so he was forced to assist her to alight. "My sister-in-law is unfortunately indisposed. I've come in her place. We met last year in New Orleans when I was a guest at the home of Henry Beauregard. You were visiting from England."

Trowbridge appeared completely unnerved, but he took her hand. She felt sure from his reaction he knew she was Cheyne Sinclair's wife. The villain was amazingly well informed.

"That's my nephew on his prize mare." She indicated Badger, who waited nearby. "The lad accompanied me, but now he'll ride back to Berkshire."

Trowbridge looked again at Mirage. "Yes. A beautiful specimen."

Laurel caught the look of grudging admiration on Trowbridge's face. He knew an exceptional animal when he saw one, she'd credit him that.

Mirage whinnied and reared, as she had been trained to do at Badger's unseen signal. Her mane whipped in the sunlight, her nostrils flared as her front hooves pawed the air. Badger tapped his quirt on her withers. The mare landed squarely, then collected herself and bent one knee in a bow. The trick was breathtaking in its disciplined beauty.

Laurel waved at the boy.

Badger waved back and reined the horse toward the gate. He had played his role to perfection.

Trowbridge now gave Laurel his undivided attention. Offering his arm and conducting her inside, he asked, "What brings you to England, Miss Caldwell?" he asked with a strained voice.

She wondered how he was feeling, escorting the wife of the Sea Falcon into his mansion. "I'm staying a few days with my aunt and uncle at Berkshire. The weather is so fine, I thought I would call on you and your wife."

"I regret my wife is in London. But I've ordered tea."

Laurel was dressed in a peach-colored silk morning dress. She wore stunning jewelry Cheyne had given her, and wished, for once, for the huge diamond she had left behind in Tangier. She knew the earl would be impressed with a show of wealth, and today she wanted every weapon she could muster to keep him off balance.

"Now what's this about Berkshire?" Trowbridge inquired. "I thought the place was abandoned after that rascal Will Cobbett died." He guided her into the grand salon.

"No," she said, not losing her smile. "The property still belongs to my aunt, Elizabeth Mackinnon. She's come to London to put it on the market. She'll do so after the horse competition next week."

"I heard the Mackinnons had left the Isle of Skye."

"Yes, but they've sold their Skye property to me. In fact, I was thinking of buying the house at Berkshire. The half Arabian mare you just saw, ridden by my nephew, is entered in Prince Albert's contest. Once Mirage wins, she'll be in such demand, I may decide to keep her here for breeding. With the prize money, I'll be able to turn the place into a beautiful estate." She held out her hand. "We would be neighbors, Lord Trowbridge. Wouldn't that be pleasant?"

His expression suggested exactly the opposite. He cleared his throat. "Are you saying you think your mare will win Prince Albert's contest?"

"I'm quite confident. We brought her from America, and she's certain to win, in my opinion. As I recall, you were looking for a horse for the contest when you were in Louisiana. Did you find one?"

He answered curtly. "I did. An excellent black stallion. A thoroughbred. I think he'll give your little mare a run for the prize money."

"Do you? Honestly?" She laced her words with utter disbelief.

She could see Trowbridge was upset. Good. That was exactly what she had hoped.

"How is your father?" he asked gruffly, offering her a wingback chair opposite his.

"Very well, thank you. He's building a new ship to add to our fleet. When you next visit Louisiana, you must tour the shipyards. I believe you'd be quite impressed."

"Ah, here is tea. Will you play the hostess?"

"It looks very nice, but actually, Lord Trowbridge, I've come here to confide in you, and ask for your assistance."

"Is that so? How can I be of help?"

Laurel scrutinized the puffy face with skin the color of a dead fish. "The fact is, I am no longer Miss Caldwell. I recently married."

This news obviously didn't surprise him. "Congratulations, I'm sure," he mumbled.

"My husband is Captain Cheyne Sinclair, who is currently occupying a cell in the Tower of London. I believe you know of whom I speak."

He scowled fiercely. Then he cocked his chin and placed his fingertips together. "So we have honesty at last. It appears you tricked me, madam. I doubt if your sister-in-law intended to visit today at all."

"You're quite right. But I do represent my entire family. I would like to come to the defense of my husband, the man you captured and imprisoned. The man against whom you press charges, despite the queen's inclination to pardon him."

He drew himself up. "I can only offer you my sympathy. Sinclair is a scoundrel."

Laurel kept her temper. "To some, he may be, but not to me. You see, I love him, and he's the father of my six-week-old son."

"More misfortune. The man has been a pirate and a blackguard for years. I know this for a fact."

"What you *think* is that your investments in slave ships may be jeopardized because of him."

"Slavery is still legal in many places—in the United States, for example."

"Yes, but not importing slaves. What I want to know is what proof you have that my husband has done anything illegal. That he served with Lafitte is no longer considered a serious crime."

If harsh looks were daggers, Laurel was pierced through and through. "I have proof. Do you think I would lie to the queen or to the judge at the hearing or to you?" He was losing his temper.

"I'm afraid I do."

Trowbridge rose and glared down his aquiline nose. "Madam, I have proof your husband is none other the infamous Sea Falcon. He steals valuable wares from innocent ships, then makes off with his prize like any pirate."

She feigned shock and horror. "That's outrageous. You couldn't possibly have proof of such a false accusation."

As she had prayed he would be, he was challenged to produce his proof. He crossed the room and unlocked the top drawer of his desk. Removing a wrapped package, he drew off the string and held up a banner. Her shock and horror became real.

Trowbridge displayed a black and white flag with a Falcon in flight. The flag Cheyne always flew from his ship.

"What does this look like to you, Mrs. Sinclair?"

She gathered her thoughts quickly. "A flag, I suppose. Perhaps a bird of prey. What makes you think it belongs to my husband?"

He pulled a paper from the drawer. "I have the signed affidavit of an acquaintance of his, a woman he knows in Morocco."

"A woman?"

He studied the document. "Yes. Her name is Shazade Amin. She once lived in his house." He curled his lip. "Presumably *before* your marriage. She lives in Spain now, but she came to England personally to deliver the flag to me. She found it in Mr. Sinclair's personal belongings in Tangier. I might add that she spoke with several individuals who swear Cheyne Sinclair and the

Sea Falcon are one and the same. If necessary, I will bring her from Spain to testify."

Laurel gripped the arms of her chair. The evidence was convincing and she was sure Shazade had found the banner at Tamerlane. Not only that, she would bet her life Shazade had spied on Cheyne and sent word of his visit to Scotland. She was forced to proceede with her plan. "I know Shazade Amin. She is of highly questionable reputation, to say the least, and her former employee was Saad, the slave trader, from Morocco."

Trowbridge went whiter than usual. He knew this kind of information would be rich gossip in the elite London circles he wished to enter. "I daresay, you're a bold young woman."

"I can be, when I have right on my side. Queen Victoria and her consort despise the slave trade because it's flagrantly immoral. It's only a matter of time till it will be completely outlawed. None of the queen's inner circle engage in the practice. Nor would anyone of class be acquainted with such a person as Shazade Amin, a woman who is nothing more than a spy and female companion for riffraff such as Saad Terraf." She watched the earl's eyes blink in alarm. That she had these details would certainly cause him to worry.

"I suppose your husband has told you these lies. I'm astonished you would dare call on me under the guise of a friend and speak in so rude a fashion. It's quite appalling. But I've heard Americans have no manners at all."

"My manners are not the problem, My Lord. The problem is that my husband is in prison. I want him released so he can return with me to Scotland."

"Your husband will be sentenced to hang."

"On the contrary, the queen is in sympathy with his cause. Even if he's proven to be the Sea Falcon, which I doubt, Victoria will likely commute his sentence."

He stuffed the paper and the banner back into the drawer and locked it. "Impossible."

"Two days ago, my mother and Mrs. Mackinnon met with the queen personally. I assure you, my husband will not hang."

He clenched his fists. "Victoria, that self-righteous light-skirt! How dare she put herself above the law!"

"She *is* the queen of England. She has the right to do such things. I'm optimistic she will give my husband a full pardon."

"Damnation." He marched toward her and eyed her from under stringy eyebrows. "So why are you telling me this? Frankly, you're wasting your time. I am doing my duty for my country, and I expect to prove the man guilty."

Laurel was nauseated by the beast's claim, but it was time to press forward. "The fact is, I am prepared to make you an offer."

"What sort of offer?"

"You saw the Mackinnon's mare, Desert Mirage. You know she is very likely to win Prince Albert's contest."

"I don't know any such thing."

"I believe you do. I've been told that were it not for Mirage, your horse would be a sure winner."

"I intend to win, regardless of your animal."

"I don't think so. Mirage is not only beautiful, she is swift and able to run great distances without tiring. She has been trained in the American West on the great plains. Her heart is huge and her stamina amazing. She will finish the twenty mile race well ahead of any competition."

Trowbridge glared at her with pure hatred. Laurel knew he was capable of murder and she knew that at this moment he would like to send her to her grave. Now was the time to strike her bargain.

"Lord Trowbridge, I'm in a position to practically guarantee that your entry wins Prince Albert's contest. There will be other horses, of course, but if I withdraw Desert Mirage, and if your stallion is fit, he will almost certainly be the victor."

His jaw worked. "Why would you do that?"

"In exchange for my husband's freedom. If you drop your charges against him, he will go free at once. The public will quickly lose interest in the Sea Falcon. And if you win Albert's prize, you will have no further need to invest in slave ships. You will be feted in royal society. Your stallion will be the toast of England. On the other hand, you have nothing to gain but a paltry reward if my husband hangs. I realize your sense of justice will be disturbed, but surely you can also see the value of forgiveness," she added with a virtuous air.

She saw the struggle in his face. He wanted to take her offer, but it stuck in his craw. She must do something now that was extremely difficult, the hardest of all. She must allow him his pride.

"Excuse me, my lord," she said softly. "I've always heard about noblesse oblige, the unwritten law practiced by noblemen. Americans stand in awe of such ideals, such charity. I can assure you that you will be forever in my prayers if you will use your power and prestige to set my husband free. He will probably never return to England. I ask this for myself and for our baby son." She almost gagged on the pleading tone in her voice, but she had to allow this monster to save face.

He paced the floor, his hands behind his back. Then he turned. "When will you withdraw from the competition?"

Her heart leaped. "I'll go to London tomorrow, if you like. We could meet there. I will withdraw the horse from the contest at the same time as you withdraw the charges against my husband."

"If I agree, you must first withdraw the horse. Once that is done, you have my word I will then withdraw the charges."

"I'm sorry, but we will act simultaneously or not at all." She knew she was implying she didn't trust him, but there was no other way. She *didn't* trust him, any farther than she could throw his great manor.

"I'm busy tomorrow."

She stood. "I'll await your convenience."

"I'll be in touch. You may go now."

She could hardly breathe as she left the house. Had she succeeded or failed? She thought he was about to agree, but then he had hesitated. She wanted to scream in frustration, but she had to stay calm. The interview had gone well and she had done her best. All she had to do now was to wait for developments.

Cheyne was surprised when, two days after Laurel's visit, he was taken from his dank cell and moved to a comparatively comfortable suite on an upper level of the Tower. He was allowed to bathe, given decent clothing, and three meals a day. Hardly excellent cuisine, but nourishing and ample.

His new bailiff was an older man who gave him a pleasant smile and a word of cheer whenever he delivered the meal tray. Clarence was his name, and he said he'd been a guard at the Tower for years and had seen all the good and bad that mankind could dredge up. He'd seen men and women face death with extraordinary courage, and he'd seen criminals dragged screaming to face the ax, while folks who were probably innocent walked to their destiny with a smile of polite resignation. Clarence had explained that the queen herself had ordered Cheyne's fair treatment. Cheyne was sure this must be the result of Elizabeth Mackinnon's request.

One morning, along with the dinner tray, Clarence delivered a letter.

Cheyne snatched it up, then waited for Clarence to leave before he read it. It was from Laurel. In it, she said she was working on a plan to free him, a plan that might involve Trowbridge withdrawing the charges against the Falcon. Unfortunately Laurel didn't give many details, but she did say that the earl had the Sea Falcon's flag as well as sworn testimony from Shazade Amin that Cheyne was the Falcon.

Cheyne cursed the day he had laid eyes on Shazade. He had thought he was doing the woman a favor, rescuing her from a terrible fate. Instead he had been the victim of Saad's clever trap. How ironic, he thought, that Saad had lost his life in a scheme to capture Cheyne, but in the end, his plotting had produced the desired results.

Shaking his head, Cheyne folded the letter and gazed through his one small window overlooking the rooftops in London. He couldn't help being despondent. For so many years, he had risked his life for the cause of ending slavery. Fighting that injustice had been the only thing that had given him real satisfaction since the disappearance of Lafitte. And now, when he had discovered the joy of love, taken a wife whom he utterly adored, created a son to bring joy to his days, he must accept the death he'd tempted for so long. Even now, he didn't fear the noose. But he was consumed with regret that he must leave life, just when it offered so much happiness.

· 39 ·

The waiting was agony. As each warm summer day passed, Laurel grew increasingly frantic. Her temper frayed and she snapped at everyone. Her family was patient, but their pitying glances only made her feel worse.

On the day before the competition, Badger came to tell her he must take Mirage to Burlington Estates near London, where the contest would take place. Accommodations for guests and horses were available at Burlington. The horses would be put on display in their stalls later today, and Prince Albert would inspect them and make his choices. The prince's selections of the three most beautiful animals would be announced the next day, then a cross-country race pitting the three finalists would take place, the winner to take the grand prize.

Laurel smiled at Badger and assured him all the family would attend and do their part to cheer him on. After all, since her plan to rescue Cheyne had evidently failed, the only thing left was to win the contest and witness Trowbridge's severe disappointment. Then she would begin again to find a way to save her husband.

Shortly after noon, Laurel, Rebecca, Shannon, and Elizabeth and Fletcher Mackinnon entered their coaches and headed toward Burlington Estates. Badger had ridden ahead on an immaculately groomed and beribboned Desert Mirage.

Lord Burlington had made his vast estate available for the most exciting horse competition ever to be held in the British Isles. His special guests had been arriving for several days, and on July nineteenth, Prince Albert himself took up residence. Queen Victoria stayed at home with her children, since after all, this type of extravaganza, with dancing till dawn and its collection of horsemen, foreigners, and gamblers was not exactly her cup of tea.

On the other hand, the prince was in his element.

July twentieth, the day of the competition, couldn't have been more perfect. During the early morning, a light shower had washed the air and heightened the country fragrances of grass and meadow and flourishing flower gardens. By midmorning, the sun beamed on the colorful assemblage, as several hundred well-turned-out visitors, dapper with wide bonnets and top hats, milled around the immaculate stables admiring the most fabulous display of horseflesh anyone had ever seen.

By far the largest group had gathered at the stall of the American entry, Desert Mirage. Although the earl of Croydon's stallion should have been a favorite, the earl was extremely unpopular, and besides, the crowd was fascinated by the exquisite perfection of the mare with a coat like burnished rose.

Laurel was numb inside. Her mother or Shannon stayed close, one or the other grasping her elbow, offering her their support. Her family kept their sympathy to themselves, but they were all heartbroken. Laurel knew it without hearing the spoken words.

At ten o'clock, the entire gathering moved to an arena where bleachers had been set up under an enormous canvas tent. Nineteen horses were paraded around the enclosure and put through their paces by their proud owners or trainers.

Seated between Fletcher and Elizabeth, Laurel watched the show in stony silence. Across the way, Prince Albert held court in his private box. Farther along, Laurel saw Franklin Trowbridge and a handful of his friends. The earl's black stallion was indeed a prime specimen, plainly superior to all the other entries save one.

"Here comes Badger," said Fletcher. "I do wish his Uncle Kyle could see him today."

Badger was only twelve, but he looked every inch a man as he rode Mirage in a display of excellent horsemanship. He was wearing a Spanish-style black suit trimmed with silver and rose-red piping. His hat was wide-brimmed black felt with a leather thong under his chin holding it in place. By now the onlookers knew young Montgomery Wyndford had English roots with connections to the Wyndfords from Northamptonshire. His deceased father, the Wyndford's second son, had gone to America and staked a claim to a property in the West that would dwarf the grandest estate in England.

By the time Badger finished his presentation with Mirage's perfect bow, the crowd had picked him as their favorite and given him a rousing ovation.

Laurel looked toward Franklin Trowbridge. He had disappeared from his box.

Within minutes, she received a note delivered by one of the many servants circulating in the area.

With shaking hands, she opened it, read it, then passed it to Fletcher.

Dear Mrs. Sinclair, it began. *Please do me the honor of meeting me at 11:00 in the gardens near the fountain of Neptune. I would prefer we meet alone. Yours, Franklin Trowbridge, earl of Croydon.*

Laurel knew as soon as she saw Trowbridge's face that she had won their war of wills. He rose from his seat in the shade beside the fountain and bent over her hand, but his expression was grim and stormy.

"You wished to see me, sir? I think we can forego any pleasantries."

"I agree," he said sharply. "I do admire the way Americans come straight to the point."

"I'm pleased there is *something* about my countrymen that pleases you." Her tone was as icy as his.

"I must admit you have an exceptional horse. No doubt it will be one of the three chosen for the final race."

"In my opinion—yes."

"So will my black stallion. I'm assured of that."

"Perhaps. Are you now considering my offer?"

"I am."

"Time is short. If my husband isn't set free before the race, my horse will run and win. Can you make the arrangements quickly?"

He removed a paper from his inner pocket and held it out for her inspection. It was addressed to a judge.

"What do you plan to do with this?" she asked, carefully concealing her rampant nervousness.

"I will deliver this note in person to the judge who was scheduled to hear your husband's case. He is here. I am withdrawing my charges and I will suggest he order your husband released from the Tower immediately, unless the queen has other ideas."

"The judge has the authority to do this?"

"Absolutely. Since the queen will not enforce the verdict from the old trial, when Sinclair was condemned in absentia, he can now be released if there are no further charges. Victoria can give him a full pardon, if she's inclined as you said."

"I'm sure she'll be pleased to do that. One more thing. I want the Sea Falcon's flag."

His eyes became angry slits. "I expected that. I'll give it to you when you withdraw your horse from the competition. It's too late to withdraw from the judging on conformation and beauty, but if you remove your mare from the cross-country event scheduled for four o'clock this afternoon, she will be disqualified from the contest. Perhaps you could say she has some kind of injury."

"Yes, that sounds plausible. I will prepare a letter to that effect and deliver it to Prince Albert."

"Do it *now,* if you please."

"Do you have paper and pen?"

He motioned to a servant standing near. "Give me the writing materials," he ordered.

The man pulled paper and quill and a tiny flask of ink from his coat.

"You're well prepared, I see."

"I was sure you'd cooperate," said Trowbridge.

Laurel sat on the bench and spread out the paper. Taking the quill, she wrote a brief note to Prince Albert, explaining that her horse was injured and would have to be withdrawn from the race. Then she said, "There, sir. Now, what assurance do I have my husband will be set free?"

"You don't trust me to do as I promise?"

"Frankly, no. I want to personally see you deliver your request to the judge. Then you can deliver my note to the prince. After that, I want the flag."

Trowbridge looked outraged, but finally controlled his temper. "I fear for the future of America," he snarled, "if all the women are as brash and demanding as you, Mrs. Sinclair. It is extremely unbecoming and will emasculate your men in time."

"We shall see, sir." She rose and looked across the garden, where refreshments were being offered to everyone. "Where is your friend, the judge? I believe I see the prince and his party near the maze."

A simmering Trowbridge looked over the crowd. "There he is. Seated beside the tennis court."

"Good." She slipped her hand through the earl's arm as they walked toward the judge.

Cheyne had left his lunch tray untouched. The weeks of waiting, of being a prisoner, regardless of the few comforts he'd been provided, were taking a heavy toll on his spirits. He had received several encouraging letters from Laurel, but they had held no details and seemed vague when it came to her plans or any progress. He couldn't help thinking her efforts, and those of her family, had been for naught.

In addition, he worried about her confrontation with Trowbridge. He had warned her about the man's evil scheming. And after all, the earl had the power of his title and connections. What if she had put herself into danger? Thank God for Fletcher Mackinnon. Surely that stalwart fellow, who had once escaped the earl's clutches, would look after Laurel and see to her safety. On the other hand . . .

Clarence unlocked the door and entered the room. He had a smile on his face and a small envelope in his hand.

Cheyne couldn't prevent the hope that swelled his heart.

"I say, Mr. Sinclair, 'tis your lucky day."

"Why is that, Clarence? Have you news?"

"Indeed I do. You've been released from prison. I don't know the particulars, but these are orders coming straight from the queen."

Cheyne was momentarily speechless, then took a look

at the document Clarence was holding. It was official. He was a free man.

"Here's your personal belongings," Clarence said, handing him an envelope.

"Clarence, you've brought the best news a man can have. I can't repay you now, but someday I will." Cheyne shook the bailiff's hand, then quickly left the room and made his way down the steps and out into the brilliant afternoon sunshine. He wasn't about to linger. He didn't know how his freedom had been gained, but he was eternally grateful for it. No doubt he owed his good fortune to Laurel and her family. They must have done something spectacular to persuade Franklin Trowbridge to drop his charges. He knew the bastard wouldn't do it after all these years of stalking him unless he had a great deal to gain. Then again, maybe this was only a temporary reprieve.

All Cheyne could think of was finding Laurel. Would she be at Berkshire, the Mackinnon's country home? Surely she hadn't returned to Scotland. What was today's date? After weeks in the Tower, he had lost all track of time. As he left the low-class district, he spotted a tavern and hurried inside.

"What is the date?" he asked the barkeep.

"July twentieth. Today is the prince's horse contest everyone's gabbing about. I'd give me last farthing to be at Burlington today."

"*Today* is the competition? Where is Burlington, if I may ask."

"An hour's ride north. But don't bother trying to see it. Only the nobles and powerful gents will be admitted. The prince will be there, and he's well guarded."

Cheyne mumbled his thanks and went back outside. The only item of value he had was the wide gold ring that had been in the envelope Clarence had given him. He would trade the ring for whatever nag was available at the nearest stable. If he guessed correctly, Laurel and her family would be at the competition. After all, that had been the primary purpose for her family's journey to the British Isles. With luck, he could be at Burlington within a couple of hours. He guessed the time was shortly after noon. He had no idea what would be happening at Burlington when he arrived, but the devil himself couldn't keep him from gaining admittance and finding his darling wife.

· 40 ·

It was half past three when Cheyne rode his exhausted mount onto the grounds at Burlington. Obviously a major event was in progress. He saw an enormous tented pavilion with flags flying and heard the sound of a band and enthusiastic applause. The area surrounding the pavilion was deserted except for one uniformed guard leaning against a tree, trying to see what was happening under the tent.

Cheyne tethered his horse in the shade and made a wide circle around the guard. Had he been an assassin bent on murdering the prince consort, he would have had an easy time of it. But all he wanted was to slip into the crowd as unobtrusively as possible and find his wife. On the other hand, he belatedly realized he couldn't possibly be unobtrusive. The gathering at Burlington was certain to be the cream of English nobility, dressed in their very best clothing to mingle with their queen's royal consort, while he looked as if he'd drifted in from a London ghetto.

Nevertheless, he made his way to the pavilion and hid in the shadows. The bleachers under the expansive vaulted canvas were packed. Both ends of the sheltered area were open, creating a wide path through the middle.

Peering from behind a support pole, he saw a rope stretched across the grass track. This must be the location of the race, or at least the start and finish of it. He remembered the horses were to run twenty miles, out through the countryside, then back again. Inching forward he studied the crowd, but didn't see a familiar face.

Suddenly the band played a trumpet fanfare. The prince consort stood and the onlookers quieted at once.

"Dear friends and horse lovers," shouted the prince. "I am proud to announce the three finalists in confirmation and beauty. These magnificent horses will run the route and finish here before us. The first horse to cross the finish line will be the winner of the contest. The finalists are De Leon, the French entry; Majestic, belonging to Irish Lord Murphy; and Black Duke, owned by the earl of Croydon."

Cheyne was surprised. What had happened to Desert Mirage? He was certain the mare would be in the finals if she had been entered. Maybe Laurel wasn't here after all.

Someone yelled from the crowd. "What about the American horse? Where's the rose-colored mare?"

The prince held up his hand. "I regret to inform you, the American entry has been withdrawn due to an injury a short time ago."

The audience moaned with one voice.

As the band launched into a stirring tune, Cheyne headed toward the stables. He was sorry to hear about Mirage, but he knew now that Laurel was here somewhere, or had been here this morning.

The barn area was deserted. The losing entries were munching oats in their elegant stalls, oblivious to their defeat.

Cheyne made his way along the rows. Then he saw a sign above a stall that said *Desert Mirage, Mackinnon—America.* When he reached the enclosure, he found Badger rubbing down the mare.

"You must be Badger Wyndford. I'm Cheyne Sinclair.

I don't believe we've met, but I've heard much about you."

Badger looked startled, then put down his brush and crossed to the stall gate. "Pleased ta meetcha, Mr. Sinclair. You're married to my Aunt Laurel, and you just got out of jail."

"That's right. I'm looking for my wife, but I'd prefer to stay as much out of sight as possible. I'm not sure what's going on and 'tis important I don't cause trouble for any of your family."

"Laurel's gone to the race. But I know she's plenty anxious to see you, sir. She was hoping you would show up this afternoon."

"She knew I was coming?"

"Yessir. She arranged everything with the earl."

"Franklin Trowbridge?"

"Yessir."

Cheyne didn't like the sound of this. "What did she arrange?"

"For you to be let out of jail. In exchange for Mirage withdrawing from the contest."

Cheyne was consumed with anger. So that was the price of his freedom. For him, it was an excellent trade, but he knew what this competition meant to Laurel's family. He had never dreamed Trowbridge would let him go free, but of course, a hundred thousand pounds was a very great incentive.

"I'm sorry, Badger. I know what this contest meant to everyone. I'd like to find some way to make it up to all of you, but I'm not sure I can." He had an idea. "Badger, is Mirage fit? Uninjured, that is?"

"She's perfect, Mr. Sinclair. She could easily win the race. The prince announced she was one of the three finalists because she's such a pretty thing. But then he had to take her out of the contest when he was told she was hurt."

"Dammit, Badger, she should be out there. When will the race start?"

"Real soon. I'd say fifteen or twenty minutes. They said at four-thirty, after the band quits playing."

"Can you saddle her quickly?"

"Sure, but—"

"Get started. I have a plan. But 'tis important no one know I'm here. Not even Laurel."

Badger needed no urging. He pulled his racing saddle from a post and tossed it across Mirage's back.

"What's happening after the race?" Cheyne asked, entering the stall to help with the bridle and bit.

"There's a fancy dress ball tonight to award the prize to the winning horse. It'll be held in the outdoor pavilion. The winner has to show up in person to get the prize."

"Perfect. With your help I can surprise Laurel, and no one will know I'm Cheyne Sinclair."

"The Sea Falcon," said Badger with enormous awe.

"You know about that too, eh?"

"Sure. I've heard that most folks think the Falcon is a hero."

"Not if they've invested in the slave trade. 'Tis better we keep my identity a secret until I'm out of England. I've had enough of greedy nobles and their prisons."

From the pavilion, the music began to swell toward a climax. "Hurry up," urged Cheyne. "Fine. Up you go." He cupped his hand to hoist the boy into the saddle. "Now here's my plan."

Laurel sat with her family and stared at the emerald green turf of the temporary track. Where was Cheyne? He should have been here by now. On the other hand, he didn't know for sure she was at Burlington, and he might have gone straight to Berkshire. Yes, that was probably what he did. She comforted herself by feeling the Sea Falcon's flag tucked into the purse dangling from her wrist. She would have preferred to go to Berkshire to wait for Cheyne, but the prince consort had given them this special box of honor. The prince had been extremely sorry to hear about Mirage's injury. In fact, he had expressed enormous interest in the mare and her unusual bloodline, and had arranged to speak with Fletcher personally before the ball tonight. He had even implied he might want to acquire Mirage for his private stables. Since her family had lost a hundred thousand pounds as a result of Cheyne's rescue, she was hoping the prince and Fletcher would come to a favorable financial agreement. At any rate, she couldn't ask them to give up this chance to meet with the prince because she was impatient. Berkshire was only two hours away and the instant Fletcher had finished his meeting, they could leave for home.

But worry gnawed at her. What if something had gone wrong? She had seen Trowbridge give the note to the judge, and the judge had promptly sent a rider to London. Everything appeared to be in order, but the earl was a sneaky devil and might yet pull some trick to thwart her plan.

The band ended its tune and played a fanfare. Three horses in racing gear, ridden by jockeys in colorful silks, rode onto the track. It was a spectacular sight, but Laurel had no interest at all. She kept gazing around the crowd, looking toward the entrance, hoping beyond hope to see Cheyne appear. Even if he came here, there was always the chance he couldn't gain admittance to Burlington Estates. After all, the royal guards were keeping out uninvited guests. It was agonizing to think Cheyne might, even now, be somewhere on the outskirts of the property, unable to come inside to look for her.

A huge cry went up all around her. The crowd was on its feet.

Fletcher cried, "By Saint Andrew, look at that!"

She stood and peered toward the track. From the stable area, a horse was galloping forward. A horse more beautiful than any other.

A gunshot started the race.

To her astonishment, Desert Mirage was galloping in the wake of the three front runners. Wearing Mackinnon red and green, Badger leaned over the flying mane.

The onlookers went wild. The race was under way and the three official entries were already disappearing out the far end of the pavilion and heading for the trees that marked their course. No one seemed to care about them; it was Mirage that had captured their fancy.

"What the hell is Badger doing?" shouted Fletcher. "What about the bargain?"

What about the bargain, indeed? Laurel felt faint. Badger must have taken it on himself to defy her instructions and race the horse after all. It was a terrible risk and she couldn't believe the lad had done such a thing. He was sensible, obedient, dependable. His Uncle Kyle had said he'd been a wild youngster, but she'd not seen his rebellious side since she'd known him. Why would he choose now, with so much at stake, to pull such a stunt?

For she had no doubt Mirage would win the race.

Two boxes away, Laurel saw Franklin Trowbridge glare at her, his face black with anger. After the horses disappeared from view, he left his seat and made his way toward her.

She wouldn't be intimidated by this evil man. As he approached, she lifted her chin and stared defiantly at him.

He eased in behind her box. She caught Fletcher's eye and shook her head to warn him not to interfere. Heavens, Fletcher would kill the man in front of everyone with very little provocation. That wouldn't help anything.

She left her seat and faced Trowbridge. This was between the two of them. She didn't want her family involved in case there should be an ugly scene.

He scowled at her. "You won't get away with this."

"I didn't plan it this way. My nephew made the decision to race. He has worked for months to get Mirage ready. I suppose he couldn't resist making the effort. Frankly I don't blame him, and I expect he will win."

"You know what that means."

"What? That an innocent man will hang?"

"Innocent?" He laughed bitterly. "Cheyne Sinclair was born in guilt and shame. He'll hang for his crimes, after all. It isn't too late for me to bring charges once again."

"It *is* too late. My husband deserves his freedom and he has it, regardless of the outcome of the race. You will never catch him this time."

"I kept my part of our bargain. You can be assured, if your horse wins, your husband will be arrested before morning, and that's an end to it. I'm still a lord in this land, and I can use my power to see that an escaping criminal is brought to justice."

She refused to feel a smidgen of guilt, even if it appeared she'd broken her promise. "And I kept my part of the bargain. But my nephew didn't agree to anything." She glanced at Fletcher, who was observing from a distance. She knew she must end this conversation before there was serious trouble. "I suggest we watch the race. If your stallion is as wonderful as you claim, he may yet win."

He shook his finger under her nose. "We'll see. But I assure you, if your mare crosses the finish line first, your husband will be on his way to Tyburn." Suddenly he grabbed her purse and tore it from her wrist. Then he spun away and headed toward his box.

She wanted to scream and call him a thief, but now was not the time. Besides if she did, Fletcher's hair-trigger temper would send him after Trowbridge. Nothing would be accomplished if Fletcher Mackinnon pummeled the earl in front of all these ladies and gentlemen. Though Fletcher might enjoy his revenge, he would certainly end up in prison or worse. No, she had to shore up her courage and appear confident, if for no other reason than to keep Fletcher calm. But terror clawed inside her. Trowbridge was a powerful lord and if Mirage won, he would use the Falcon's flag to destroy Cheyne. Even if Cheyne managed to escape, he could never return to the British Isles. She prayed now that Cheyne wouldn't come to Burlington, but would stay safely at Berkshire until they were reunited. Then they would escape from England and sail to Tangier or America on her ship, anchored now at Skye.

Ignoring the questioning looks of her family, Laurel returned to her box. The minutes ticked by as the band played merrily. The horses had a rough trail to ride, up hill and down hill, across moors and streams.

She couldn't focus on the conversations going on around her. She just stood with the others and stared at the far side of the pavilion where the horses would reappear.

After what seemed forever, the crowd at the far end began to shout. A horse was approaching. Like a wave, the noise grew and rolled across the audience.

With her heart tripping crazily, Laurel strained her eyes. Yes, a horse was coming. Only one horse.

It was Desert Mirage. He was winning the race—and dooming Cheyne to hang or spend his life as a wanted man.

Racing down the track, Badger was bent over the gleaming mare's neck, riding with ease, his crop tucked under his arm. Mirage was the picture of controlled power and beauty.

The onlookers went wild with delight.

As they neared the finish line, Badger suddenly rose in his saddle and reined in the horse.

The crowd hushed, staring in shock and amazement.

"What's he doing?" cried Shannon at Laurel's elbow.

Badger halted Mirage inches before the horse's nose touched the finish line. He stood in the stirrups and jogged the mare in a wide circle.

The audience began to clap a rhythm and shout, "Cross—cross—cross!"

With Mirage prancing along the turf, Badger swept his cap from his head and acknowledged the cheers.

A black horse galloped into the pavilion. Close behind him came the French gray, followed closely by the Irish blood bay.

The earl's black stallion swept past Mirage and raced across the finish line.

The entire assembly was on its feet, clapping, yelling, thrilled and excited by the unexpected turn of events.

Badger coolly replaced his cap and trotted toward the exit leading to the stables. He hadn't crossed the finish line, but no one could say he hadn't won the race.

Laurel and Fletcher bounded from their box and rushed toward the stables. When they reached Mirage's stall, Badger had already dismounted and was walking the mare to cool her down.

"Well done," shouted Fletcher. "You've set the place on its ear, young man. And still you kept the bargain."

Badger looked incredibly pleased with himself. His eyes twinkled in his sweaty and dirt-smudged face. "It was a snap, Fletcher. We got ahead right away, and Mirage was never pushed. She's surely a wonder!"

With tumbling emotions, Laurel ran to the boy and embraced him. "Goodness, Badger, you were grand. How did you think of such a thing? Trowbridge will get his reward and my bargain with him is still intact. But everyone in England knows who the real winner is today."

Holding the reins, Badger stared down at his boots. His answer was unintelligible, and Laurel assumed he was overcome with sudden modesty.

"Make way for His Highness, Prince Albert."

Laurel looked up to see an entourage arriving in the stable. The prince himself led the way. She dropped into a curtsy and elbowed Badger in the ribs. The boy merely stood gaping at his first close encounter with a ruling monarch.

"Congratulations, young man," offered the prince

graciously and shook Badger's hand as if they were equals. "I understand you trained this horse in America, then readied her for the race after a long sea voyage."

Badger's cheeks were flushed, but he smiled and said, "Yes, sir, but the credit goes to the mare, I reckon."

"Well spoken, lad." The prince turned to Fletcher. *"Laird* Mackinnon, is that correct?"

"Aye, Your Highness. Though I don't use the title since I now make my home in America."

"I see. Well, Mr. Mackinnon, I've never seen a more beautiful horse. She should be winning the prize, but plainly something went amiss at the finish."

"That was my idea," piped up Badger. "I knew she had been withdrawn and wasn't a legal entry, so I thought I'd just show her off, then let one of the others win the prize."

"Very interesting." The prince stroked his sideburn. "Well, lad, you've put me in an awkward position. The earl of Croydon's stallion officially won the race, but my subjects are demanding a reward for your horse, too. Old King Solomon had answers to this sort of dilemma, but I'm not sure I have his wisdom."

"I'm sorry," said Badger shyly. "I didn't mean to cause so much trouble."

A man approached the prince. "Pardon, Your Highness, but the black stallion has arrived in the stable. The earl of Croydon is awaiting your pleasure."

"Yes, yes," the prince waved his hand impatiently. "I'll stop by shortly to congratulate him." He looked down at Badger. "Tell you what I'm going to do, young Wyndford. Solomon was known for dividing things, and that seems fair to me. I instigated this contest and made up the rules myself. You and your mare have made the event more exciting than I ever expected. I believe I'll just divide the reward between you and Trowbridge. After all, his horse would have been a distant second if things had gone as they should have."

Laurel caught her breath. Was this possible?

Fletcher stepped forward. "We would be extremely grateful, Your Highness. When we withdrew Desert Mirage, we thought it was absolutely necessary to do so."

"I'm sure you had the animal's welfare in mind. But your mare looks fit. I believe she could have run the course twice without tiring."

"I'm sure of it," said Fletcher.

"Very well. It's my race, and I say the prize money will be divided equally. I'll expect you at the ball tonight to collect your fifty thousand pounds. In the meantime, wash and groom your mare. The ball is to be held in the pavilion and I want Desert Mirage and Black Duke to be present as the guests of honor."

Laurel bowed as the prince left to make his way toward Croydon's stall. She could just imagine how annoyed the earl would be at losing half his prize. But since he didn't deserve any prize at all, he should count himself lucky. More important, how would this affect his view of the bargain they had made? And when could she retrieve Cheyne's flag?

·41·

Cheyne had watched the race from a shadowed spot near the bleachers. It had gone exactly as he and Badger had planned. But when he kept his rendezvous with Badger, after everyone had gone to the house to change for the ball, he had been stunned to hear about the prince's decision to split the prize money. Stunned and extremely gratified.

Standing in the shadowy barn, Badger looked pleased as punch. "What are ya gonna do now, Mr. Sinclair?"

"First, I'm going to ask you to call me Cheyne. After

all, we're related in a roundabout way. Laurel always says *relatives are relatives,* no matter how distant or how they got that way."

Badger grinned and whispered, "I'd like to call you Falcon, but I wouldn't dare."

"Not around here, lad," Cheyne said grinning. "Not even if we're in Louisiana. No, I think we'd better keep that name a secret."

"Are you going to find Laurel?"

"Not just yet. She's gone to the mansion to change for the ball. But I do need you to do me a favor. Will you find Fletcher Mackinnon? I'm going to find the jockey's quarters and clean up a bit. I could do with a better looking suit of clothes that don't stink of the Tower. Mackinnon and I are about the same size. I don't care about fashionable evening wear, just something presentable so I can meet Laurel at the ball."

"Sure. I can do that."

"And swear Fletcher to secrecy."

"I get it. You're gonna surprise Laurel."

"Possibly." He winked at the boy.

"Sure thing. See you later—Cheyne."

Laurel turned before the mirror in the small but elegant room she'd been given for the evening. She had tried to rest on the single bed, but she had been far too excited and nervous to relax even a minute. A short time ago, a maid had brought her a glass of wine and stayed to help her with her toilette and her gown. She considered the ball merely an ordeal to get through before they could return to Berkshire. She had made up her mind that Cheyne must be waiting there for her. After all, Trowbridge had been furious over her failure to live up to their bargain. That indicated he had done his part and withdrawn his charges.

Her dress for this special occasion was pale blue taffeta with puffed sleeves and delicate ivory lace collar and cuffs. Beneath the yards of skirt, she wore a fitted corset and five starched petticoats. The maid had pinned up her hair and woven flowers through the layers of golden curls. To complete the ensemble, she wore a necklace created of sapphires and pearls and a pair of matching earrings. She was satisfied with her appearance, but her mind wandered constantly to Berkshire, where Cheyne could be waiting.

When Shannon arrived, Laurel was momentarily distracted from her concerns by the lady's outrageous appearance. Shannon's dress was purple silk, dappled with rhinestones. Her upswept hair was held in place by several immense pink feathers that tickled her neck and wrapped around her shoulders. Diamonds sparkled from her ears and neck and on several fingers. Laurel loved her sister all the more because Shannon never allowed fashionable good taste to stand in the way of having fun.

"Is it time to go?" asked Laurel.

"Yes, I heard the band start playing a few minutes ago. We'll collect Mother and Elizabeth on our way downstairs."

"Where is Fletcher?"

"He left some time ago for his meeting with the prince. He said he would see us at our table in the pavilion. It seems the race track has been magically turned into a ballroom with tables reserved for all the guests. Aren't we lucky it isn't pouring rain?

"Yes indeed." Laurel glanced one last time in the mirror. "Let's be on our way. I want to get this over with and escape for home as soon as we can."

Cheyne stayed out of sight in the stables until he saw Fletcher approaching, carrying a sizeable package. Stepping into the light, he reached for Fletcher's hand. "Good to see you again, Mackinnon. A hell of a lot has happened since we last met in New Orleans."

"You do lead an exciting life, my old friend. Congratulations on your marriage, your new son, and on your escape from jail. Did I miss anything?"

"That covers it pretty well. I owe all of you a huge debt for securing my freedom. Thank God, you're getting something for all your efforts with the horse."

"Laurel arranged everything. If it had been up to me, I'd have shot Trowbridge and that would be that."

"Not a bad idea."

Fletcher handed him the package. "I wrapped the clothes as you suggested, so no one would guess what you're up to, but I fear they suffered from the wrapping. They're not evening clothes, but perhaps they will do."

"Take a look at what I'm wearing. Anything is an improvement. I'm in your debt." Cheyne unwrapped the paper and removed a pair of trousers, a white shirt, and a beige frock coat and satin cravat. To his surprise, under the coat was an enamel brooch bearing the Sinclair coat of arms.

"What's this?"

Fletcher was grinning ear to ear. "A brooch to secure your clan tartan. I borrowed it for the evening from one of your distant Sinclair kinsmen who's here at the contest."

"A pretty trinket, but I'd dare not wear it in public, much less the tartan itself. Any legitimate Sinclair would take immediate offense."

"Maybe not. Let me explain. I met with Prince Albert earlier this evening so he could instruct me in tonight's procedures. I do think His Highness is having the time of his life directing all this activity."

"No doubt. But you've something up your sleeve. What is it?"

"When Badger delivered your request for the clothes, he explained you planned to surprise Laurel at the ball."

"Aye. I have that in mind."

"But I have an even bigger surprise for you."

"Good lord, what?"

Fletcher pulled a paper from his pocket. "The prince himself slipped this to me. He looked sly as a fox, very pleased with himself."

Cheyne laid the clothes over a railing and opened the paper. Holding it near a lantern, he read with increasing astonishment. It contained a full pardon for all his crimes, signed by the queen and carrying the royal seal. After absorbing the news, he stared at Fletcher. "You've brought me a new life, Mackinnon. This is more than I'd dare hope for. I'm—astounded."

"You once saved my life. 'Tis a small favor in return for that."

"Nevertheless, I won't forget it, my friend."

"You can thank the prince and the queen. When Trowbridge accused you of being the Falcon, they privately considered you a hero, not a pirate."

"Are they aware I've married your niece?"

"My wife and Rebecca Caldwell explained that when they met with Queen Victoria. Tonight I merely pointed out to His Highness that you could now lay claim to the property on Skye that had once been mine. The man didn't have any problem with a switch from Mackinnon to Sinclair. In fact, he said the Sinclairs of Ulbster were personal favorites of his."

"My connection to that illustrious clan is not the noblest. As you know, I was produced on the wrong side of the blanket."

"So was many a powerful gent. But you're legitimate now."

"What do you mean?"

"That's the rest of my good news. When the prince heard your wife owned Strathmor, he said you should be the new laird of Skye. I quite agree."

Cheyne couldn't believe his ears. "Me? A *laird?*" He shook his head in amazement. "I can't believe it. I bloody well can't believe it."

"The prince is much in favor. But he suggested we keep this under our hats for now. Later the announcement will be made through official channels. Then the clan will have to accept you."

Cheyne reached to shake Fletcher's hand. "If ever you felt in my debt, you're free of it now. How can a man say thank you for receiving a new life, a name free of scandal, and a legitimate title? Not just for me, but for my son."

"We're square, 'tis true. Now I must go to the ball. And you must tidy yourself a mite or your wife may not have you, after all." With a parting grin, he left Cheyne in the stable.

Laurel, Shannon, Elizabeth Mackinnon, and Rebecca Caldwell entered the pavilion, escorted by a servant in elegant livery. They took their seats at their reserved table, noting the empty chair reserved for Fletcher.

The night air was like sweet gossamer, perfumed by the flowers on each table and the breeze drifting from nearby gardens.

Crystal chandeliers were suspended overhead to give the area the luminescent glow of a true ballroom. The bleachers and the racing turf were gone, replaced by a large wooden floor, polished and ready for dancing. At one end, a raised dais held the tables for Prince Albert, his entourage, and Lord and Lady Burlington, their close friends and family.

As the four ladies sipped from glasses of champagne, they listened to the orchestra and watched couples participating in an elaborate cotillion. Several female guests stopped by the table to introduce themselves to Elizabeth Mackinnon and politely request her autograph on their napkins as they exclaimed over her novels.

Laurel squirmed in her chair. Where was Fletcher? When would the prince make the awards? Thinking of Badger, who had gone with several boys to explore the estate, she hoped the lad wouldn't stray too far. As soon as Fletcher had the prize money and Desert Mirage had been presented to the gathering, they would leave at once for Berkshire.

As time passed, the party grew more boisterous.

"When will Fletcher arrive?" Laurel impatiently asked the ladies.

"I thought he would be here by now," Elizabeth said. "I saw him briefly after he met with Prince Albert. He was in a rush to go to the stable to check on Desert Mirage. Badger promised to have the horse groomed and gleaming for tonight's presentation, but sometimes boys can be careless."

Lavish hors d'oeuvres were passed and glasses refilled. On the dais, the prince, wearing his trademark black frock coat and trousers, was holding forth with great merriment. Dancers now crowded the floor, enjoying lively quadrilles and graceful waltzes.

When Laurel could sit still no longer, she stood and circled the table. She had twisted her lace handkerchief into a moist ball, and now she dropped it carelessly to the floor. She started to retrieve it when she heard Shannon say, "There he is. Fletcher's coming."

She rose and breathed a sigh of relief when she saw Fletcher making his way from the far side of the pavilion. With his large frame encased in his beige coat, he was easy to spot, even in the uncertain light from above.

Searching again for her hanky, she wasn't aware he had arrived beside her until she heard him speak.

"Lady Sinclair, may I have this waltz?"

Laurel's heart stopped beating. Cheyne was gazing down at her, his sea-green eyes alight with pleasure.

She heard tittering from the ladies behind her, but she couldn't move or speak. The shock of seeing him so unexpectedly kept her frozen and silent. How absolutely marvelous he looked, despite the thinness of his face. His hair was longer than usual, a bit more gray at the temples, and there were new lines at the corners of his eyes. None of that mattered. He was here at last.

"Cheyne," she whispered, too overwrought to say more.

"Aye, Cheyne Sinclair, your wayward husband," he

commented with a twinkle in his eyes. "Or Hammond Brown, if you prefer. 'Tis quite some time since we waltzed together, Laurel. Perhaps a lifetime ago." He held out his hand.

In a trance, she grasped it and walked with him to the dance floor. As her spirits leaped, she realized vaguely she had mistaken him for Fletcher since he was wearing Fletcher's suit. He appeared amazingly well groomed and stylish for a man who had been in prison a few hours ago.

His arm went around her waist; his eyes held hers. As if the intervening years had never existed between this waltz and their first dance in New Orleans, they turned slowly, revolving, oblivious to everything but the nearness of each other, the ecstasy of seeing, hearing, touching, absorbing. Laurel was sure her slippers didn't touch the ground as she floated in his arms. Only when the music ended did her mind begin to work. She longed to rush into his embrace, to smother him with kisses, but that was hardly possible with so many people surrounding them.

As if reading her thoughts, he smiled rather wickedly and led her out of the pavilion and strolled toward the stables. Once inside, he pulled her into his arms and crushed her to him, claiming her lips, melding the two of them into one soul, sending her senses skyrocketing into a rapture of joy and passion. She found it pleasurable agony to hold him so close, and yet to desire so much more, to know that fulfillment would come in time, but not yet, not quite yet.

His breathing was ragged when he released her. "My darling lass, how I've dreamed of this moment. I thought it would never happen, but imagining it has kept me alive."

She stroked his cheek. "I've been terribly worried, Cheyne. Just look how thin you are. You came so close to death, I thought—" The words caught in her throat.

"I owe my life to you and your family. Badger told me the details of your plan. I'll never forget what you've done—all of you."

With sudden concern, she said, "But Cheyne, are you in danger here? Who are you tonight? Sinclair or Brown?" Her gaze swept over him. "Surely not the gypsy tinker. You're wearing Fletcher's suit, if I'm not mistaken. Should we slip away? The others can manage without us. I don't care if—"

"Slow down, my love, and let me explain." He couldn't keep his hands from her as he spoke. "I have wonderful news. When the queen discovered Trowbridge had dropped his charges, she issued a full pardon for any of my past crimes. Fletcher just received the document from the prince an hour ago." He patted his coat pocket. "I have it right here."

She flung her arms around him and kissed him again. When she could finally tear herself from his embrace, she said, "I knew she would do it," she said. "I never thought I'd adore an English monarch, but I do tonight."

"Nor I, but indeed she seems to have a good heart. 'Tis about time the throne was occupied by such an intelligent person."

"Then you have no need for subterfuge?"

"Only in one thing. 'Tis best I not reveal to anyone I'm the Sea Falcon. That gent has such a questionable reputation, even Her Majesty prefers to pretend he doesn't exist."

Laurel laughed through her tears. "The Sea Falcon is a dangerous man, I can attest to that. By the way, have you heard from Rafi?"

"No, but I expect by now he's in Tangier. As I told you, I gave him orders that should I not survive, he was to carry on the Falcon's work."

"Wonderful. His courage and skill may rival the man who was his mentor."

"I don't doubt it."

She glanced at his lapel. She hadn't noticed the badge he wore until now. "What's this?" She fingered the colorful brooch.

"That, my lady, is the symbol of my new status in life, and yours as well. That is the Sinclair coat of arms. Fletcher Mackinnon borrowed the item for this one evening, but I'll be acquiring a permanent tartan before long. I must announce, my dear, you are looking at the new laird of Skye, assuming the people will have me as their leader."

Her heart soared. "*Laird* Sinclair? Can it be true?"

"Prince Albert has declared it, and will make it official ere long. That means you will be a titled lady, as well as being the most beautiful lady in Louisiana, or maybe in America—hell, maybe anywhere in the world." His grin swept over her, warming her from head to toe.

"As long as I belong to you, I would be as happy to be a beggar as a lady."

He hugged her to him. "To my relief and joy, that won't be necessary. Nor will I need to fear for your reputation, or that of our sons. How is Scott, by the way?"

"He's safely at Berkshire with two doting ladies. He's growing, Cheyne. Just wait till you see him!"

"I'm counting the minutes."

"We can leave for Berkshire as soon as Fletcher receives his prize. Have you heard about what happened here today?"

"I watched the race from behind the bleachers."

"Cheyne Sinclair, you've been here all this time and didn't tell me? Goodness, I might have expired from worry. Then what would you have done?"

"Been consumed with remorse, I expect. But here you are, pink cheeked and lovely as always. And I did want to surprise you." With great tenderness, he brushed her hair fleetingly with his lips, then abruptly raised his head. "Did you hear something?"

"Someone's coming, I think. Let's duck into that empty stall."

The two were out of sight when Franklin Trowbridge walked by, reading the signs on each stall. He was carrying a bucket and a box, and he was muttering curses under his breath.

·42·

Cheyne peered between the slats. Trowbridge had stopped to look at Desert Mirage. Then stealthily the earl started to unlatch the stall door.

In an instant, Cheyne moved to confront him. "What the hell are you doing, Trowbridge?"

Laurel was right behind him. Cheyne grabbed the earl by his collar.

Trowbridge was white as death. He coughed and sputtered and rolled his eyes, looking for help, but the barn was deserted. "Let me go," he rasped.

Cheyne snatched the bucket from Trowbridge's hand and inspected the contents. "Oats. That's all?"

"I—I came to feed Duke. I just wanted a closer look at your mare."

Dropping the bucket, Cheyne grabbed the small box Trowbridge was trying to hide behind his back and held it up to the light. Fury ignited inside him. "Rat poison!" he said between clenched teeth.

"No!" Laurel cried. "No one could be so cruel."

Fletcher pushed Trowbridge against the wall. "This piece of slime is capable of anything. You're a dead man, Trowbridge." He put the poison on a shelf and reached for his pistol, his knife, anything, but recalled he had no weapons. "Strangling's too good for you, but it will have to do." He wrapped both hands around the man's throat.

"No, don't!" Laurel tugged on his arm. "Don't do it, Cheyne, please. If you kill him, you'll hang for sure."

Slowly Cheyne eased his grip.

Gasping for air, Trowbridge sank to his knees in the dirt.

"He doesn't deserve to live. Give me the poison. I'll stuff it down his throat." He reached for the box.

"I know how you feel, but we could both hang if you kill him."

Cheyne hesitated, then stepped back. "What'll we do with him? We caught him red-handed. We can file charges."

"You'll never prove anything," croaked Trowbridge. "I'm a peer of the realm and you are nobodies. Just a pirate and a foolish American woman. Nobodies!" he railed, struggling to his feet. "A British court would never take your word against mine."

"He has a point, Cheyne," Laurel said. "Maybe we should let him go. But he must return your flag."

"You mean, he still has the Falcon's flag?"

"I got it back from him when he agreed to withdraw the charges, but he yanked my purse from my arm when Mirage entered the race. He guessed the flag was in it." She glared at the earl, who gaped at them with bulging, terrified eyes.

Cheyne was seething. "Trowbridge, Saad, and Shazade Amin. A kettle of rotten fish, those three."

"You're exactly right."

Cheyne tightened his one-handed grip around the earl's neck. He hadn't killed a man in years, but the urge at this moment was almost irresistible. "Where is the flag, Trowbridge? Produce it now or the rat poison is going down your gullet."

"In—my coat pocket," Trowbridge squeaked.

Cheyne jerked open the coat and pulled out Laurel's purse, along with a document. He handed them to

Laurel. "See if the flag's inside. What does the paper say?"

"Yes, here it is." She removed the black and white banner. "And the paper is the affidavit signed by Shazade explaining where she found it."

"Excellent. We'll burn them both when we get a chance. But what in hell are we going to do with this— this villain? He deserves a slow and miserable death."

"I'm afraid we'll have to let him go. We have no choice. I do hate the thought that he'll win so much money and go free after what he's done, but we can't risk any more trouble." She slipped her arm around Cheyne's waist. "Let's just leave England. I want to go home."

Her heartfelt plea touched him deeply. He thought for a minute. "I have an idea. Do you know where the stable office is located?"

"Yes. It's right next to the barn."

"Go there and find paper and pen. Bring it quickly, before someone comes." He looked down at Trowbridge, who appeared to be near fainting. "You'll do what I command, My Lord, or I'll kill you, I swear."

Laurel returned in less than a minute. Cheyne shoved the earl to a bench beneath a lantern and spread the paper before him. "Write exactly what I say. Then sign it. Laurel, darling, do you think you can throw a bridle and saddle on Trowbridge's stallion and lead him here? I know ladies don't—"

"Cheyne Sinclair, I've been saddling horses since I was five. You knew me then. Do you doubt what I say?"

He chuckled at their shared memory. "Aye, I believe you."

She was off in a flash and returned within a short time, leading the tired stallion along the hay-strewn passage between the stalls.

Mirage snorted and came to her door to see what the commotion was about.

Cheyne tucked the earl's note safely into his coat pocket.

Trowbridge struggled weakly, but Cheyne tied his hands before him and wrapped the man's own silk handkerchief over his mouth, then hoisted him atop the stallion. Working swiftly and silently, he bound him firmly in place, leaving him just enough slack to reach the reins.

Laurel watched in the dim light. Finally she whispered, "What are you doing, Cheyne? Won't you tell me?"

"Nay, dear wife. You'll have to trust me."

"Very well, but do hurry," she murmured. "We're lucky we haven't been discovered."

"Aye. I guess everyone is at the ball, and the guards are in their cups at this hour." Holding the stallion's bridle, Cheyne glared up at the earl, whose eyes were wide and terrified above the handkerchief. "My Lord Trowbridge, we could easily have killed you, but we'll give you one last chance to escape your well deserved fate. Go home, immediately. Ride as fast as you can to your estate and count your good fortune every step of the way. Stay out of our lives forever, do you understand?"

Trowbridge nodded vigorously.

Cheyne led the horse into the night and slapped it briskly on its rump. It leaped away, carrying its owner toward home.

Turning to Laurel, he put his arm around her.

"You're a sly one, Cheyne Sinclair," she quipped.

He gave her a quick hug and a crooked smile. "We'd better go. Guard your purse well. The proof of the Sea Falcon's true identity is inside."

She tied the strings around her wrist and stood on tiptoe to lightly kiss his lips. "With my life," she said as they strolled arm in arm toward the pavilion. "With my very life."

As they crossed the grassy strip surrounding the raised dance floor, they saw Badger running toward them.

"Hey, Cheyne! I see you got some clothes from Fletcher. Hi, Laurel."

Cheyne clapped his hand on the boy's shoulder. "You did a fine job, lad. I'm much obliged to you. Now I have another favor, one very much more important."

"Sure thing."

Cheyne handed Badger the paper the earl had written on. "Go to Prince Albert's table and hand him this. Tell anyone who tries to stop you 'tis a matter of life and death."

"You bet." Badger grinned and charged straight across the dance floor, causing several swaying couples to halt their manuevers and send him annoyed glances.

Keeping an eye on the boy, Cheyne took Laurel in his arms and moved in time to the music.

The tune was still playing when Badger approached the prince and handed him the note.

After Prince Albert read it, he rose and motioned for the band to cease.

The dancers halted in place to face the dais.

The prince's husky voice boomed in the silence. "It is time we pay tribute to our winning entries. I have a surprising announcement. His Lordship, Franklin Trowbridge, the earl of Croydon, the winner of today's race, has unexpectedly returned home. Unfortunately he won't be here in person to collect his prize, one half of the purse of one hundred thousand pounds. I say *unfortunate* because I would like to thank him personally for his extremely magnanimous gesture. I have just received a personal note from the earl advising me he wishes to contribute his entire winnings to the hospital for women in a certain difficulty in London. In addition, the earl says he and his wife are going into complete seclusion for the foreseeable future, due to a sudden call to a life of religious contemplation."

A collective gasp went up from the crowd. Both Trowbridge's prize money and any hope of climbing the social ladder evaporated together as if they'd never existed.

Laurel looked admiringly at Cheyne. "Lord Sinclair,

how very clever. And what a wonderful choice of a charity."

His eyebrow cocked. "Such establishments usually need extra funds. If I'd been in luck, I could have been born in one." He hugged her to him. "But I was saving all my luck for my old age."

"Old? You?" She actually winked at him and whispered, "The Sea Falcon could not possibly be described as *old*. I know that for a fact."

Badger returned to their side, his face full of pride. "I did it. That prince is a pretty nice fellow. I can't wait to tell my friends in Dakota about how we made friends."

Trumpets sounded a fanfare.

"Where is Fletcher, anyway?" Badger asked. "He's supposed to show off Mirage and get the prize."

The orchestra began to play "Yankee Doodle," a tribute to the American horse who had stolen everyone's hearts. All heads turned to the entrance of the pavilion.

Along the narrow track surrounding the dance floor came Desert Mirage, ridden by Fletcher Mackinnon, former laird of the Skye Mackinnons, and now a cattle baron in the American West.

Fletcher wore buckskin from head to toe, and he straddled a bright colored blanket rather than a saddle. In true Lakota style, his hair was shoulder length and flowing, and around his neck he wore a bear claw, which he had earned as a youth in the land of his mother's people.

The band stopped playing except for the drums, which took up a steady beat in time with the flying hooves of the magnificent mare.

Fletcher circled the pavilion at a brisk pace as the audience recovered from its surprise and began to clap a cadence. As he rode past the table where his wife, Elizabeth, was seated, he pulled a rose from inside his shirt and tossed it into her waiting hands. The onlookers broke into wild cheers of delight.

Reining up before the prince, Fletcher raised one arm in salute to the English royal consort.

Prince Albert grinned broadly as he leaned down and tossed a pouch to Fletcher.

Fletcher caught his prize and shouted a Lakota victory whoop, then without retrieving his reins, he kneed the mare into a gallop and circled the pavilion once more. As he disappeared toward the stables, the applause and cheers under the canvas roof became deafening.

In the excitement, no one noticed as Cheyne turned to his beloved Laurel and pressed her against him, taking her lips once more.

AUTHOR'S NOTE

Skye Laurel brings to a close the trilogy of the Mackinnon family of the Isle of Skye. Their story has taken my research from the land of the Lakota Sioux during the early 1820s, through the Regency period in England, to New Orleans in the days prior to the Civil War.

The Isle of Skye fired my imagination with its remote windswept beauty and its dramatic setting as a part of the Scottish Highlands and as an island in the Hebrides.

The hero of Book I, originally White Arrow, who becomes Fletcher Mackinnon, Laird of the Mackinnons on Skye, continues to be a catalyst in Books Two and Three. As the Mackinnons move from Skye to Dakota in the American West, the English cattle baron, Kyle Wyndford, enters their lives and changes their destiny. In *Skye Laurel*, the reader returns to the Isle of Skye with a Mackinnon cousin, Laurel Caldwell, who encounters the lusty ex-pirate, Cheyne Sinclair, before she can reclaim the Mackinnon castle of Strathmor.

The Skye Trilogy has filled my thoughts for many months. I've lived the adventures of my heroes and heroines and enjoyed getting acquainted with secondary characters, whether they were precocious youngsters, dreadful villains, or beloved pets. It's always difficult to say good-bye.

I hope you have enjoyed reading the Skye Trilogy as much as I have loved writing it. A special thanks to all those readers who have sent your thoughts to me regarding the trilogy.

Krista Janssen

KRISTA JANSSEN

Creole Cavalier	87464-0/$5.50
Indigo Fire	51907-7/$5.99
Wind Rose	74499-2/$5.50
Skye Lakota	51908-5/$5.99
Skye Legacy	00217-1/$5.99
Skye Laurel	00218-X/$5.99

Available from Pocket Books